With You Always

Also by Rena Olsen

The Girl Before

RENA OLSEN

With You Always

G. P. Putnam's Sons

New York

G. P. PUTNAM'S SONS

Publishers Since 1838
An imprint of Penguin Random House LLC
375 Hudson Street
New York, New York 10014

Copyright © 2018 by Renata Olsen
Penguin supports copyright. Copyright fuels creativity, encourages diverse voices,
promotes free speech, and creates a vibrant culture. Thank you for buying an authorized
edition of this book and for complying with copyright laws by not reproducing, scanning,
or distributing any part of it in any form without permission. You are supporting writers
and allowing Penguin to continue to publish books for every reader.

Library of Congress Cataloging-in-Publication Data

Names: Olsen, Rena, author.
Title: With you always / Rena Olsen.
Description: New York : G. P. Putnam's Sons, [2018]
Identifiers: LCCN 2017027824 (print) | LCCN 2017032559 (ebook) |
ISBN 9781101982402 (ePub) | ISBN 9781101982396 (softcover)
Classification: LCC PS3615.L7315 (ebook) | LCC PS3615.L7315 H57 2018 (print)
| DDC 813/.6—dc23
LC record available at https://lccn.loc.gov/2017027824

Printed in the United States of America
1   3   5   7   9   10   8   6   4   2

For my grandparents, Lyle and Roberta Riebe,
who have lived lives worth aspiring to.

With You Always

The drip drip drip of the faucet echoes throughout the large bathroom, and she lifts a toe to intercept the droplets, her foot barely reaching across the expanse of the whirlpool-style tub. The water ripples as the movement disturbs the glassy surface. Her head rests on the porcelain lip, her neck too tired to hold the weight of it any longer. The water has taken on a pinkish tinge, and she can't help but feel some relief that it is over. She has found her escape. He can't change this, can't control her anymore.

PART I

ONCE UPON A TIME

It may have been a mistake to bring my work outside with me. It seemed like a good idea at the time. My stuffy desk area barely got sunlight from the window at the end of the hall, and I was feeling claustrophobic. I imagined myself as one of those urbane business-women, sitting on the edge of the fountain at the park across the street, sipping coffee from a well-worn travel mug while flipping through very important reports, pausing to smile at the children playing at the park. Passersby would notice me, respect my tenacity to work through the lunch hour. "How sophisticated she must be," they would say to each other.

The reality, unfortunately, was far from my fantasy. The sun, dim from my desk, was brighter than I expected, and I had to squint against the blinding whiteness of the paper to make out the columns of numbers that made up my boss's expense report. The coffee I'd picked up was already cold in the paper cup next to me, and the wind was threatening to snatch the reports right out of my hands. Not to mention the brats who were splashing on the other side of the fountain. If I got hit with cold droplets one more time, I was going to lose it. But I refused to give up and go back inside just yet. Blowing my hair out of my face once again, I reached for my cup. Even the bitter bite of the lukewarm coffee would be worth the kick of caffeine to get me through the afternoon.

What happened next seemed to take place in slow motion. A

particularly large splash of water connected with my back, drenching my new suit jacket from collar to hem. I arched and sucked in a breath at the sudden chill, knocking my coffee over onto my slightly wrinkled dress pants. At that exact moment, a gust of wind finally succeeded in ripping the pile of papers from my hands, sending them flying across the busy sidewalk.

Swearing under my breath, I scrambled up, ignoring the dampness of my back and pants, and chased the papers as they danced away from me and each other, in every direction, swirling as if playing a game. People stepped around me as I ran, half-crouched, clutching the mischievous papers to my chest. Finally I had gathered them all, and I knelt in the grass, muttering as I tried to smooth out the creases my mad grabbing had created.

I didn't notice at first when a pair of shiny black loafers stopped in front of me. I jumped as a deep chuckle floated down from above me. I followed the length of his legs, clad in expensive slacks, up his torso, sheathed by a crisp white shirt and decorated with a sharp purple tie, up to his mouth, where full lips were forming words. I was entranced by their movement, and their perfect placement on his symmetrical face, which itself was devoid of any facial hair, not even a shadow.

"Are you okay, miss?" His words finally penetrated the haze surrounding my brain, and my mouth, which had dropped open at some point, snapped shut. I looked up to meet crystal blue eyes.

"I'm sorry, what?" My first words were less than intelligent, but the way his eyes sparkled showed me he didn't care. He was amused.

"I asked if you were okay." His eyes crinkled at the corners when he smiled, and I had to catch my breath again.

Wind gusts pulled insistently at my papers, and I used it as an excuse to break eye contact and look down at my stack of now ratty reports. "Um, yes. I'm fine. These reports tried to stage a coup, but I got 'em." I laughed at my own corny joke, and was pleasantly surprised when he laughed with me.

"I'm afraid you may have missed one," he said, holding out a piece of paper with my boss's familiar unreadable scratches scrawled across the surface.

My eyes widened. It was a list of all of her client dinners, probably the most important report in the stack. Of course that would be the one that almost got away. I reached for it, grateful for my rescuer.

"Thank you so much, you have no idea. You've saved my life."

He waited for me to grab the paper in his hand, but instead of releasing it, he used it to tug me a step closer. A hint of his cologne, rich and expensive, reached my nose. "Saved your life?" he asked, eyes glinting with amusement and something deeper. Curiosity? Attraction? "This must be a pretty important paper." A lock of dark hair escaped from his impeccable coif, falling onto his forehead.

A shaky laugh fell from my mouth. "Yes, extremely," I said, tugging on the paper again. His hold remained steady, and my stomach churned with excitement or discomfort. I didn't know how to act in this situation. Should I pull harder? Let go of the report and run screaming? Step toward him and see if he smelled even better up close?

"It must be worth something then," he said. "Dinner, perhaps?"

My cheeks warmed. I glanced down at my coffee-stained pants. Was he asking me out? After he witnessed perhaps the most ridiculous moment of my life? More ridiculous than my first day at the marketing firm, when I spent the day with my brand-new designer blouse misbuttoned. I had assumed the smiles directed my way were in welcome, not because people were laughing at me. I couldn't even market myself. "Um," I stammered, "I don't know if that's . . ."

He flashed straight white teeth as his voice took on a teasing tone. "Too much, too soon?"

I nodded. "I don't even know your name."

"That is a dilemma," he said, his face turning serious. "I guess the question is, do you *want* to know my name?"

Did I? No question. But this was all suddenly too much. I

pursed my lips. The best course of action would be to turn him down flat. I'd had enough experience with men like him to know it wouldn't lead anywhere good.

Undeterred, he grinned. "Fair enough. Drinks then? Meet me here after work. Around six? We can exchange names then, if you're interested."

It was on the tip of my tongue to say no. After all, what did I know about him other than he had a symmetrical face and was good at catching papers? The way he was looking at me, though . . . there was an earnestness to his expression, as if this wasn't just a game. Like he actually wanted me to say yes. What could it hurt? Lately I'd been having a glass of wine in the evening to wind down after long days. Why not go out for one? And the company would be nice, even if just to look at. I couldn't deny that I found him alluring. I nodded. "Okay. Yes."

His eyes sparked with excitement as he finally relinquished the paper. "Fantastic. Until then." He inclined his head toward me and strode away.

"Until then," I whispered, clasping my sheaf of papers to my chest, reports forgotten as my heart raced.

The shout of a child running past brought me out of my trance and I shook my head, smiling to myself. My adrenaline pumped from the encounter, and, bolstered by the idea that a random man could recognize that I was worth spending time around, I turned and strode back into the building. I attempted to organize the stack as the elevator rose to my fourteenth-floor office, but they were pretty much a mess. If only Elaine would get on board with an electronic system for all these reports. At least it would save me the trouble of trying to decipher her scrawling handwriting. I'd gotten pretty good at it, but it still took more time than it needed to.

Dumping the pile on my desk, I glanced up to see that Elaine was at her computer, tapping away at her keyboard, her forehead smooth and relaxed instead of wrinkled concentration. Maybe today was my day to be brave. With a deep breath, I smoothed my stained pants and walked into her office, praying I looked as confident as I felt.

I tapped on the door and waited for Elaine to glance at me before stepping inside.

"Do you have those reports?" she asked before I could formulate the words I wanted to say.

"What?" I glanced back at the crinkled pile on my desk. "Oh, yes, almost finished."

"Good, I'll need them first thing tomorrow."

"Of course."

Elaine's focus was on her computer monitor, fingers flying over the keys in a dance, no doubt corresponding with important people. I fantasized about being one of those people, instead of being at the beck and call of one. As my mind wandered, Elaine's fingers slowed, and I looked up to find her watching me. "Was there something else, Julia?"

This was my time to be brave. I took a deep breath. "Actually, Elaine," I began, "I was going through your reports and almost lost one to the wind, and it got me thinking—"

"You had my reports outside?" Good thing I didn't tell her just how many I almost lost.

"Yes," I continued, "but it gave me an idea."

Her brow creased, but she leaned forward, listening as I outlined my proposal, nodding along to my suggestions. I knew that by the end of my speech, Elaine would start to see me in a whole new light. And it would only be the beginning.

"I can't believe you're actually going." My sister's voice sounded tinny through the speaker of my cell phone as I held up one dress after another in front of the mirror. I couldn't go out with my mystery man in a damp jacket and coffee pants, so I'd snuck out a half hour early to run home and change. I hadn't really taken a lunch anyway. My sister called as I surveyed my woefully inadequate wardrobe, and was now hounding me for details about my mystery man.

"Of course I'm going, Kate. You should have seen this guy. It's like a Ken doll came to life." The yellow dress had some promise. Flirty, fun, a bit flashy.

"It's so unlike you, Jules," Kate said. "You don't even know his name."

It was too bad Kate couldn't see how hard I rolled my eyes at that. "Maybe it's time for me to step out of my box." I dropped the dress on the bed and rummaged through my makeup. A smoky eye was probably too much for drinks. Maybe I should have said yes to dinner. "Besides, it's probably just his random act of kindness for the day. Trust me, this man *does not* have problems getting dates."

"Don't sell yourself short. You said he had good taste. Clearly that extends to women as well."

I shook my head, though Kate couldn't see me through the phone. "That's very sweet, Kate. Maybe you're right."

"Okay, don't believe me, but I'm proud of you, little sis. Just make sure you stick to public places." There was a teasing note in her voice, and I laughed.

"I'll be careful. I've got pepper spray in my purse."

Kate's laugh was interrupted by my nephew Kyle running into the room. "Moooom!" I could hear the whine in his voice.

"Wait a sec, Ky," Kate said. "I'm talking to Auntie JJ." The noises continued in the background, but Kate ignored them. "Tell me what happened with Elaine! Your text was very cryptic."

My eyes shone with excitement as I held the yellow dress in front of myself again. "I pitched her an idea to look into streamlining some of our data form entry and going electronic. There's this great program I was researching called Sibyl that was created by an amazing woman, which I thought would appeal to Elaine, and even though it's pretty new, all the reviews coming back are phenomenal . . ." I trailed off, able to detect Kate's waning interest even over the phone. Laughing, I jumped back into my story. She tended to space out when I went into detail about my job. Kate always wanted to hear every detail about any office drama, but when it came to the actual work I did, the CliffsNotes version was the best way to keep her attention. "I wasn't prepared at all, I just sorta marched in there and blurted it out, but she said she'd consider it, and asked me to put together some ideas for other systems we could consider as well."

"That's great," Kate said. "Maybe if you're not spending all that time shuffling paper, you'll get a chance to actually use your marketing degree."

"We can only hope," I said, keeping my voice light, though Kate's words stung. She didn't mean anything by it, but I didn't need a reminder that I wasn't living up to my "potential." I hadn't moved up as quickly as I'd hoped, and Kate was the usual recipient of my complaints about the lack of larger responsibilities. "Elaine said she knew someone would come in someday and take the firm out of the Stone Age. Honestly, I'm not sure how we're keeping up as it is."

"By overworking poor overqualified assistants," Kate said.

She wasn't wrong. If we could become more efficient on the paper end, I could take on more duties with clients and actual campaigns. As it was, just keeping Elaine organized took up the majority of my time. Before I could respond, my other nephew, Scott, came bellowing in on the other end of the phone. "MOM!"

"I'll let you go," I said. "Let's get drinks this weekend, though. Make Eddie take the kids for an evening."

"It's a deal," Kate said. "Have fun tonight. Make bad choices."

"The worst," I said. "Love you." I blew a kiss into the phone before ending the call. Surveying my shoe collection, I picked out a pair of almost-new red pumps. Kate bought them for a girls' weekend and wore them once before passing them along to me. This seemed like the perfect opportunity to take them out again. Satisfied with my choices, I checked the time. I'd talked to Kate longer than I thought.

I hung the dress in the bathroom to steam out the wrinkles and jumped in the shower, my feet dancing their way through my getting-ready routine as I hummed under my breath.

Chapter 2

It was a few minutes after six when I seated myself at the fountain again. I had tried to be a little late, not to seem overeager, but it appeared Prince Charming was playing the fashionably late card himself, and better. The children from earlier were gone, and most of the foot traffic left was office workers, straggling out of tall buildings, heading home to families or pets or possibly out to happy hour with coworkers. A group of the assistants from my office piled out of the building across from the fountain and headed for the nearest bar. They went out about once a week, and usually invited me to join, but I often declined. I was on good terms with most of the other assistants, and we shared the woes of working our way up the ladder, dealing with menial tasks better suited to an intern until we got the opportunity to take on more responsibility. I used to go out with them more, but I had seen too many promoted above me, and while I was happy for them, it was too hard to maintain close relationships in a workplace that encouraged competition, even if it was friendly. Watching the group disappear around the corner, I didn't notice when he walked up next to me.

"Hello again." His voice both electrified and calmed me. The cadence was musical, soothing, the voice of a man completely at ease with himself. There was no hesitation. He wasn't surprised I was here. He had been certain I would come. I decided to borrow some of that confidence for the evening.

Glancing coyly over my shoulder, I looked him up and down. "You're late."

He laughed. "I was actually early. I've been sitting over there"— he gestured to a bench on the other side of the fountain—"trying to come up with the perfect opening line."

I cocked my head. "And you came up with 'Hello again'?"

His teeth were so white. It made me want to keep him smiling as much as possible. "How'd I do?"

It was impossible not to return that smile. I stood and turned to face him. "Nailed it."

Conversation flowed much more easily than I had expected with my mystery man, whose name was Bryce. Bryce Covington. It was such a regal name, I thought it should always be said in a British accent, though I resisted repeating it back to him that way. And Bryce lived up to the charm of his moniker. He was a complete gentleman.

We headed for the Burrier, the fanciest hotel in the city. Bryce kept a respectable distance between us, though he didn't move away when I casually brushed his arm with mine. When we arrived, he placed a hand on the small of my back as the doorman held the door open for us, and my entire body heated from that point of contact. When he removed his hand, I shivered.

"Are you cold?" he asked, shrugging off his suit coat before I could even answer. "Here, take this." The soft fabric smelled of him, clean, citrusy. I didn't want to admit that I was just missing the contact with his hand, so I pulled the coat more tightly around my shoulders.

"Thanks."

The inside of the hotel was gorgeous, all high ceilings and sweeping fabrics in rich golden hues. A grand piano stood in the corner, and a petite woman in an elegant dress played a piece so intricate that it seemed her fingers barely touched the keys. Bellhops rushed from desk to elevator to the front doors, doing the bidding of one important guest or another. I tried to keep my face as neutral as possible, to mask the awe I felt at being here. Though I'd worked down the street from this building for four years, I had never set foot inside. I'd made reservations for my boss too many times to count, but had never been invited along. Why would a lowly assistant attend a lavish business dinner, anyway? I was confident that would be changing soon. With Elaine's attitude when I'd pitched her my idea today, I knew she would be calling on me to take more responsibility before long. I could almost picture us wining and dining a client together in the splendor of the Burrier dining room.

"Stunning, isn't it?" Bryce's breath whispered across my ear, and I jumped. He laughed. "Sorry, I didn't mean to startle you. I take it this is your first visit to the Burrier?"

"Am I that obvious?" I asked, disappointed to have been found out. This was why I was never in drama club in high school. Couldn't act worth a lick.

"In a good way," Bryce said. "Most people who are used to this place just walk past everything. The way you slowed down and really *looked* at it, really *appreciated* what a special place it is . . . that says a lot about who you are."

"Or just my lack of experience," I said, rolling my eyes.

Bryce stopped and took my shoulders in his hands, turning me to face him. "No. Somehow I think that even if you'd been here a thousand times, you would still stop to appreciate the details."

My cheeks flushed as Bryce released my shoulders. He didn't wait for a response, which didn't matter because all coherent thoughts and word-forming abilities had fled for the moment. Instead, he placed his hand on the small of my back and led me to the hotel bar. A small table in the corner had a RESERVED sign on it, and as soon as the host caught sight of Bryce, he rushed over to lead us in that direction.

"I didn't know you could reserve tables in the bar," I said, lowering myself into the chair Bryce held out for me.

"Most people can't," he said simply, taking his seat across from me. After he had put in an order for a bottle of wine, he folded his hands and pierced me with those incredible eyes. "Now, Julia, I want to hear all about you."

I laughed. "Really? Not much to tell." His eyebrow quirked, and I groaned. "That's really cliché, isn't it?"

"A little." His teeth flashed white. "Maybe I can narrow it down for you, though."

"Please."

"What's one thing on your bucket list?"

I stared at him. "Really? You don't want to know about my job or my family or whether I have pets or not?"

He waved a hand dismissively. "I'll learn all that stuff. I prefer to jump right in."

It was going to be hard not to fall for this guy. As I talked about the things I wanted to do—visit Ireland, climb a mountain, be an extra in a movie—his entire focus was on me. He asked pertinent questions, responded in the exact right way to everything I said, and never interrupted. It was as if no one else existed. It seemed like only minutes later when I wound down, and I was shocked to see that I had been talking for over an hour.

"Oh my goodness," I said, embarrassed. "I'm so sorry I talked so long. I want to hear about you." I leaned forward, attempting to emulate his listening pose.

Two dimples appeared when he smiled. "If I may make a suggestion?"

I nodded, hoping this wasn't the beginning of a kind brush-off. The evening had gone so well, and Bryce had a way of making me feel completely at ease. I was already more myself with him than I'd been in any of my previous relationships. Still, that small negative voice inside my head whispered that he was going to end our time together, that he'd realized in the midst of my monologue that he didn't care to spend any more time with me. When he didn't continue right away, I lowered my eyes to the table in front of me, where my fingers anxiously smoothed over the designs in the wood.

"Can we extend drinks into dinner?"

My eyes flashed up to meet his. "Really?"

"I know you just wanted to do drinks, and I understand if you'd rather call it a night, but I would really like to spend more time with you."

"Absolutely," I said, standing, surprised but pleased at his suggestion, and at his directness. In past relationships I always wondered what was going on in the man's head. The lack of games was refreshing.

Bryce hopped up from his chair and rushed to pull mine out. His suit coat, still hanging from my shoulders, slipped as I came to my feet. "Oh," I said, pulling it off. "I'm not cold anymore. You probably want this back."

"Nah," he said, taking the coat from me and putting it back in place. "It's colder in the restaurant. You might as well keep it. Put your arms through the sleeves if you'd like."

I started to protest. The coat was covering up my cute dress, which I really wanted him to appreciate, and I didn't want to get anything on his clothes, which I was bound to do if I tried to eat while wearing it. However, one look at his eager face and I shrugged and stuffed my arms through the sleeves. "Thanks." The brilliant smile I got in return made the extra hassle worth it. Besides, he'd seen my dress earlier, and I didn't care if anyone else saw it.

When we were immediately led to a table at the back of the restaurant, I realized Bryce had anticipated that the evening would lead to dinner. I wondered where else he anticipated it leading, and the butterflies in my stomach took flight. I took a deep breath and reminded myself that I had boundaries. No matter how charming the man, I would not sleep with him on the first date.

Probably.

"What's good here?" I asked after Bryce had settled into the booth across from me. Opening the menu, I was overwhelmed with the choices.

"Everything is good, but I can suggest something for you if you'd like."

Relieved, I nodded. "Sure, I trust you."

Bryce signaled for the waitress. She rushed over as if she had been waiting for his call. I wondered briefly if every patron at this restaurant received the same deferential treatment, but a quick glance around the restaurant proved that, while the other patrons were treated with respect and efficiency, there were several waitstaff paying particular attention to our table even as they served other guests.

After Bryce had placed our order for baked salmon and wild rice, I leaned forward, keeping my voice low. "So who are you really?" I asked. "I mean, a reserved spot in the bar, this table waiting, everyone so eager to do your bidding. Are you a mob leader or something?" I winked to show him I was teasing, but I was genuinely curious.

He laughed, and I relaxed, glad he hadn't been offended by my observations. "Nothing so sinister," he said, leaning back in his chair and studying me. "I'm a lawyer. I represent the owner of the hotel. Actually, I represent all of his holdings."

Impressed, I nodded. "That makes more sense, I guess. How did you get such a big name on your list?"

"That," Bryce said, leaning his arms on the table, "is a story for another time."

"Sure." I sipped at my water, trying not to focus too much on yet another indication that he was planning to spend more time with me beyond tonight.

Two hours later, I sat back in my chair, glad for Bryce's coat as I wrapped my arms around myself. "That was the most amazing meal I've had in a long time," I said. "Thank you for bringing me here."

"I'm glad you enjoyed it," Bryce said. He stood and held out a hand. "Walk with me?"

This was it. The moment I needed to be strong and tell Bryce in no uncertain terms that I would not be staying in one of the beautiful rooms with him tonight, as much as the sweet wine and delicious food I'd consumed might try to convince me otherwise. Although I would love to see one of the rooms. I'd heard they were spectacular. I didn't realize I'd said as much to Bryce out loud until he nodded.

"The rooms are great here. Best in the city." But instead of leading me to the desk to inquire about whether there were any vacancies, Bryce led me back out into the chilly night air. We walked in silence for a few minutes, and I couldn't tell if the tension in the air was my imagination or if he was feeling it, too.

"I had a great time tonight, Bryce," I said. "I'm really glad the wind blew that report into your path."

"I don't believe in coincidences, Julia," Bryce said, his tone serious. He stopped and turned to face me, taking both of my hands in his. "I believe we were meant to meet by that fountain today. It wasn't an accident."

I liked the sound of that. The idea that we were somehow fated to meet, even while I was coffee-stained and damp, seemed incredibly romantic. "I think you're right, Bryce Covington."

"I'd really like to ask you out again, Julia."

"I'd really like you to ask me out again, Bryce."

He smiled, and I was hit with the realization that I would do anything to keep that smile on his face. The emotion toward Bryce surprised me in its intensity, and I worked to push it to the back of my mind to examine later. We continued talking as we walked, eventually making it back to the fountain, where we sat and watched the nightlife in the city fly by. Bryce talked a little more about his job, though he couldn't divulge too much information about his clients. It sounded like he had some extremely influential people on his roster, and my respect for him grew.

"It's getting late," I said finally, standing. "I usually don't go out when I have to work the next day, but this was great."

Bryce stood as well. "Let me walk you to your car." I nodded, and we walked to the parking garage behind my office building, where I'd been able to park for free. "Next time," Bryce said as I dug through my purse for my keys, "I'll pick you up."

"It's okay," I said, fishing the keys out. "I don't mind meeting places."

"I insist," he said, tone firm. "It's only right that I pick you up. How's this weekend?"

Charming to the core, this man. It was second nature to me to make things as easy as possible for my dates, to avoid being annoying. Bryce clearly didn't see me that way. It was as if he wanted to make things as easy on me as possible. And I decided I would let him. "Sounds good." We exchanged numbers so I could text him my address.

"I'll call you," he said, reaching behind me to open the car door.

I started to shrug his coat off my shoulders to give back to him, but he waved it away. "You can give it back to me this weekend. Stay warm on your drive home."

He leaned in, and I knew this was it. The kiss. The perfect end to the perfect date. I sucked in a breath as my eyes fluttered closed.

"Goodnight, sweet Julia," he whispered, his breath brushing across my lips. He leaned back, and my eyes opened, staring at him. It wasn't a kiss, but it was almost as powerful. He waited for me to climb into the driver's seat of my car and shut the door behind me. He was still staring after me when I checked the rearview mirror before turning the corner out of the garage and heading home.

That night I laid his suit coat carefully on the chair next to my bed, and my dreams were peppered with ocean-blue eyes and the hearty, happy laugh of the man I was already falling for.

The light grows dimmer through the skylight. Night is falling, and still she lies, submerged in the rapidly cooling water. Somewhere outside, a dog barks. It is unusual to hear noises from their house. He would be so upset to know someone has ventured so close. He always claimed the tall fence, the secure gate, were for privacy, and they were. But there were some things he wished to be more private than others. Some things that were meant to be kept, if not loved. Owned. Controlled. And happily so. Happily, naïvely possessed.

Chapter 3

"Tell me again." Kate's voice had taken on an almost breathless quality that came across even over the phone. "What did he say when he told you goodbye?"

I sighed, pretending to be exasperated, but I couldn't keep the giddiness out of my voice as I repeated Bryce's parting words to me the night before. "'Goodnight, sweet Julia.'"

Kate's groan was quiet but still audible. "He sounds incredible. When are you seeing him again?"

My sister hadn't wasted any time calling for details on my date. Unfortunately, her timing wasn't the greatest, since I'd slept through my alarm that morning. This was why I didn't usually go out on work nights. I knew myself, and I needed my eight hours of sleep in order to function.

"Kate, can we talk about this later? When we have drinks this weekend? I'm going to be late for work." I was dying to share all the details of my date, but I was already way behind schedule, and I didn't want to undo the progress I'd made with Elaine yesterday.

"Ugh, I want to know everything *now*. What are you doing after work? Want to come over for dinner? The boys would love to see you."

"I don't know, Kate, I'm not sure I can handle a dinner of mac and cheese and chicken nuggets after experiencing all that the Burrier restaurant has to offer."

"You've changed," Kate said, her tone falsely wistful.

"I didn't choose this life," I said, cracking up before I could go further. "Dinner sounds great. I'll just come straight from work, okay?"

"See ya!"

I rushed into work twenty minutes later, frazzled and dreading the lecture I would get from Elaine. When I reached my desk, I was surprised to find my computer on and piles of reports and review copy neatly stacked and waiting for me. Elaine was on the phone in her office, and she simply waved at me as I scooted behind my desk, stowing my purse in the bottom drawer.

Thoroughly confused, I logged in to my computer and started going through e-mails.

"Psst!" I jumped as a hiss came from my right. I looked over to see Micah, one of the other assistants, leaning over, giving me a sly look. "Hey, don't worry, I covered you this morning."

Torn between gratitude and suspicion, I asked the first question that popped into my head. "Why?" Micah had never been particularly friendly toward me. She had been at the agency nearly as long as I had, and tried to organize the other assistants like some sort of adult version of *Mean Girls*. Few of us played her games, but most of our coworkers still showed her some deference because of her seniority. Since I had technically started before her, I had no such obligation, and it seemed she resented me for that, despite the obvious fact that I wasn't being promoted anyway.

She laughed. "I saw you with Mr. Hottie at the Burrier last night. I wouldn't have been too quick to get out of bed, either." She waggled her eyebrows suggestively. Ah. Apparently being seen with Bryce had somehow elevated me in her eyes. If it resulted in her being more pleasant to be around, I was glad she'd spotted us. "Don't worry, Elaine thinks you were running a special errand for the big boss." She looked toward Elaine's office. "I may have hinted that it had to do with her ten-year anniversary with the company, so now you have to throw her a party, but I'm sure the guy was worth it."

Great. I knew there would be a catch to her help. And she had the total wrong idea about how I'd spent the night, but it really wasn't her business, so I didn't bother correcting her. "Thanks for covering, Micah."

"Come have lunch with us today. You can tell us about your mystery man." She turned her attention back to her computer without waiting for a response. Apparently she assumed I would just do what she asked. And she was probably right. I might not have had any interest in playing her games, but I was happy to do what it took to keep things friendly with her. Besides, I liked the other people she typically ate with well enough. We might not even have to speak.

My phone buzzed, and I glanced down at it automatically. Thanks for last night. Hope your day is going well so far. -B

That man could make my stomach flutter even from a distance. It was a pretty tame message, but I felt it to my bones. He cared enough to check in the next day. Proof that he wasn't into games.

Overslept but everything's fine, I responded. Someone kept me out past my bedtime.

I would apologize but I'm not actually sorry. ;) Hope you're not in trouble.

I chuckled quietly. Not yet, but I might be if I don't get to work. Have a good day!

I'll call you tonight.

With something else to look forward to, I happily returned to my e-mails, humming through the normally monotonous work and dreaming in the background.

I pulled up to Kate's house hours later, still smiling. Bryce had texted me a couple more times throughout the day, and I was flying high. I even managed to keep my cool when Derrick, the office copy boy, once again stapled all my reports in the wrong spot, requiring me to redo them. I suspected he did it on purpose, but today it didn't faze me.

Have fun with your sister tonight. -B

I didn't respond to Bryce's text, but I hummed a little tune as I stowed the phone in my purse and climbed out of the car. Kate's street was filled with all the typical sounds of a suburban neighborhood. Kids playing a pickup game of basketball next door trash-talked each other, snippets of the evening news floated from an open window, and in the distance, a mower roared to life. The smell of fresh-cut grass permeated the air, and I breathed deeply. I loved this neighborhood. Kate and I joked that as soon as I settled down, I could buy a house nearby, and our kids would be able to play together.

My smile fell a bit as I realized that, at this rate, her boys would have zero interest in hanging out with any kids I had. But they'd be great older cousins, anyway. For the first time in a long while, I allowed myself to believe that our little fantasy might become a reality. I just knew Bryce would love this neighborhood, with its quaint old houses and friendly neighbors. I shook my head, laughing that after one date I was already picking out a house. Slow down, Jules.

I could hear the familiar sounds of chaos as I approached the front door to Kate's house and entered without knocking. As usual, her two boys were running around in their *Star Wars* gear, brandishing light sabers and trying to beat the crap out of each other.

"Boys!" Kate yelled over their happy shouts. "Aunt Julia is here! Time to put the light sabers away and sit at the table."

"Never!" Both boys turned to me and stalked closer. "That's no aunt, that's Rey, and she's come to try to beat Kyle Ren again!" Eight-year-old Scott pointed his light saber at me. "But even if he falls, Supreme Leader Snoke never will!"

"Scott! My name is Kylo Ren!" Six-year-old Kyle was indignant. "Kyle Ren doesn't sound like a Jedi name at all."

"But it's your name."

"Nuh-uh."

"Boys!" Kate sounded exasperated. I loved visiting, but there was something to be said for going home to a quiet apartment and putting my feet up at the end of the day. Taking pity on her, I stretched both arms out.

"Neither of you can resist the power of the Force," I said, waving my fingers in the air. "You *will* drop your light sabers and go sit at the table."

I could see the conflict in Scott's eyes. Even though he liked to play the bad guy, he knew the good guy was stronger. Finally, he stiffened and dropped his light saber. "I will drop my light saber and go sit at the table." He walked like a robot toward the table and sat.

Kyle, ever trying to stay in Scott's favor, followed suit.

"Bless you," Kate said. "I never imagined parenting would involve so many swords."

"Light sabers!" Scott corrected, falling silent when I held up a hand again.

Kate crossed the room, giving me a quick hug and then threading her arm through mine. "So, now that we have peace and quiet for a few minutes, I want to hear all about last night."

I took a seat at the table and peeked at my curious nephews. "Maybe we should wait until Kylo Ren and the Supreme Leader have finished."

"Fine, but you're not getting out of telling me," Kate said, disappearing into the kitchen and reappearing with a pan of lasagna. "I need details, woman."

I rolled my eyes. "Where's Eddie?"

"Working late. Again." There was an edge to Kate's voice. She and Eddie were the perfect couple at times, but lately he'd been working a lot of overtime for no extra money, and the wear on the marriage was showing. Not to anyone outside the family, of course, but I knew them too well. I let it slide for now, but Kate wasn't the only one who would be pressing for details later.

"Ahhh, peace and quiet," Kate said. She was lounging on the couch when I came out to the living room after tucking my nephews into bed. Scott was still clutching his light saber as he drifted off to sleep, despite our argument over whether the Supreme Leader actually used a light saber or not. Spending time with my nephews made my heart ache for kids of my own, and I couldn't help picturing what my babies with Bryce might look like. I definitely had it bad already.

"Did Eddie come home?" I asked, jumping in before Kate could divert attention to my date.

She jerked her head toward the basement door. "Came home, grabbed a slice of cold lasagna, and went downstairs. He won't come back up until one a.m. or so."

I frowned. "Is this normal?"

"Lately," Kate said, sighing. She looked at the basement door as if she wanted to say more, but instead took a deep breath and forced a pleasant look onto her face. "But enough about the boring old married couple. I want to know more about this guy who has clearly swept you off your feet." She studied me, a smirk on her lips. "Seriously, Jules, you've hardly stopped smiling since you got here."

"Scott and Kyle," I began, but Kate shushed me.

"Don't even try it. I know you love my kids, but they've never made you glow quite like that. And that's a good thing. So. Spill." She leaned forward, eyes eager, and that was all it took for me to launch into a step-by-step playback of my date.

After I finished, Kate flopped back onto the cushions, sighing. "Seriously, Jules, he sounds fantastic." She eyed me, a thoughtful look on her face. "I'd wondered if you would ever let yourself like someone again after Jake . . ."

"Ugh, and this conversation was going so well," I said. I had no desire to talk about my ex-fiancé.

Jake had promised me the world. We'd met in college, and he had seemed so different from the other guys. He took an entirely different approach to life. He expected that good things would happen for him, and he was usually right. He told me once that he just listened to his heart, and he knew what to do. I'd ended up taking the assistant job instead of moving to a different city and a more promising position because he didn't want to leave. He'd proposed to me when I'd told him I wasn't moving, and I trusted him when he said he felt that he needed to stay put.

Two months later, he was inspired to take a six-month assignment learning how to work on an organic farm. After that, he wanted to hike the Appalachian Trail. And all the while I waited, certain that he would come back to me so we could start our life together.

When he broke off the engagement, Jake told me that he assumed I knew that we were headed in different directions, that we were no longer on the same page. He said that we existed in different worlds, that I was stuck, and would only hold him back. He laughed when I suggested we try to work it out. Laughed at me even as I cried and handed the ring back.

Now he was living abroad with his childhood sweetheart, doing humanitarian work in some developing country. I saw updates sometimes from mutual friends. I was glad to still be by Kate and the boys, but it had been a big blow to my confidence. Only recently had I started to think I might be open to the idea of a relationship again.

"Fine," Kate said, bringing me back to the present. "You're right, we won't talk about that douche-canoe. Let's focus more on your fairy-tale prince. What did you say he did for a living?"

I breathed a sigh of relief as the topic moved away from the pain of my past. I was over it, mostly, but it still wasn't fun to think about. No one likes to be reminded that they weren't good enough. But even as I told Kate about the importance of Bryce's job, doubts started creeping in. Jake had seemed so wonderful at first, too. A little selfish, maybe. A bit shallow. But we were young. We didn't know better. Now I was older and wiser. Wasn't I?

It was almost eleven by the time I drove home. I was going to pay for it in the morning, but it was worth it for some real girl talk with my sister. It seemed lately we mostly talked about her kids, and before that it was Eddie. I hadn't had much more than my job to talk about since Jake took off. I probably needed to get some hobbies.

I was climbing into bed when I realized I'd almost forgotten to set the alarm on my phone, which was still in my purse. I wasn't sure I could count on Micah to cover for me two days in a row, so I planned to set at least three alarms.

When I unlocked the phone I saw the text from Bryce still open on the screen. Bryce couldn't be a hobby, but maybe he could help me find some.

Not wanting to wake him if he was already asleep, I texted. Hey, just got home. Thanks for the texts. We had a nice time, but we talked longer than planned. Don't want to wake you, but give me a call tomorrow when you get this.

I hit send and plugged the phone in, preparing to turn out the light and go to sleep, but the phone rang almost immediately. My heart fluttered when Bryce's name lit up the display.

"Hey," I said, smiling into the phone, glad he was awake. "I thought you'd be sleeping already."

"Nah, I was hoping you'd call," Bryce replied. "I wanted to hear how your evening went."

"It was good." I paused, and decided I wasn't ready to open up to Bryce about my concerns about my sister's marriage. "We mostly talked about boring stuff. Work, the kids, you know."

His laughter vibrated the earpiece on the phone. "Nothing else?"

"Hmm," I said. "Nope, can't think of anything else interesting there was to talk about."

He laughed again. "Sure, sure. Okay. I just wanted to check in, but I'll let you go to bed. For someone who claims to not stay out late on weeknights, you've sure been a night owl the past couple of days!"

I laughed. "This is rare for me, I promise you. I'm going to pay for it at work tomorrow, and probably fall face-first on the couch when I get home."

"No plans tomorrow?" His voice rang with the smooth confidence that I associated with him already.

"Nope. I'm simply too exhausted from my busy social life this week," I teased.

"What about Friday?" he asked. "Plans then?"

"Hmmm." I pretended to think about it, knowing full well my calendar was wide open. "I had considered doing some of my complicated chores on Friday. Cleaning behind the stove, scrubbing the grout in the bathroom. You know, exciting stuff."

He laughed. "Perhaps I could persuade you to postpone those plans and spend the evening with me instead?"

I sighed. "Well. I suppose I could move those things to Saturday. If I had to."

"I appreciate your sacrifice."

Settling back into my pillow, I reached over and turned the light off. "I should probably go to sleep. My boss prefers me when I'm conscious at work. Sweet dreams."

He didn't say anything for a moment, and I thought he might have drifted off himself. Finally, he spoke. "My dreams will be sweet as long as you're in them, Julia Hawthorne."

Pleasure rushed through me at his words. "Keep saying things like that and I'll keep you around for a while."

"I'm counting on it," he said, chuckling. "Sleep well, Julia. I'll talk to you tomorrow."

"Goodnight, Bryce."

Chapter 4

I was beginning to wonder if I was in the middle of some elaborate dream. As things with Bryce continued to go well, things at work also improved. Whereas Elaine had been generally dismissive of me in the past, since our discussion about electronic filing and databases, she had been practically friendly. She started sending me on small errands, not just to pick up lunch or coffee. I even ran a message to the president of the company, who very few of us had access to. On Friday, she called me into her office to ask my opinion on a design she'd been working on.

"I like the font in this one, but the colors are so much better over here," she said, wrinkling her nose as she studied the options for the ad she was creating.

Biting my lip, I contemplated whether I should actually offer a suggestion or just agree with her. I had an idea, but I didn't want to overstep.

"Spit it out, Julia," Elaine said. "You'll never get anywhere in this company if you don't speak your mind."

I also wouldn't get anywhere if I said something Elaine didn't like, but I definitely couldn't speak my mind about that. Instead, I nodded and pointed to the computer. "May I?"

"Go ahead," she said, gesturing to the keyboard.

I saved what she had and then merged the two options.

"That won't work," Elaine said. "The font doesn't fit right."

"Hold on," I said. "Just give me a minute."

Elaine's intake of breath told me that she wasn't used to assistants speaking to her like that, and I cringed internally, but then again, she was the one who had told me to speak my mind. I selected a font similar to the one she liked but better suited to the design, moved it into place, and stepped back.

The room was silent as Elaine stepped forward, leaning in until her nose was almost touching the screen, studying my work. I held my breath.

"This . . . this is actually quite good," Elaine said finally, and I sagged in relief. "Do you know much about graphic design?"

"No," I said. "Not really. I took a couple classes in undergrad, but most of what I know I've learned here, from you and some of the other designers."

Elaine studied me. "How would you like to learn more? You have an eye for this, but could use some refinement. The company would pay for some classes if you could give us a commitment to stick around for a few years after you're properly trained."

I was speechless, and clenched my teeth to keep my jaw from dropping. After snagging the job here, my interest in advertising and graphic design had grown, but I'd never been able to spare money to take more classes. It really was like a dream. When I was sure I could speak calmly, I cleared my throat. "I would love that."

"I'll see what's coming up and let you know," Elaine said, sitting back at her desk and turning to her work. It was her way of dismissing me. I turned to leave. "Julia?"

I looked back, working to keep my expression smooth and professional. "Good work today. You're destined for greater things than that desk out there."

It was higher praise than I'd ever expected from Elaine. She wasn't the type to dole out compliments just for doing a job, even if it was done well. In fact, she was more likely to find the smallest possible error and point it out. Loudly.

"Thank you, Elaine," I said before exiting her office and heading straight for the break room. As soon as the door closed behind me, I jumped up and down, squealing quietly. It was an entirely inappropriate display, but I was bursting. I couldn't wait to tell Kate. I couldn't wait to tell Bryce. I stopped jumping as his name crossed my mind. How quickly he had become one of the first people I wanted to share good news with. I knew he'd be just as excited as I was. I could hardly wait.

A knock sounded on my door at exactly six that evening. I had just slipped the charm bracelet that matched my sister's over my wrist, and I took one final look before hurrying to the door. I'd dressed a little more subdued that night, but I prayed I looked elegant and classy and not like I was on the way to a funeral in my black sleeveless dress. The skirt was just a little swishy, and fell to the top of my knees, and I jazzed it up with a red belt. I hated high heels, and my feet were still a little sore from wearing them the other night, so I slipped into a pair of flat strappy sandals before swinging the door open. My mouth dropped.

Bryce looked incredible. He wore a suit, making me grateful I had chosen something more formal. He had skipped the tie, and his dress shirt lay open at his throat. He stood with his hands in his pockets, looking as if he'd just stepped off the cover of a men's fashion magazine, and when my eyes finally made it to his face, it was to see him laughing at me.

"Should I change?" he asked. "You seem pretty distracted."

"Don't you dare," I said, reaching for my purse. "Oh, I have something for you!" I was a little reluctant to give up the jacket he'd loaned me the other night, but I hoped I'd have an opportunity to borrow another one at some point. Plucking the jacket from the coat-rack by the door, I presented it to him with a flourish.

He laughed. "You shouldn't have."

"Oh, but I insist," I said, teasing.

"I wouldn't be a gentleman to refuse a gift from such a lady." He held out an arm for me to take. "Shall we?"

I double-checked the locks and then threaded my arm through his, appreciating the solidness of his bicep against mine. The fabric of his suit coat was rough against my bare skin, and I shivered at the contrast.

"Cold already?" he asked, removing his arm so he could open the front door of my building.

"Nope, just excited," I said, smiling at him. "What do you have planned for tonight?"

Bryce shook his head. "That, dear Julia, is a surprise."

I started to respond, but my voice caught in my throat when I saw the limousine parked in the street. Swallowing my surprise, I asked, "Is that for us?"

"Only the best!" Bryce took my arm again and led me forward. A rotund man in a driver's cap hopped out of the front seat and hurried over to open the back door for us.

"Thank you," I murmured as Bryce motioned me in before him. I slid across the seat and barely noticed as Bryce climbed in behind me. I'd never been in a limo before, but it was exactly like every movie I'd seen, down to the moonroof that I was dying to poke my head out of. Probably not proper for a second date, but I was sorely tempted. I wondered what Bryce would say if I did. If I opened the moonroof, stood tall, threw my hands in the air, and screamed my joy to the city. Would he join me, or would he be embarrassed by such a juvenile display? I decided not to find out, at least not this time.

The entire night was already taking on a dreamy quality. None of the dates I'd been on had ever come close to this level of extravagance. The back of the car was bathed in a soft bluish glow from tiny spotlights dotted around the interior. I could imagine myself stretching out on the buttery leather seat in front of me and taking a small nap on the way to wherever we were going. Of course, that would require moving away from the incredible man beside me, and I had no intention of doing that unless forced.

"So what's the deal?" I asked, looking over at Bryce. "You have a limo?"

He leaned in. "Can I tell you a secret?"

I swallowed, flustered by his nearness. "Of course."

"It's a loaner," he said, his voice low. "I really wanted to impress this amazing girl I met, so I called in a favor from an associate."

Laughing, I shoved his shoulder gently, creating space between us so that I could breathe and think coherently. "Can I tell you a secret?"

He inclined his head. "Of course," he said, echoing my earlier answer.

I lowered my voice to a whisper. "You don't have to work too hard. She's already impressed."

His dimples popped. "Well then, how about we ditch the fancy dinner plans and go bowling?"

"As long as I'm with you," I said, and immediately regretted it. Too much, Jules. Simmer down.

But the look in Bryce's eyes said that he didn't mind my declaration. I relaxed. Bryce had a way of making me think and say things even I didn't expect, but he also seemed to appreciate it. I was so used to censoring myself, it was a strange feeling to be so free with someone, especially someone I'd just met.

The car was slowing by now, and I realized we were back in the city, just a few blocks from where I worked. This was an area heavily populated with office buildings, fairly quiet at this time of night. "What are we doing here?" I asked. "I didn't know there were restaurants around here."

"There aren't," Bryce said as the door opened and he stepped out. He offered me a hand, and I craned my neck to see the top of the tall building we stood in front of. "This is my office building."

"Wow," I said. I felt a little guilty that I'd never thought to ask which building he worked in, but then I remembered it was only our second date. I didn't need every detail yet. "Which floor?"

"Top," he said, pulling me forward. He pulled out a card and waved it in front of a keypad. There was a click and he pushed the door open, ushering me inside ahead of him.

The lobby of the building was dimly lit, and a security guard sat at the front desk, working on a crossword puzzle. He looked up as we approached. "Good evening, Mr. Covington. The chopper is prepped and ready to go."

Chopper?

"Thanks, Sid," Bryce said, his tone pleasant and familiar. "How are the kids?"

"Doin' great, Mr. Covington. April won her class spelling bee and Nathan just started basketball camp, thanks to that scholarship the church got him."

"That's good to hear, Sid. Have a good evening."

"You too, Mr. Covington," Sid said, and nodded at me. "Ma'am."

Bryce chuckled as we got into the elevator, waiting to speak until the doors had separated us from the lobby. "Why the frown? Do you not like the building?" He was teasing, but there was a hint of concern in his voice as well.

"He called me 'ma'am,'" I said, pouting. "When did I become old enough to be a ma'am?"

This elicited an even larger laugh from Bryce. "He was just being polite. I don't think he meant it in a derogatory way."

"Clearly you are not a woman," I said, crossing my arms across my chest. I was being dramatic on purpose, and I knew he knew it from the twinkle in his eye.

"You're right, I'm not a woman. I'm sorry you were offended." Bryce took my arms, uncrossing them and sliding his hands down to clasp mine. "Would you rather he asked for ID?"

I rolled my eyes. "Okay, I get it. Dramatics off." I winked at him, which seemed to surprise him for a moment, and his brow creased before smoothing out again.

"Now that's settled, *miss*," he said, teasing. "Are you ready for your surprise?"

My stomach lurched. "Sid mentioned a chopper. He meant for salad, right?"

Bryce bit the corner of his lip, his expression amused. "How does a nighttime helicopter ride sound?"

"Terrifying," I answered honestly, before I could put my filter in place. Bryce wasn't offended, however.

"Have you ever been in one?"

"No." For good reason. I didn't need to be enclosed in a metal death bird. I'd seen enough movies about what happened if things went wrong.

"You should try things before you diss them."

"'Diss'?" I asked, raising an eyebrow. "Did you really just use the word 'diss'?"

"Did it distract you?"

"A little."

"Then my plan is working."

"But now I just remembered that you have a helicopter. Maybe I do need to clean behind my stove tonight."

"It's not my helicopter. It belongs to the company."

"Well, maybe we shouldn't use it. We wouldn't want to scratch the paint job."

Bryce only shook his head in amusement and took my hand.

The elevator stopped at the top floor, and I followed Bryce to a door at the end of the hallway. I barely noticed any of the details of the top floor, where Bryce said he worked, so focused was I on what was coming next. I would have to come back and visit. If I survived the helicopter ride, of course.

There wasn't much opportunity for private conversations once we were ushered into our seats. I was given headphones with a mouthpiece to communicate with Bryce and the pilot, but once we were in the air, I wasn't interested in conversation. Even as I gripped Bryce's hand, I couldn't tear my eyes from the view. The city at night was majestic, especially from the air. It was a clear evening, and I was certain no one could ever appreciate the view of the city as I did in those moments.

"You were right," I shouted into my mouthpiece. "This is fantastic."

"What?" Bryce said.

"You were right," I repeated.

"What?"

I turned to find him watching me, a mischievous look on his face. Of course he'd heard me the first time. I made a face at him without repeating myself before turning back to the window.

Too soon, we were landing in a different part of the city. Bryce jumped out first and took my waist to lift me down. As soon as I was on solid ground, he released me to adjust my dress and hair. When I was put together again, Bryce's hand settled at the small of my back, the heat burning through the fabric of my dress as he led me forward.

We'd landed a little ways down from a small seafood restaurant on the river, which ended up being our destination. As it had been at the Burrier, the waitstaff seemed to know Bryce well and deferred to him, leading us to a quiet table overlooking the water. Bryce ordered for us without asking for menus, and I took in the general ambiance of the place.

"I've never been here before," I said. "It's charming."

"One of my favorite places," Bryce said. "The owners attend my church and I helped them secure the financing to open it."

"Wow," I said, looking around. The place was packed, even for a Friday night. Clearly they did good business here. "So, Bryce," I said, folding my hands on the table. "You let me talk for hours the other night about every part of my life. I want to know more about you. Tell me about your family. Are your parents still around?"

I saw the walls go up before Bryce even spoke, his voice guarded but sad. "I don't really talk about my parents, Julia." He paused, as if searching for the right words. "My childhood was not a happy time, and I'd like to steer clear of unpleasant topics tonight." He reached out and touched the tips of my fingers. "I want this night to be special for you."

My smile was forced. I wondered what had happened with his family to cause that reaction in a man whom I had already grown used to being open and genuine. I was reminded that I didn't really know Bryce at all yet. Instead of deterring me, however, that realization only fueled my desire to know more. Bryce was a puzzle I was dying to piece together, and I would start tonight.

Chapter 5

Almost a week later I hadn't been able to learn much more about my mystery man, and he was doing everything in his power to distract me from trying. While he wasn't closed off, exactly, it just seemed that he always veered the conversation back to me when I started to ask personal questions. And it was working. I reasoned with myself that we had only just started dating, though our connection was real and stronger than anything I had experienced before, even with Jake. I'd seen him every night that week, and when we weren't together, I was thinking about him.

I'd even done my best to track him down online, but he had zero social media presence. When I mentioned to him that I couldn't locate him to connect, Bryce just shook his head and made a comment about everyone putting their business out on social media before advising me to shut mine down. An Internet search only yielded his law firm's website, which I bookmarked because of the picture on his bio page. Even the bio was generic, filled with information that could be applied to almost any male of the species.

"Ahem." I jumped as Micah cleared her throat. "You've got that goo-goo look on your face again," she said, rolling her eyes. "Thinking about Prince Charming?"

I scrunched my nose, annoyed at being caught in a daydream. "No, just trying to visualize this new project Elaine has me working on," I lied, knowing it would shut Micah up. After her initial show of goodwill, covering up for me with Elaine when I ran in late, she'd gotten frostier with each new project Elaine asked my input on. There had only been a couple, but Micah's questions about Bryce had become more snarky than curious. She still wanted all the details, of course, but was especially skilled at pointing out the worst possible reason for any action.

"You went for tacos?" she'd asked after I recounted the highlights of my Taco Tuesday adventure with Bryce. "That's so tacky. Did he wear a sombrero?"

It was pretty easy to ignore her remarks, and I even brought them up with Bryce, who brushed them off. "Jealousy isn't very attractive," he'd said. "Not that I blame her for being jealous of such an amazing woman."

I smiled now at the memory. Bryce had a way of making me feel secure, making me feel like things that bothered me were just small things that were easily shrugged off instead of the boulders I made them into.

"It's creepy when you smile like that," Micah said.

Laughing, I took out my phone. I needed a break from Bryce, because as wonderful as he was, I wasn't focusing on anything else, and I was self-aware enough to know that wasn't healthy. I sent a quick text to my friend Savannah, ignoring the pang of guilt that it had been several weeks since I'd texted her. Even living in the same city, it was hard to get together often. I hadn't even told her anything about Bryce yet. Not that I wanted to spend my evening talking about him. Just the highlights.

Hey, Van, what are you up to tonight?

The response came almost immediately. Footie pajamas and Netflix, but I could be persuaded to change my plans if the right offer came along.

Mickey's?

Hell yeah! I'll call the Cat Pack.

Perfect. See you at 7?

You're on.

I felt lighter as I texted Bryce to let him know I had other plans that evening. We hadn't set anything up, but over the past few days it had seemed almost unspoken that we would see each other every day. He responded quickly to have fun and he'd call me tomorrow, and even that short text sent happy chills down my body.

With a night of girl time ahead of me, I was finally able to focus on completing the sample portion of the Sibyl program Elaine had allowed me to purchase after our conversation, completely blocking out Micah's sighs and death glares as I hummed happily.

It was a little after seven by the time I made it into Mickey Finn's, the bar Savannah and I used to practically live in during college. Along with the rest of the "Cat Pack," as we christened ourselves, we'd celebrated highs and mourned lows at our favorite corner booth, which I was happy to see Savannah had snagged for us. I spotted her as soon as I walked in, her dark curls unmistakable even from across the room.

"JULES!" she cried, weaving her way through the crowd and throwing her arms around me when she reached me. "I've missed you!"

"It's only been a few weeks, Van," I said, linking arms with her as we made our way back to the table.

"That is forEVER in Cat years," she said, scooching into the large round booth and pulling me in after her.

"Hey!" I exchanged hellos with the others at the table. Kara, Darci, Joni, and Amanda made up the rest of our "pack." Even as I settled into the worn leather booth and into the natural flow of conversation that never seemed to lag, no matter how much time we spent apart, I realized how much I missed these girls who had seen me through the crazy college years and beyond. Through finals and through my broken engagement, even as I watched each of them grow and reach milestones while my own life remained stagnant. Not that I begrudged their success and happiness. I was just ready for my own life to begin. Bryce's blue eyes flashed through my mind and I started to believe that my time had finally come.

Shaking my head, I kicked my mushy thoughts away to focus on the group. "So how'd you score our booth?" I asked. "Joni, are you still seeing the bartender?"

"Nope," she said, laughing. "Van did it!"

I looked at Van, raising an eyebrow. "When did you get so much pull?"

Tossing her hair, she shrugged. "You know Mickey loves me. I called ahead and he reserved it."

"Uh huh," I said. "Even after you broke his heart all those times in college."

"Please," she said, laughing. "A little harmless flirting never hurt anyone, and it got us our booth back."

"I'm telling Austin," I teased.

"He's the one who suggested it," she said with a wave of her hand. "My man knows how things work."

The bar filled up as we spent time catching up. It didn't take long for them to worm information about Bryce out of me. Not like it was hard. As much as I was enjoying the evening, I couldn't quite push him completely out of my mind. By the time I'd finished talking about our meeting and first date, all the girls were staring at me with versions of starry-eyed optimism and goofy grins.

"You've got it bad," Savannah said finally. "I haven't seen you like this since . . . well . . . ever. Even with He-Who-Shall-Not-Be-Named."

I squared my shoulders. "Jake," I said, and Savannah's mouth dropped open before curving into an approving expression. "It's fine to say his name. I am over it, over him. I'm so over him. Moving forward. Maybe with Bryce, maybe not, but definitely forward."

The girls looked at each other. "With Bryce!" they said in unison, and the bartender chose that moment to bring us a round of shots, sent from a table of fraternity-looking guys. We toasted them before downing our drinks, and it was like we were back in college.

"You guys! We have to karaoke!" Darci said. "Like we used to!"

"I have the perfect song," Savannah said, eyes sparkling. "Hold on, I'll go put us on the list."

I leaned into Amanda as Savannah skipped away. "I've missed you guys."

"Same," she said, patting my head at an awkward angle. Amanda was the quiet one, probably the most steady of all of us. And the first one of us to get married. We jokingly called her Mama Amanda after she got married, even though Savannah said her "I dos" only a few months later. I'd have to call Amanda to have coffee soon. She was more comfortable one-on-one.

"Let's go, girls!" Savannah was back, tugging on my arm, pulling me out of the booth. I grabbed Amanda, who grabbed Darci, and so on down the line until we were a human chain, winding our way up to the stage.

As the first strains of the Spice Girls' "Wannabe" blasted from the speakers, we all hooted and hollered. There wasn't a more perfect song at this point. *"If you wanna be my lover, you gotta get with my friends!"* I screamed into the microphone. I was usually a fairly decent singer, but for tonight, I was all about letting loose with everything I had, playing up my role as Ginger Spice to Van's Scary Spice.

Too soon, the song ended, and we exited the stage to raucous applause, making our way back to the table. I collapsed, signaling for water.

"Don't look now, girl," Savannah said, whisper-shouting to be heard over the next act, crooning along to "Genie in a Bottle," "but I think Bryce has some competition. Dude hasn't stopped staring at you since we were up on stage."

Savannah tended to exaggerate, but I decided to look anyway, figuring I'd send a flirty wave and then get back to my night with the girls. Instead, my stomach dropped as I saw the man now making his way over to the table.

"Bryce?"

Bryce's face was fixed in a casual expression as he approached. "Hey," he said, reaching the table. "I wasn't sure if I should come over or not." Despite his claims to be unsure, he looked completely confident in his decision, his gaze zeroed in on me.

Flustered, I did my best to sit up straight and smooth out my hair and clothing. "Of course you should, but what are you doing here?"

He ran a hand through his hair, which was decidedly more mussed than usual. It was a good look for him. "I thought I'd have a drink with some of my friends," he said. "I didn't realize we'd end up at the same place." I craned my neck to look back the way he'd come, trying to get a glimpse of this group of friends. He mentioned friends from time to time, but not by name.

An elbow gouged my side, and I remembered my friends were all still sitting at the table. My world had once again been all Bryce for those few seconds.

"Bryce," I said, "this is Savannah, Darci, Amanda, Kara, and Joni. Guys, this is Bryce."

Everyone said hello, and then continued to watch the two of us like we were a reality television show.

"Listen, ladies," Bryce began, his natural charm sparking from every syllable. "I know this is girls' night and everything, but do you mind if I borrow Julia for a few minutes?"

"Take her," Savannah said, shoving me out of the booth. I practically fell into Bryce's arms. He caught me and set me upright before taking my hand and leading me away.

"I'll bring her right back," he called over his shoulder.

Sorry, I mouthed at the group as I allowed Bryce to pull me through the crowd. Savannah made a hand gesture that caused my cheeks to heat. I was glad for the dim lighting in the bar.

Bryce let me up a side staircase to the rooftop patio. It was much quieter away from the crowd. Small pockets of people dotted the area, but there was plenty of privacy. We found a small corner partially blocked from the rest of the rooftop by a canopy and sat on the chaise longue set up for optimal nighttime city viewing.

We sat for several minutes, not speaking. It was surprisingly peaceful, with the sounds from the bar muted and the lights winking at us from all directions. The silence between us was a comfortable one, not pressured. In fact, I felt more settled with him than I did away from him, which both surprised and calmed me. Shifting in his seat, Bryce turned to me, taking my hands. "Julia," he said, "I'm really sorry for interrupting your night with your friends, but I saw you up on stage and I had to tell you something."

Ducking my head, I blushed. I hadn't exactly planned for Bryce to see *that* part of me just yet, though he was bound to see my silly side eventually. "Yeah, it's a little different from how I usually act," I said. "I guess you got to witness a whole different side of me tonight." I laughed, trying to inject levity into the moment.

Brushing a finger under my chin, Bryce raised my face to look at him. "If I'm honest, I wasn't a fan of all those guys in there staring at you dancing around onstage." Embarrassed, I tried to look away, but his gaze held mine. "But you were absolutely beautiful. I couldn't take my eyes off you."

At that moment a meteor streaked across the sky. "Make a wish," he whispered, leaning close.

"I don't have to. Everything I need is right here."

He leaned in. "Julia."

"Yes?" I could barely breathe, so close were our lips.

"I love you."

Most people would say it was insane to fall in love so quickly, but as soon as he said it, I knew it was true for me as well. We were one of those stories, the ones young girls talk about. The whirlwind romances where both people just *knew* without needing more time. As those words left his lips, I knew that this was the man I wanted to spend my life with.

"I love you, too."

His lips closed the distance to mine, and when they met a thousand shooting stars exploded behind my closed eyelids as fireworks danced across my skin. He cradled the back of my head, holding me in place as if I would have any desire to leave this spot. My fingers clutched at his sleeves, moved to his chest, rested there, felt his heart racing in time with my own.

We fell, together, as bright and dramatic as the meteor falling to its fiery death above us.

He's not sure which is worse: the walk home or actually arriving home. In the distance, the outline of a run-down shack shimmers in the afternoon heat. From here, it looks abandoned, as if some tragedy drove its inhabitants off in the middle of the night, leaving a shell of a life behind.

Unfortunately, the tragedy still exists in those walls.

Behind him, a group of boys from his grade shuffles as if using one mind. He smirks. They don't have enough smarts to make up an entire brain between them. Still, his footsteps grow, longer and faster, his gangly legs finally serving a purpose. Used to be those boys would have caught him and roughed him up already. But he's found ways to outsmart them.

By the time he reaches the front gate, the illusion, and his secret hope, that the house is actually abandoned is shattered. The TV screams through the open windows, the voices distorted, words garbled. The only thing more grating is the sound of his mom and her latest live-in yelling at each other. The topic of the argument doesn't matter. It always ends the same.

He steps inside the gate, picks his away across the grass scattered with piles the dog left behind, and swings up into a towering tree, the only one of its size for miles. Remnants of a long-forgotten attempt at a tree house rot in the deepest part of the tree, and he settles in what would have been the lookout tower, opening his bag and pulling out his homework. He tunes out the cacophony of the world and focuses on his singular goal: escape.

PART II

FIRST COMES LOVE

Chapter 6

K ate picked up on the first ring.

"I can't do this," I said, not giving her a chance to greet me. "I'm going to say something stupid and Bryce will realize he made a huge mistake and dump me on the spot."

An amused sigh preceded Kate's laugh. "You'll do fine, Julia. Bryce's family will love you."

"I am pretty great," I said, nodding at my reflection in the mirror as I surveyed my blue, knee-length dress from every angle. "And my fashion sense is impeccable."

"Lead with that," Kate said. "Get them on board early."

Just joking around with my sister had the desired calming effect on my nerves. "Did I tell you it's not even his real family?"

"What does that mean?"

I frowned, recalling the conversation with Bryce. He refused to talk about his biological family, but had gone on and on about this man and his wife who he said had changed his life. "I'm not really sure," I answered Kate. "He calls them the Reverend and Nancy." I thought for a moment. "I don't think he's ever even mentioned the Reverend's first name. Anyway, I guess they lead some church in the Sheridan Heights area. We're going to the service before brunch."

"Really? Interesting. I hadn't pegged Bryce for a church boy."

I rolled my eyes, though Kate couldn't see me. "He goes to

church, but I don't know if that classifies him as a 'church boy,'" I said. "Besides, how do you know? You've never even met the guy."

"And whose fault is that? Savannah and the Cats got to meet him. I'm beginning to think you're ashamed of me."

"It's time you knew, Kate."

"Brat."

A knock at the door interrupted my response.

"He's here, gotta go."

"Have fun, and Jules?"

"Yeah?"

"Relax, they're going to love you." Sincerity warmed her tone, and I smiled into the phone.

"Thanks. I'll call you tomorrow."

Bryce was leaning casually against the wall in the hallway when I opened the door. As usual, he took my breath away at first glance. At second glace, I let out a surprised laugh. "They're going to think we planned this."

He was dressed in dark pressed slacks, which he paired with a shirt almost the exact blue of my dress. Of course, they brought out the brilliant blue of his eyes, which was why I'd picked the color for myself.

Pushing off the wall and closing the distance between us, Bryce took my face in his hands and gave me a chaste kiss in greeting. "Great minds think alike, love."

My lips tingled where his had brushed them, and I wondered if I'd ever get used to the feeling. My confidence grew and I leaned forward to place a not-so-chaste kiss on his surprised mouth. "Indeed," I whispered against his lips.

Bryce cleared his throat, and I was happy to recognize the effect I had on him. "We'd better get going," he said. "Do you have a sweater?"

I glanced down at my bare arms. After our greeting, putting on a sweater was the last thing on my mind, but since we were going to church, I had set out a cardigan. "Just a second." I stepped back into the apartment, collected my purse, and shrugged on the white cardigan as we headed back out the door. "Is this okay, though?" I asked, suddenly nervous again about being presentable for the people he called family.

"You look perfect," Bryce said, his voice encouraging. "You'll fit right in."

The wave of relief I felt at that statement held me all the way until we pulled up in front of the huge building that housed Bryce's church. A sign declaring CHURCH OF THE LIFE in tall, bold letters hung over the entrance, surrounded by great pillars that gave it a regal feel. Bryce pulled up into the half-circle drive and my door popped open as soon as the car came to a halt. A smiling man offered his hand to help me out of the car. I glanced at Bryce, but he was already out and handing his keys off to another man. The two shook hands, and I allowed myself to be pulled from the passenger side. Bryce jogged around and took my hand from the man who had helped me, tucking it into his elbow.

"Thank you, Peter," Bryce said, shaking the man's hand. I nodded at Peter as Bryce led me away, and Peter gave a small wave before jogging to the next car to assist its passengers.

"Valet service?" I asked.

Bryce gazed down at me. "It's one of the ministries of the church. It's meant to be welcoming. Besides," he said, gesturing to the right, "would you want to walk from over there?"

Across the street was a giant parking lot, several football fields wide and deep. In the distance, golf carts ran valets back toward the entrance. The synchronicity of it was beautiful, but I shook my head. "Thank goodness for valet service."

We walked through the massive double doors and were immediately greeted by no fewer than five different people. Most knew Bryce by name, and he shook hands and introduced me to each one. The names flew past me and refused to stick in my brain, which was otherwise occupied taking in the interior of the building. Giant screens flashed announcements everywhere I looked. The smell of coffee wafted over from a café to the left, and groups of kids disappeared into the kids' church area on the right. An information booth dominated the center of the room, and the mass of people teemed around it.

"What do you think?" Bryce whispered in my ear.

"It's . . . a little overwhelming," I said, looking up at him. A frown creased his brow. "But everyone seems so nice," I continued, trying to avoid offending him. "I've never been to a church like this."

His brow smoothed, and he smiled, pride evident across his face. "There aren't many like it," he said, and began pointing out the different areas, giving me a mini-tour. As we walked, a door opened and a group of girls spilled out.

"Wow, so many young people," I said, impressed.

"Those are the girls from our school," Bryce said. "They live there full-time. I'll show you around there someday. I think you'd really appreciate it."

No wonder the building was so large. A church and a school and any number of other things. I was suitably impressed. At the entrance to the sanctuary, a smiling woman handed me a booklet outlining the service and listing all the activities going on at the church. It was substantial.

"You guys do a lot here," I said, flipping through.

"We try." Bryce took my hand and led me farther into the room. The soaring ceilings held my attention for a moment before I caught sight of a table in the back.

"Bill shredder?"

"We believe in freedom from financial burdens," Bryce explained. As he spoke, a woman walked up to the shredder, fed a bill through, and picked up a bell sitting next to the shredder, ringing it loudly. Immediately, everyone in the vicinity began clapping, and several people ran up and embraced the woman, offering her congratulations.

This was certainly not what I expected at a church, but it fit Bryce. With him, everything had been unexpected from the moment we met. He tugged my hand and I followed him down the center aisle toward the front of the church. It was almost completely filled up already, but there were two empty seats in the middle of the second row that had obviously been saved for us. It took us a bit to get to them, as Bryce hugged each person we passed and introduced me. I forgot most names except for the woman I sat next to, Stacy. Her blonde hair shone in the bright lights surrounding the stage in front of us, and I self-consciously smoothed my dress as I took in her perfectly pressed skirt-and-blouse ensemble.

"It's so nice to meet you, Julia," Stacy said. "Bryce speaks highly of you, and we've all been excited to meet you."

I smiled at her, unsure of how to respond, since I was sure Bryce had never mentioned her to me by name. In fact, Bryce had only ever talked about the Reverend and his wife in any of his stories. "I'm very excited to meet everyone," I said. "Bryce says such nice things about the people at church." That was vague enough, and seemed to satisfy her.

"We'll have to get together for coffee sometime," Stacy said. "I'd love to learn more about you, and see if Bryce has been exaggerating!"

"Sure, yes, of course," I said. "Do you want my e-mail?"

"I'll just get your number from Bryce," she said, and before I had a chance to respond, loud music blasted through the sanctuary. Everyone hopped to their feet and before I knew it, I was swept into the excitement of the service.

The church had a full band, and it was almost like attending a rock concert where everyone knew the songs except me. Bryce and Stacy swayed and clapped on either side of me, and all throughout the room people fell to their knees and raised their hands in the air. I'd never seen anything like it, and it fascinated me. Between songs, the bandleader invited everyone in the congregation to greet each other, and people milled about the room for almost ten minutes, hugging and shaking hands, before the music started again. I had never seen Bryce so animated, so in his element, and I had never been so attracted to him. This was where his charismatic confidence came from. I found myself watching him more than paying attention to the music.

A gnawing need to know more about what drove Bryce, what made him tick, grew in my heart, at the same time as a sinking feeling in my stomach made me realize that I didn't belong in this world. This wasn't me. This was exciting and fascinating, but I wasn't a part of it. I didn't quite fit. Fears and questions about what Bryce saw in me reared up as I observed all the perfectly put-together people around me. That was another thing I had noticed. Everyone looked as if they had stepped off the pages of *Jesus Today* magazine. Graceful, classy, not a hair out of place, even as they danced and jumped to the music.

I was generally pretty confident about my looks. Jake had done everything he could to erode my self-confidence, and if he'd stuck around he probably could have done a great deal more damage. Being with Jake was the most self-conscious I had ever been about my appearance. Until now. Surrounded by these perfect people. And, as I looked around more, I realized that it wasn't just in the clothes or the hairstyles, the perfect makeup on the women and the neatly trimmed facial hair on the men. It was more something in how they held themselves, the same way Bryce held himself. As if they were untouchable. Unflappable. So sure of their place that the idea of questioning it would have been foreign.

My thoughts must have been reflected in my expression, because when Bryce looked down at me between songs, the elation on his face faded. He leaned down and spoke directly into my ear, his warm breath raising goose bumps down my arms. "Everything okay?"

I nodded. *Fine,* I mouthed, as the next song started, and forced my lips into the semblance of a happy expression. I turned toward the stage and started clapping, trying to keep in time with Stacy, who appeared to have perfect rhythm. From the corner of my eye, I could see that Bryce continued to watch me for several moments before turning his attention back to the music. Inside, I sagged with relief, though I kept clapping, not wanting to draw Bryce's attention back to me. He didn't need to be worried about my insecurities when he was sharing this part of his life with me.

My feet ached by the time we were invited to sit down after a full forty-five minutes of singing. I'd never heard any of the songs before, but most were pretty easy to catch on to, especially with the words flashing on the screens. As we settled back in, Bryce reached over and took my hand gently, resting our clasped hands on his knee. I was grateful for the contact. It tethered me back into the moment, to Bryce and the reason I was here, rather than allowing my thoughts to run wild with why I didn't belong. I could save those musings for later. This was a side of Bryce I'd never seen before, and I wanted to enjoy the moment.

A man walked onto the stage, dressed in a long robe of deep purple. His brown hair was shot through with silver, which glinted in the lights from the stage. When he spoke, I found myself leaning forward, almost unconsciously. His tone was magnetic, his words powerful, even the simplest ones. I knew without asking that this was the Reverend whom Bryce spoke about so enthusiastically.

I didn't understand much of what the Reverend said, but I was amazed when he said a final prayer and stepped down and I realized that over an hour had passed. Soft music played over the speakers, the lights in the sanctuary brightened, and everyone began shifting, gathering their belongings as the low rumble of conversations rose through the room. A man tapped Bryce on the shoulder, and he released my hand to turn and greet him. I sat, still and contemplative, trying to process what had happened over the past two hours.

"What did you think?" I jumped as Stacy leaned over, touching my arm to get my attention.

"I don't know," I said honestly, before I could stop myself. I clapped a hand over my mouth. "I mean . . . uhhh . . ."

Stacy laughed. "It's okay, Julia, nobody really knows what to think the first time they hear the Reverend. He's a very gifted speaker."

I nodded. "He is. I'm not sure I understood everything he said, but I know it was very good."

"You'll learn," she said, leaning back and giving me an appraising look. "I think you'll fit in just fine here, Julia."

My heart leapt, both in elation and in fear. How did she know what I had been thinking? Was it so obvious that I didn't fit, but that I wanted to? If she'd seen it, had Bryce seen it, too? But her words brought comfort. Maybe she saw something in me that I didn't. I had many questions for her, but before I could voice any of them, Bryce touched my elbow.

"Are you ready?"

"Yes," I said, smiling at Stacy. "It was nice to meet you."

"You too, Julia." Stacy gave a small wave and turned in the opposite direction as Bryce led me out of the row and down the aisle toward the front of the church. A woman who looked to be about my mother's age stood near the stage, greeting people who came up to her with a handshake or a hug. Her chestnut hair was parted severely down the middle, but fell in soft waves to her shoulders. As with all the other women, her face was perfectly made up, and her smile was practiced but friendly.

As we approached, her face lit up. "Bryce!" she said, walking toward him with open arms. He released me to envelop her in a hug.

"Good morning, Nancy," Bryce said, releasing her from the hug but holding her shoulders as he stepped back. "How is everything?"

"Better now that you're here, as always," Nancy said, laughing. "What did you think of the Reverend's sermon?"

"Very moving," Bryce said. He removed his hands from Nancy's shoulders and reached back for my hand, pulling me forward. "Nancy, this is Julia, the woman I told you about."

It seemed that Nancy's eyes tightened just a bit at the corners as she looked at me, reminding me of the feelings of inadequacy that had flooded me during the service. This was the woman Bryce considered a mother figure. Would she think I was good enough for him?

So quickly that I convinced myself I had imagined it, Nancy's face lost the pinched look and brightened into a megawatt smile. She reached out and pulled me into a hug. I returned it gently, realizing as we embraced that the woman felt very fragile, as if I could break her if I squeezed too hard.

"Julia," Nancy said, pulling back. "We have heard so much about you. The Reverend and I have been so anxious to meet you. Bryce talks about you constantly."

"I've been anxious to meet you as well," I said, trying to mimic the smooth confidence of her voice. "Bryce lights up when he talks about you."

Nancy looked over at Bryce, a genuine smile on her face. "We're very proud of Bryce, and very happy that he seems to have found someone he . . . cares about." The pause was subtle, but I caught it, and Bryce's corresponding squeeze of my hand told me that he caught it as well and was trying to reassure me.

"Nancy and I have a meeting to attend before brunch," he said, steering the conversation another way in order to alleviate the bits of tension that had just sprung up. "But after that we'll head over to the dining room."

I looked up at him, my eyebrows rising. "There's a dining room here?"

He laughed. "The Reverend's house is attached to the church. The church actually grew up around their house. They built it from the ground up. It's an inspiring story."

"We'll get to that later," Nancy said, interrupting. "We'd better get to our *meeting* so they don't start without us."

Bryce frowned. "They can't start without you."

"Still," Nancy said. "It's rude to keep them waiting."

Something passed between them, almost too quickly for me to catch, and Bryce turned to me, picking up my other hand as he faced me. "The meeting shouldn't take long. Will you wait for me in the café?"

"What meeting do you have?" It was maybe a little nosy, but Nancy's attitude had made me curious.

"Just our leadership. We meet every week after service," Bryce said, releasing my hands to dig out his wallet. "Grab yourself a coffee while you wait, and I'll be there soon."

"Sure," I said, taking the bill he held out for me. "No problem."

Bryce didn't look at me again as he and Nancy headed for a side door off the sanctuary. I stood for a moment before heading back up the aisle toward the back of the large room, which had mostly emptied out, though there were pockets of people laughing or praying together. People smiled as I passed, but did not stop to engage me in conversation. Apparently I was less interesting without Bryce by my side.

There were still a fair number of people outside the sanctuary, and the café was more crowded than I expected it to be. Several groups gathered at the round tables and in comfortable soft chairs, talking quietly. I ordered my coffee and took it to a small chair in the corner. It was situated so that I could watch for Bryce, but also allowed me to observe the other people in the café.

They fascinated me. I'd never been to a church where people stuck around so long after the final hymn was sung. Usually people were ready to be done with their weekly duty and move on with their weekend, watch that football game, get those last Sunday chores done before heading back to work. The members of this church, however, seemed more settled, ready to spend the entire day in this building if they needed to.

That reminded me of the school that Bryce said was attached, as well as the Reverend's home. I wondered if that was part of it, that homey feeling. People actually lived here, but there wasn't a feeling of intrusion, at least not in these public areas. Just enough of a welcoming atmosphere without being overwhelming.

"Hey!" A perky voice dragged me from my observations, although if I had been truly observant I should have noticed her approaching. The woman in front of me was small and blonde, and wore a wide smile that lit up her entire face.

"Hello," I said, smiling back. It was impossible not to. I wondered if I had met her earlier and just forgotten, but I didn't know how I'd forget someone like her. She positively sparkled.

"I'm Jenny. We saw you sitting over here alone and thought you might like to join us." Jenny gestured to a cluster of couches and chairs across the café, where a small group of women watched our interaction with expectant looks on their faces. "Is this your first time here?"

I nodded. "Yes, I came with someone. Uh. My boyfriend. He had a meeting or something so I'm just waiting for him."

"That's cool," Jenny said. "Welcome! I can leave you alone if you want, but feel free to wait with us."

I had a feeling Jenny was used to people saying yes, and it wasn't hard to see why. And her friends looked just as happy and hopeful that I would join them. It felt as if I were the best friend they'd never met, but had always known was coming.

"Sure, I'd like that," I said, standing. "I'm Julia."

Jenny led me to the group and made introductions. I promptly forgot each of their names except for Jenny and Maryann, a quiet brunette with brown eyes that locked on mine during our introduction. Everyone was friendly, but it was as if Maryann, in her quiet ease, really *saw* me. I didn't know how else to explain it.

"We're all part of a weekly Bible study," Jenny explained. "But we like to have coffee after church most weeks to discuss the sermon as well. It's best when it's fresh!"

As I sat back and listened to the women talk, I was struck again by the ease of it, the sense of familiarity even though this was my first visit. Whereas during worship I'd felt out of place, I could almost believe I fit here. I felt comfortable with this group, happy and content. I was even brave enough to venture a few questions of my own about things I'd heard the Reverend say in his sermon, and the women were all anxious to answer anything I asked.

By the time Bryce arrived, I felt as if I'd made a good start at some friendships, which would be important if I continued coming with Bryce. Knowing how important this church was to him, I figured he would be pleased. The women here were different from my other friends, but not in a bad way. Just . . . different. I waved excitedly at Bryce when I spotted him at the café entrance, and stood as he wound his way through the tables to our spot.

"It was so nice to meet all of you," I said. I thought I had a grasp on all their names by now.

"Let me grab your number, Julia," Jenny said, pulling out her phone. "We'd love for you to join us for study sometime."

"That sounds great," I said, and rattled off my number for her.

"I'll call you."

Bryce reached us by that point and took my elbow. "Ready for lunch, Julia?"

"Yes, I'm starving," I said. "Bryce, do you know all these ladies? They kept me company while I waited."

His mouth was tight, not the friendly and open expression I was used to. "Hello," he said, addressing the group. "I trust you all enjoyed the message today."

There was a chorus of agreement throughout the circle and I puzzled at the change in atmosphere. Where things had been light and easy before, tension had descended, an unacknowledged wall between Bryce and these women. Before I could think too much on it, Bryce led me away. " 'Bye!" I called over my shoulder. "Thanks again!"

As soon as we were clear of the café, Bryce's shoulders relaxed. I hadn't realized how tense his entire body had been. "Everything okay?" I asked.

"Fine," he said. "Meeting just went longer than we planned. I'm sorry I kept you waiting."

"Don't worry about it," I said. "I was fine."

"I can see that."

I frowned. "Do you have a problem with the people I was talking to?"

"Of course not," Bryce said, laughing. "I don't even know them."

"You were a little rude."

"Was I? I certainly didn't mean to be. I just don't want to be any later for lunch than we already are."

I raised an eyebrow at his tone.

"Do you want me to go back in and apologize?" he asked.

Searching his face for mirth and finding only sincerity, I shook my head. "It's fine. I'll just remember that you get a little testy when you're hungry."

He laughed again, his familiar Bryce laugh. "Are you making a list?"

I scoffed. "A list? I have an entire book by now."

Grabbing my hand, he lifted it to his lips. "You make me laugh, Julia. Thank you for coming today."

"I'm having a great time, Bryce. Thank you for showing me a little of your world."

"Ready for more?"

"Absolutely."

Chapter 7

Bryce led me through an office area, down a carpeted hallway, to a large door. He opened it without knocking, and as the door closed behind us, all sounds of the church were cut off. We were in a small room, occupied only by a love seat and a chair.

"The outer welcoming room," Bryce said. He pulled me across the room to another door. "Just sets off the house a little bit from the church."

Through the next door, I could immediately tell that we were in a home. We stood in another hallway, this one with dark wood floors, covered by an elegant runner down the center. Several closed doors lined the hallway, but the walls were dotted with pictures, family portraits. Bryce walked slowly beside me, giving me time to examine them.

"Who are all these people?"

"Family," Bryce said. "Not all by blood, but all considered family. Most of them attend church here."

I smiled at him. "I love how close everyone is. I've never experienced anything like it."

"You've only scratched the surface," he said. "I knew you would appreciate it. Eventually I hope you start to think of the people here as your family as well."

I wasn't so sure about that. Everyone was nice, and it was lovely how close he was to them, but I already had a family. Though Bryce hadn't said it outright, I got the feeling that he didn't have anyone other than the Reverend and Nancy, and the people at the church. I had my parents and Kate and her family.

We emerged from the hallway into a well-lit great room. Floor-to-ceiling windows made up one wall, with a view overlooking a small pond that wasn't visible from the front of the church. It appeared we were at the rear of the property. To the left, tall bookshelves flanked a massive fireplace. To the right, a long dining table set with elegant china and utensils took up a large amount of space. The high ceilings kept the room from feeling cramped, and the cushy furniture made it feel comfortable.

"You found her." Nancy walked into the room, a genuine smile on her face. I paused before returning it, so different was it from her earlier expression, when I had felt more tolerated than welcomed.

"She was chatting with Jenny's group," Bryce said, and a glance passed between Bryce and Nancy so quickly that I might have imagined it. "They invited her to join their study."

"How lovely." Nancy sounded sincere. "You make friends fast, Julia."

Pleasure at her praise fluttered through me, and I was surprised that I was so eager to please her. "To be fair, she approached me," I said. "After that, they were all very easy to talk to. Everyone is so nice here, Nancy. You have something really special."

Nancy reached out and touched my hand. "I'm so glad you think so. We do, too."

She looked as if she was going to say more, but the door at the end of the hallway opened, distracting her.

"Reverend," she said, her tone bright. "Welcome home." She rushed to greet him, and I was bemused by her fawning. She took his suit jacket, then bent to pick up his discarded shoes, scurrying through one of the doorways off the hall before returning empty-handed. She took the Reverend's arm in an almost formal way and led him forward.

"Reverend, this is Julia, the woman Bryce has been telling us about."

The Reverend's eyes were emerald green and sparkling with humor, despite the fact that there was nothing funny happening at the moment. Laugh lines radiated from the corners of his eyes and connected a road map across his face, a story that told of a happy life. He smiled, revealing teeth that were white, but not blindingly so, and just a little crooked, which endeared him to me immediately. He had a confidence about him, an aura that at once made me feel safe and heard, though I hadn't spoken. He was what I imagined a religious leader should be. Approachable, graceful, relatable. I found myself drawn to him even before he spoke.

"Julia," the Reverend said, coming forward and clasping my hands in both of his. His grip was firm and warm, his hands soft. "We are so glad you could join us at last."

It was natural to smile back, and my face heated at his rapt attention. "I'm glad to be here. It's, uh . . . been a while since I attended a church service." I looked down, feeling a sudden wash of shame.

"We're just happy you're here now, Julia," he said, and relief ran through my veins, straight to my heart. I looked up to meet his eyes again and saw only acceptance and compassion. Joy. No sarcasm or judgment.

"It was a nice service," I said. "I've never been to one with a band and lights and screens and all that. It made me feel like I was at a show, but, like, one I was a part of, too, if that makes sense." I realized I was babbling as the Reverend, Nancy, and Bryce all chuckled around me. I ducked my head. "I just really liked it."

The Reverend looked like he was going to say something else, but a bell chimed from the other room.

"That'll be lunch ready," Nancy said. "Margot made meat loaf."

The Reverend squeezed my hands once more and then relinquished them to Bryce, who took one and tucked it into his elbow.

"You did good," Bryce said, leaning down to whisper in my ear. "Meeting the Reverend can be a little intimidating."

I nodded my head, shaking off the feeling of awe. "He does have a presence."

Bryce's eyes twinkled. "That's an understatement. It's why he's so successful."

By then we were at the beautiful dining table. Bryce pulled a seat out for me and took the one next to it, to the right of the Reverend. Nancy sat on the other side, across from Bryce.

"We thought it would be nice just to have a small lunch with Julia today," Nancy said, and I looked down the long table, wondering how many people usually joined them after church. "We really want to get to know you," she said, turning to me. She noticed my glance and explained, "The table is often full after services. It's our way of giving back and really getting to know the members of the church. Margot, our cook, prepares enough to feed an army every week."

As if she heard her name, a slim woman dressed neatly in a knee-length black skirt and a white blouse appeared through the swinging door that I assumed led to the kitchen. She was lovely, perfectly pressed, her shining brown hair falling to her shoulders, framing her heart-shaped face set with large brown eyes. There was a skip in her step as she brought out the serving dishes, and I thought I heard her humming as she went about her work.

"Good afternoon, Reverend," Margot said, her tone respectful. "I enjoyed service today. I hope you're hungry."

"This smells great, Margot," the Reverend said. "Where's Joseph? Isn't he helping serve?"

"He got caught up," Margot said. "But it's no problem. I've got it."

"Do you need help?" I offered without thinking. The tray Margot was balancing seemed almost too large for her, though she handled it with ease. Margot's wide smile faltered when I made the offer.

"No, dear," Nancy said from across the table. "You're the guest.

We wouldn't dream of imposing." I was surprised at the edge to her voice, but when I looked over, her expression was as pleasant as ever, and I decided I must have imagined it.

"Precisely," Margot said, smile back to full wattage. She set the tray on the table and went back for more. It took her four trips to bring all the dishes out, and then she came back to fill the water glasses. No one else spoke up to help her, but she continued to hum as she worked. She removed the lids from the food with a flourish, and when the steam cleared, a colorful and mouthwatering array of food waited. And then she was gone.

The Reverend cleared his throat. "Why don't I pray?" he said, and we all bowed our heads. After the prayer, Bryce patted my knee under the table and began piling food onto my plate.

"You might be wondering, Julia, why we didn't offer to help Margot."

I feigned surprise at the Reverend's observation, though there was nothing surprising about it. We had all been witness to my failed attempt to help, and the tension afterwards obviously wasn't just my imagination. "I'm not sure what you mean, Reverend."

"Making us Sunday dinner is one of Margot's Acts of Service. You see, we're all given gifts, things that we can do to bless others, and it's a blessing to *us* to use those gifts. Margot has been given culinary gifts as well as hospitality gifts, and she generously shares those gifts with us a few times a week. When one of our members is performing an Act of Service, we don't step in. It is theirs to attend to, and trying to step in would be an insult to their work for God."

My cheeks heated again. "I'm so sorry," I said. "I had no idea." It seemed a little odd to me, not to be allowed to help someone out, because that in itself seemed to be an act of service . . . What if my Act of Service was to help others with theirs? When I posed this question, the Reverend laughed.

"You have a thinker here, Bryce," he said. "I like that. Questions are good, especially at the beginning, as long as you understand that there comes a point where it just has to come down to faith."

We spent the rest of lunch in easy conversation. I asked a couple more questions, but soon the conversation steered to me and my life. The Reverend was very interested in my family and my job.

"Bryce was telling us that you're doing quite well at your job these days."

I shot Bryce a look, and he shrugged. "We talk a lot."

"He may have exaggerated," I said, laughing. "But there have definitely been some good things happening. My boss is giving me some more responsibilities, and I'm hoping to get a chance to move out of an assistant position sometime in the next year. I'd love to have more of a hand in actual marketing and design work."

"That's all fascinating," Nancy said. "You know, I work with some of the ladies on our outreach teams. Perhaps you could help us with designing logos and event materials."

"Nancy," Bryce said, warning in his voice. "This is her first time here. Give her a chance to get acclimated before you pull her in and put her to work."

"Best way to get involved is to dive right in," Nancy said, unapologetic. "She's clearly skilled in this area. And it could be fun."

Bryce started to say something else, but I interrupted. "It does sound fun," I said. "I'm definitely open to helping out sometime, maybe after I've come a few more times?" I tried to appease both Bryce and Nancy, unsure who I wanted to impress more.

Nancy looked at me, her gaze piercing, for several moments, and then nodded. "Of course. I can introduce you to some people next week."

That wasn't exactly a few times, but she wasn't talking about dragging me down this week, so I counted it as a win. Conversation moved on to family, and I learned that the Reverend and Nancy had never had children of their own.

"We've always felt that this church is our child, that all the people who go here are our legacy. And then along came Bryce." The Reverend looked at Bryce like a proud father. "He's as much of a son as we could have ever asked for. More, in fact, than we could have dreamed of."

I looked at Bryce. The matter of his family was still a bit of a mystery to me, but I was relatively certain that he wasn't adopted. "When did you guys meet?"

The Reverend leaned back in his chair. "Hmm. Must have been . . . eighteen years ago? Nineteen? Bryce was just a scrawny little troublemaker back then. Nothing like the impressive young man he's become." The Reverend's eyes glossed over, and I felt for a moment that he was no longer with us, that the Bryce he was seeing wasn't the one whose hand rested on mine between our plates, but the boy he'd been when their paths had crossed for the first time.

Bryce cleared his throat. "Enough about that," he said, voice almost too bright, fake. He was clearly uncomfortable, and while I felt for him, I was also incredibly curious about what his life had been like before the Reverend and Nancy came into it.

Before I could follow any of those lines of thought, I found myself being pulled to my feet. "I'm going to take Julia on a tour of the grounds, Reverend," Bryce said. "I pointed out the main parts of the building earlier, but I think she'd really love your gardens."

"Excellent plan," the Reverend said. "Joseph should be in to clean up soon, and by the time you get back we'll be ready for afternoon tea."

"Okay," Bryce said, and then he was pulling me toward the beautiful French doors and out into the sunlight.

Stunning. It was the only word I could think of to describe the gardens that Bryce and I strolled through in the afternoon sun. Rock paths snaked through seemingly endless swaths of greenery. Benches offered rest along the way, but Bryce and I continued walking. It was like an entirely different world, and I could hardly believe this existed in the middle of the city. It was the suburbs, but still, it was an oasis in the middle of a bustling area. It was impossible to even hear traffic.

After a while, we settled into a swing on a gazebo somewhere in what I assumed was the center of the garden. I sat close to Bryce, and his arm curled around my shoulders. We didn't even pretend to be formal anymore. I laid my head on his shoulder and sighed.

"This has been an incredible day, Bryce. Thank you."

"You've been incredible," he said. "You fit in so easily. With the church people, with the Reverend and Nancy . . . It's like you're meant to be here."

His statement pleased me so much that I decided not to bring up my many faux pas from the day. If what he wanted was to remember me fitting seamlessly into his world, who was I to argue? Besides, as he said it, I realized how much I wanted it to be true. I wanted to be part of this world, part of this church family, part of Bryce's family. It was like they possessed some secret that I simply had to know. I wanted to stay here, learn more, soak it all in. I remembered the feeling I had during the sermon, and then again after church with Jenny and her group. If I could be that comfortable all the time, I wanted to be a part of it.

"I can't believe places like this exist in the city," I said, meaning both the garden and the church.

"You can always find a place to belong, Julia. You just have to know where to look."

I thought about my workplace, how I didn't quite fit there, but then remembered that I was finding my way. And my family fit together as effortlessly as Bryce fit with the Reverend and Nancy, though we had maybe a little more drama. I was sure there was drama here, too, but I enjoyed the fact that I knew nothing about it and didn't even have to think about my own drama.

My family would like it here, too, I decided. A place with so many wonderful people and groups would be right up their alley. I wondered if they had any sort of couples counseling program or study for Kate and her husband. Maybe they could finally talk things out.

I realized I was being fairly optimistic about life in general, but I found that I liked it. I spent my life being pessimistic and expecting the worst from people, especially after everything with Jake. Being in this church, being in this place, being with this man . . . it made me reconsider how I saw the world, and I liked the way it felt. It was hopeful, happy. Maybe the joy I saw in the Reverend, in Bryce, in so many of the people I'd met today . . . maybe it was attainable for me as well.

Bryce broke me out of my reverie when he landed a soft kiss on my forehead, and gently showered kisses along my jawbone. I raised my face to meet his, and I stopped thinking about anything aside from Bryce for quite some time.

The library is his retreat when the tree house can't be, on days like today, with a violent storm surging outside. Fortunately, the pouring rain also discouraged the group of boys from following him home. He wonders if they have any hobbies other than tormenting him. If only they knew that their harassment was more like being tickled with a feather compared to the horror he lives in every day. Last week they changed tack and split up, cornering him by the old barn. He laughed as they struck him, and eventually they stopped and backed away. He was sure they thought he was mentally unstable, but that was okay. He grinned at them through his swelling eyes, blood flowing freely from his smashed nose. And he laughed some more. They ran then, but were back the next day, stalking his steps through town. They didn't learn. He'd received the switch for the bloodstains on his shirt, but he separated from the pain, floated out of his body, imagined the looks on their dumb faces to soften the sharp needles over his back.

Most of the time in the library he spends studying. The only way out of this town and this life is by getting a scholarship or being good at sports. Even then, most of the sports "stars" peak in high school and come back home to live with their parents before moving next door, or down the street, destined to stay put for the rest of their lives, unable to hack it outside the bubble of small-town life.

He is different. Once he can leave, he'll never return. For anything.

Today, a stranger lounges in one of the chairs in the reading area, rustling the newspaper as he turns the pages. The man is well-dressed, his clothing clearly not from the Happy

Mart or any stores of that ilk. And he reads the paper as if he's truly analyzing it, not just looking for quotes to pull out to sound smart at the bar this weekend. The boy is intrigued. Strangers don't come here often, and they rarely spend time in the library. Maybe at the café, just off the highway, which boasts of the best apple pie since Granny made it, but even then few are willing to venture into the grungy interior to test the food.

He watches the man for a while, and then goes back to his studies. His skin feels itchy, like he's being watched, but every time he looks up, no one pays him a bit of mind. It's the same feeling he gets when one of the horde are lurking, too afraid to approach him on their own, but keeping tabs just in case the rest of the group shows up. He shifts in his chair uncomfortably.

After a time, the man folds his paper and gets up to leave. He passes the boy with the barest of nods in his direction, and is gone. In his absence, the itchy feeling dissipates, and the boy wonders if the paper was the only thing being analyzed.

Chapter 8

I was still mulling over my visit with Bryce's family the next day at work, processing all the interactions even as I worked on a presentation for Elaine. The positivity from the visit hadn't exactly dissipated overnight, but I found myself craving more, while still feeling the effects of my time with the Reverend and the church family. I was excited at the prospect of learning more and spending more time with the people who attended there. At the same time, I was nervous that no matter how much I wanted to fit in, or how much Bryce's influence helped, I still wouldn't be able to find my place. Many parts of me clung steadfastly to the beliefs I'd developed while I was with Jake. Every time that optimism surged, especially when I was with Bryce, Jake's voice barged in to tamp it down, to remind me that I wasn't worth the effort and that they'd all figure it out soon enough.

My family had never really attended church growing up. We'd go with grandparents on the holidays, but it wasn't a big part of my life. When we did go, I mostly remembered having to wear uncomfortable shoes and sitting on hard pews and listening to an old man drone on and on. And while I got the idea behind Communion, which we seemed to do almost every time we visited, it always weirded me out that they talked about it like flesh and blood. When I was with Jake, even the occasional visits stopped because he staunchly refused to set foot in a church. He was a proud atheist and got frustrated when I wouldn't renounce all things religion. It wasn't that I believed or didn't believe. I just didn't know, and I wasn't willing to put my foot firmly on either side of the fence I had become so adept at balancing on.

After yesterday, I was teetering.

It still seemed too good to be true. The simple faith that the Reverend and Bryce and Nancy all shared. And Jenny and her Bible study. It was like they knew a secret, something that filled them with light, and I desperately wanted to know what it was.

"Hey, earth to Julia." I became aware that Micah was hissing at me in a loud whisper. "You've been staring at that slide for like ten minutes. Elaine wanted it by five, right?"

Crap. I'd been doing so well at balancing, but I was incredibly distracted. I decided to try the prayer thing the Reverend had talked about, and sent up a quick missive for focus on my project, with a plea at the end for Elaine to love it enough to continue giving me more responsibilities.

At 4:30, I hit send on the presentation and pinged Elaine through our messaging system to let her know it was on its way. I stood and stretched, shocked at how much time had passed. I'd been so focused that I'd forgotten to stop for lunch. My stomach grumbled as I pulled out my phone and headed for the break room.

Dinner tonight?

The text was from Savannah and I typed out an affirmative response. I'd gotten a couple of texts from Bryce that day, but I knew he was helping with a project at the church that night. He hadn't invited me to help, but maybe I should have offered. I hoped they didn't think less of me for not offering, but I also didn't want to step on toes, especially given the response when I'd tried to help Margot the day before. Besides, some girl time would do me good. Savannah attended church regularly. Maybe she could give me some insight into my experience.

We met at a tiny café that had been a favorite throughout our college years. We used to come to Sankofa to study, since it was open all night. All they asked was that patrons buy something every hour or so if they were using the electricity and Wi-Fi. They had a pretty good selection of sandwiches, and when I walked in and inhaled the scent of coffee and pastries, I was transported back to our under-graduate days, when the most pressing concern was the quiz in Me-dieval Lit that neither of us had studied for.

Van already had a table, a tiny round number on rickety legs, surrounded by mismatched chairs. I was half convinced that Sankofa just picked up their furniture from the side of the road, as new things appeared frequently and old things disappeared, prob-ably broken by an overenthusiastic football player treating them like they were sturdier than they actually were, but the entire aesthetic worked well.

"I ordered you a BLT and chips," Van said as I sat down. "My treat."

"You didn't have to do that, V," I said, gingerly lowering myself into a metal chair with spindly legs that I wasn't sure would hold a cat, let alone my body. I breathed a sigh of relief as the chair only groaned slightly and then settled in. "I could have gotten it."

She waved a hand. "I know, but I wanted to treat. It's been too long since we've hung out just the two of us."

It was an old argument that wasn't actually an argument. We were both creatures of habit and got the same thing at all our favor-ite haunts, so it had become a tradition for whoever arrived first to order for both. Back when we were hanging out more regularly, it had gotten a little out of hand, with one of us arriving up to an hour early and putting in the order. Old habits die hard. I was fifteen minutes early and she'd still beaten me. I loved my friendship with Savannah. I knew that no matter what came, we would be able to come back here, to our roots, and be right back where we started.

Our food came and we chatted about work and family, catching up in a way that we hadn't been able to when we went out a couple of weekends ago. I was perusing the dessert menu, looking for something to share, when Savannah got down to business.

"So. Jules. You haven't mentioned the guy once tonight. What's up? He break your heart already? You break his? Do I need to break something else of his?"

I laughed. She was always the first to my defense. "Actually, things are good, Van. Really, really good." I paused, trying to figure out how to fully encompass all the emotions I had toward Bryce and his world, and my desire to become more a part of it. "He brought me to his church yesterday."

It wasn't what Savannah expected to hear. She blinked at me. "Girl, I've been trying to get you to my church for years. What makes him so special?"

I shrugged. "The guy who runs the church is sort of like a father figure to Bryce. I couldn't exactly meet them and *not* go to church."

Savannah leaned forward. "And?"

"And . . . it was good, Van. It was nothing like anything I'd experienced before." The words rushed out of my mouth now as I described what the service had been like, how it had made me feel, how friendly and welcoming everyone had been.

"Which church was this?" she asked when I paused for a breath.

"Church of the Life."

Her brow furrowed for a moment, and then she frowned. "That big one with all those gardens and the school and stuff?"

"That's the one." I wasn't sure how to read her reaction. "You've heard of it."

"I've heard things."

It was my turn to frown. "You've heard what things?"

"Just things," she said. "People who go there are a little . . ." She made a swirling hand gesture by her ear, and a surge of irritation rushed to my fingertips.

"Have you ever been there, Savannah?"

She must have heard the annoyance in my voice, because she looked a little stunned at my reaction. Plus, I rarely called her by her full name.

"No, I haven't," she said, her voice careful. "But, Jules—"

"Then do you really think you should be judging the people?" I was angry now, and hurt. I had been so excited to share with her, so certain that she would understand and be happy for me, happy that I'd found a church after she had bugged me for so long. Instead, she was insinuating ridiculous things about Bryce's church, and, by extension, his family. "Just because it's not *your* church doesn't mean it's a bad place, or that people are crazy for going there."

"That's not what I meant, Julia."

"I thought you church people were supposed to keep from judging others, and accept people who are different. But I guess if it's not how you do it, it's not right." I dropped the dessert menu and began gathering my things.

"You know that's not true," Savannah said, laying a hand on my arm. "Please, just hold on a moment."

I took a deep breath, raising my eyebrows, refusing to say more. I wanted nothing more than to storm out in a fit of righteous anger, but I also didn't want to leave things like that with Savannah. We would recover, of course, but even in my agitated state I knew I would sleep better if we talked things through tonight.

"I'm sorry, okay?" she said, and the apology sounded genuine. "Look, I've just heard that people from there can be a little weird, a little Stepford, but you're right, I shouldn't judge it if I've never been there."

I slumped back into my chair. "I thought you'd be happy for

me, V. I thought you've been wanting me to find a church for so long that you would be glad that I'm excited for the first time."

"I am, I swear. Just . . . it seems like it happened really fast. Like, boom, you're dating this guy and then you're going to church and after one Sunday you're willing to get into a fight with me about it."

"We wouldn't have to fight if you were nicer." I tilted my head toward her in mock challenge.

"I'd be nicer if you didn't always try to fight me," she responded, teasing. The tension dissipated almost immediately.

"Listen, I appreciate that you're concerned, because I know you're looking out for me, but I need you to trust me. Bryce's family runs the church, and I spent the afternoon with them and they're really great. I just want to know them better and find out more about the church. I promise I'll look at everything carefully, and maybe you can help me talk through some things?"

Savannah's golden eyes sparkled. "I'd really love that."

"And maybe you can come with me sometime if it's something I decide to continue with."

She smiled. "I'd like that, too. Then I can make informed judgments." She winked at me, and I just shook my head at her.

Despite our easy resolution, a small sliver of doubt crept in after our conversation, and stayed with me. I wanted to talk to Bryce when I got home, but he had texted to say he was hung up with the cleanup from the event he'd helped with, and would talk to me tomorrow. So instead, I tried talking to God again. Still, it took me a while to fall asleep that night.

Chapter 9

S orry about last night. The text arrived from Bryce as I sat down at my desk the next morning.

> It's fine. I got to hang out with Savannah. I told her about your church.

> ??

> She had some questions. But I think she's happy for me.

I got a message from Elaine asking me to come into her office before I could see Bryce's reply. He knew I was at work, so I didn't bother signing off before throwing my phone into my desk.

Elaine was studying her computer screen as I knocked on the open door, entering without waiting for a response. "You needed something?"

She looked up at me and her face creased in a rare smile. "Yes, Julia, please sit down."

Elaine never asked me to sit, so this was new. "Should I close the door?" I asked, aware that Micah's head was tipped toward Elaine's office. She had her standard earbuds in, but I was well aware that she rarely had music playing in them. I overheard her saying once that people got overly careless about what they said when they thought she was listening to music. It's how she knew all the gossip.

"Yes, please. Let's keep this meeting private," Elaine said, and I saw her glance through the window at Micah as well. Apparently I wasn't the only one who was onto her. I hid my amusement as I sat across from Elaine.

It was another minute before Elaine spoke again. "I've been looking over your presentation, Julia."

My stomach fluttered, and I clenched my fists to keep my fingers from twitching in anxiety. I didn't even respond, just nodded, for fear that my voice would betray my nerves.

"This is very good work, Julia," Elaine said, turning her computer screen so that I could see my work on full display. "It needs a few tweaks, but I think together we can make a presentation the client will be happy with."

"Together?" I asked, wondering if that meant what I thought it meant, not daring to dream it.

"Yes, I have a couple hours this afternoon. We can set up in the boardroom and talk through some changes."

"Okay," I said, biting my cheek. "That sounds fine."

"Excellent."

I stood to leave, and Elaine's voice stopped me.

"And, Julia?"

"Yes?"

"I'd also like you to be there for the presentation. I think you deserve to see the client's reaction to your hard work."

This time I didn't try to hold back my grin. "I would love that," I said. "Thank you so much, Elaine."

"You earned it." With those words, Elaine turned back to her computer and I was dismissed.

I practically skipped all the way back to my desk, hardly able to believe what had just happened. Within a few weeks of doing this extra work for Elaine, I was already attending a client presentation.

Of course, this followed years of hard work on the more menial, but necessary, tasks of the office. I had always seen Elaine as cold and aloof, not really paying attention to anything I did unless I messed it up. I had a feeling she had been keeping an eye on me for longer than I suspected, assessing my potential.

Remembering I had been texting Bryce, I pulled my phone out of my desk to check in and share my news. My eyes widened as I saw his stream of texts.

> You think she's happy? What does that mean?
>
> Why wouldn't your best friend be happy for you?
>
> What did she say?
>
> Julia? Are you getting my messages?
>
> Did she say anything about the church?

My meeting with Elaine hadn't lasted that long, but Bryce had been busy. It was sweet that he was worried about how my friend saw his church, since it was such an important part of his life. He had expressed similar concerns about my family, and what I would tell them, since it wasn't part of our family tradition.

> Sorry, Elaine needed me. You'll never guess what she's letting me do!
>
> You can tell me in a minute. Help me understand your conversation with Savannah first.

I rolled my eyes. Men could be so single-minded. Look at one thing completely before moving on to the next. What's the fun in that? I shoved my excitement down for a moment so I could explain, but just then the elevator bell dinged and I looked up to see Elaine's boss stepping off the lift.

> *Big boss is in the building, I gotta go.*
> *I'll explain later, promise!*

I shoved my phone back into my drawer before Mr. Roberts turned in my direction. I pinged Elaine through the messaging program and she immediately started stacking her haphazard piles more neatly on her desk. She stood and smoothed her skirt and hair, and then sat back down with an air of professionalism. Elaine always appeared put-together, but it seemed that even the most composed person has someone they are intimidated by.

"Hello, Mr. Roberts, are you here to see Elaine?" I stood and greeted the man.

"Yes, errrr . . ." His eyes hunted for my nameplate, which was buried under my own pile of papers.

"Julia," I supplied, holding out a hand. "I'll just let Elaine know you're here."

"Thank you," he said, clasping his hands behind his back. His small eyes took in the details of our work area, and I had a feeling he didn't miss a thing. I rushed to Elaine's office.

"Elaine, Mr. Roberts is here to see you."

"Thank you, Julia," Elaine said, as if I hadn't forewarned her. "Please do see him in."

"Right this way, sir," I said, gesturing into the office.

"Julia, why don't you stay and take notes?" Elaine said. "This pertains to our presentation."

I flushed with pride that she was already describing it that way. I ran to my desk to grab a notebook, ignoring Micah's envious stares stabbing into me. Maybe if she spent less time gossiping she would be in a similar position. She wasn't untalented, just unmotivated.

I paused. That was a rather pompous thought, but not untrue, at least not in my opinion. I sent up a quick prayer for Micah, and for my own fast fingers, remembering how well I had focused after my prayer before, and how that presentation was turning out. Maybe there was something to this church thing after all, even if I didn't really know what I was doing quite yet.

It was almost two hours before I reopened the door to Elaine's office. I was exhausted, but happily so. Mr. Roberts shook my hand enthusiastically before taking his leave, and I shuffled to my desk and dropped my notebook onto its surface. The pages of the notebook were filled with scribbles and ideas and my own brainstorming. I had expected to sit in the corner and take notes, but the meeting had gone an entirely different way. Mr. Roberts had asked for my input, had been genuinely enthusiastic about my ideas, and before I knew it, he was calling his office manager to set me up with classes on design and DMA certification. I was so deliriously happy, I almost forgot about my hastily typed message to Bryce from earlier.

My lunch hour had started already, but before I could dig out my lunch and go call Bryce from the break room, Micah cleared her throat.

"You have a . . . umm . . . visitor, Julia." I looked over at her and she nodded toward the small waiting area near the elevators, which actually consisted of two chairs perpendicular to each other with a square table in between them. Out-of-date magazines spread over the surface of the table, along with a basket of fake flowers, and Bryce sat in the chair facing my desk, the picture of practiced calm.

Butterflies took flight in my stomach, and I jumped to my feet and rushed over, my tiredness of a few seconds ago forgotten. I bounced right up to him and raised my face for a quick kiss. His mouth curved and he leaned down to peck me on the cheek. I could feel Micah watching us, and I flushed. I knew he probably didn't want to make a public scene, but it definitely felt like a brush-off, and in front of Micah no less.

He reached down to pick up a basket from the floor with one hand and gripped my hand with the other. "I brought lunch. Is there somewhere we can have some privacy?"

Micah snorted, and I shot her a look. "There are probably others in the break room, but there's usually a table in the corner that's a little set apart," I said. "Not complete privacy, but the best we've got." I shot him a bright smile, hoping to elicit one in response, but all I got was a furrowed brow.

"That's fine, I suppose," he said. As we walked past Micah, he nodded at her, and she gave a finger wave. I wondered how much they had spoken while I was in my meeting.

We made our way to the break room, which was indeed buzzing with activity. We got a few glances, but people mostly stuck to their groups. They tended to congregate around the larger tables in the center of the room, rather than the smaller ones on the outskirts. Micah walked in a few seconds behind us as we claimed the table farthest from the crowd, and immediately began whispering to her minions, who snuck looks in our direction.

I ignored their stares and turned to find Bryce staring at me intently. "What's going on, Bryce? I'm glad you surprised me, of course, but is everything okay?"

"I didn't surprise you," he said, still staring. "I texted and asked if I could bring you lunch so we could talk about Savannah."

"Savannah?" So much had happened this morning, my casual mention of Savannah seemed like a distant memory. Obviously not to him, though. "I just told her about going to church with you. She was curious about it."

"Curious about what?"

I took a deep breath. It was understandable that Bryce would be interested and anxious about someone's reaction regarding the church. It was so important to him, and I loved that passion, so I wanted to be very clear. "Van has been trying to get me to go to church for years. Years, Bryce."

He leaned forward, listening, but didn't say anything.

"I always found excuses not to go. We've been friends for such a long time, I think she figured if she kept inviting me, eventually I would cave, if for no other reason than to shut her up."

This earned me a small smile.

"I think at first she was a little hurt that after years of her asking me to go to church and me refusing, you were able to get me to go with you after only a few weeks." I shrugged. "We talked about it and the Reverend and Nancy and how they're leaders of the church, and how I went really out of a desire to meet your family more than a desire to attend church."

Bryce shifted and I could tell he wanted to say something, so I quickly continued, holding up a hand to keep him from interrupting.

"That's probably not the best reason to decide to go to church, but I want to be completely honest with you. It's not that I don't believe in God, but it's never been a big part of my life. My ex absolutely refused to go to church, and I let that influence my decision to stay away as well. Once I knew how important your church was to you, I wanted to honor that."

"And what did Savannah say when you told her that?"

"It took a little bit of explaining, and I think she got it by the end, but I also think she was still annoyed that you were the one who got me to go."

Bryce's shoulders had lost some of their tension, but he still didn't look completely okay. I wasn't sure why he was so freaked out by my conversation with Van, but I felt the need to reassure him.

"I wasn't lying before," I said, reaching over to cover his hand with mine. He flipped his hand palm-up and enclosed my fingers in his warm grip. "I've never been to a church service like that before.

I felt things I've never experienced, and I mean that in the best way possible."

He reached over and grabbed my other hand. "Really?"

I nodded. "Really." I squeezed his fingers. "It's not that I don't have a lot of questions. I'm still a little skeptical. But I felt something while I was there, during worship for sure, but especially after dinner with your . . . uhhh . . . the Reverend and Nancy."

He laughed. "You can call them my parents, Julia. I consider them to be my parents, and they look at me as a son. It's easier. Less confusing."

"And your real parents . . ." I knew it was a risk, but I was very curious about the part of himself that Bryce kept closed off from me.

"Not in the picture," he said, his tone final. I would probably ask again another time, but a brooding look crossed his face, wrinkling his forehead and bringing the corners of his mouth down in a frown.

That look needed to go. "Guess what," I said, and his eyes met mine again. "I tried praying yesterday and you won't believe what happened."

Immediately his entire body shifted, became energized. His eyes lit up and his reaction was enough for me to gush about my day yesterday and the crazy morning I'd had. I wanted to do everything in my power to keep him just like he was in that moment. Like a live wire, a coil of energy, full of life and excitement.

"That's amazing, Julia," Bryce said when I'd finished filling him in. He raised my hands to his lips, kissing the fingers. "You are so talented, I never doubted your boss would see your genius."

I laughed. "You've only known me a few weeks."

"Yes, but I knew right away you were special. I'm shocked it took her this long to realize."

I flushed, and was glad for the chatter in the rest of the room that kept our conversation private. "I don't know how much responsibility she's giving me for the actual presentation, but just being there is a huge deal. This could be the start of my career. The *real* start of my career."

Bryce's eyes twinkled, and I was struck by how important this man was to me already. He was the first one I wanted to tell about all the good things happening. He hadn't been around long, but I already knew that I didn't want a life without him. I didn't dare speak in that moment, because I didn't want to let on how intensely I was feeling. From the look in his eyes, however, he knew, and felt the same way. Though we had professed our love already, this was something different. Something more than love. And I was feeling it in the crowded break room in the middle of a workday. It was probably for the best that we didn't have more privacy.

Clearing his throat, Bryce released my hands and reached into the basket. "I just grabbed some stuff from Gustafson's," he said, referencing a high-class eatery a few blocks away. They had amazing breads and cheeses, a great selection of wine, and the best chocolate in the city. Bryce pulled item after item out of the basket, and my mouth watered more with every reveal.

Soon we had a spread fit for royalty on the tiny table between us, and we didn't even notice as the room cleared out, leaving us alone. We were already in our own little world, and it was a place I wanted to live forever.

Chapter 10

Kate's house was in chaos. Scott and Kyle ran around, chasing each other with light sabers, much to the entertainment of our parents, who were settled in on the couches in the living room. Kate fussed around the kitchen, peeking at the roast every minute and flittering between the side dishes, checking for taste and temperature. I hovered in the doorway, anxiously glancing between Kate and the basement door, which Eddie had disappeared through over an hour ago.

"Are you sure I can't do anything?" I asked. The table had been set, Kate had been cooking all day, but I still felt like I should be doing something. "Pour water?"

"Nope, Eddie can help me," Kate said, her smile just a little too cheerful. Her eyes slid to the basement door as well. Eddie had said he was going to bring up an extra table from the basement to set the sides on, but somehow I doubted it took that long to dig out a table. Kate kept the basement clean and organized.

"I can go check—"

"No." The doorbell rang, and Kate motioned toward the door with a jerk of her head. "There's Loverboy now! You can help by answering the door before Scott gets there, or your boyfriend will find himself challenged to a duel."

That got me moving, and I just barely got to the door behind Scott, who threw it open and pointed his light saber straight at Bryce's chest.

"It's Darth Vader!" he said, his voice a little too excited to be facing his mortal enemy. "Prepare to duel, O Dark Lord of Evil."

Bryce's expression was bemused, and he looked up at me.

"You don't have to," I said. "Scott, Bryce just got here, and—"

"You got another light saber, buddy?" Bryce's face was earnest.

"Yeah!" Scott ran off to get another weapon, giving Bryce time to give me a proper kiss in greeting.

"You just scored about ten thousand points for not calling it a sword," I whispered as Scott came back, followed by Kyle.

"A light saber is *not* a sword, Julia," Bryce said with mock seriousness.

I laughed as Scott barreled over to Bryce with his spare light saber, the red one he always used when he was playing the Dark Side, and Bryce barely had time to grasp it before both boys went on the attack. They parried into the living room, the boys shouting in delight and Bryce making heavy breathing sounds like Darth Vader. Bryce sent a wave toward my parents, who watched in amusement, but was too busy to say hello in that moment.

Kate came to stand beside me, arms crossed. "You had to bring another kid," she said, nudging me with her shoulder. There was an edge to her words. Kate had been progressively less enthusiastic about my relationship with Bryce with every conversation we had about him. I wasn't sure why, and I knew I needed to ask her about it, but there never seemed to be a good time. It had been weeks since I'd had a chance to talk with her alone, where one or both of us wasn't distracted.

I shrugged. "It doesn't hurt to be young at heart."

Just then, Bryce rushed to my side, grabbing me around the waist. "Get back, young Jedi, the princess is mine!"

"Never!" Scott yelled, echoed by his brother. "Don't worry, Aunt Julia, we'll save you!"

Bryce tried to hide behind me, but was too slow for Scott, who managed to get a good jab in.

"I'm hit!" Bryce said, holding Scott's light saber as if it were sticking out of his body. He stumbled back and forth, falling to his knees. "But . . . I'm . . . your . . . fath . . ." He fell to the floor in a dramatic death scene, sticking his tongue out to prove that he was truly dead.

Scott and Kyle cheered. "We saved the princess!" Kyle said as they jumped in circles around me. "Long live the Jedi!"

Loud clapping broke through their celebration, and I looked to see Kate standing at the entrance to the dining room. "Okay, well done, Jedi, now please go wash your hands and come to the table." The boys immediately complied, which was impressive, but since they'd been able to finish their play this time, there wasn't much reason to argue.

While the boys had been playing, Eddie had reappeared and the table he'd brought up was heavy with all the dishes Kate had prepared. Everything was in perfectly matched serving dishes, steaming and ready to be devoured.

"After you, Mr. and Mrs. Hawthorne," said Bryce, who had come in from the living room, and it occurred to me that I hadn't bothered to introduce them yet.

"Oh! Sorry!" I backtracked to where my parents had paused by Bryce. "Mom, Dad, this is Bryce Covington. Bryce, my parents, Allison and Dan Hawthorne."

Bryce shook their hands. "It's great to meet you at last. I've heard so many good things about you from Julia." He placed an arm around my shoulders. "You've raised a good daughter here."

From the direction of the kitchen, I heard what sounded suspiciously like a laugh, quickly covered up with a cough, and I shot Kate a look. She raised an eyebrow at me before walking over to us.

"And this brat is my big sister, Kate," I said, nodding in her direction.

Kate wiped her hand before reaching out to clasp Bryce's. "That's *older* sister," she said, smiling. "But much more fun."

Bryce laughed. "I'm not sure I can agree with that," he said. "But I can see that beauty certainly runs in the family."

I could practically feel the effort Kate put into not rolling her eyes, and I narrowed my eyes at her. Bryce was being very charming, and trying to fit in. Since I'd done this with his family not long ago, I felt for him. Maybe it was a little cheesy, but I didn't doubt his sincerity.

Kate checked that Bryce and our parents weren't looking and stuck her tongue out at me before clapping her hands again. "Okay, let's all sit down! Scott and Kyle should be done pretty quick."

We took our places at the table after a quick introduction between Bryce and Eddie, and sure enough, the boys came racing in seconds later. Kate had stuck them on the end with Eddie, placing me between Bryce and Scott and my parents across from us. She took the other end of the table.

"Should we get started?" she asked, reaching back for the first dish to pass.

Bryce's hand grabbed mine under the table, and I looked up to find him staring at me. I tried to discern what he was trying to tell me, and then it hit me.

"Hey, guys, can we hold on a sec?"

Activity stopped, except the boys, who were whining about when they would get the dish with their mom's homemade mac and cheese. Everyone stared at me.

"Uh." I cleared my throat. "Do you mind if we pray first?"

Now they really stared. I wasn't sure my family had ever prayed before a meal, except possibly some Easter or Christmas Eve feasts. It wasn't something that came naturally. Bryce had always prayed before meals since we'd been dating, and while I'd been trying to get in the habit, being back with my family had pushed it completely out of my mind. Gradually, eyes shifted from me to Bryce, and understanding dawned. Of course they weren't surprised. I'd filled them all in on my visit to Bryce's church.

Kate slowly set down the dish she'd been about to pass. "Of course, Julia. Go ahead."

I looked at Bryce, feeling panicked, and he nodded in encouragement. Everyone bowed their heads, and I took a deep breath.

"Uhhh, God? Thank you for this food. And, um, for everyone at the table." I racked my brain, trying to remember how the prayer had gone when the Reverend blessed our meal. His had been long and flowery and beautiful. Mine was . . . less so. "Thank you for Bryce meeting my family, and please let Scott and Kyle behave for the meal." This elicited giggles from the boys. I was glad they were paying attention. "Bless this evening. Thank you." I peeked through squinted eyes at the rest of the table. Everyone else's head remained bowed respectfully. "Oh. Amen."

A chorus of amens echoed mine and Bryce squeezed my hand again. "Nice job," he whispered, leaning over so only I could hear. "Thank you."

I squeezed back as the dishes started making their way around the table. Kate was a great cook, and soon the only sounds were chewing and the occasional exclamation about how heavenly the food tasted. Eventually, conversation started up again.

Bryce asked most of the questions, expertly keeping the focus on my family instead of delving too deeply into his own story. He talked with my dad about the job he'd worked for thirty-five years, asked my mom for gardening tips, discussed all things *Star Wars* with my nephews, and was even able to talk computers and gaming with Eddie. I watched him insert himself gracefully and seamlessly into my family, and it felt right. Hope and love swelled in my chest as all my favorite people got to know each other. There was laughter and gentle ribbing, mixed with serious topics.

My family was interested in the Church of the Life, and Bryce was happy to tell them about it, though he seemed more restrained than he usually did with me. He had told me once that sometimes people were put off by his devotion, and I wondered if he was holding back because he wasn't sure how it would be received. He had certainly noticed my family's surprise when I'd requested that we pray before eating. I hoped that hadn't made him uncomfortable. If it did, he wasn't letting it show.

Kate was the only one who remained mostly silent through the meal, other than to graciously accept the compliments on her cooking. She spent most of the time studying Bryce and looking between the two of us. I wasn't sure Bryce had noticed, but it was starting to make me uncomfortable. I was usually good at reading my sister, but she had her poker face on tonight and wasn't giving away a thing.

Soon the plates were scraped clean and the boys requested to be excused, off on their next adventure before their parents even had the words out of their mouths.

"Should we move to the living room?" my mom asked, pushing her chair out.

"I'm going to get a head start on cleanup," Kate said, starting to stack plates.

"I'll help," Mom said.

"No, no," Kate said, waving her hand dismissively. "Go relax and get to know Bryce better. Julia will help me."

I shot her a look. "Julia will?"

"She will."

"But what if I want to—"

"You already know Bryce. Come help your old sister."

I rolled my eyes and turned to Bryce. "I'll be in in a little bit. Go enjoy yourself."

He stood, pulled my chair out, and pulled me up, then leaned down and dropped a kiss on my cheek. "I'll keep a spot warm for you."

He waited for my parents and Eddie to come around the table, and then followed them into the living room. I stacked dishes silently with Kate, making neat piles on the counter by the sink.

"Do you want these in the dishwasher?" I asked.

"No! This is my good china. It has to be washed by hand."

"Are you serious?"

She laughed. "You really are hopeless sometimes, Julia."

"I just live in the real world, not a magazine," I said, bumping her with my hip as I brought another load in from the dining room.

"Real people use china."

"Real people use sturdy plates. Or paper plates if they haven't run the dishwasher in a while. Why would you want to own dishes that don't go in the dishwasher?"

"Because I'm classy."

I laughed as I went out to wipe down the table. I poked my head in the living room. "The extra table can be brought down whenever you go back down, Eddie," I said.

Eddie looked up from what seemed to be an intense conversation with Bryce. "Thanks, Julia. I'll bring it down later."

"You can do it now," Bryce said. "We can pick this up when you get back. Or I can help you."

"Uh, no, that's fine," Eddie said. "It's not a two-person job. I'll be right back."

My mouth almost fell open in shock that he had taken Bryce's suggestion. I watched him fold up the table in bemusement before looking back at Bryce, who winked at me. He knew exactly what he was doing. I blew him a quick kiss before returning to the kitchen to help Kate *hand wash* the mountain of dishes we had dirtied.

"Eddie is bringing the table back downstairs," I told her as I rolled up my sleeves and grabbed a towel to dry the dripping dishes she handed me.

"He's disappearing already? Ugh," she said. "I would have thought he could stay at least a while longer for tonight."

"Actually," I said, "I think he was going to bring it down and come back up. He and Bryce were in some sort of deep conversation." I turned to stack the plates on the counter. Kate remained silent, and when I turned back, her back was to me, her hands submerged in the sudsy water. Steam still rose from it, so it couldn't have been comfortable to leave them in there, but she didn't move. "Kate?"

"Bryce got Eddie to stay upstairs?"

"Yeah. But I'm sure Eddie is just trying to impress him." I knew immediately it was the wrong thing to say.

"Why would he need to impress Bryce?" Kate asked, and there was venom in her voice. "When he doesn't make any sort of effort to impress me? What's so great about Bryce?"

"That's not fair."

"What's not fair about it? We've spent half the evening with him and we know nothing about him, Julia. Can you not see that? See how he avoids talking about himself?"

My heart sped up as I realized the implication of her words. Bryce had spent the evening trying to learn about the family, and she saw it as something shady instead of something selfless. "He was trying to be polite," I said. "No thanks to your silence." In fact, Bryce had tried to engage Kate several times, and she had responded in short sentences, not offering any additional information. Eventually he would move on, but he never stopped trying to bring her into the conversation. "You've been weird ever since he got here. Just because the boys like him and Eddie wants to stay up here and talk to him doesn't mean there's something wrong with him."

"He's too . . . shiny," Kate said, finally pulling her hands out of the water and spinning to face me, splashing bubbles across the kitchen floor. "Everything he says about himself is a cliché. Even his compliments are clichés." She wasn't speaking loudly, for which I was grateful, but each word hit me like a punch in the stomach. "You are so smitten with the *idea* of Bryce, I wonder if you even really know him at all."

"I know plenty," I said, frost dripping over my words. "Bryce has been nothing but good to me, and nothing but kind and charming to the family tonight. How dare you question his motives? How dare you question my judgment?" The towel twisted in my hands.

"Just because your marriage is in the toilet doesn't mean you can dump all over my relationship." She gasped, but I didn't give her time to respond, throwing the towel on the counter. "I think I'm done helping. My boyfriend is waiting for me."

I spun on my heel and stalked out of the kitchen, bypassing the living room and heading straight for the bathroom. I needed a few minutes. Leaning against the porcelain sink, I willed my pulse to slow down. *Deep breaths, Julia,* I chanted to myself. *She's just jealous. She and Eddie are going through a rough patch and she can't stand to see me in a healthy relationship.* Gradually my pulse slowed and I calmed down. In fact, I started to feel sorry for Kate. I had never been happy with Jake, and she'd walked me through every step of that while her relationship with Eddie seemed like the stuff of dreams. Now our roles were flip-flopped, and I couldn't imagine it would be comfortable for her to be the sister in need of relationship help.

Still, I wasn't sorry enough to apologize to her that night. I still needed time. A quick glance in the mirror showed that my face was no longer flushed, and my teary eyes were now dry, no evidence that they had almost spilled over. I made my way back out into the living room and found Bryce, Eddie, my parents, and the boys gathered around a board game.

"Come play with us, Auntie Julia," Kyle called. Bryce patted the spot next to him on the couch, and I plopped down next to him, as close as possible without actually sitting in his lap, which I thought would be inappropriate at this stage.

"We already started," Bryce said. "But you can be on my team."

"That's very nice of you, but I'm terrible at board games," I said. "Are you sure you want me on your team?"

He looked at me, and his expression was playful, but his eyes were serious. "Always."

He wakes up with his sister on the floor next to his bed again. She often finds her way there when the fighting gets bad. She's quite a bit younger, five to his fourteen, and he is the most stable man in her life. Mama isn't even sure who her daddy is, so it's whoever's living in the house this week. Sissy calls all adult males "Daddy," and he has long since given up trying to correct her. It caused a bit of a stir when she called the principal "Daddy" at the start of her kindergarten year, but he got her back on track and talk died down soon enough.

Though the fighting went late into the night, a glass breaks in the kitchen and the squabbling starts up again. He leans down, gently nudging Sissy awake, and helps her climb out his window. He prefers to run most places, but this time he places her on the handles of his rusty old bike and pedals toward town. The café owner sometimes takes pity on them, and his mouth waters at the thought of a stack of the pancakes she makes.

Ten minutes later, he's sitting across from Sissy, who is shoveling pancakes into her mouth as if she hasn't eaten in days while the gentle-eyed café owner looks on. It probably has been days since she had anything of substance, and may be several more before Mama makes it to the store, so he eats his stack more conservatively. The café owner clucks and shakes her head before returning to the other customers.

His skin starts itching again, right at the back of his neck, and he looks up to find the stranger from the library watching him. The man does not look away, and the boy stares defiantly back. There is no judgment in the man's eyes, but the boy knows what he's thinking. Freeloaders. Dirty urchins. He knows what the people in town whisper under their breath. He's only started to become more acceptable by excelling in school and doing his own laundry. He does Sissy's, too, and insists she bathes at least three times a week. Most of the kids didn't even realize what family she belonged to for the first few weeks of school.

The man doesn't move until they're finished, and the boy bustles Sissy back out into the sunshine, scooping her up as she squeals with delight before depositing her back on the handlebars and biking them both toward school. He doesn't have to look back to know the man has followed them out of the café, and watches them until they are out of sight.

Chapter 11

I had fallen asleep in the middle of the game the night before, so I was confused when I woke up in Kate's guest room. It was still early, and the house was quiet. There was a handwritten note on the side table, and Bryce's sharp, economical handwriting was visible.

> *Didn't want to wake you, princess. Give me a call in the morning. Thanks for a wonderful evening. Your family is charming.*

I lifted the paper to my nose, as if I could get a whiff of Bryce's cologne, but of course it was paper from Kate's notebook, so it had more of a floral scent. I realized I was sniffing paper and decided it was time to get up and go home before anyone else was up so I could shower and call Bryce. He had mentioned something about a fun activity today, but wouldn't tell me what it was. I certainly wasn't trying to slip out to avoid an inevitable confrontation with Kate. That would be juvenile and I was definitely above that.

I splashed my face with water, straightened my dress, which had been surprisingly comfortable to sleep in, and opened the guest room door. Sunlight spilled into the hallway from the large living room windows. I was halfway down the hallway before I realized the smell of fresh-brewed coffee hung in the air, and it was too late when I realized that meant someone was awake.

There was no way to sneak past without being obvious at this point, so I said a little prayer that somehow it would miraculously be Eddie up early, and stuck my head in the kitchen. Kate sat at the kitchen table, fingers wrapped around a mug of coffee, staring at nothing. She hadn't seen me yet, far off in her other world as she was.

This was a Kate I didn't see much anymore. She wore a gray robe, belted tightly at her waist. Her hair was pulled on top of her head in a messy bun, her face clean of makeup. This was the Kate the rest of the world never saw, all pretenses gone, all masks waiting to be donned for the day. This was my Kate.

"Good morning," I said, keeping my voice quiet. She jumped anyway. "You always did like to stare at the wall in the morning."

She gave me a small smile. "Just booting up," she said, a joke our dad had started back when computers took endless minutes to warm up when they were turned on.

I stepped into the kitchen and headed for the coffeepot, pulling my favorite travel mug from the cupboard.

"You're not sticking around?" Kate asked, eyeing the mug.

"I need to get home and shower," I said. "I'm meeting Bryce for lunch and I have a couple things to do at home first."

Kate didn't say anything for a moment. "About last night," she started after the pause. "Julia, I—"

"It's fine, Katie," I said, filling up the mug. "Water under the bridge. I really appreciate you hosting. That's a lot of stress, so you can't be held responsible for everything you said."

Kate didn't take the bait to let it go. "No, Julia, I stand by what I said, but I probably could have said it a little nicer."

I took a deep breath before turning back to her. "I don't want to do this again."

"Me neither, but, Julia, I'm worried about you. You've fallen for this guy so hard in just a few weeks and I don't really trust him."

Closing my eyes and counting to ten, I gripped my mug. "You have absolutely no reason not to trust him."

"He's too polished."

"That's not a reason. Give me a solid reason, something he has said that's untrue, something he's done that was rude or inappropriate."

Kate pursed her lips. "I can't."

"See?"

She slammed her mug on the table. "I can't because he doesn't *say* anything! He talks a lot but there's no substance. It's all surface."

"Your husband was having a pretty in-depth conversation last night. Did you ask him what they talked about?"

More silence.

"I can't do this, Kate. I'm sorry you didn't like Bryce. It actually makes me really sad. But I do like him, and so does the rest of the family. I don't know why you can't just let me be happy, but it's not my problem right now." I stomped toward the door.

"Don't you trust my judgment?" she called after me.

I opened the door and turned around. She looked so small sitting at the table alone, and her eyes were sad, though I guessed it was because I wasn't letting her get her way this time. "No. I don't," I said. "Not anymore." And I stepped out into the cool morning air.

It took thirty minutes in the shower for me to feel normal after my second round with Kate. Anyone else I could have argued with and moved on as if nothing had happened. Even Savannah, who was closest to me aside from Kate, couldn't get under my skin the way Kate did.

Maybe it was because I had always looked up to Kate. She always seemed to have it together. She had all the boyfriends and the friends and the good grades and the sports trophies. All-star everything. But she'd never looked down on me. Never questioned my judgment about anything. Until now.

It may have stemmed from what happened the last time I got drawn in by a charming guy, except Jake's charm really was all fake. None of us had realized it at the time. Even Kate had fallen under his spell. And when he cheated on me the first time, she'd been angry right along with me, but had supported my decision to give him another chance. By the third time he'd cheated, she'd been ready to go beat him up for me, but had respected my wishes and had stayed out of it. Maybe this time around she wanted to make sure no one was fooled, that I couldn't be hurt again.

I tried to focus elsewhere as I did a few chores around the apartment and paid bills. I called Bryce, and he gave me an address to meet him at for lunch. "I have to go into work for a bit this morning," he said. "But take a taxi to the address. I'll bring you home. I'd come and get you, but . . ."

"It's fine," I said. "I have been able to get myself around the city pretty successfully up to this point."

He laughed. "But a gentleman would make sure."

"You're always a gentleman," I said. "Even when you can't pick me up."

I ordered an Uber, which took me back into the neighborhood of Bryce's church, and I was surprised when we pulled up to a tall, modern-looking building right across the vast parking lot. Bryce was waiting outside, and jumped up to open the door for me.

"Thanks," I said, and then repeated my thanks to the driver. He had been a chatterbox, but he spoke about his kids with such affection that I hadn't minded at all.

"Did you take care of him?" Bryce asked, and it took me a moment to realize he meant payment.

"Oh, yeah, it's all through the app," I said, pulling out my phone. I pulled up the app and left the driver a quick glowing rating before turning back to Bryce.

"I don't know if I like you taking rides from strangers," he said. "It makes me nervous."

"It's perfectly safe," I said, waving off his concerns. "It's just normal people like you and me. This guy has five kids." I laughed. "He said they're all under the age of six, and when he gets a job driving it's like taking a break. He only drives on the weekends, though."

The lines around Bryce's mouth were still taut. I knew why he was concerned, but I wanted to reassure him that he didn't need to be. "I'm safe, and I'm here, Bryce," I said, looping my arm through his. "Now are you going to tell me where 'here' is?"

His face relaxed and he led me up to the front of the building. "This is where I live."

I knew Bryce lived in the same neighborhood as the church, but I hadn't been to his place yet. The neighborhood was well tended, Bryce's building towering over the other homes on the street and yet fitting seamlessly into the family-friendly feel. Children's laughter echoed down the street as we entered the lobby, which was just as clean and well maintained as the outside. A doorman waved at Bryce as we passed.

We rode the elevator up to the eighth floor. "It's not the penthouse," Bryce said. "But it's pretty comfortable for me."

The inside of the apartment was all clean lines and fresh colors, blues and grays and modern furniture. Tall windows gave plenty of natural light. The apartment was a studio, with a half wall separating the bed area from the rest of the room. Bryce watched as I wandered through the room, inhaling the scent that was all male, all Bryce. A decent-sized bathroom jutted off from the area by the bed, and I was amazed at how clean it was. Kate and Savannah were both forever complaining about how gross it was to share a bathroom with a man. I wondered if it was always like this, or if he had made a special effort to clean it for me today. Either way, it was a good sign.

"This is nice," I said. "How long have you lived here?"

"Since they built it five years ago," he said, moving over to the couch and sitting down. He patted the spot next to him and I joined him. "Before that I still lived with the Reverend and Nancy."

I did the math. That meant he was still living with his surrogate parents in his mid-twenties. A little weird, but not completely un-heard-of, especially these days.

"I didn't have to live with them. I made enough to live on my own," Bryce continued. I was careful not to make any sounds, just nodded that I was listening. I didn't want to break the spell. This was as much as Bryce had talked about his past, other than his church activities. "Their house is so big, and I came to live with them while I was still in high school, so it made sense for me to save up money."

"That does sound logical," I said. "And you were able to get such a nice place with your savings."

He laughed. "Actually, this apartment is one of the benefits when you work for the Church of the Life. Rent and utilities paid, though if I wanted cable, I'd have to get that on my own."

My eyes widened. "I thought you worked for a law firm down-town," I said, confused.

"I do, but the Church of the Life is our biggest client. The Rev-erend helped secure me the job with the understanding that I would be the primary attorney for the church. So they consider me one of their employees. I manage a few other accounts, too, some busi-nesses of other members from the church, like the Burrier, but most of my time is spent on the church."

I had no idea about lawyering, so I didn't know if it was possible to spend all your time on one client, no matter how big they were. "Does that really take up all of your time?"

Bryce shifted. "You have to understand, Julia. When I say I represent the Church of the Life, I mean all the members. The church keeps me on retainer and pays all the legal fees for anyone in the church who is in need of help. I don't specialize in everything that comes up, but that's where it's beneficial to work for a firm with a wide variety of attorneys with a wide array of experiences and knowledge."

That made a lot more sense. Suddenly it seemed like an enormous job for one person. "How do you have enough time to do all of that?"

He laughed. "The others help out as needed, but it's not like I'm in court all the time. I do a lot of advising. Sometimes I have office hours at the church on the weekends, since that's the only time people have. That's what I was doing this morning."

I nodded and glanced out the window. The church was perfectly framed across the parking lot, and the gardens were out of sight, but I still felt like I could be there. This building was almost like an extension of the church. "So are all the residents employees of the church?"

"No." Bryce chuckled. "We don't have a large number of employees, and many of those we do have own their own houses. Mostly the employees who live here are those who are single, and a few married couples. Very few children."

"But the church owns the building?"

"Yes. Most of the tenants are members of the church, but of course we don't turn anyone away. It just seems logical that people who go to the church would want to live here. Or that if someone was able to get an apartment here, they would attend the church."

I nodded. "I got the feeling that everyone was super close. I didn't realize that meant physically as well," I said, my tone joking.

"Community is important," Bryce said, his voice serious. "We are nothing if we are alone. We need to stick together, hold each other up. It's laid out in the Bible."

"Of course," I said, a little taken aback that he had responded so seriously to my joke. "I think it's nice, actually."

His expression was gratified. "I'm glad."

I patted his knee. "So where is this fancy bistro you're taking me to this afternoon?"

"You're sitting in it," he said, spreading his arms wide. "You treated me to a home-cooked meal last night, I wanted to do the same."

"Well, that was Kate's doing," I said. "If I had been in charge, we probably would have had spaghetti and meatballs or taco salad or something equally as 'classless,' as Kate would say." All of the feelings of the morning rushed back in, and I could feel my forehead creasing.

Bryce rubbed a thumb over the wrinkles, smoothing them out. "Want to talk about it? We can have a picnic on the floor and eat the sandwiches I made."

"That sounds good," I said. Bryce stood and went to the fridge to remove a platter from the refrigerator, along with a few sides. He laid out a simple but delicious-looking meal on the coffee table, and I slid to the floor to move in closer.

As we ate, I confessed to him about my conversation with Kate, and all the things she'd said about him. He didn't react in a negative way, just let my story pour out, including my musings on how my relationship with Jake had led to her reaction. He was particularly interested in Jake, and what our relationship had been like.

"Were you in love?"

I thought about it. "I thought we were at the time. Now, I'm sure we were just infatuated. Puppy love."

"And Kate didn't have a problem with that?" he asked. He wasn't angry. There was only curiosity in his voice.

"She was in her own love haze at the time. I don't think I ever realized how much she lets her personal experience in the moment affect how she sees everything else. She was in love, so it made sense that I was, too. And now she's unhappy and assumes no one could be happy if she's not." I didn't realize until I said it that all my musings were leading there, but once it came out, everything clicked into place.

I looked at Bryce with wide eyes. "I can't believe I just said that, but it really makes a lot of sense. You asked just the right questions to help me get there."

He shrugged. "I won't pretend it wasn't somewhat selfish. I'm interested in you and a little jealous of any guy who got to be with you in any way."

"Bryce," I started, but he held up a hand.

"Another thing that doesn't make a lot of sense. I don't have a right to be jealous of people you knew before you met me, but I've learned you can't always control your feelings, nor should you."

I was continually impressed by this man. I'd never met another man so in touch with his emotions, let alone willing to talk about them. Impulsively, I leaned over and kissed him. He responded immediately, moving closer until there was no space between us.

The heat increased, and soon he was lowering me to the carpet, and I was going willingly. Time ceased to exist. All that mattered was Bryce, and his lips, and his hands. I paid no attention to the hard floor beneath me, only the solid weight above me. I would have let it continue, except Bryce broke away, breathing hard. He didn't move from where he was, but rested his forehead on mine, eyes closed. I willed my breathing to slow, my heartbeat to calm. Eventually, he kissed my forehead and moved away from me.

"I'm sorry, Julia," he said, scooting so there was a little space between us. "I lost control a little there."

"Don't be sorry," I said. "I wanted it, too."

"But it's my job to hold your honor," he said, looking away. "Ravaging you on the living room floor isn't appropriate."

"But it's kinda sexy," I said, trying to joke with him.

He looked at me, gaze dark. "I'm serious about this relationship, Julia. You're not just some fun tumble."

"I know," I said quietly. "I never believed you thought of me that way."

"You are worth more than what just happened."

My emotions were a jumble of contradictions. On the one hand,

I was flattered that he thought so much of me, that he considered a future with me, that he held me in such high esteem. On the other, to me, what had just happened was exciting, and a step in our relationship. We hadn't spoken of the physical side of things, and I didn't know where he stood, considering his devotion to his church, but I was happy to go as far as he would let us. Apparently we'd already crossed that spot, if the tense lines of his body as he began cleaning up lunch were any indication.

Bryce moved closer again. "I'm sorry," he said, leaning over to plant a small kiss on my lips. "Just because I said we went too far doesn't mean I didn't enjoy it. You are irresistible, but I have to resist you. At least for now."

I leaned against him, thinking about the last man I'd been with. Jake. What if he'd respected me the way Bryce did? I suddenly felt dirty, used, and I scooted away from Bryce.

"Hey," he said, reaching out to stop me from moving farther away. "What's wrong?"

"Do you . . . do you think less of me for not waiting, Bryce?" I blurted it out before I lost my nerve. I had to know now if this would be a deal breaker for him. I was falling for this man, and I couldn't take it if down the road he decided he wasn't interested in used goods.

"What do you mean?"

"I mean Jake," I said. "We slept together. We lived together. All these things that you have been so careful to avoid out of respect."

Bryce pressed his lips together. "It seems like you're talking about more than just sex."

A surprised laugh burst out of me at his bluntness, despite the seriousness of the conversation and the pounding of my heart. "Now this sounds like a therapy session, although I never made out with my last therapist."

"Julia."

I sighed. "Okay, O perceptive one, I guess you're right. Jake was the love of my life . . . at least I thought he was, as I said before. He was spontaneous and adventurous and always kept me laughing. But even now I'm remembering ways that he showed me that I was far more invested than he was. He never came to pick me up unless it was on his way, and even then he'd sit outside and honk. It was just convenient for us to live together so we weren't driving separately everywhere. Whenever we talked about our future, even after we were engaged, it was *his* plans. *His* dreams. Never ours, and definitely not mine."

Bryce's arm had found its way around my shoulders again, and he rubbed slow circles into my upper arm with his thumb, encouraging me to continue. "Being with him became habit, I think. I can look back now and see everything that was wrong, but sometimes I still convince myself it was my fault, that if I'd done something more, *been* something more, he wouldn't have cheated." Bryce tensed, and I realized I hadn't shared that tidbit yet, but he said nothing. I continued, "I've always secretly thought that if I was enough, he wouldn't have left." I turned to look at Bryce. "But if he hadn't left, I probably would have stayed with him forever, and we wouldn't be here."

"Now that's a silver lining I can get behind," Bryce said, leaning over and pressing his lips to my cheek. "God always has a plan, Julia," he breathed into my ear, sending shivers down my spine.

We sat like that for a while, close together, our souls contentedly intertwined. Finally, he straightened and turned to me, an excited look transforming his face.

"So, do you want to go on an adventure?"

The adventure, as it turned out, was looking at houses. "I decided it was time to invest," Bryce said. "I hope you don't mind tagging along. I'd love your input, though if you'd rather go home . . ."

"No, no," I said, schooling my face into a pleasant expression to mask my inward celebrating. "It's fine! I really enjoy looking at houses, actually. Kate and I watch those house-hunting shows all the time." He was bringing me house hunting and wanted my input. I didn't need to be a mind reader to figure out what that meant. Was he already planning a house for us? If he saw me in his future, it would make sense for me to have a say, and I appreciated the gesture, especially if he had been planning this before we met.

The houses we looked at were all in the Sheridan Heights neighborhood, same as the church. "Are you looking to see anything outside this neighborhood?" the Realtor asked.

"No." Bryce's answer was firm. "I'd like to stay here. It's close to my family and the schools are good."

The Realtor looked between the two of us with a knowing smile, but didn't say anything. Though Bryce had introduced me as his girlfriend, she knew, as I did, that it was only a matter of time.

That thought stopped me in the middle of my perusal of a walk-in closet. Was I really having these thoughts so soon? We'd only known each other a handful of weeks. Of course, it seemed much longer, but in reality, it was barely a blip. Were we still in the honeymoon phase? Would this feeling fade? And if it did, would it grow pale and translucent, like an old cotton shirt washed too many times? Or would it become comfortable, natural, like a well-worn pair of jeans?

Relationships are not clothing, Julia, I scolded myself. Still, I hoped for the jeans.

We had one house left to see, and Bryce was practically vibrating with excitement. "Something on your mind, Mr. Covington?" I teased.

"Saved the best for last," he said, and I immediately craned my neck to catch sight of the house. Everything we had seen today was lovely, expensive, and not really my style. They were nice, and Bryce had pointed out the merits of each one, but none of them felt like home. Now we were in a tree-lined neighborhood, where the oaks towered high enough to create a canopy of flickering shade over the pavement. Most of the houses here were set far back from the road, and guarded by tall iron gates. I wasn't sure how I felt about being gated in, but it did lend an air of old-world charm to the area.

The Realtor must have given Bryce the pass code for the gate, because he punched it in as if he already lived there. The gate slid open smoothly and he drove up the shaded drive. The house was set so far back from the street that I didn't get my first look at it until we crested a small hill.

It took my breath away.

The old stone house stood tall and proud in front of a wide fountain, cheerfully bubbling in the sunshine, the water droplets catching the light and giving the entire scene a fairy-tale look. Bryce pulled up behind the Realtor's car in the circular drive. He turned off the engine and looked at me. "Well?"

"It's gorgeous," I breathed. "At least on the outside." Though I couldn't imagine the inside would disappoint, either. It was like a castle from one of my childhood storybooks. Rounded corners on either end that sprouted three floors tall reminded me of the turrets, and the towering double doors could just as well release a drawbridge to get over the moat.

There was no moat, of course, and no drawbridge, but the inside was just as spectacular. A library filled the bottom portion of one of the rounded towers, and stretched back farther into the house. A window seat occupied the curved part of the wall, and I could already picture myself sitting on the plush cushions, reading for hours. Or sitting with a child in my lap, picking out our favorite picture books for afternoon story time. An office took up the other rounded side on the ground floor, with plenty of bookshelves and dark wood molding. I could see Bryce working here, even seeing clients here if he needed to. He fit here.

At the back of the house, an enormous kitchen with white cupboards and high-tech appliances made me anxious about testing my mediocre cooking skills. Maybe if I had a kitchen like this I would be more motivated to learn to cook. I would love to learn to cook for Bryce. The kitchen led into a breakfast nook, situated next to French doors that led out onto a deck overlooking a lush green yard. There were a couple of trees that looked close enough to hang a hammock, and there was plenty of room for a sandbox or a playhouse. At the bottom of the deck was a patio with a fire pit, and around the side yard, I saw the edge of a pool.

I could have wandered the house for hours, imagining, dreaming. There was a theater room in the basement, a smaller office off the large office on the ground floor, a dining room that could fit a table almost as large as the Reverend's, a large living room and an upstairs parlor, and five bedrooms, the largest of which made me want to move in immediately.

The whirlpool tub was something out of my dreams, and the double shower could send the water bill skyrocketing. The walk-in closet was as large as my bedroom in my apartment, possibly larger, and the main area of the bedroom was large enough to fit a king-sized bed with room to spare.

A bed. To share with Bryce.

I shook my head. I had to get those thoughts out of my head. This was Bryce's house, or could be, if he chose to buy it, and while I had hopes for a future together, I had no claim to anything here. In fact, I didn't have enough money to rent a guest room in the house for the night. Everything was so extravagant, and I wouldn't know how to live in a place like this, as much as it would be a dream to do so.

"What do you think?" Bryce's voice startled me, and I jumped, eliciting an amused laugh from him.

"It's gorgeous, Bryce. I love every inch." I paused. "It's . . . it's terribly expensive, isn't it?"

He frowned. "Money isn't an issue."

Money isn't an issue? That had never been my experience, and I had a hard time believing that it could be true. Real people didn't live in houses like this. Except . . . Bryce could. Everything about him screamed that he would be right at home here. Maybe it was because he'd grown up in the beautiful mansion the Reverend and Nancy had, at least for some of his teen years. He was used to opulence.

"You fit here," I said.

"And you?" Bryce asked, moving closer, taking my hands. "Could you see yourself here?"

I didn't meet his eyes. "I don't know," I said, trying to be honest. "I have never even set foot in a place like this, let alone imagined living someplace this fancy." I looked up at him. "I mean, I always imagined living in Cinderella's castle as a little girl, but I'm not sure that even lives up to this house."

Instead of being disappointed, Bryce threw his head back in a hearty laugh. "You're comparing this house to Cinderella's castle."

I nodded. "Except this house is better."

He laughed again. "If I fit here, why don't you?"

I shrugged and looked away.

Bryce put a finger under my chin, raising my face so that I met his gaze. "You fit with me. If I fit here, so you do."

His gaze was hypnotic, and I almost believed him, almost believed that I could deserve to live in a place like this with a man like him. It was exactly what I wanted to hear, exactly what I craved, to belong here, with him, in his world. But that part of me, that damaged part that still believed the lies Jake had told me—the part that, in a small way, agreed that I wasn't worthy of a life that included a house like this, that included a man like this— wondered if it all really was too good to be true.

"Julia, I told you earlier that I was serious about this relationship. I know you feel it, too. Whatever house I buy, I want you to be in love with it, too. Not just because you think I fit, but because you think you could fit, too, if that's where this relationship ends up going." He paused. "I don't think it's a secret that I see it going in that direction. Otherwise I wouldn't have brought you."

Even though I'd known it, hearing the words directly from him almost had me coming off the floor in excitement. At the same time, I felt grounded suddenly, like I wasn't in this alone. Bryce was right here with me, feeling the things I was feeling, dreaming the dreams that had been filling my quiet moments lately.

"You fit here," I said slowly. "And if you fit here, so do I." I echoed his sentiment from moments before, and joy filled his face. He leaned down to kiss me, not the passionate kisses of earlier, or the timid ones that followed. This kiss was a promise, a commitment, an understanding. And it was the most powerful kiss yet.

She catches sight of her reflection in the mirrored wall. It was his idea to install mirrors that could be used from any vantage point. He was always vain like that, she realizes, though at the time she mistook it for confidence. The woman who stares back at her is a shadow of the woman she used to be, the woman she remembers as being vibrant and full of life, quick to laugh. The woman in the mirror now is too gaunt, her hair too processed, the bags beneath her lower lashes too purple. Only the eyes remain the same, and even they are dimmed, empty of the spark that used to make them shine, the hope that used to fill them, the playfulness that hinted at secrets untold.

Her fingers dance along the surface of the water, making swirling designs as the pink color deepens. It won't be long now.

PART III

THEN COMES MARRIAGE

Three months into my relationship with Bryce, and we were completely in sync. We'd entered the muggy days of summer, but the nights remained cool. The cicadas whirred in the trees during the day, and rather than annoying me as usual, I embraced the sound.

I embraced most everything these days. Initially I had thought it was a love haze, and it would diminish, but if anything it had grown stronger. I attended church regularly with Bryce now, and had begun volunteering some of my time for various graphic design assignments. I'd joined the Bible study that Jenny had invited me to, and had found some wonderful friends in the women who attended. They'd helped me integrate into the world of the church, learn the different language, and didn't laugh when I asked questions, like some of Bryce's other friends did.

At work, Elaine had been hinting at a promotion, and even Micah's jealous stares couldn't dampen my enthusiasm. Despite the intensity of my relationship with Bryce, I was able to focus at work more than ever. I'd taken a class at the church about goal setting and how to make the most of your career, and I had learned so much. Elaine had been impressed before, but now she counted me almost as an equal. There was an empty office next to hers I hoped would be mine within the next few months.

Bryce continued to fit in well with my family. Even Kate was friendlier, though I could tell she was doing it for my benefit, which I appreciated. Our relationship was tenuous at best. It was the only dark spot in my life. She had been my best friend, but now we rarely talked, because inevitably the conversation turned to Bryce and her objections to him, and I was tired of defending him and our relationship to her. Things with her and Eddie had gone from bad to worse, and they were talking about separation. Eddie had fully embraced Bryce, and I wouldn't be surprised if that was part of Kate's objection and the growing divide between them. I couldn't imagine why she was letting this come between her and everyone she loved, but she was adamant that she didn't trust Bryce. I missed my nephews, but I couldn't handle much of Kate anymore.

"That is a fancy necklace, girl," Savannah said from her spot on the couch in my living room. She was sprawled out, comfortable as if it was her own home. With Kate's role in my life temporarily suspended, Van had stepped in to help fill the gaps. She and I had grown closer than ever, and she loved hanging out with Bryce. Her husband, Austin, also got along well with Bryce, and we enjoyed many summer evenings by the pool at Bryce's new house.

He had gone with the beautiful castle, as I knew he would. We were slowly decorating, and it was assumed I would have a hand in all decisions. After the day he made the offer, we continued on with a purpose, with an end goal. Just as it was important to have goals in your career, it was important to have goals in your personal life, and to work toward them. Bryce and I were headed to the same place, it was only a matter of time before it was official.

"You sure you don't want to come see the yacht?" I asked Savannah. "I'm sure it would be fine with Bryce, even if you just wanted to stop by quick."

"Are you kidding? Moonlight on a yacht? I don't think Bryce wants me anywhere near that romantic date." She paused. "Will there be seafood?"

I turned and threw a pillow at her, laughing. Bryce had helped a client out of a jam a few years back, a member of the church, and in return he'd given Bryce full access to his yacht. All Bryce had to do was let him know when he wanted to use it, and the guy would staff it and have someone take it out. I didn't ask what the jam was, but I figured it had to have been pretty significant for that kind of reward.

Bryce didn't talk about his cases. He wasn't allowed to, of course, but I knew he made a difference from the sheer number of people who approached him every week to tell him just that. They also approached me and told me things Bryce had done for them. Getting them out of a bad contract, referring them to a colleague for a custody battle, setting up a new business. He did as much as he could, and worked long hours, but I was proud of him.

There was a knock on the door, and I quickly threw my shawl around my shoulders and took one last look in the mirror before pirouetting in front of Van. "How do I look?" I asked.

"Stunning," she answered sincerely. "You'll knock his socks off. And maybe his pants, too." She snickered and my face heated.

"You know our relationship isn't like that," I murmured, and she cackled an apology, though it was significantly less sincere than her appraisal of my outfit had been.

Bryce and I hadn't come close to crossing the physical boundary again, as much as I had wanted to. He held himself very carefully, and knew when to take a break and get some space so that he wouldn't be tempted, though he told me I tempted him constantly. One time was after we'd gone for a long hike. My face was sweaty, my hair plastered to my cheeks and neck, my shirt clinging to my back, and he'd hauled me close and kissed me until I saw stars. "You are so beautiful, all the time," he'd said. "You could tempt a man to do many things if he wasn't careful."

It was a compliment, I knew, but it did make me feel a little uncomfortable to be reminded that just being me, in any situation, had the potential to cause negative thoughts. Not that sex was negative, but one thing I'd learned in my Bible study was about the importance of our bodies being temples, and keeping those boundaries in place outside of the institution of marriage. I understood now what Bryce had meant about how it was his responsibility to protect my honor. I was grateful that he was so much stronger than I was, and that he was teaching me patience and restraint. It was even more important to me to avoid crossing those lines, given that I hadn't been so careful with Jake, and Bryce had forgiven me that past. Savannah thought it was all crazy, of course. She'd learned to stay pure until marriage in her church, but as she said, she hadn't exactly followed that rule, and she hadn't been struck by lightning, and neither had I when it was Jake. But I hadn't had the same beliefs back then. It was different. I was different.

I took a deep breath, shot Savannah a dirty look, and swung open the door. Bryce leaned against the doorframe, looking like an angelic James Bond in his tux, and I was more grateful than ever that he was determined to keep us honest, because I wasn't sure I could keep myself from jumping him otherwise. He swallowed hard, and I realized I probably had the same effect on him. I wore a long beaded black dress that shimmered when I moved. The neckline was a high halter, and the back dipped low, but not indecently so. A chain ran between my shoulder blades to keep it from slipping off my shoulders.

Bryce cleared his throat. "You look . . . miraculous."

I laughed. "That might be the highest compliment you've ever paid me." I reached up and smoothed his lapels. "You look pretty miraculous as well. Are you sure you're real?"

"You wanna pinch me and find out?"

"Maybe later." I winked, and his eyes widened.

"Oh, just go on and get it over with," Savannah called from behind me. "I'll close my eyes so I don't see you make out."

Bryce grinned. "Have a good night, Savannah," he called, then pulled me out in the hallway and shut the door, barely giving me time to grab my matching beaded purse. He held my shoulders for a moment, the look in his eyes intense, and I almost expected him to shove me against the door and kiss me senseless, but he only placed a very chaste kiss on my lips before hooking my arm in his elbow and leading me downstairs.

Waiting out front was a sleek black limousine, complete with a driver who jumped out of the car and rushed to open the door as we exited my building. A happy sigh escaped my lips as I remembered the limo from our second date, the first time he'd picked me up from my apartment. It seemed like so long ago, but also like no time at all.

"Savannah is going to be really mad she didn't decide to come along," I said, smiling up at Bryce. "A girl could get used to this."

He laughed. "Don't get too used to it. It's a rental."

I slid into the plush interior, appreciating the dimly lit luxury of the backseat. "Not a loaner from a church person this time?"

Bryce chuckled again. "Not this time."

I didn't let on, but this gratified me. I wasn't opposed to Bryce using his congregational connections, but it seemed like many of the things we did were thanks to one member or another. The congregation shared everything, but with the sharing of assets came the sharing of information. Half the congregation seemed to have a stake in our relationship at this point, and while I appreciated the support, sometimes I wanted things to be between the two of us. And since the yacht we were heading to was a church member's, not having our entire date financed by others seemed like a win.

Bryce took my hand and held it through our drive to the marina. We didn't speak, but the silence was comfortable, as always. Bryce had pointed out to me once that I seemed to have a need to fill silences with noise, and while I was offended at first, I realized that he was right. Now I waited in the silence to decide if what I wanted to say really needed to be said. Bryce had complimented me on the quality of our conversations, and I was using the technique at work as well. It was a lesson Bryce said he'd learned from the Reverend long ago, when he had needed to learn what was important to say, and what could be left alone.

Bryce still didn't talk much about his life before meeting the Reverend and Nancy. What I had gathered was that they had met Bryce when he was a teenager, and had helped him through school. Bryce always spoke of meeting the Reverend as if it had been a miracle, with a reverence that made it seem as if he'd run into God Himself. After several months of getting to know the Reverend, I understood. There was something about him . . . I wondered sometimes if he did have a more direct connection with God than others. He certainly seemed to have an aura of peace and wisdom about him. Nothing ruffled him. I had come to admire him almost as much as I admired Bryce, though in a completely different way.

"Here we are!" Bryce's voice had taken on the tone of a child on Christmas morning. I knew he was excited about spending time on the yacht, and I smiled at his enthusiasm. He slid out the opposite door of the car and held a hand out to help me. Offering his arm, he escorted me down the wide dock until a beautifully lit boat came into view.

"Is that it?" I asked, my excitement level chasing Bryce's. "We get that to ourselves?"

"Us and a crew." He gazed down at me. "Do you like it?"

"It's completely amazing," I said, and meant it. I'd never spent time on anything more than a speedboat. As we climbed the gangplank to the deck, I realized I never really knew what a boat was before that moment. This was what a boat was meant to be. We walked through the luxurious cabins and living area belowdecks, and strolled the walkways. It seemed bigger on the inside than it looked on the outside. I laughed to myself, wishing Savannah was around to appreciate my *Doctor Who* reference.

The captain came and introduced himself to us, and soon the engines were revving up and we were headed out to cruise the river.

I leaned against the railing, marveling at the twilit night. The city stood stark against a backdrop of purples and pinks, and as I watched, lights and stars winked on from skyline to horizon. Bryce stood behind me, sheltering me on either side with his arms. "Beautiful, isn't it?" he breathed into my ear.

"It's like a whole new world," I replied, my voice hushed with respect for the pristine beauty of the city at sunset. Of course, I knew that it wasn't perfect, that some of the areas I admired from afar were, in reality, dirty and smelly and noisy areas that wouldn't be conducive to a romantic evening, but from this distance, on this beauty of a boat, everything appeared calm and peaceful.

We stood like that for several minutes, until one of the crew came to tell us dinner was ready. I took Bryce's arm again and we walked to the back of the boat, where a small table had been set. The only lighting was from twinkle lights strung back and forth across the ceiling, and a bit of light spilling from the door the servers moved through.

"I wanted candlelight," Bryce said. "But it's a little windy for that."

"It's perfect," I said, smiling as he pulled out my chair. "Everything looks amazing."

And it was. The food was delicious, and conversation moved easily. I found myself staring at Bryce at one point, and I wondered how I got so lucky. God must have been looking down on me that day. I laughed to myself as I pictured God blowing on my stack of papers, putting me in Bryce's path. If it weren't for that gust of wind, we might never have met. And I would never have found the church or the Reverend. So many of the most important things in my life wouldn't exist but for that one moment in time. It was amazing to consider.

Bryce looked up as I stared, and one side of his mouth turned up. "Do I have something on my face?"

I shook my head. "Nope. Just admiring the view."

His cheeks colored, and I felt my own follow suit. Bryce was confident and intelligent, but he wasn't very comfortable with compliments, at least from me. I was trying to help him become better at accepting them. He normally said that he didn't need compliments, that his worth came from elsewhere, but he had improved, and tonight he just reached across the table and took my hand. "Are you finished?"

"I am," I said, laying my fork on my plate and removing my napkin from my lap with my free hand.

"Want to go look at the lights some more?"

"Yes."

Bryce jumped up and rounded the table to pull out my chair before I could stand, and we strolled toward the front of the ship, fingers entwined. When we reached the bow, he placed me in front of him again, but instead of bracing his hands on the railing as he had before, he wrapped both arms tightly around my waist, tangling his fingers with mine and resting his chin on my shoulder. As beautiful as the night had become, clear and cool, I closed my eyes to savor the moment, to savor the closeness of the man behind me. I concentrated on our heartbeats, so often in sync.

While my heart beat along at a calm rate, steady and safe, Bryce's galloped along at twice the pace. Sometimes his pulse picked up when we were close, but not like this, and not in moments like this, mostly void of sexual tension. At least I'd thought so. I wondered if I'd read the situation wrong, if Bryce was struggling in this moment, and I was making things worse by snuggling into the warmth of his body.

"Are you okay?" I whispered, turning my head slightly so he could hear me.

"Never better," he responded, but his pulse jumped again at my question. Reluctantly, I untangled our fingers and loosened his arms around me, turning in his embrace. Immediately I realized it was probably the wrong move, now that our bodies were flush against each other, but I needed to see his face.

Reaching up, I smoothed my hand down his cheek. He closed his eyes and leaned into the palm. "Your heart is racing," I said. His cheek felt cool, so he wasn't sick. "Are you sure you're okay?"

His eyes popped open, the blue piercing me with its intensity. "I want this moment to last forever," he said. He turned his face to kiss my palm. "Or maybe the next moment."

My heart rate picked up. "What happens in the next moment?"

As he dropped to one knee, I understood why he had been so nervous or excited or maybe a combination of the two. He had been waiting for this moment, and I also understood why he wanted to keep it forever. Although I did disagree on one thing. The moment I wanted to last forever was the one that came after. The one that didn't wait for whatever speech he had planned, didn't even wait for the question.

The moment that I said, "Yes."

I was still euphoric as we approached the dock again. I admired the way the diamond Bryce placed on my finger sparkled in the moonlight, by the light of the twinkle lights, and even how it caught random reflections in the dark corner where Bryce pulled me and kissed me until I was breathless. We were giddy as two teenagers. I was going to be Mrs. Bryce Covington. I couldn't wait to announce it to the world, and yet my shoulders stooped as the crew began their tasks for docking.

Bryce, who hadn't released me since I'd said yes, noticed, and rubbed his hand on my back under my shawl. "What's wrong?"

Momentarily distracted by the feel of his smooth palm on the bare skin of my back, I didn't answer right away.

"Julia?"

"Hmm? Oh," I laughed, my neck flushing in embarrassment. "I'm just a little disappointed to be going back to dry land. You were right. I wanted these moments to last forever."

He pulled me toward him for another kiss, this one less exuberant than those from earlier. Leaning back just far enough to look into my eyes, he said, "The party's not over yet." He nodded toward the dock, where I could now see a crowd of people gathered, holding up signs. Their cheering danced across the water toward us.

"Who is that?"

"Look closer."

I leaned away to turn more fully toward the approaching dock, and Bryce adjusted his body closer to mine as I did so. We were already so in tune with each other. Pulling my focus from the location of Bryce's body, a task in itself, I squinted into the dim moonlight to see who was waiting to greet us.

I gasped as the faces came into focus. My parents, the Reverend and Nancy, Van and the gang, Jenny and the Bible study girls . . . even Kate and her family stood, cheering and waving as we drew closer. I turned back to Bryce. "You had all this planned, too?"

"I'd do anything to make you happy, Julia," he said. "I knew you'd want to celebrate with your friends and family as soon as possible."

Tears pricked my eyes at the gesture. He was amazing, this man who was going to be my husband.

It seemed to take forever for the yacht to dock and the ramp to be secured so we could exit, but when we did, I skipped down to the dock and straight into the arms of the Reverend and Nancy, who were at the front of the group.

"We're so proud," the Reverend said. "Congratulations." Even Nancy had tears in her eyes as she squeezed me and kissed my cheek, her dry lips warm on my skin. They turned to Bryce, handing me off to my parents, who hugged me tightly. Next, Van grabbed my hands and we squealed together.

"You *knew*," I accused. "The whole time I was getting ready!"

"Girl, I've known for weeks. I know how to keep a secret!"

"I'd be annoyed if I wasn't so excited," I said, pulling her in for another hug.

"That was my plan all along." She winked at me. "Now are you going to let me see that rock?"

And so it went, through all the well-wishers. We gradually made our way back to shore, where a party had been set up in an outdoor area of one of the restaurants overlooking the water. We drank champagne and laughed and Bryce and I were separated for most of the evening, much to my chagrin. Everyone seemed to want to speak with us at once, and the best way to accomplish that was to divide and conquer. There were plenty of steamy looks across the patio, though, a wink here, a raised eyebrow there. Though we couldn't be touching, we were constantly aware of each other. I wondered if this was how marriage would be, if this connection would grow stronger or fade away with time.

I finally broke away to get some air after chatting with some people from the church who knew Bryce fairly well, but whom I had only met a couple of times. It was dawning on me how many people I would need to know better now that Bryce and I would be married. I wasn't the greatest with names, so I was trying to commit these people's stats to memory when I saw a dark figure silhouetted against the night.

Kate.

I had only spoken to her briefly when we'd arrived at the dock. She had given me a perfunctory hug when I reached her, and then stepped back to allow her boys to jump all over me and exclaim their joy at "Uncle Bryce" officially marrying me. She'd melted into the crowd before I could say anything else to her, and we'd seemed to be on opposite ends of the room all night tonight. I was grateful she had come, and I was ready to clear the air. I cleared my throat as I approached.

Kate swung around, surprise filling her face when she saw me. "What are you doing out here?"

"Getting some air," I said, smiling. "There are so many people in there. I needed a break."

"Lots of well-wishers," Kate agreed, and I was taken aback at the bitterness in her voice. I'd thought her attendance tonight had been an olive branch, but her tone suggested otherwise.

"I'm glad you came, Kate," I said, trying again to bring peace back to our relationship. "It means a lot. I've missed you."

Kate's shoulders slumped. "I've missed you, too."

I stepped forward, relieved by her response. "This is going to be so great, Kate. I know once you get to know Bryce . . ."

She held up a hand to stop me. "I don't want you to think that because I'm here it means I approve of this."

It was like a bucket of ice water had been splashed over my entire body. "What do you mean?"

Kate looked behind me, lowering her voice though we were the only ones around. "What do you really know about him, Jules? You've been dating, what, a couple months?"

"Three and a half."

"And you think you're ready to commit to marrying him? You're still in the honeymoon period!"

If Kate had deigned to actually have a conversation with me over the past few months, she would have realized just how much Bryce and I knew about each other, just how strong our connection was. But instead she had separated herself from us, put up a wall that was impossible to break through, communicated only enough to be considered polite.

"I'm more than ready," I said. "I can't wait to spend the rest of my life with him."

"You didn't answer my question," Kate said. "Other than his job and his church, what do you really know about him? Where are his parents? Why are that pastor and his wife always hanging around? What's that church all about, even?"

My anger rose as she spoke. I ignored the discomfort that I didn't know the answer to the questions about his past, which was easy because it was quickly eclipsed by anger over her accusations against the church and the people who had been nothing but warm and welcoming to me since my first visit.

"I know that I love him and he loves me and he would do anything to make me happy," I said, spitting the words at her.

"He doesn't love you," Kate said. "He controls you."

"How dare you?" My gut tightened and my heart raced. I couldn't believe what I was hearing.

"You're a different person since you met him, Julia. You can't see it, and maybe everyone else is too relieved that you finally met someone to care. Everything you say and do revolves around that man. You don't take a shit without asking him for permission."

"That's not fair."

"It's true!" Kate threw her hands in the air. "It's like I'm screaming at a brick wall. There's something wrong with him, Julia. He looks at you like he owns you."

"He does own me," I said. "He owns my heart, he owns all of me, and I own all of him. That's what a relationship is."

"That's a really messed-up way to look at a relationship."

I reached the end of my temper. "He loves me, Kate. Just because you ended up with someone you hate and are completely miserable with doesn't mean that you can sabotage my life to keep me as miserable as you."

Kate stared at me, and I wanted to take the words back immediately. She had said some terrible things, but I knew what things were like with Eddie. "Kate," I began, but at that moment Kate's eyes widened and Bryce called out from behind me.

"There you are, my love!" The happiness in his voice brought me back to the reality of the moment, and my anger rose again. Not at Bryce, but at Kate for ruining what should have been a perfect night. We continued to stare at each other until Bryce reached us and threw an arm over my shoulder. "Are you coming back to the party?"

Taking a deep breath, I mustered a smile for my fiancé. "Yes, of course."

He looked at Kate. "Kate? You coming?"

Kate didn't say a word, just looked at me for a beat longer, then turned and walked into the night. I watched until she disappeared into darkness and then turned my back on her, allowing Bryce to lead me back to the lights and laughter of the party. Before we joined everyone again, he turned and pulled me into his embrace.

"We're in this for the long haul now, right? Together forever?" There was a vulnerability in his question that was foreign to his usual tone.

I placed a hand on his cheek and looked deeply into his eyes.

"Till death do us part."

Chapter 13

The next morning, Bryce and I were surrounded as soon as we entered the church building. Word had spread fast about our engagement, and it seemed the entire congregation was eager to extend their congratulations and well-wishes. The music was already starting by the time we slipped into our row near the front of the sanctuary. Stacy squeezed my hand as we sat, and I squeezed back. I didn't fully connect with Stacy still, but she had always been nice to me, and I knew she was close with Bryce. I vowed to do a better job of cultivating that friendship, for Bryce's sake if for no other reason. I'd asked Bryce about his friendship with Stacy once, and he'd admitted that they had considered dating a few years back, but the Reverend had foreseen that it would not be a good match. Within a few weeks, Stacy had met the man she would end up marrying, though she remained close with Bryce. I couldn't imagine remaining so close with a man I'd had strong feelings for, but my only experience was with Jake, so I was perhaps not the best judge of those sorts of relationships. Still, there were times when their history and close friendship brought up feelings of jealousy in me, which fueled my desire to become closer with Stacy.

I'd also learned that Bryce wasn't a huge fan of Jenny and the rest of my Bible study, but he was friendly to them because they were important to me. He didn't give much of an explanation for why he didn't like them, only mentioning that it was a large church and not everyone's beliefs meshed as well as they would like. He followed it up by stressing the importance of allowing many different people to worship together, but I still felt that tension whenever I spoke about the group, even though he made an effort to ask questions and was always polite when he retrieved me from the café after his weekly meeting. I thought it was a great testament to our relationship that we were both making such an effort to blend into each other's life. We were a unit now.

As always, the music carried me away from my stray thoughts and straight into worship, and by the time the Reverend took the stage, I was leaning forward, eager to hear what he had to say this week. I was startled when he turned and spoke directly to me.

It often felt like the Reverend was speaking to me in his sermons. They were always surprisingly relevant, and he was the sort of speaker who would make eye contact with you and hold it for several beats instead of skipping over to the next person, but this time he was actually speaking to me, and to Bryce.

"Bryce and Julia, I know we didn't talk about this ahead of time, but the Lord was speaking to me last night, and I thought it would be prudent to listen to the Creator of the world." The congregation laughed at this. "He told me that this sermon is for you, and I rewrote everything I had planned, so if you could come on up here, we'll have some chairs brought out."

My entire body was on fire as I stood and made my way to the aisle, followed closely by Bryce. "Don't worry," he whispered in my ear. "He mentioned it briefly to me this morning. I told him it was fine."

Why hadn't Bryce run it by me? I supposed it had happened too quickly, and there wasn't time to check in. Still, I wasn't happy to be in front of a thousand people with no sense of what was going to happen next. As we climbed the stairs to the stage, the Reverend looked at me and smiled.

"No need to be worried, Julia," he said, his voice taking on the calming tone I was familiar with. "We're just going to have a conversation."

My fingers shook as the Reverend reached out to lead me to one of the stools that had materialized from backstage. His thumbs rubbed over the backs of my hands, soothing my nerves. I climbed up on one of the stools, and Bryce took the one next to me, quickly claiming my hand.

"Isn't that sweet, folks?" the Reverend said, and there were murmurs of agreement all through the congregation. "Now, for those who weren't aware"—he paused for a chuckle to spread through the room, because who wouldn't know what he was about to say—"this man up here is Bryce Covington, a son to me in every way that matters."

Bryce raised his free hand in a small wave, acknowledging the smattering of applause he received for being himself. He didn't seem the least bit nervous, and I concentrated on where our hands were joined to draw strength from him.

"And this lovely lady here is Julia Hawthorne. Julia just started coming to our little church"—another pause for laughter—"a few months ago, but already she has become an integral part of our community . . . as well as an integral part of our family." I tried my own version of Bryce's jaunty wave, though I was certain my face was ten shades of red.

"Last night," the Reverend continued, "Bryce asked Julia to be his wife." The Reverend looked over at Bryce, who grinned and raised our clasped hands, where my engagement ring winked brilliantly in the stage lights.

"She said yes!" he called before the Reverend could announce it.

It took a full two minutes before the applause died down. The entire congregation stood in support, and Bryce pulled me to my feet. We stood waving at the people as if we were celebrities, and I felt both ridiculous and empowered as I looked over the crowd. They knew very little about me, but I had the approval of Bryce and, more importantly, the Reverend, and that was all it took for them to accept me. It was a strange and heady phenomenon, and though I still wasn't fully comfortable in front of so many people, I didn't hate the feeling that came over me as we stood there.

Finally the congregation calmed down and we all sat again, Bryce and me still in our spots on the stage.

"In case you didn't catch that," the Reverend said. "Congratulations."

My cheeks hurt from smiling so wide, and Bryce's expression matched my own.

"The Word the Lord brought to me last night comes from the New Testament," the Reverend said, slipping smoothly from proud father to magnanimous leader. "The Bible talks about marriage several times, but for today we're going to focus on Ephesians. A verse often quoted, but little understood . . ."

Forty-five minutes later, the Reverend wrapped up his sermon and motioned for us to follow him backstage instead of heading to our seats as the band came back on to lead the final songs. My heart was back to its normal speed, though I hadn't released Bryce's hand since we sat down. During the sermon I was as entranced as ever, especially as it applied to me in more ways than usual. In my few months of study, I hadn't paid much attention to verses about marriage, and now I was both anxious and eager to learn more.

Once we were clear and the Reverend had removed his microphone, he turned to us. "I'm sorry for springing that on you, but I didn't feel like I had much of a choice." He raised his eyes heavenward and I wondered what it would be like to hear the voice of God so clearly. Bryce said he had heard it the day we met, and Nancy, once she warmed up to me, told me that God had spoken to her about me as well. The women in my Bible study talked about God speaking to them, but it was more symbolic, in the words of friends or dreams. Not these very vivid instances of hearing the voice of God. I longed for that experience.

"It's fine, Reverend," Bryce said. "It was such a good message. Thank you for sharing it with us."

"Yes," I said, smiling. "I'm honored to have inspired such passionate teaching."

"Well, God inspired it," the Reverend corrected. "It was just prompted by your engagement."

"Of course," I said, embarrassed to have spoken out of turn.

"Bryce," the Reverend said. "Would you mind letting everyone know that the Gathering will start a bit late? I wish to speak to Julia."

"I'd be happy to," Bryce said, squeezing my hand once more before extricating his fingers from mine and walking down the hallway. I looked around the backstage area. I'd never actually been back here, as many times as I had been in this building over the past several months. The offices, where I helped with graphic design projects, were housed in another part of the building, and the Bible study met in homes where the women lived. This was where Bryce always disappeared to after church, for the "Gathering" that was held every week after the service. He never spoke of it, or who else attended. I was never invited, and I didn't ask questions. I'd learned that the one area regarding his faith that Bryce didn't talk about was these Gatherings. The one time I did ask, Bryce reacted more negatively than when I'd asked about his family. It was clearly a closed topic.

"Come this way, please, Julia," the Reverend said, leading the way down a hallway, away from all the sound equipment and extra instruments stored in the area where we'd been standing. The hum of backstage and the echoes of the music still going on in the sanctuary faded as we crossed into a carpeted area, much more dimly lit. It was like crossing a portal into the sacred, and I felt the urge to whisper and make as little noise as possible.

The Reverend opened one of the thick wooden doors and gestured for me to precede him into the room. Inside, the lighting was muted, giving the entire room a serene atmosphere. Two chairs and a couch were grouped around a coffee table. All it was missing was a TV and it could have been my living room growing up. Landscape pictures dotted the walls, each embellished with a quote or a Bible verse. Some of the quotes seemed to be attributed to the Reverend, but I didn't get a chance to look too closely before the man himself spoke again. "Please, sit, Julia. Let's talk."

My anxiety spiked. I was usually pretty calm with the Reverend, but after this morning, I was already on edge, and this sounded serious. I'd never had a conversation with the Reverend without Bryce. It felt odd. Not wrong, just . . . different.

I took a seat in one of the chairs, crossing my legs and folding my hands and trying not to look as if I were ready to jump up and run for the door. While I was still nervous, I also recognized that being brought to this part of the church was an honor, and I wanted to be respectful of the gesture as well.

"This is nice," I said, motioning around the room. "Very homey."

The Reverend followed my gaze, taking in the room as if seeing it with new eyes, and nodded. "That's good to hear. We do try to make things as comfortable as possible." He studied me for a moment, and I sat up straighter. "I wanted to have a chance to sit down with you, Julia, because I know you're new to our church, and to the faith in general. Because of this, I'm not certain you know the way of things yet, and I want to make sure you're on the right track to be the best wife for Bryce and the best addition to our church family."

My brow wrinkled. I was new to the church, yes, but I wasn't sure how that would hinder my ability to be a good wife. The best wife. And Bryce hadn't said anything about rules regarding marriage. Although, when I thought about it, though we had both seemed to know the direction we were headed, we never explicitly discussed marriage until the proposal. On my part, I didn't want to ruin it, especially by talking about it too early. And the old-fashioned part of me wanted him to bring it up first. Which he had. By proposing.

"I'm not sure I understand, Reverend," I said. "I'm sure whatever I need to learn, Bryce can help me with. Or Nancy, or even my Bible study." I knew the Reverend had good intentions, and was trying to help, but part of me wasn't sure this topic was one I wanted to discuss with him on my own. While he knew a great deal about me, I didn't know much about him, and though I was sure he had a lot of great advice for a successful marriage, I was proud of how Bryce and I had been finding our own way to this point. Anything I wasn't comfortable discussing with Bryce, I couldn't imagine I'd be more comfortable talking about with the Reverend, at least not without Bryce there.

It was the Reverend's turn to frown, a foreign expression on his face. He always looked calm and peaceful, or joyous. When he was passionate about something, or discussing the evils of the world, he got this intense look on his face that could be interpreted as anger, but it was so animated that I would have hated to taint it with that label. This expression was more concerned than sad or angry.

"You've been attending the study Jenny Peters runs, is that correct?"

"Yes, sir. They've been so nice and welcoming. Usually I sit with them while Bryce is at the Gathering after service. They invited me to join the first week I visited, and I've learned so much from them."

"Yes, I see," the Reverend said, the corners of his eyes wrinkling just slightly. "I'm very glad to hear my parishioners are so friendly." He paused. "But I wonder if that's the best group for you to be in."

"Why?" The question came out before I could wonder if it was rude. I was genuinely curious about why the Reverend would have a problem with Jenny's group, though I suspected his answer would mirror Bryce's feelings on the matter.

He smiled indulgently. "You see, Julia, that group, while a wonderful example of how welcoming our church is, is not the sort of group you should be associating with as Bryce's wife."

Confusion with a hint of irritation flared in my gut, and I spoke again before thinking. "Are you saying that group isn't good enough?"

The Reverend held up his hands. "No, no, of course not. That's preposterous. I'm simply saying that as Bryce's wife, you will be part of the Gathering, and your duties will expand to the point that an extra group such as Jenny's would not be fulfilling to your mission with the church."

There were more questions I had about that, because it didn't sound quite right, but I was stuck on something else. "I'm going to become part of the Gathering?" The secretive group that met after service every week. Where Bryce and Nancy and Stacy all went, leaving me behind each week. It would certainly help in my vow to become closer with Stacy. And would be one less thing I had to avoid bringing up with Bryce.

"Of course! You will join today, in fact. No time to lose. It is imperative to your relationship with Bryce that you share this experience."

Excitement bubbled in my stomach. I was ready to go right in that moment, but I could tell that the Reverend wasn't quite finished. "Thank you. I appreciate the opportunity," I said, and I could tell it was the right response as the Reverend's eyes lit up. "I'll be sad to leave my Bible study, but if you think it's best, I suppose I can see the women other times." I ignored that guilt I felt at giving in to the Reverend's demand so quickly, especially when it seemed he was being a bit unfair. He hadn't exactly said anything negative about my Bible study, but there was that same underlying tension when he talked about them as I heard in Bryce's voice when we discussed the women in the group.

"You'll see them at church, for sure," the Reverend said. "Now, on to the other things we need to discuss." The topic of my Bible study was clearly closed. "I'm not sure Bryce had time to talk to you about how everything works with engagements here." He looked at me expectantly.

"Um, no, we didn't get a chance. I'm assuming some premarital counseling?" Kate and Eddie had done premarital counseling. She'd said it was a waste of time because they were so in love. See how much good that had done them.

The Reverend shifted, his pleasant expression not changing. "It's a bit more involved than that, Julia. We take marriage very seriously in our church. We do not want mismatched couples joining their lives. It's not good for their souls and it's not good for the family."

"I agree," I said, nodding. "I take marriage very seriously as well."

"Good." The Reverend inclined his head toward me. "Now. Bryce played his part beautifully. He came and requested permission to date you, which we granted after he told us of the time you'd spent together. That was before we'd even met you. When we did meet you, I'm going to be really honest, Julia, we weren't sure. I was frankly surprised that Bryce had chosen someone who didn't share his beliefs. He has always been so devout, at least since I've known him. I had always pictured him with someone from the congregation, someone in a position similar to his own."

I looked down at my hands. I had gotten the feeling from Nancy that I didn't quite measure up when they met me, but the Reverend had never given that impression at all. I'd felt accepted and loved from our first introduction. It was painful to think that he hadn't wanted Bryce to be with me in that first meeting. My instincts that first week about not fitting in had been more accurate than even I'd believed. I wondered if they'd regretted saying no to Bryce's relationship with Stacy, if they thought that he would have been better off with someone like her.

The Reverend placed a finger under my chin and raised my head to look at him. "I will always be honest with you, Julia, even when the truth is painful. That is the truth of when we first met you, but that is not the truth of today. Today Nancy and I couldn't be happier that Bryce found you. I truly believe it was God's hand in your life that put you in Bryce's path. You were lost, and we found you. You have proven your dedication over these past months, and when Bryce came to request permission to propose, I was only too happy to grant that as well."

It was astonishing how much influence this man had over my life that I was completely unaware of. Bryce had to ask permission both to date me and to propose? But it made sense when I thought about it. The Reverend heard from God more than anyone. He had wisdom I couldn't even fathom. Instead of feeling violated, as others might (I pictured Van's reaction and almost started laughing), I felt protected, cherished. The church really took into consideration every aspect. They cared so deeply for their members, their *family*, that they had a hand even in this. I couldn't help but wonder, if more people had been involved in my relationship with Jake, if things would have turned out differently, if they could have helped me see the ways it wasn't working sooner.

I smiled at the Reverend. "So what's next? I've said yes, but I'm guessing it's not just on to the wedding planning now."

He laughed. "There will be plenty of time for that, my dear. Nancy is very excited to get started with helping you plan. But in addition to joining the Gathering, you and Bryce will be attending twice-weekly counseling sessions with myself and Nancy. We will also connect you with a mentor couple, with whom you will be expected to meet weekly. In addition, I'd like you to come here, to our spiritual counseling center, to learn more about your individual gifts and how you will use them in your marriage and in the church." He paused and leaned forward. "Your dedication to all of these things and your ability to balance your faith and personal lives will help me to determine whether you are truly the best match for Bryce."

My mind was spinning. I attempted to calculate the sheer time commitment of all of those meetings and sent up a prayer to God to extend the days by a few hours until the wedding. "That's . . . a lot," I said. "With work and other commitments . . ."

"This has to be the most important thing, Julia." The Reverend's voice grew sharper than I'd ever heard it. "Not just the engagement, but your commitment to the church and to God. I've mentioned this to Bryce, but you'll need to look at your priorities in activities outside the church, such as your job. I'd hate to see you make an idol out of your work there. I understand you're doing quite well, and I have seen others go down the path of putting work above family and faith."

"I would never do that," I said, but at the same time I knew that I had been working longer hours as Elaine depended on me more. A promotion would mean later evenings and travel, even some weekend commitments. We worked when the clients wanted us to work. "I have faith that God will help me organize my life and make the decisions that need to be made," I said, sounding more confident than I felt.

"I'm glad to hear it," the Reverend said. "Learning to balance your time is a key skill to have." He rubbed his hands together. "There's more to discuss, but it can wait until later. For now, why don't we make our way to the Gathering?"

I jumped up, my excitement evident.

"You'll sit in the back and observe at first, Julia," the Reverend said, leading the way to the door. "When you're ready to join fully, I will let you know. It could be only weeks, but maybe longer."

Observing was better than sitting in the café, waiting. With a skip in my step, I followed the Reverend from the room, leaving the troubling aspects of our conversation behind me.

Chapter 14

At the end of the hallway, double doors opened into a large circular room. A mural splashed over the domed ceiling, and I wanted to take some time to study it, but my attention was drawn to the group of people gathered in the center of the room. The Reverend touched my arm.

"You can stay back here and observe," he said, his voice low. He nodded toward a small grouping of chairs near the door. "Please do not interrupt or ask questions. There will be time for that later."

I almost laughed at the idea that I would draw attention to myself by interrupting whatever they did in this room, but I only inclined my head to indicate that I understood, then turned and made my way to the chairs and sat in one facing the room.

By now the group had noticed our entrance, and the low rumble of conversation extinguished as the Reverend made his way toward them. I caught Bryce's eye and he winked at me before turning his attention back to the Reverend. That small gesture showed me that I belonged here, even if I was still somewhat on the outside, and settled whatever nerves I had following my conversation with the Reverend.

I recognized several of the people in this group, though I knew few by name. I'd been introduced to all of them, I was sure, but I had gravitated elsewhere, toward the women in my Bible study and those who surrounded them. The only time Bryce and I spent much time with large groups of people from the church was at the Sunday dinners that had become our weekly routine with the Reverend and Nancy. I regretted not paying better attention before to all the people who had paraded through the house from week to week.

There were no windows in the room, and once the door was closed, someone came over and pulled a heavy black curtain over the doorway so that no light from the cracks could sneak in. The electric sconces along the wall were extinguished and candles were lit on tables around the large space. I was amazed at the size of the room. It must be located at the back of the church, the same side as the Reverend's house, not visible from the road or from Bryce's apartment. I couldn't imagine having missed a part of the building like this. There were about fifty people in the room, and they stood in loose groups of three or four.

The Reverend stood at the front of the room, and everyone's attention turned to him as he raised his hands. "We thank You for Your Word at the service this morning, O Lord. Now we request Your presence."

In unison, everyone else in the room repeated his words like a prayer, or a chant. They turned to each other and clasped hands in their small groups. Nancy, who had been standing to the right of the Reverend, walked to a corner to a small round table that held only a silver goblet and a small silver plate, similar to what we used during Communion. As she lifted the goblet, candlelight reflected off curved markings on the side, but I couldn't tell if it was writing or just a flowing design. The plate held small discs of varying neutral colors, some a dark tan, almost brown, others lighter beige, almost white. She walked to the first group and handed each person a disc as they held their hands cupped to received it. Nancy exchanged low words with each recipient, but I couldn't decipher what was said. Next, they passed the goblet around and each took a sip. Nancy moved from group to group and repeated the same ritual before returning to her spot next to the Reverend. He reached for her hand and they continued praying.

The room filled with sound now, but it was no longer in unison. Some continued the prayer from before, while others moved their lips, no sound coming out. A couple were speaking audibly but almost as if in another language, and on one side of the room raucous laughter broke out. From my perch, the situation was devolving into chaos, and now I understood why the Reverend had told me not to interrupt. I searched for Bryce, and found him standing in the center of the room, his hands in the air, face raised to the ceiling. His mouth opened wide and he started laughing. When he turned his head, I gasped at the size of his pupils. None of the blue was visible from where I sat. His eyes were pools of black, transforming his handsome face into something maniacal, and I couldn't decide if I was drawn to him or repelled.

This was nothing like what I'd expected. I had been picturing a board meeting, or an extra-elite Bible study of some sort. This was terrifying, and growing more intense by the minute. The groups had split by now, and those who were speaking gibberish or chanting or laughing converged around Bryce in the center, while others moved to the outer edges of the room. A woman whose name I couldn't recall fell into the seat next to mine.

"Didn't happen this time," she commented. "It's been over a month." She looked distraught, but I had no idea how to comfort her. I had no idea what was happening. She glanced at me, then reached over and patted my knee. "Almost over now."

Almost as if her words had triggered it, a rumbling sounded from the floor. I looked at the woman in a panic, and she just smiled reassuringly. The rumble grew louder and from nowhere a strong gust of wind swirled through the room, extinguishing all the candles.

"Better get the lights," the disembodied voice of the woman said, and the fabric of the chair rustled as she rose and moved away. As the lights came back on, my eyes were drawn to the group in the center of the room. They had huddled together, some standing, some who had clearly fallen to the floor being gently helped to sitting positions. The Reverend stood over them, holding his hands over them and saying a quiet blessing.

I stood as the group dispersed, waiting for Bryce to come over to me. By the time he reached me, he was back to normal, looking as fresh-pressed as he had when he picked me up this morning.

"Ready for lunch?" he asked, as if everything that I had just witnessed hadn't happened. I stared at him with wide eyes.

"Bryce—"

He lowered his head to speak directly into my ear. "Now is not the time to talk about it."

I opened my mouth, desperate for some sort of explanation, but closed it again at his look, my teeth clicking together with the force. Bryce brushed a kiss over my forehead and then took my hand and led me from the room.

We passed the café, but it was dark this time. The Reverend's conversation with me had delayed the Gathering, and I had honestly lost track of time in there anyway. The café always stayed open as long as it took for Bryce to come back, whether it was ten minutes or an hour. I missed my weekly check-in with Jenny, and realized I wouldn't get to see her much at all anymore if I was attending the Gathering every week and needed to leave the Bible study. I'd call her this week to see about lunch.

Part of my brain was screaming at me, asking why I was thinking about lunch plans after everything that I had just witnessed. But the bigger part of me wasn't ready to process it quite yet. I had questions, but I was afraid of what answers I might receive.

It was tempting to tell Bryce I wasn't feeling well and to bow out of lunch, but it would have been too obvious. I wasn't sure what I was supposed to do next. We weren't supposed to talk about it, but everything had changed now. I followed Bryce silently to the now familiar door to the Reverend's house and took my seat at the table. I smiled at the woman who served me, but did not attempt to start a conversation. A few of the people from the Gathering joined us this week, so there wasn't much pressure on me to speak. Bryce glanced at me regularly, worry evident on his face, but it was the Reverend's gaze that weighed on me.

In that moment, I realized this was part of the test. This was part of my vetting to be Bryce's wife. My reaction to what had gone on at the Gathering and how I dealt with the aftermath would determine whether or not I received the Reverend's blessing on the marriage. I was sure Bryce knew it as well by the way he tried to engage me in normal conversation while trying to hide the concern in his eyes. The Reverend had pretty much told me that my ability to deal with everything that was coming would determine whether they would continue to bless my union with Bryce.

Taking a deep breath, I reached over and took Bryce's hand. He looked at me and squeezed my fingers without interrupting the conversation he was having. I moved into it seamlessly, though I felt as if I were coming out of a trance. I suddenly found myself eager to prove that I could handle whatever had happened. In fact, instead of anxiety, I now felt only curiosity at what I had witnessed. After a bit, I also felt the weight of the Reverend's gaze lift from me. When I glanced over at him, he was engaged in conversation with one of the musicians from the band. I hoped that meant I had passed.

As usual, we were the last ones remaining after the meal. I sat on the couch, watching Bryce say goodbye to the last of the other guests, when Nancy approached and sat in the chair across from me.

"We need to sit down and start discussing wedding plans," she said, her voice excited. Though we had been on good terms for several months, I couldn't help thinking back to our first meeting, and what the Reverend had said about their reservations toward me. The fact that they'd been negative about our relationship at the beginning and Nancy was now eager to discuss wedding plans for my union with Bryce was nothing short of miraculous. It all came down to Bryce. He knew from the beginning that I would fit, and made sure that I did. He had cemented my place with this family.

"We haven't even talked about a date yet," I said, smiling at her. "But as soon as we iron out some details, I'd love your help. My mom has been excited for wedding planning since my first boyfriend, so I know she will be ecstatic to get started as well."

Nancy's face fell slightly. "I'm sure we can discuss dates today, and," she cleared her throat, "of course your mother will be involved in the planning." She didn't sound certain, but I attributed it to having just met my mother. Once they got to know each other, I knew they would get along famously, as we did.

Bryce and the Reverend joined us a couple of minutes later. Bryce sat next to me on the couch, wrapping an arm around me and pulling me close. He pressed a kiss to my temple and sighed happily. Nancy stood, allowing the Reverend to sit in the chair. She perched on the arm, and he rested a hand on her knee.

"I'm glad you stuck around today, Julia," the Reverend said, jumping right in. "I was worried you would try to disappear. I'd hoped you would stay, but it's a lot to take in at once."

"A warning might have been nice," I said carefully, not wanting to upset them.

Bryce squeezed my shoulder as the Reverend smiled. "There's no way to fully prepare for the Gathering. We've found the best way is to just allow one to observe." He leaned forward, hands clasped, eyes bright. "Tell me, Julia, what do *you* think happened in that room today?"

This moment was almost worse than being brought up onstage during the morning service. The spotlight was on me again, with three expectant sets of eyes waiting for me to give a satisfactory answer.

"I—I'm not sure," I said. I wanted to take a guess, but I decided honesty was the best option. "I heard a lot of prayers and gibberish and laughing and . . . it almost seemed like everyone was drunk." I shrugged apologetically, hoping they didn't eject me from the house immediately for that observation.

The Reverend was the first to start laughing. Giant belly laughs exploded from him, and he leaned back as Bryce and Nancy joined in. "That's great," he said, trying to catch his breath. "That's the best description I've ever heard of the Gathering."

I laughed along with them, though not as enthusiastically. I wasn't sure what I had said that was quite so funny.

After he'd calmed down, the Reverend leaned forward again. "What you witnessed, dear Julia, was a group of devoted servants in the very presence of God."

A shiver ran up and down my body at his words. Was it true? Had God been there? I sensed that he didn't mean in the way we talked about God always being with us, but in a real and tangible way.

"We take the Eucharist to open ourselves up to the Oneness," the Reverend continued. "Only by accepting the Gift can you truly feel His presence."

The chaos I had witnessed came into sharper focus, not as chaos but as a celebration. The laughter, the people falling . . . it made sense in the context of God's presence.

"So . . . people were speaking gibberish because they couldn't speak in His presence?"

"They were speaking in tongues. Those were other languages." The Reverend became more animated. "We have witnessed many miracles in the Oneness, Julia. The experience is different for everyone." He looked at Bryce.

Bryce turned to me. "For me, it's usually pure joy and euphoria. Better than I've ever known, each time over again. Other times the feeling is so overwhelming that none of the muscles in my body work and I find myself on the floor, still enraptured." He rubbed a hand through his hair. "It truly defies explanation. I can't wait for you to experience it for yourself."

My eyes widened. "When will that be?"

"When you're ready, you will join the Gathering. It will be up to

God to decide if you are ready for Oneness with Him. Some experience it every time, some only sporadically. It can depend on your devotion and what is going on in your personal life. When you are at your purest, so will be your connection to God."

I nodded, excitement filling me. "I know I'll be ready with your help."

"One more thing, Julia," the Reverend said, and there was warning in his voice. "You must not speak of what goes on during the Gathering with anyone. Not your family, not your friends. You may speak with Bryce about it when the two of you are alone, or in your counseling sessions, but that's it. It's a very intimate experience that not all are ready to experience or worthy of experiencing."

"How do you know who is worthy?" I asked.

"God tells me," the Reverend replied, as if it were the most obvious answer in the world. And I suppose, to him, it was. For me, it would still take time to understand all of this, but the secrecy of it all added to the excitement.

We left soon after, and while I could tell Bryce wanted to talk more, I wasn't quite ready. I wanted to go home and bask in what I had learned and seen. I also wanted to look through my Bible to find the verses the Reverend had spoken of today. This week marked the beginning of a new path for me, even brighter than the one I had been on before. I couldn't wait to see what came next.

Chapter 15

Everyone was just as excited as I'd expected at work the following day. Elaine crowed with joy and Micah's face took on a pinched look when she caught sight of my ring.

"So how'd he do it?" Micah asked, trying to maintain a casual tone, but failing.

"On a yacht," I said. "After a moonlit cruise. And then our family and friends were waiting back onshore to celebrate with us." I sighed. "It was pretty perfect."

The women gathered around sighed with me, either remembering their own proposals or imagining what it would be like. Before too long, they had to disperse to do actual work.

Elaine called me into her office that afternoon and congratulated me again. "I'd hoped what I wanted to say next would be the most exciting thing to happen this week, but I'm afraid it may take second place," she said, smiling. "A new project coordinator position has opened, and I'd like to offer it to you."

My eyes widened and my heart leapt as I sent a prayer of thanks up. "Elaine, I—"

She held up a hand. "It comes with that office I know you've been eyeing, but also with more hours. There will be more overnight trips and weekend obligations." A pause. "The position requires many of the classes you're signed up for, so you'll need to make sure to follow through on those. I got the board to make an exception to allow me to offer you the position now. We couldn't wait until you'd finished, and I didn't want you to miss this opportunity."

"I won't let you down, Elaine," I said, even as echoes of my conversation with the Reverend reverberated through my head. I could do this. I could plan for a wedding and grow deeper in my faith while taking a new position and attending classes. I wouldn't have much time for myself, but it would be worth it in the end. Besides, I knew that this was what God wanted. He wouldn't have opened all these doors if that wasn't the case.

"It's all about balance, Julia," Elaine said, as if she could read my mind. "You've shown me over the past few months that you can handle this. I have every confidence in you." She gave me a smile before dismissing me.

I couldn't wait to tell Bryce, but I decided I wanted to do it in person instead of over the phone.

Dinner tonight? I sent a quick text. His response was almost immediate.

Your place or ours?

Pleasure sliced through me. Our place. That beautiful house that would be mine, too. Ours. Be there by 7.

See you then!

I put my phone away and started with the task of cleaning out my desk. My new office was waiting for me, and I couldn't wait to move in.

I was unloading the Chinese takeout onto the dining room table when the back door clicked open and Bryce walked in. I stopped what I was doing and ran to him, throwing my arms around his neck and kissing him enthusiastically.

"Whoa!" he said, dropping his keys and briefcase to wrap his arms around my waist. "I could get used to this sort of greeting!"

I laughed. "I just had a really good day. And I missed you."

He pulled me close. "I missed you, too." And then we didn't talk for several minutes. Finally, I pulled away.

"Our food is getting cold."

Bryce sniffed the air. "What'd you make?"

"Oh, I had to stay late today, so I didn't get a chance to stop by the grocery store. I wanted to make chicken, but I picked up Chinese instead." As I'd hoped, the kitchen in this house had inspired me to learn more about cooking. I had been trying all sorts of new recipes, and found that I was actually a pretty decent cook when I tried.

"Ah," Bryce said, and I sensed disappointment in his voice.

"I'll make chicken later this week," I promised. "I just wanted to be sure you'd be able to eat right when you got home instead of having to wait for me to cook."

"That's very sweet of you, Julia," Bryce said. "But I would have waited. Besides"—he winked—"we could have passed the cooking time somehow."

"Ha ha, very funny," I said, extricating myself from his arms. "We're not married yet, buddy." I dished out the food onto plates Bryce had brought from his apartment. I made a mental note to talk about going to register for gifts, and got excited flutters thinking about building a life with this man. A little thing like dinnerware could get me going again, and while I was tempted to mention it so we could be giddy together, I decided to share my news with him instead.

"I had a very interesting day today," I said, looking up at Bryce after we said our prayer. "Of course everyone was very excited about the engagement."

He raised an eyebrow. "Even Micah?"

I laughed. "She at least pretended to be."

"I wouldn't expect anything less," he said, and we shared an eye roll.

"Anyway, this afternoon Elaine called me into her office, and you'll never guess what she said."

Bryce put a finger to his chin as if considering what his guess should be. "She wants to be a bridesmaid?"

The mental image this elicited almost caused me to choke on the bite I'd just taken. "No! Can you imagine?"

He pretended to think about it. "Well, you'll have to pick your dresses first, then I can give you a real answer."

"Bryce!" He was in a silly mood, and I was glad. He would be so excited. "No! She wanted to offer me a promotion! It comes with an office and everything. Of course, I have to take those classes she had me sign up for, but I was going to do that anyway. But it's everything I've worked for, and I couldn't have done it without your support!"

As I babbled, I realized that Bryce had not really reacted when I shared the news. A slight pause in the motion of bringing his fork to his mouth, but otherwise he continued eating, the movement almost mechanical.

"Bryce?"

He looked up at me. "That's great, Julia. I'm glad she recognizes your talent. I always knew she would." A pause. "I was under the impression that you'd spoken with the Reverend yesterday before the Gathering about your work."

"Yes," I said slowly. "He said that I would have to think about my job carefully and make sure it doesn't become an idol that takes away from the church or my personal life."

"And what do you think will happen once you're taking classes and working a more demanding job?" His tone was conversational, but I bristled at the words. I took a deep breath to calm my anger, reminding myself that Bryce always had my best interests at heart.

Like the Reverend, he was only concerned about how I would deal with everything. Still, it stung, and my throat tightened. I took a deep breath, attempting to steady myself.

"I can handle it, Bryce. It will be crazy for a while, sure, but it'll be worth it in the end." My voice cracked on the last word as I worked to hold back tears. I'd been sure he would be just as excited for me as I had been when Elaine offered me the position, but his reaction was nothing like I'd expected. It almost seemed as if he wanted me to turn the job down, stay an assistant.

"I know you're capable, Julia, but look at tonight. You aren't even working this job yet and you had to stay too late to cook a dinner for us."

"I'll do a better job of planning ahead. We can take turns cooking. I can cook on the weekends." Except when I'm working, I didn't add.

"Weekends that should be devoted to the church! Especially with the extra counseling sessions and meetings we're going to be doing in preparation for our marriage. Our marriage, Julia. I can't be the only one in this."

"That's not fair."

"Isn't it? Everything we do right now is under scrutiny. You were just invited to the Gathering, but if the Reverend senses your devotion waning, he could put an end to all of this."

My mouth dropped open. "And you would allow that to happen?" Stacy's face flashed through my mind. He had allowed it to happen before. Why did I think he wouldn't let it happen again?

"My first priority is to the church." Bryce's voice was calm but full of conviction. "You knew that soon after we started dating, and you certainly knew it when you agreed to marry me. If God tells the Reverend that you aren't devoted to Him and to our mission, he will have every right to demand that our engagement come to an end."

I couldn't believe what I was hearing. It was practically an ultimatum, except played off as someone else's decision. Tears pricked my eyes and I couldn't hold them back any longer. "All I wanted tonight was to hear that you were proud of me and that we'd make it work. This is my dream, Bryce, and you know it. I can't believe you'd treat it like this." With that, I stood and marched out of the room.

"Julia!" Bryce called after me, but I ignored him. We'd never fought like this, but he'd never shown such disregard for my dreams before. I understood that the church had to be a priority, but many of the parishioners were able to be devoted and also successful in their careers. Look at Bryce, the hypocrite. He was extremely successful, but he worked long hours. How was he any more devoted than I was? I walked out the front door and stood on the porch, looking at the lights from the neighboring houses twinkling in the distance. We were so very isolated here. I wanted to leave, but I'd left my things inside. At some point I'd have to swallow my pride and go back in, but I wasn't ready yet.

The door opened behind me and light spilled from the house before being snuffed out as the door swung back into place. I didn't turn around as footsteps approached, and I didn't move when Bryce's arms came around me from behind.

"I'm sorry," he whispered in my ear, his lips close enough that his breath disturbed my hair and sent chills down my body. "I'm so sorry, Julia. I'm so proud of you, and you can do anything you put your mind to. I should have celebrated with you. You're right. We can figure out the rest later. For now, let's just go back in and toast to the fact that Elaine recognized what a treasure she has. It's something I need to remember as well."

Tears continued to slip down my cheeks as I turned to face him. His eyes were distressed as he used the pads of his thumbs to wipe them away.

"I'm sorry," he said again.

I nodded. "I know. Let's go back inside."

We went back in and finished our meal, but though we both

pasted on smiles and forced laughter, the tone of the evening had changed. I knew it wasn't the end of the conversation, and I also knew I needed to figure out what sacrifices I was willing to make for Bryce and for the church. I knew what the answer should be, but I didn't know if I had the strength to face it yet.

Her body alternates between shivering and feeling very, very warm. As if now that it's free, it can't decide how to regulate itself. Even her basic biological functions have fallen into order, following his instructions to a fault for fear of retribution. There is almost no temperature difference between the water and the air of the bathroom, no longer steamy, but still damp.

A headache is edging in, creeping along the corners of her skull, sending whispers of pain from the base of her neck to the space behind her eyes. Her thoughts become fuzzy, and she almost forgets what she is waiting for. Instead, she wonders how life would have been different, had she not lost her report to the wind that day. He would have kept on walking, she would have kept on reading, and there would have been little chance of their ever meeting.

Chapter 16

"It was awful, Van," I said into the phone the next day. I'd left work a little early in order to meet Nancy and my mother to do some preliminary dress shopping. Nancy insisted that we needed to start right away. It already felt like my mom and I were just along for the ride. "I've never seen him that way, like I'd failed him by doing well at my job. I'm so confused."

"That is really strange," Van said. "I always thought he was really supportive of you moving up in the ranks. What changed?"

I sighed. "I don't know. We got engaged? I had a chat with the Reverend about what it means to be a good wife?"

"Wait, what?"

"Oh, I didn't tell you about that?" I laughed, but it was humorless. I couldn't talk to Van about the Gathering, but I could talk about being pulled up onto the stage during the service on Sunday. Hundreds of people saw that happen. Quickly I explained the situation and what the Reverend had said, and gave a short version of our conversation after the service. "I mean, I don't think he was wrong about what we talked about, but . . ."

"But nothing," Van said. "That is some weird shit."

I was glad I hadn't told her about the Gathering, even if I had been allowed.

"You've been to my church, right?" Van said. When I responded that I had, she continued, "We've talked about those verses and, girl,

I think he interprets them very differently. It's about mutual respect, not about the wife always obeying and giving up everything for her husband. The husband is supposed to sacrifice for his wife, too."

My defenses leapt into action. "I don't think he was saying that the husband shouldn't sacrifice anything. I think his point was that I have a lot to learn about sacrifice and balancing my church life with my non-church life. He wanted to make sure that I didn't become so engrossed in one to the detriment of the other."

Van was quiet for a moment. "Sounds like they only have a problem if the church part suffers. Not if your job, your passion, your dream suffers."

"I don't think that's true, either. Bryce apologized for his reaction."

"But you said you think it'll come up again."

I was regretting telling her anything now. I wanted to talk through it with her, but when she gave voice to the concerns bouncing around in my own head, I found myself defending Bryce and the Reverend's positions. Maybe they had a point after all. Or maybe I wanted Van to continue to point out to me that I was getting the short end of the stick. My mind went to the Gathering again. If I could truly be One with God, if I could hear Him and commune with Him, wouldn't it be worth the sacrifice? Wasn't that what they were trying to help me understand, trying to get me to see? If I let go of my own dreams, and let God fully take control, there would be no telling what my life would bring. It was terrifying and exciting. Really, Bryce and the Reverend were trying to prepare me for a better life, one too amazing for me to dream for myself.

"I gotta go, Van," I said. "I'm meeting Mom and Nancy in twenty minutes. Thanks for listening."

"Jules . . ."

"I'll talk to you later!" I hung up before she could respond again. It was rude, but I felt a certain clarity from our conversation, though not in the direction I'd expected. Maybe I was starting to hear the voice of God after all.

———

Thursday was my first individual counseling session at the church. My counselor's name was Susie, and she was spunky and fun. She wore a denim skirt, and told me right away that she pretty much exclusively wore skirts because it's what her husband liked, but that she ended up really liking them, too. "It's freeing," she said. "Lots of movement and air circulation, plus there are so many cute ones out there. I know some women feel empowered by pants, but I feel most like myself in a skirt."

I didn't think she was trying to convert me to skirts, but I shifted in my seat, smoothing my dress pants self-consciously. "Does your husband have a say in everything you wear?" I asked.

She thought for a moment. She wasn't offended by my questions, and rather than a typical therapy session, this had run more like a conversation, with both of us contributing equally. This fact alone had reduced my anxiety by a thousand percent. I was sure these sessions would be all about exploring my childhood and seeing if I was really cut out to be a wife, but so far we'd mostly spent time getting to know each other, and Susie had talked a lot about what being a wife of a devoted church member was like. She, too, hadn't been part of a church before meeting her husband. Now she regularly attended the Gathering and achieved Oneness almost every time.

"I guess in many ways he does," she said in answer to my question. "After honoring God, the most important thing to me is honoring my husband, so I always keep that in mind when choosing clothes to buy and wear. And if he has an opinion, I take it very seriously. I got some yoga pants to wear just around the house, and he came to me and very gently pointed out how tempting it was for me to wear them. If neighbors saw or a deliveryman came to the door, I would be responsible for that temptation. And even for him, when he needed to be focused on other things, it was very distracting for me to be wearing them. So now they only come out on special occasions." She winked, and my face heated. I knew we'd have to talk about sex eventually, but as comfortable as I was with Susie in this first conversation, I wasn't ready to go there yet. Besides, I'd rather talk to Kate or Van about that part of marriage.

My heart twinged when I thought of Kate. It hadn't even been a week, but her silence seemed louder this time than it ever had. I'd looked at bridesmaid dresses with Mom and Nancy the other night, and Mom evaded the question when I asked if she thought Kate would agree to be my matron of honor.

It had always been assumed she would stand with me on my wedding day, but after our fight, I wasn't sure anymore.

"Give her some time," Mom had said. "She'll come around. Kate is Kate. You know how she gets."

I did know how she got, which was why I was worried. No one I knew could hold a grudge like Kate. We'd never had a fight this huge. Apparently I was breaking a lot of records this week. Biggest fight with Kate, first real fight with Bryce.

"Where'd you go?" Susie asked, and I blinked at her, startled from my thoughts. "I think I lost you for a few minutes."

I sighed. "Sorry. I was thinking about a couple things that happened this week. But you were talking about yoga pants."

She leaned forward, suddenly serious. "I'm done talking about yoga pants. Let's talk about what's on your mind." And just like that we slipped into our roles. She was still easy to talk to, but instead of interjecting with her own stories, as she had earlier, she simply listened and nodded and made the appropriate noises. When I'd finished, she pursed her lips.

"Family can be hard," she said. "Especially when they see you moving in a direction they're not willing to follow. It seems to me that Kate is jealous of you."

"That's what I thought! Bryce is so great compared to Eddie."

"Not just in that," Susie said, "though I agree with you. She's also seeing you move toward this faith, move closer to God. You'll often find this with your non-believing or other-believing friends and family. They see the changes in you, and they fight to keep you down when you're meant to rise."

"You think Kate wants to keep me from God?"

Susie shrugged. "I don't know Kate, but I've seen this before. You have something that she can't attain, so she'll do whatever she can to sow seeds of doubt. She's not the only one. Your friend Savannah seems skeptical of the changes in you as well."

I'd barely mentioned Van. "What do you mean? Van is a regular church attender."

Susie's words were gentle, but firm. "Not all churches are created equal, Julia. You've seen the power here. Anything else . . . well, those from other churches would also seek to dilute the power of the message you receive here. It's terrifying to them because they don't understand it. I saw you at the Gathering on Sunday. You were suitably anxious, but also intrigued. I jumped at the chance to counsel you because I know you were meant for this, meant for us, meant to be truly One with God. And part of that is surrounding yourself with the right people and learning how to be a true and righteous member of the church, and a virtuous wife to Bryce."

When she said those things, they seemed obvious. I'd been attributing so many of the good things in my life to the church, so it made sense that Kate would be jealous of that. I'd focused only on Bryce, but my entire way of looking at the world had shifted. I had joy that she couldn't comprehend. I'd wanted to share it with her, but maybe Susie was right. Maybe it was better to surround myself with those who understood it, rather than be in anguish over those who never could.

"Aren't . . . aren't we called to bring others to God as well? Be disciples?"

"Yes." Susie nodded. "But there's also a time to let go and trust in God. There's nothing He can't do, but sometimes He chooses not to move in someone's life. You see how small the Gathering is compared to the size of the church. Only so many can be Chosen."

Pride surged through me to be one of the Chosen. "What makes us different?" I asked, placing myself firmly in the Chosen group for the first time.

"There are rewards for all who believe," Susie said. "But for those who are Chosen, the rewards are beyond our imagining. No one who believes will be forgotten, but those who have been One with God will be One forever, ecstasy in paradise beyond our wildest dreams." A rapturous look took over Susie's face, and I knew she was imagining it. "No fear, no death, no pain . . . Think of it, Julia. How could you turn that promise down for anything here on earth?"

She was right. I couldn't imagine turning it down. Not for Kate. Not for Van. Maybe not even for Bryce.

Bryce had driven me to the church and was waiting when I emerged from my session with Susie. I felt like we'd covered so little of what we needed to get to, but at the same time I'd learned so much. "I think these counseling sessions are going to be incredible," I said. "Susie is great, and she really helps me to put things in perspective."

"I'm so glad," Bryce said, taking my hand and leading me to the parking lot.

"Did you stop by to see the Reverend?" I asked.

"I did." Bryce looked troubled.

"Everything okay?"

He shook his head. "Not really. A former member of the congregation is suing him."

I gasped. "What? Over what?"

"I don't have all the details. The worst part is that he was part of the Gathering. The Reverend is worried that details of the Gathering will be made public, and that God will decide to remove Himself. That means no more Oneness."

"That's awful," I said, a sinking feeling in my stomach. "I thought everyone went through rigorous screening before being invited in."

"The Devil is clever, Julia," Bryce said, opening the car door for me. He rounded the hood and slid in behind the wheel. "Even the Reverend has been fooled from time to time." He paused as he started the car and made his way out of the parking lot. "I do remember he was hesitant about this member. He was a bit arrogant, and then upset when he couldn't achieve Oneness. He left, and we had to ask the counselor who approved him to leave as well. We'd all been fooled, but the counselor was supposed to be our safeguard."

I couldn't imagine experiencing that and then being asked to leave. The guilt that poor counselor must have felt. I shook my head, sadness filling me for no reason. If I failed at achieving Oneness, did that mean Susie would risk being kicked out as well?

"This is why it's important to surround yourself with people who understand you, Julia. And for your environment to be conducive to your faith. That's why I had concerns about your job." He raised a hand when I opened my mouth to argue. "I don't want to get into it tonight. I'm still proud of your accomplishments, but I want you to understand where my hesitancy lies."

I nodded. I did understand that it came from a place of caring and concern. I also couldn't ignore the fact that he was giving me a very similar message to the one I had received from Susie tonight. Again, I wondered if I was becoming more sensitive to the voice and will of God. From what I'd learned, it tended to come through other people first. I definitely needed to pay attention.

Bryce walked me to my door and kissed me goodnight. "I'll pick you up from work tomorrow for our dinner with our mentor couple." Despite the gloomy news from earlier, excitement sparked in his eyes now. "Maybe we'll get a glimpse of how we'll be in twenty years."

I kissed him once more before unlocking my door. "I'll count the minutes," I said before slipping inside, already thinking about what skirt I would wear to work tomorrow.

Chapter 17

I glanced at the user manual again, trying to figure out how to fix a glitch in the new Sibyl program I was piloting for the firm. I'd gotten the go-ahead to purchase the full system, but it was proving to be more complicated than the sample I'd tested had been.

`Error OP99—Talk to network administrator`

"Ugh." I slammed my hand onto the thick pages, rather than shoving my computer monitor off my desk like I wanted. The impact still unsettled a carefully balanced stack of papers on my desk, sending the entire pile crashing to the floor.

I slapped a hand over my mouth to prevent the curse words that bubbled up inside of me, and sent up a small prayer for peace as I stared at the papers, which I had just organized before taking on Sibyl again.

"You okay?" Micah asked, and I glanced to where she sat, not far outside my office door, a look of amusement playing on her face. She'd moved to my old desk, which was between Elaine's office and mine, to be available to both of us. To say she wasn't happy about the arrangement would be an understatement, though right now she looked pretty pleased.

"I'm fine," I said, kneeling on the floor to gather the papers. I wouldn't have time to reorganize. I needed to leave in a few minutes to meet Nancy and my mom for my dress fitting. I'd hoped Elaine would keep her regular hair appointment and leave before me so she wouldn't see me ducking out early again, but the last time I'd peeked she still sat in her office, frowning at her computer as she typed away.

Micah arched a brow. "If this is you okay, I'd hate to see you on a bad day."

"Shut up, Micah," I mumbled, low enough that she couldn't hear me. Immediately I felt guilty. Micah wasn't my favorite person, but snapping at her was beneath me.

"What was that?" she asked, eyes narrowed now.

"Nothing," I said. "Just trying to get this stuff back in order."

My computer beeped before she could respond, and I gathered all the papers in my arms and dumped them on my desk before checking my messages.

Come see me.

From Elaine. No clues about the reason, but my heart thumped rapidly anyway. Gone were the days when I looked forward to my summonses into Elaine's office, or her visits to mine. When I was excited about the projects I'd shown her, or the new clients she wanted to talk to me about.

There hadn't been any new clients for me in weeks.

I tapped tentatively on the door to Elaine's office before entering. She looked up at me and my stomach dropped at her grim expression. "Have a seat, Julia," she said. "I'm just finishing up this e-mail."

Closing the door to avoid having an audience for whatever came next, I sat in the chair nearest the exit, better for a quick escape if needed.

Elaine tapped a few more keys and then turned to me. "There's a potential new client with a base in Omaha. I need someone to go out there and spend a few days learning about the business and convincing them to sign with us." She pulled out a folder. "You'll leave early Sunday morning and return Thursday. I'm sending Jeff with you."

This was a test, one that I knew I was going to fail. Elaine had mentioned the possibility of more travel, but so far it had only taken me a couple of hours away, and never overnight. Bryce would never go for it, not to mention going with another man. Also, we had church on Sunday and appointments every night next week.

"Elaine, thank you so much for this opportunity—"

"You're welcome," she said, her eyes holding a warning about continuing with what I was going to say next. I ignored it despite the hammering of my heart.

"But I can't go to Omaha."

Elaine sighed the sigh of the truly weary, a long-suffering boss who can't seem to keep her star employee in line. I hated disappointing her. "And what is the excuse this time?"

Irritation fluttered through me, but I tamped it down, praying for the right words to say to preserve my pride and my job. "It's just really short notice," I said. "I have obligations with my fiancé for our wedding and for the church."

"You knew what this position would entail before you accepted the promotion, did you not?" Elaine asked, rubbing a hand over her forehead and closing her eyes. "Travel, late nights, long hours. You said you were on board."

"I was," I said. "I am. It's just a really busy time right now with the wedding planning and other church stuff."

"I don't want to hear about your church stuff right now, Julia. I want to hear about why you are failing to uphold your end of the deal on this promotion. Your grades in your marketing classes are abysmal, and I know you're an intelligent woman. You have refused to stay late most of the nights I've requested it due to 'obligations.' I understand this is a busy time, but I need to know that you understand that this is still a business, that this is still your job, and I need

you to start acting like the young woman I hired. I took a chance offering you this position, and I don't want to regret it. I still have high
hopes for you, Julia. Don't let my faith in you be misplaced."

It was like being punched in the gut. I almost doubled over from
the pain and shock of her words, though they weren't totally unexpected, and weren't at all unfair. I deserved every one of them. I was
failing. Failing at classes, failing at almost every aspect of this job.
My eyes stung as tears threatened to fall, and I blinked them back.

"I'm sorry, Elaine," I said, my voice barely above a whisper. I
wasn't even sure she could hear me, but she inclined her head as if I
should continue. "I know I haven't been as present as I should have
been lately. My focus has been split, and that's not fair to you or to
the company."

"Thank you for that apology, Julia, but I need more from you
than that. I need your word that you're going to step things up, catch
up in your classes, be present when you're here in the office, stay late
if necessary. And I need you to go to Omaha."

Taking a deep breath, I looked at my hands. "I will, I promise.
I'll do better. I'll study harder and my focus here will be single-
minded. But, Elaine," I said, looking up at her, "I can't go to Omaha.
And I can't let my job completely take over my time, especially when
I'm just starting a life with my fiancé."

Elaine's face was a road map of lines, though she was not an old
woman. Her face didn't tell her age, but rather her dedication to her
job, and her willingness to put it above everything else. Every one of
those hard-won lines was etched with disappointment at my words.
But I couldn't be Elaine. I could learn from her, I could emulate her
in many ways, but ultimately I knew that the major difference between the two of us was that this job was her life, while the job was
only a portion of mine.

"I see," she said finally, looking away from me and back to her
computer screen. "Perhaps Micah would like to take your place, try
her hand at wooing a client."

A sour taste filled my mouth. Elaine knew which buttons to push. But I wouldn't let her see that she got to me. "I think she'd appreciate the opportunity," I said. I looked at my watch. "I need to get going for a dress fitting. I'll be in early tomorrow to make up the time."

Elaine didn't say another word as I left her office, though as I passed by her window on my way out minutes later I could feel her eyes on me, a weight I carried onto the elevator and all the way to the dress shop.

"I'm sorry," I said, rushing into the counseling room at the church, breathless from my flight from the parking lot. "Things ran late with Nancy," I explained to Bryce, who was sitting across from the Reverend.

Bryce waved a hand. "It's okay, sweetheart. Nancy called and said you left your phone with her. She sounded excited about the fitting."

Gratefulness filled me that Nancy had thought to call. She'd been holding all of my things and taking pictures on my phone of the final alterations for my wedding dress, but when I'd seen the time, I'd rushed out without grabbing the phone from her. Good thing she lived nearby.

I took my seat on the couch next to Bryce and gave him a small peck on the cheek. "It went great. I'm so excited, but I haven't had time to process. I really am sorry about being late."

The past few months had been a whirlwind of dress fittings and wedding decisions. I worked especially hard not to stay too late at work, as Elaine had pointed out earlier, because Bryce was always crabbier when dinner was late. I spent most of my time at his house now, except for sleeping there, and had begun the slow process of going through my things in my apartment and moving what I was keeping over to the house. The wedding was two months away. With everything going on, I had considered suggesting that we pick a date a little further out, maybe in the summer, but Nancy and the

Reverend thought it would be nice for us to marry on their anniversary in May.

Nancy had pretty much taken over the wedding planning, which I knew bothered my mom a bit, but I was grateful. Between all the extra classes I was doing for church and for work, I was glad to let someone else make decisions about the wedding. She ran everything by me, of course, and her taste was exquisite. It would be a fabulous event.

"You look tired, Julia," the Reverend commented. "Is everything okay?"

I sent him a sunny smile. "Of course! I'm learning so much here, and in my marketing classes, but it's all working out really well."

He looked at me. "Do you really believe that?"

My heart sank as I interpreted that look. I really thought it was going fine, but apparently the Reverend felt differently. "It's been weird getting rid of stuff in my apartment," I said. "More emotional than I expected."

"We talked about that, Jules," Bryce said. "It makes more sense for us to start fresh together."

I patted his knee. "Yes, I know. And my stuff is old. But it has a lot of sentimental value. Honestly, that's almost as draining as anything else."

"Would you like Nancy to come over and help?" the Reverend offered. "She's a whiz at organization."

"I'm aware," I said, picturing Nancy's lists and notebooks for the wedding. "She's whipped the wedding right into shape. But maybe I'll have Van come over and help. We can reminisce over the college memorabilia." I hadn't seen Van since her bridesmaid dress fitting a couple of weeks ago, and we hadn't had any alone time since before the engagement. It seemed that every time we planned to hang out, something came up. It would be nice to spend time with her face-to-face instead of grabbing a few minutes on the phone.

Van had also agreed to step in as my matron of honor, since Kate had told my mom in no uncertain terms that she would not be attending my wedding to "that man." Her rejection stung, but I'd talked through it with Susie and with Bryce, and both assured me that taking a break from that relationship was for the best. I still hoped we could repair it one day, but giving it time seemed like the best option for now.

The Reverend leaned forward. "Is that the best use of your time, Julia? With work and classes and wedding planning and moving and all of your commitments here, do you really have an evening to spare going through old junk knowing that you probably won't get much done?"

That was harsh, and I sat back, a little stunned. "Isn't it important to take time to rest as well? To recharge?"

"You've done this, Julia," the Reverend said. "You've stacked your plate so high that you don't have the luxury of taking it easy unless you're willing to give something up."

I crossed my arms. "You mean my job." It was an old conversation that kept recycling, and I was tired of it, not only because I could feel my resolve weakening every time we discussed it.

"Just hear him out," Bryce said, placing a hand on my shoulder. I wanted to shrug it off, but I also drew comfort from his touch.

"You want me to hear him out because he's on your side."

"Whoa," Bryce removed his hand. "Since when are there sides? Aren't we on the same side?"

"I'm a little concerned about your hostility, Julia," the Reverend said. "All we're doing is having a conversation. That's what premarital counseling is about. Talking through issues and coming to solutions."

"And I'm concerned that my job has been considered an 'issue' since the night Bryce put this ring on my hand," I said, spinning the offending jewelry on my finger. I turned to Bryce. "You said that I've known about your dedication to church and God from the start. Well, you've known about my passion for my work and my dream to have a long career since we met."

Bryce took both my hands, looking deeply in my eyes. "Dreams can change, Julia. God never will. He's a constant. And I wonder if your moods lately have to do with Him nudging you in a direction you hadn't planned."

"Why is it always my dreams that need to change?"

Bryce and the Reverend exchanged a look, which irritated me more. I tugged my hands free.

The Reverend gave me an appraising look, which he had perfected. It was as if he could see into my very soul. Maybe he could. I had rarely been angry at the Reverend. He just didn't bring out those feelings in me. But tonight I felt as if he and Bryce were ganging up on me.

"How is work going, Julia?" the Reverend asked.

"Great."

He sighed. "I'm going to ask again. How is work going?"

And I broke. I started crying and told them about my conversation with Elaine that afternoon. "She said that she took a chance on me and she was regretting it. I haven't stayed late most of the times she's asked me to because I had to come to meetings or sessions here, or we had an appointment with Ron and Shirley." Our mentor couple had been wonderful, but they had also wanted to meet more often than I was first told, just adding to my list of things to keep track of. "I completely missed a meeting yesterday because I just spaced it off. I feel pulled in every direction and I don't even think I know what I want anymore."

There it was. I'd said it. I had been clinging so fiercely to the path I'd put myself on years ago, and I'd been ignoring how unhappy it made me. Work was a series of unfinished tasks and resentful stares from those I'd been promoted above, and while Elaine appreciated some of the work I'd been doing, she'd noticed my split focus. She hadn't given me any indication that my job was in jeopardy, but I felt the stress of it in every e-mail, every request to meet. She still wanted me as her protégé, but I knew she was frustrated with my lack of progress. And if I didn't pass the classes, it was a moot point anyway. I couldn't do the job without my DMA certification.

Bryce rubbed my back in slow circles as I cried myself out. "I knew something was up," he said, though he wasn't talking to me. He addressed the Reverend. "She's been so snappy at home, always working on something. We're not even married and I feel like I never see her." He sighed. "I miss her."

There was the guilt. The guilt that I felt whenever I had to pick something up instead of making dinner for us. Whenever I had to leave early to get home and do homework or attend a study group, though I skipped most of those. Bryce was busy as well, helping the Reverend with his court case, but we hadn't even had time to talk about it. It wasn't healthy.

"Julia," the Reverend said, his voice soft. "There's a reason you haven't been invited to participate in the Gathering yet. God has told me that there's a blockage, and I think we just found the source. He cannot be One with you until you sort it out."

I nodded. I thought as much. I'd been observing the Gathering for months now, but the Reverend hadn't even shown an inkling to invite me to participate. Each week that I was passed over added to my feelings of inadequacy. Taking a deep breath, I sat up, leaning into Bryce, who kept a protective arm around me.

"I think you know what you need to do, Julia," the Reverend said, his pale eyes piercing mine.

I nodded. I did know.

The next day I walked into Elaine's office and quit my job. I cleaned out my desk, e-mailed my instructors to drop my certification classes, and walked out of the office without a backward glance. I had a new dream.

Chapter 18

My wedding day dawned clear and bright. It was the perfect spring day, and I was grateful for the sunshine. I'd barely slept the night before, due to a mix of excitement and anxiety. I had no second thoughts about becoming Mrs. Bryce Covington, but after the bachelorette party last night, which mainly consisted of doing facials and eating snacks with my bridesmaids, I'd been hit with a wave of sadness. I pulled out my phone and typed out a text.

> *Wish you were here. It's not too late to come to the wedding.*

Before I could think twice, I sent the message off to Kate and rolled out of my bed, or rather, off my mattress. The apartment was basically empty at this point, with only a few pieces of furniture that would be collected next week to go to Goodwill. I stumbled out into the living room to find Van sprawled on my couch, and I smiled.

"Hey," I said, nudging her with my knee. "Good morning. Time to rise and shine and focus on me for an entire day."

Van rolled over and swatted at my legs. "Go away."

"I'm pretty sure you're supposed to call me 'Your Highness' today," I mused, stepping out of her reach. That got me a pillow to the face. It didn't take long for it to devolve into a full-on pillow fight. Even as I attacked, I relished this easy play between us. The only shadow was the knowledge that I hadn't yet told her that I'd left my position at the firm. I worried that she wouldn't be happy for me, wouldn't understand. The secret had acted like a wedge in our friendship. I'd never shut Van out of anything before.

Still, I felt so much lighter since leaving my job. I suddenly had time to do all the other things I needed to do, and I barely missed it, especially with the wedding planning. I spent much of my time at the church now, planning with Nancy or helping with design things, so I wouldn't have had much extra time for Van anyway. Susie thought that Van was probably jealous of my devotion. I'd told her about the time soon after my engagement when Van pulled me aside and asked if I was sure about Bryce. It wasn't malicious, like with Kate. She was genuinely concerned I was moving too fast for my first relationship after Jake. But she supported me, was standing with me today no matter what reservations she might have held at one time.

Unfortunately, even Bryce had suggested that I step back from my friendship with Van. I had refused him just as I had refused Susie when she suggested it, just as I had ignored Nancy's pointed look when I made Van my matron of honor. I knew we would get back to where we'd been. Just because we didn't see eye to eye on everything and just because we didn't see each other all the time didn't mean we had to end the friendship. Bryce and I had almost had another fight when he suggested replacing her as matron of honor. He thought Stacy was a better option to stand with me, since she "truly understood our faith." But there was no way I was replacing Van.

A knock at the door interrupted our giggling fight, and I called a truce while I stumbled to answer it. I opened the door to find Nancy and Stacy waiting for me. Nancy strode in and looked at Van on the floor, still breathing hard, and raised an eyebrow at me.

"Good morning, ladies. Stacy tells me the party went well last night."

"It was great," I said, smiling at Stacy. I had been making an effort to get to know her better, and had made her a bridesmaid out of deference to Bryce after his failed attempt to insert her as my matron of honor, but I still couldn't quite connect with her. I was surprised when I was trying to build my wedding party at how few friends from the past I was still in touch with. Even the Cat Pack didn't get together anymore, though they were all invited to the wedding. But Bryce preferred a small wedding party anyway, so we kept the attendant list small, two each.

Once Nancy arrived, the games were over. Van usually avoided being around at the same time as any of my church friends, but especially Nancy, and when I asked her about it she just said that Nancy gave her a weird vibe. It saddened me because I loved them both, but they were very different. Case in point, Nancy immediately took charge and started ordering us around. She was as determined to make this day perfect as I was, so it didn't bother me.

Nancy had offered to drive us all to the salon, but Van declined. "I'd rather have my own car," she said, "in case I need to run out for anything for Julia."

"I'm not sure why you would need to, dear," Nancy said. "I've taken care of everything."

"Still," Van said, keeping her voice even, though I could tell she was irritated. "Just in case."

"Very well. We'll see you over there."

"I'll ride with you, Van," I said, moving to join her on her walk to her car, parked down the block.

"Oh, I need to discuss a few last-minute details with you, Julia. We won't have much time once everything gets rolling," Nancy said, opening the passenger door to her car. Stacy was already in the backseat, buckled in and ready to go.

"It's only a quick drive, Nancy," I said. Van stood on the sidewalk, waiting on my decision.

"Precisely," Nancy said. "Which is why we need to use every minute."

I shrugged an apology at Van, who shook her head and took off jogging toward her car. I got into Nancy's car, and she immediately shoved a photographer's pamphlet in my hands.

"I need you to double-check our choices on which poses and portraits we want of the wedding party."

I stared at her. "Nancy, we spent hours deciding on this weeks ago. We went over it at least three times."

"And now that it's your wedding day, I want to be sure you're still sure. We won't be able to go back and make these decisions again, Julia."

I sighed. "Of course." But as soon as I started looking through the sample poses, I got excited again. I was getting married.

The day passed in a blur. Nancy seemed to have everything under control, but she kept double-checking my opinion on everything. I appreciated her attention to detail, but I did get slightly irritated when she interrupted my moment with my mom, who hadn't been included in any of the morning activities. It was time for pictures, and we had just a few minutes together before Nancy bustled in.

"Are you ready for your reveal with Bryce?" Nancy asked. "I thought the garden would be the perfect spot for some photos."

We'd discussed whether we wanted to do a reveal and pictures ahead of time or after, but in the end, for the sake of time, we decided to do a private time with Bryce seeing me for the first time, and then most of the family and wedding party pictures before the ceremony.

I looked at my mom and leaned forward to give her one more hug.

"You are so beautiful," she whispered, and tears pricked my eyes. I knew we were both thinking of the last time we were in this situation, and it was the three of us on Kate's wedding day. I hadn't gotten a text back, and Mom said Kate wasn't responding to her, either. She'd hoped my sister would swallow her pride and show up, but I wasn't holding my breath. I patted the small purse that held the charm bracelet that matched Kate's. We'd gotten them at a flea market years ago. I'd wanted to wear it today, to feel as if Kate was with me at least in spirit, but Nancy had wrinkled her nose at the colorful jangling charms and presented me with a sparkling diamond bracelet instead, a gift from her and the Reverend. I had slipped the charm bracelet into my purse, knowing it would still keep Kate close. Blinking back the tears, I released my mother and got up to follow Nancy to the garden.

The moment I saw Bryce for the first time on our wedding day, he took my breath away. By his hard swallow, he was similarly affected. I was glad it was only the photographer and the bridal party witnessing this moment, though to me it seemed that Bryce and I were the only two in the world. He approached me and took my hands reverently, as if he didn't want to break me. He leaned his forehead on mine and began to pray, and I closed my eyes and thanked God for bringing this man into my life.

Though I'd seen him before, he took my breath away again when I saw him standing at the front of the church a couple of hours later. The sanctuary was packed, as if the entire congregation had shown up, but I could only see him. I remembered little of the service, so lost was I in Bryce's eyes, swimming with tears that reflected my own. With our vows, and our rings, we promised ourselves to each other, and sealed it with a kiss. I knew in that moment that I would do anything for this man. My husband.

The reception flew by. I danced the night away, and didn't even see Van or my parents slip out. And when Bryce and I stumbled into our house, our home, in the late hours of the night, no words were necessary as we made our way to our bedroom for the first time as husband and wife. And then I was finally, completely and totally, his.

Raising her left hand above the surface of the water, she examines the large diamond adorning her third finger. Given the choice, would he have chosen her over this ring? Would he have put her ahead of everything he had built for himself? She doesn't know. And doesn't care. She has taken the choice out of his hands. She is the one doing the choosing now.

PART IV

HONOR AND OBEY

The water lapped against the dock as I sat on the bench at the end, appreciating the small ripples in the lake. It was almost sunset, which had become my favorite time of day on our honeymoon, and this was our final evening. The wind was a little chilly, and I wrapped the blanket I'd brought down more tightly around me. Bryce was up in the cabin, reading. We had spent most of the past week together, alone in the cabin, and though I'd only been down on the dock for fifteen minutes or so, I already missed him.

As if conjured from my mind, large hands fell onto my shoulders, and Bryce leaned down to drop a kiss on my hair before coming around to sit close to me on the bench. I opened the blanket to share, and with two of us in the cocoon it was almost too warm. Not that I was complaining.

Initially I had wanted to go someplace more exotic for our honeymoon. Either to Europe or someplace tropical. I'd researched all sorts of packages and exciting trips, but in the end Bryce reminded me that our honeymoon was about spending time together as husband and wife. The Reverend and Nancy owned a beautiful cabin a couple of hours away, and the lake would be fairly empty at this time of year. He'd been right, of course. The secluded cabin had been the perfect romantic backdrop for our first week as a married couple. We had full days free to do whatever we wished. We prayed together, went for walks, and spent plenty of time getting to know each other more . . . intimately. It was better than anything I could have planned, and I was thankful Bryce had taken the initiative to overrule what I thought I wanted.

"Are you ready to go back?" Bryce asked, leaning in and nuzzling my neck, sending tingles down my spine. It was freeing being able to express ourselves physically. After our first night together, it was like a giant pressure valve had been released. I hadn't realized how much we both had pent up before then.

I shivered. "No, not really. I think we need another week."

He chuckled, running his lips up to my ear. "But you'd miss the Gathering on Sunday."

Arching my neck, I sighed. I was finally invited to participate in the Gathering this week. I'd been ecstatic when the Reverend had announced it to me before we left for our honeymoon, but in this moment I was having a difficult time drumming up that excitement.

"It'll be there next week," I said, turning my face to Bryce's, attempting to capture his lips.

He sat back abruptly. "It'll be there next week?" he repeated, his tone incredulous.

"Bryce. I was kidding," I said, reaching a hand to his face.

He leaned away, ducking my touch. "You are being given the opportunity to be One with God and you're so easily swayed by the thought of more sex. Honestly, Julia, I thought better of you."

My heart dropped. That wasn't what I meant at all. "I was just teasing, Bryce," I said, reaching for him as he stood, admitting the cool evening air into our cocoon. "Of course I'm excited and anxious to get back for the Gathering. You know that."

"Do I?" He looked at me as if disgusted with what he saw. "I won't talk to the Reverend about this, Julia, but you might want to spend some time reading the Bible tonight to get your heart ready. I'll sleep in the other room."

Tears pricked my eyes, but I nodded as he turned and walked back toward shore. I didn't allow them to fall until he was on his way up the stairs to the cabin. Clearly I'd failed in some way, responded incorrectly to my husband. I stared into the sunset, which had turned the sky a spectacular mix of pinks and purples and oranges, but didn't really see it as I replayed our conversation.

It was almost completely dark by the time I returned to the cabin. The bed in the master suite was made as neatly as it had been that morning, and there was a sliver of light showing from the second bedroom down the hall, though no sound came from within. My Bible, which Bryce had given me soon after I'd started attending church, sat on the bed with several passages marked for me on the importance of putting God first, and how a woman who feared the Lord was to be revered. Sighing, I prepared for bed, climbed in, and began to read.

I followed Bryce into the church on Sunday with a mix of anticipation and anxiety. He gripped my hand tightly as we made our way through the morning crowd. Everything was fine between us. He'd made me breakfast our final morning at the cabin, and I'd apologized for not taking my participation in the Gathering more seriously. I sometimes reverted to humor about things that were no laughing matter, and I vowed to talk with Susie about it in my next counseling session.

Bryce and I had determined that I would continue with individual counseling, but cut back on our couple work now that we were married. We'd still meet with our mentor couple from time to time, but honestly I considered the Reverend and Nancy more of an ideal marriage to emulate than the couple we'd been meeting with. They were nice, but there was very little life to them. They were serious about everything, and while I understood there were things that needed respect at all times, I couldn't deal with the complete lack of humor I saw in their marriage, though I could tell that they treated each other well. They were suited for each other, just in a different way than Bryce and I were. I saw us much more like the Reverend and Nancy, and since Bryce was in many ways like a son to them, it made sense to pattern our relationship after theirs instead of after some practical strangers.

"Julia!" I looked around to see where my name had come from and saw Jenny working her way through the crowd toward us. I smiled and started to pull away from Bryce to meet her halfway, but though he stopped, he didn't release my hand, so I waited for her to reach us instead.

"Jenny, hey!" I said, giving her a one-armed hug, since Bryce still clutched my hand. "How are you? I didn't get to see much of you at the wedding."

She squeezed my fingers as she pulled away from the awkward hug. "You looked so beautiful. I tried to come say hi but you were always surrounded by people, so I figured I'd just catch you another time. Dinner this week?"

"That sounds great. I'll call you, okay?"

"Definitely." Jenny opened her mouth to say something else, but Bryce interrupted.

"We'd better get going, Julia. I need to talk with someone before the service."

I wanted to tell him that he could go and I'd catch up, but the look in his eyes told me that he would rather I stayed with him, so I waved goodbye to Jenny and followed Bryce. We made our way into the sanctuary and down to our seats. Once we were in our normal spots, I turned to Bryce.

"I thought you needed to talk to someone."

"Hm? Oh." He looked around. "I don't see him. I'll try and catch him later."

My brow wrinkled, but before I could say anything more, Stacy arrived. "Julia! Bryce! Welcome back!" She threw her arms around me in a tight hug, and I patted her arm. I'd never seen her so exuberant. "Are you excited about today?" she asked, her voice low.

I nodded. "A little nervous, but mostly excited."

"You'll be great," she said, and then settled into her seat. We didn't talk any more about it. Technically even her question was out of line, though she could have been referring to just about anything. Still, it was best to be safe and not mention the Gathering out in the larger church.

Bryce had cautioned me against overthinking the Gathering as it approached, so I threw myself fully into worship, hoping that would keep me open. I was desperate to achieve Oneness my first time. I had waited so long, been preparing for so long, and Bryce had told me his story of achieving it on the first try. In some ways I felt like I needed to be able to get there right away to prove that I was a suitable wife for Bryce.

That was where my real fears hid. Despite all the counseling, despite quitting my job to focus on Bryce and the church, and despite the Reverend's blessing to become Bryce's wife, I still worried that I wasn't worthy. Our misunderstanding at the cabin over our honeymoon proved to me that I still had a lot of work to do to avoid more slipups. I wanted to be worthy. I wanted Bryce to be proud of me.

I also desperately wanted the Reverend to think well of me. I wanted to become one of his shining stars, like Bryce, like Stacy, like the others he spoke of in respectful and reverent tones. He had an incredible connection to God, and if I had favor in his eyes, I knew, I just *knew*, I would achieve Oneness with little difficulty.

So I poured my heart into worship, and when the Reverend got up to speak, I took notes, scribbling every bit of wisdom I could fit on my paper. He made eye contact with me several times during his sermon, and I was pleased at the approval I saw there. Bryce stretched his arm along the back of my chair and squeezed my shoulder. When I looked at him, there was pride in his eyes, and I was filled to bursting with joy. I knew in that moment that the Gathering, my first as a participant, would be unforgettable.

After the service, Bryce whisked me to the back chapel without giving us time to greet anyone. We were the first to arrive, and he pulled me to the center of the room and clasped my hands.

"Are you ready, Julia?" he asked, his tone solemn, but his eyes shining.

"I've never been more ready," I said. "I thought waiting was awful, but now I know why it was important. Because this moment is even more special for having longed for it." I dropped his hands to wind my arms around his neck. "Thank you, Bryce. For all of this. I'd never imagined a life like this was possible."

He grinned and pulled me close. "Just wait," he whispered into my mouth before claiming it in a brief but potent kiss.

By the time others arrived just minutes later, we were simply standing in the center of the room, holding hands at a respectful distance, sharing secret looks.

"You're such newlyweds," Nancy said, nudging Bryce's shoulder as she passed. "Time to center."

"Of course," Bryce said. He led me to a spot near Stacy. "We should be separate for this so we're not distracted. Stacy will keep an eye on you."

It was disappointing to be apart from him, but I could still see him from where I stood, and he was right. I was here to be One with God, not to ogle my husband. I angled so that I couldn't see Bryce anymore and faced the Reverend, who had taken his spot up front.

As happened every time, the crowd of people drifted into groups of three or four. I stuck close to Stacy, as Bryce had directed. The Reverend raised his hands skyward and said, "We thank You for Your Word at the service this morning, O Lord, now we request Your presence."

"We thank You for Your Word at the service this morning, O Lord, now we request Your presence," I murmured along with everyone else, and then turned to my group. We clasped hands and repeated the words, and I found myself gently swaying to the rhythm. Soon, Nancy approached our group with the plate and goblet. Again, there was a selection of darker wafers and lighter wafers. I held my hands out as I did for Communion when we did it during the regular church service. Nancy placed a dark-colored disc in my cupped palms and nodded at me encouragingly. Taking a deep breath, I placed it on my tongue. It dissolved almost instantly, leaving behind the taste of apricots and copper. Next, I took the goblet and sipped the wine, a bitter brew that the Reverend had said represented the sacrifices God made for us.

"Some churches provide sweet wines, or grape juice, as we do for our regular parishioners during our monthly Communion," the Reverend had said. "But at the Gathering, we understand that true sacrifice was required, and is required, in order to open up the connection with God. Drinking bitter wine is a small discomfort, but it is symbolic."

I kept my features neutral as the liquid poured down my throat, determined not to show weakness, as God did not show weakness in His sacrifice. Nancy nodded approvingly and moved on, and I turned back to my group.

It happened gradually. A slight buzz at the back of my skull. I continued chanting, but faltered when chills rushed through my body. It was as if I'd been attached to a live wire and was being electrocuted, but in a good way. I *was* a live wire, vibrating, sparking, and I was energy, pure energy, pure joy. I was One. He was here. I felt Him. From the top of my head through my fingertips, even my toes buzzed with light. Ethereal light. I opened my eyes and all I saw was light, and I knew it was Him. Tears leaked from my eyes, but I barely noticed. I reached out my hands, longing to touch him. Bodies pushed in from all around, all of us trying to touch the light.

I knew why Bryce had never been able to explain what I was seeing as an outsider. It was beyond explanation, beyond words, beyond the human capability to communicate. It was like every cell in my body was suddenly aware, and straining, searching, basking in the glow. And then it was everywhere, surrounding me. I spun in a circle, losing my balance and falling back, but not caring because He was here. With us. Visible and tangible and everywhere. And I was loved and I was worthy and nothing, *nothing*, would ever be worth more than this feeling.

"Julia," a soft voice called to me from somewhere in the distance. The light was fading. I didn't want it to go, but I knew it would be back. My consciousness rose to the surface as if awaking from the best night of sleep I'd ever had. Gentle hands wrapped around my arms and helped me to my feet, and through heavy eyelids I saw my husband's face, his glorious, handsome, beloved face. I threw my arms around his neck, buried my head in his shoulder, and sobbed.

"The adjustment can be difficult sometimes."

"Hm?" I looked up at Susie. I hadn't realized she was talking, though it made sense, since I was in the middle of my counseling session.

It had been three days since the Gathering, and I still felt as if I were walking half in this world, half in Oneness. Bryce had taken me straight home after the Gathering, and I'd spent most of the day marveling at the view from our window, until I was distracted by the view of Bryce reading and pulled him to our bedroom. Our lovemaking had been more satisfying than ever that night. I had spent the next two days reading my Bible, soaking in the Word, relishing in the fact that I had been with God, that He had chosen me to commune with.

"It can be difficult after your first couple of experiences with Oneness to go back to regular life," Susie said. "It's one of the reasons I know the Reverend wanted you to leave your job before participating. Can you imagine trying to work in the state you're in?"

I laughed, imagining how Micah or Elaine would react to me pulling out my Bible every ten minutes, imagining trying to explain to them what it was like.

"But how do you go back to reality?" I asked. "I mean, full reality. You seem focused, Bryce is always focused . . . and the Reverend's connection is stronger than any of ours, and he is always focused on others and doing what needs to be done. How do you do it?"

Susie sat back to think about it. "I imagine it's like anything else that you grow accustomed to. It doesn't make it any less of a big deal, but you learn to live with it."

"What do you mean?"

"For example, if you were in an accident and lost the ability to walk."

I frowned at her. "That's a terrible example."

"Stay with me," she said, the corner of her mouth turning up in amusement. "Right away, life would be so different. Daily activities would be more difficult, things that seemed so easy would become practically impossible."

I nodded. "Okay, yeah, like relearning to do things with your new reality."

"Exactly." Susie smiled, pleased I was tracking with her. "But eventually you would learn to work with the change in your life. It would always be there, a constant, but you would do things intentionally with the change in mind."

"That makes sense, I guess."

"It's a lifestyle change, Julia. You had one when you started coming to church, started making your faith more of a commitment in your life, right?"

"I did."

"And is that hard now?"

I shook my head. "Not at all. It feels natural."

She nodded. "See? Now, this is another change, a deeper change, but it works the same way. Now that you've communed with God, that connection will be present in everything you do. It's how you live your life according to His will. Everything you do should be in honor of God, pleasing to God, an act of worship, even down to cooking dinner for your husband. You honor God by being a faithful member of this church. You honor God by being a faithful wife to Bryce. We talked about this before, but now that you've experienced Oneness, it takes on an entirely new urgency."

"So if I can concentrate my energy in day-to-day life on doing things for God's glory, it will be easier to have that focus?"

"Yes." Susie clapped her hands once, as if I was a child who had just understood a brand-new concept, which, in a way, I was. "That's where that focus comes from that you were talking about with the Reverend or with Bryce. Everything they do is worship, is service. So it's not ignoring the experience, but leaning into it, taking it even further."

A new sense of purpose filled me, and I sat up straight. Tomorrow I would start working on finding direction in every activity. I couldn't wait to get home and talk to Bryce.

Chapter 20

I had no purpose. At least that's how it felt. Two weeks and three Gatherings later, I was still trying to figure out how to live each moment as an act of worship. I understood what Susie had said, but the long days spent at home seemed to blend into each other and I found myself spending most of the time wandering aimlessly. Housework was finished in the morning, supper supplies set out in the afternoon, but I found myself with a lot of time in between, and an itch to do more.

One interesting thing had come up as I shambled about the empty house. Bryce had some boxes that he'd brought home from a storage locker he'd kept for years. He said he'd forgotten about it, because his apartment wasn't large enough to keep much extra stuff around.

"You became such an expert at figuring out what would fit in our house and what needed to be donated, I thought you could go through these," he said, and I was more than happy to oblige, to have something to do. In reality, I'd ended up getting rid of all of my things from my apartment. The few things I'd tried to keep, Bryce had vetoed.

"This is *our* house, Julia; I want to fill it with *our* things, not your memories from another life."

And so it went into boxes and into the donation bin at the church. I didn't mention the items that he brought from his apartment. He had pointed out that my ex had been in my apartment, so the items from it could hold those memories, while he hadn't brought a woman to his apartment before me. He made a good point, and I was glad to be rid of my things once I realized what they meant to him.

While going through his boxes, I found a lot of things that were easy to decide to donate. Old sports balls, some novels that he would have no interest in rereading, clothes that wouldn't even fit his broad shoulders anymore. I held up one shirt, a simple green T-shirt, and was astonished at how small it was. He must have been a very slight teenager.

One box in particular caught my attention. Under piles of old clothes, buried deep at the bottom of the box, was a bundled stack of old letters, with postmarks from over fifteen years ago. All in the same flowery handwriting. All with the same return address, a small town named Meadowsville, which I'd never heard of.

I weighed the pros and cons of opening the letters. I should probably give them to Bryce, and respect his privacy. But what if they contained painful memories? He'd spoken so little about his family before coming to live with the Reverend. Part of me wanted to respect that privacy, but the other part of me was burning to know about his past, to know what his life was like before he found the Reverend. Before the Reverend found him. Rescued him.

Setting the letters aside, I repacked the box, wrote "Donate" on the top, and carried it downstairs to put in the back room. I had three more boxes to go through. I told myself that if I could focus on those, I could decide what to do about the letters. I prayed as I sorted out the last of Bryce's things. There was about a box's worth of items for him to look through to decide whether he wanted to keep them or not. The letters should have gone in that box. Better, I should hand him the letters as soon as he walked in the door that night, so he wouldn't miss them, no matter what he wanted to do with them.

Instead, I tucked the stack under my arm and scurried to my

parlor. Bryce rarely went into that room. They'd be safe there, and I could decide what to do later. I set the letters on the table and stared at them, thinking. Finally, with shaking hands, I untied the stack, took the letter on top, and slipped it out of its envelope. The same writing from the front of the envelope covered the sheet of paper inside.

> *Dear Bruce,*
>
> *Thank you for the letter, and for the money. Sissy was able to get new shoes for school. The kids don't tease her so much now. Daddy is back and still looking for a job, but he's got a couple leads that look promising. Old Lady Sherman hired me to clean her house once a week, so that helps.*
>
> *Everyone's been asking about you. They still have questions about Dwayne. I told them it was an accident and you had nothing to do with it but they still want to talk. I wish you'd tell me where you really are. You know I'd keep it a secret. I haven't told anyone about your letters. We miss you here. You can come home, you know. I'd protect you. Daddy wouldn't let anything happen to you. He told the cops you were with him that night.*
>
> *Please come visit soon. Sissy says she doesn't remember what you look like anymore.*
>
> *Love, Mama*

I sat back in the chair, short of breath though I'd been sitting. Who was Bruce? Was that Bryce? Why would he change his name? Was this his family? If so, it sounded as if Bryce had continued taking care of them even after he'd left, which was very much like him. Scenarios raced through my brain about why Bryce had left this family, why he had changed his name, assuming this letter was even for him, and I wished more than ever that he would open up to me, share about his childhood. But I couldn't ask him now.

Standing up to pace the room, I searched for a suitable hiding spot. There was a basket on the top shelf where I kept extra stationery. The envelopes would fit in perfectly there. I pulled a stool to the shelf to reach, and soon the letters were hidden. Out of sight. But not out of my mind. I breathed deeply and tried to call back the feeling from the Gathering last weekend. It had been the most intense experience yet, but Susie was right. I was getting better at living with it in the back of my mind instead of fixating on it throughout the week.

Sending up a prayer asking for forgiveness, I hurried downstairs to start dinner. When Bryce came home an hour later and asked about my day, I lied to my husband for the first time. "Same as ever. Nothing out of the ordinary."

Best if he didn't know for now.

The following week, after the Gathering, we were settling in for lunch with the Reverend when Nancy turned to me. "Julia, Bryce says that since you've organized the house, you've been eager for more to do."

I smiled. "I have been. I had thought to maybe look for a part-time job, one that won't take away from my time here at the church."

When I had mentioned it to Bryce, he'd been upset. He didn't want me working outside the home, especially with my new discovery of Oneness. He thought it was important to stick close, away from outside influences. But I was going stir-crazy, and even the plans I tried to set up with Van always seemed to fall through. She'd been pretty distant since the wedding, but every time we set up for lunch, something seemed to come up for her work or for me at the church. We had plans to go out for drinks this week, but I hadn't told Bryce yet. He was adamant about these "outside influences," but I was pretty sure he didn't mean Van. Still, I scheduled it for a night when I knew he had a meeting so it wouldn't take away from any of our time together. He would be proud of my efficiency when I told him.

"Well," Nancy was saying. "It so happens that we have need of a tutor at our school. Nothing too strenuous, but I think you'd be great as a mentor for some of our girls."

I had taken a quick tour of the school once, before Bryce and I were married, but hadn't been back since. Much of the time I forgot it was there, and in this moment I felt a little guilty about that. These were mostly girls whose mothers couldn't take care of them. It was a private alternative placement to foster care or, in some cases, juvenile detention. Each girl was sponsored by a family in the church, and the school was staffed entirely by church members, mostly on a volunteer basis, with a few paid employees. As I'd been told my first weekend at the church, everyone in the church took their tithe of time and Acts of Service very seriously.

"What would I need to do?" I asked. "I mean, do you think I'd know enough to tutor?"

Nancy waved a hand, dismissing my concerns. "You'd be given the material ahead of time to study and understand. You'll have access to the teachers as well, to make sure that you have a resource if you come across difficult material. But in general, it's pretty basic. We're training these girls to be able to function in the world as wives and mothers. Most won't go to college, and you won't be tutoring any of those on that track."

I was slightly taken aback at her casual tone, as if being a wife or mother didn't require education and dedication. They'd spent months drilling into me the importance of being a wife, my irreplaceable role within my family and the church family, and now Nancy spoke of these girls and their futures as if they were inconsequential. My shock must have shown on my face.

"Please don't misunderstand, Julia," the Reverend jumped in. "We hold these girls in the highest regard. We want the best life for them. That's why they're training to be wives and mothers. Unfortunately we can't afford to send most of them to college, and we don't want to start them out with massive debt from loans."

"But what if they don't find anyone?"

"We have plenty of groups here at the church, and we help set them up with jobs and an apartment in our buildings until they find their spouses."

I nodded slowly. "I guess that makes sense." I thought for a moment. "What if they really want to go to college?"

"If that's what they want, and we think it's a good fit, we work with them to make it happen. But most are content with the path we've set for them."

I wondered if the girls truly felt the same way. Immediately I mentally slapped myself. I remembered the person I was before meeting Bryce and compared her to myself now. I was much better off now than I had been, and some of the decisions I'd made I would never have considered before.

"When do I start?"

Chapter 21

I searched the bar for Van's familiar curls in the crowd at Mickey Finn's and had a flashback to the last time we were here. Karaoke night almost a year ago, when I'd first started seeing Bryce. Amazing what changes a year could bring.

"Julia!" I barely had time to register Van's smiling face before she crushed me into a hug. "I didn't think you were going to make it!"

"I'm here!" I said. I didn't tell her that I almost had to cancel. Bryce had decided to come home for dinner before his meeting. He usually ate with the Reverend if he had a meeting at the church, so I was already getting ready to go out when I heard him come in. I'd wiped my face and rushed downstairs, smiling as he brandished takeout containers.

"I figured you wouldn't have planned dinner," Bryce said. "But I wanted to surprise you so you didn't have to cook for one!"

It was a very sweet gesture, but his presence pushed my timeline back. I hadn't lied to him exactly, but for some reason I hadn't told him about my plans to see Van. I wrote a note in case he returned home before me, but mostly I planned to drop it into casual conversation later, as we got ready for bed. He wouldn't be upset, most likely. Maybe a little, since I didn't tell him ahead of time. Still, I hadn't wanted to risk having to cancel, as seemed to happen a lot. I didn't want to jinx it.

Van pulled me to a booth in the corner and looked me up and down. "You look different."

I fussed with my hair and smoothed my skirt. Stacy had taken me shopping before the wedding, insisting that I needed a new wardrobe to be Mrs. Bryce Covington. She'd also talked me into getting my hair lightened. "Just some subtle highlights," she'd said, but the effect on my dark auburn hair was striking.

"Do you like it?" I asked.

"Sure," Van said. "You're gorgeous as ever, just different. More like those rich folks you've been hanging out with."

I laughed. "Van, those people are my friends! And my church family. Be nice."

"Okay, okay, I'll be good. But fill me in! Tell me about your honeymoon. And your job!"

I winced, remembering that I'd never actually told Van that I'd left my job at the marketing firm. Before the wedding, I'd been worried about her reaction, and in the weeks since, our short text conversations never opened up the opportunity to really talk about the big things. Thinking about it now, I realized how bad it looked, how strange that I hadn't mentioned it. She was supposed to be my best friend, but I had kept this monumental news from her. I wasn't ashamed of quitting, but I knew what she would say.

"The honeymoon was amazing," I said, my cheeks warming as she gave me that look. "Stop it, Van, you're not getting details."

"Party pooper," she joked. "So how about that job? That fancy promotion working out?"

I bit my lip. "Actually . . . I left the firm."

"What? When? Why?"

"Um, before the wedding."

Van sat back as if I'd punched her. "And you didn't tell me? Why the hell would you leave? All you ever wanted was that promotion!"

I nodded. "That's what I thought, but it wasn't what I expected it to be." I paused, trying to figure out how to summarize everything that had happened at work leading up to my resignation. "I was stressed-out all the time, the hours were grueling, and I wasn't at my best in any area of my life. Bryce thought it was important . . ." I trailed off at the look on Van's face, like she'd stepped in something nasty. "What?"

"You let Bryce tell you to quit your job?"

"It's not like that, Van. He and the Reverend just helped me focus on where I wanted my priorities to be, and they weren't at that firm."

This time Van actually rolled her eyes. "That smarmy 'Reverend'"—she used air quotes—"could sell ice to a Canadian in the dead of winter. I can't believe you fell for that."

My stomach felt like it was filled with rocks. I got that she wouldn't understand why I left the job at first, but that was my family she was talking about. "He only wants what's best for me. I thought you would, too."

Van leaned forward, her expression earnest. "I do, Jules, that's why I'm worried. You're so different since you got with Bryce, and I should have said more before you were married, but you need to be careful."

"I know I've changed, but I think it's for the better."

"I liked who you were before."

"Maybe I didn't."

She looked at me. "Was it you who didn't, or was it Bryce who told you that who you were wasn't good enough?"

Pressure built behind my eyelids. I couldn't believe this was Van, my best friend, talking this way about my husband. Maybe Bryce had been right about outside influences. Maybe Susie had been right about Van in particular. She went to church, but she didn't get it. She wasn't Chosen. I wilted at the thought.

"Hey." Van reached across the table. "I'm sorry, okay? I just want you to be happy. Are you happy, Julia?"

I nodded. "I am."

"Okay, then." She smiled. "That's that."

I took a deep breath. "Okay. So tell me about you." We could move past this. We believed different things, but the core of our friendship was solid. And I would need to learn to deal with outside influences at some point. I couldn't stay sequestered in the church and at home forever.

Van was in the middle of an epic tale about her failure to read the directions on a cake box correctly, when my phone buzzed. My heart sank when I looked at the caller ID and saw it was Bryce.

"Hold on a sec," I said to Van. "Hey," I said into the phone, turning a bit away so I wasn't looking directly at my friend as I spoke to Bryce. "What's up?"

"Where are you?" Bryce's voice was measured. Not angry, but it held none of its usual richness.

"Ummm, Mickey's? With Van. I left you a note."

"You left a note saying you'd gone out with Van. You're at a *bar*?"

"Yeah, the same one we came to the night we first kissed. I sang karaoke, remember?"

He was silent for a moment. "I remember." His voice was husky, and I hoped it was because he was remembering our kiss on the rooftop just like I was.

"I'll be home in a while."

"I need you to come home now."

I pulled the phone away from my ear and stared at it for a moment before putting it back in place. "What? Why?"

"Because I don't like the idea of you being at a bar. Are you drinking?"

"Just some wine."

"And what happens if you get drunk and some guy takes advantage of you?"

"Bryce, that won't happen. It's one glass, like we have almost every night."

"Yes. Every night while we're home. Safe."

I turned even further in the booth, feeling the weight of Van's stare on my face. "I'll switch to water. I just need some more time—"

"Julia Covington, come home right now or I will come there and bring you home myself."

Suddenly I felt like I was being scolded by my father. "Bryce."

"Now." He hung up.

There was no doubt in my mind that if I wasn't home in twenty minutes, he would come after me. "I have to go," I said to Van.

She raised an eyebrow. "When hubby calls, you answer, no questions asked?"

Pulling out money to cover our drinks and the tip, I shrugged. "You would go if Austin called."

"The difference is that Austin wouldn't call to demand I come home."

It was clear she had overheard the conversation.

"I'll call you next week," I mumbled, scooting out of the booth. "Maybe we can all go out together."

"Sure," Van said, but I heard the doubt in her voice. The look on her face as I left seared itself into my brain. Confusion, pity, sadness . . . terror. Like she was watching me walk away for the last time. That was just dramatic, though. We'd see each other again soon. I'd make sure of it.

When I got home, Bryce was waiting in his study. "Thank you for coming home," he said. "And so quickly."

"I didn't want you to jump in the car and come after me," I said. "We could have passed each other on the road."

"I knew you were on your way," he said calmly.

I squinted at him. "How? You hung up before I could tell you I was coming."

"Your phone. I looked up where it was."

"You *tracked* me?"

"It's precautionary, Julia. Don't be dramatic. It's part of the phone plan, and it was useful tonight. I knew where you were before I called, and I'm very pleased that you told me the truth."

"What reason would I have to lie?"

He steepled his fingers under his chin and looked at me, that piercing look he gave as if he were trying to see into my soul. "I'm not sure, Julia. What reason would you have for not telling me your plans before my meeting?"

It was my turn to be defensive. Or maybe I was the only one being defensive. He certainly didn't seem at all ashamed of any of his behavior tonight. "I didn't want to jinx it," I said. "Every time I plan something with Van, something else comes up."

Bryce frowned. "Believing in superstitions shows a lack of faith, Julia. I'm going to have Susie talk more about that with you in your next session."

"Fine," I said, standing. "I'm going to get ready for bed." I started for the door. "By the way, my mother called again and would really like to have us over for dinner. We haven't seen them since the wedding." At his furrowed brow, I added, "Kate won't be there. She told my mother she doesn't approve of the person I've become, whatever that means."

Bryce stood and stretched. "I'll look at my calendar and let you know, but the next few weeks are pretty busy."

I nodded. "It would mean a lot for us to see them," I said. "For them and for me."

He walked toward me. "Do you know what I can't stop thinking about?"

Ignoring his change in subject, I tried to plead my case to see my parents again. "We could even have them over here. I'd be happy to cook."

His finger came over my lips as he stepped close. "Ever since you mentioned it, I can't stop thinking about our first kiss on that rooftop."

My pulse sped up as his other hand trailed up my arm, leaving goose bumps in its wake. "Oh, yeah?" I whispered, forgetting what we'd been talking about entirely as he lowered his face toward my own.

"It was torture," he said. "Glorious torture to only have your lips." His hand found its way down my front, cupping my breast, kneading gently. "And it's a miracle now to have all of you." With that, he claimed my mouth, and any thoughts apart from my husband fled for the remainder of the night.

This is not the day to mess with him. He stayed after school to talk his teacher into raising his grade, but to no avail. Now the boys follow him, tossing pebbles at his back, and he has little desire to speed his steps, and little patience. As yet another pebble nicks his ear, he spins, fists clenched, breathing hard. The boys stop a few feet away, their leader grinning, relaxed, pleased with himself. He calls an insult, nothing the boy hasn't heard before, but a rage builds up inside of him. In seconds he is on the leader, and the element of surprise is to his advantage. He straddles the larger boy, pummeling his face, knocking back his cronies when they try to interfere. Blood covers his knuckles, but he doesn't care.

Behind him, brakes squeal, and he feels rather than sees the circle around them part. A tall figure blocks the sun, but doesn't move to stop the boy's fists. He slows on his own, curiosity overtaking his bloodlust. He squints at the dark silhouette, immediately recognizing the refined stance. "That's enough," the man says quietly, and motions for the boy to follow him. He rises, mechanically, leaving the other boy's friends to take care of the aftermath of his rage.

The interior of the man's car is dark leather, plush enough that even his slight body sinks into the seat. The man hands him a wet wipe and the boy is aware of how much blood covers his skin, some of it from his own split knuckles. He uses several wipes to clean it off, and the man is silent as he drives to the only hotel in town.

The boy is nervous about what the man wants, but he only offers him a chance to shower and clean up. The boy locks the bathroom door securely, but when he emerges the stranger is nowhere to be found. He flips through the channels on the TV, finding something he wants to watch for once, and jumps when the key turns in the lock and the man enters the room bearing carryout boxes from the café. Through mouthfuls of cheeseburger, the boy answers all the man's questions about his life, his schooling, his family, the boys who torment him, though his answers are mostly half-truths or total fabrications. He has the eerie feeling that the man knows he's lying, but he says nothing. When he's finished, the man offers to drive him home.

He has the man drop him off in a housing development a mile from his actual house, and the small smile on the stranger's face tells him that he has fooled no one. Before he gets out of the car, he asks who the man is, for he hasn't spoken a word of himself the entire time they have been together.

"You may call me Reverend."

Chapter 22

"Math is stupid." Sydney covered her face with her hands, and frustration radiated off her entire body.

"It is," I agreed, placing a hand on her arm. "But lucky for us, you've got this."

She dropped her hands so she could roll her eyes at me, and I smiled. "Do you need a break?"

Without responding, she reached into her bag and pulled out a book. The library was pretty limited at the school, the books closely screened by the Reverend and the volunteer librarian, but the girls seemed to be fine with the selection. Not that they had much of a choice, as personal electronic devices weren't allowed.

"I'll give you a few minutes, but then we're back at it, okay?" I stood as Sydney pointedly ignored me. She had been my biggest challenge so far, but after several months working with these girls, I was fairly adept at dealing with their attitudes. I had learned early that many of the girls who attended this school had come here because they were considered "difficult" at home, as opposed to those who were here as a foster or alternative placement. Sydney was one of those whose parents had placed her here voluntarily. The lucky ones had parents who visited every weekend when they came to church. Sydney was not one of the lucky ones, so I forgave her the chip on her shoulder. I was sure I could get through to her.

"How are things going?" Nancy checked in with me a few times a day, always making sure I was still happy with what I was doing. I had gotten into a rhythm with my life, and I felt like I had purpose. I worked at the church three days a week, either tutoring at the school or helping with marketing-related tasks. I attended my counseling sessions on one or two of those days. The weekends were for Bryce and church, and we made the most of our time together. The only difficult part was still the time I spent at home, now down to two days a week. Mostly I was able to keep myself busy with housekeeping tasks or independent Bible study, but there were still moments when my mind wandered to the letters I'd found in Bryce's things. I had read through a couple more in a moment of weakness, but they didn't shed any more light on who these people were, why they weren't together, or if Bruce and Bryce were even the same person.

I knew I needed to confess to Bryce, but at this point I was worried about his reaction. I'd kept this secret for so long . . . he would be angry, and I'd discovered that angry Bryce frightened me just a bit. He stormed through the house and slammed doors. He rarely raised his voice, but his entire body was coiled as if ready to spring. The first time he got angry enough to break a glass, he looked stricken before stalking off. Usually a couple of hours in his office would calm him down, but I didn't relish the thought of calling forth his angry side. It had emerged more often as the court case with the Reverend heated up. I didn't know the details, but it was on the news as well. Bryce didn't like the way the media spun the story, and cursed them at every turn. He always came back and apologized for his behavior, and I knew he was under stress, but I didn't want to poke the dragon if I could help it. I wished he would share more of what was going on with me, but I had to be content with watching and reading what I could of the coverage, keeping in mind that it was likely not an accurate representation. What I learned was that the former parishioner was a veterinarian in the area, quite well-known, and he claimed that the Reverend and the church had taken money from him with false promises. No wonder Bryce was so angry with how the story was being relayed.

"Things are okay," I said to answer Nancy's question. I nodded at Sydney. "My student is a bit of a handful today."

Nancy's face filled with concern. "Do you need help? Sydney comes from a very difficult background."

I shook my head. "I'll be fine. I think I can get through to her. Whether she'll actually learn any math . . . ?" I shrugged and Nancy laughed.

"While you're giving her a break, why don't you go give Bryce a call? He called a while ago but said you didn't pick up."

Since the girls weren't allowed to have electronics, I didn't want to rub it in their faces by having my phone with me. I'd left it in the office with the office manager. "I'll go give him a call. Can you keep an eye out here for me?"

Nancy nodded, and I hurried to the office. Bryce rarely called me during the day on my church days, though he checked in often on my days at home. Sometimes I thought he suspected I was up to something, but I hadn't gone anywhere without telling him since the night I saw Van.

I hadn't talked to Van since that night, which pained me, but she hadn't reached out, either, so maybe it was that drifting apart that Susie had talked about.

"Hey, Julia." I was surprised to see Stacy in the office when I arrived. "Did you hear?"

I shook my head. Stacy had been around a lot more, more than any of my other friends, actually. I was hesitant to call her my closest friend, but she was certainly the one I spent the most time with. She even came over some days when I was at the house, and we would have tea and talk about the church, since that was pretty much central to both of our lives. Stacy had some pretty good ideas about some programs for girls in the church, both those at the school and those in the youth program. She thought it would be nice to pair them up more, set up the girls from the school with positive friendship mentors to set them on the right path.

"You should call Bryce right away." The look she gave me was coy, secretive, and I tried not to resent that she knew something about him that I didn't. I again wondered why she and Bryce hadn't ended up together, and sometimes I wanted to ask if she realized they hadn't. I struck that thought from my head as soon as it arrived and asked for forgiveness. It was mean-spirited and jealous. I made a mental note to discuss it with Susie later.

I scooted behind the desk and dug my purse out from the drawer the office manager shared with me. Sure enough, when I looked at my phone I had several missed calls and texts from Bryce. I was sure I'd told him I didn't keep my phone on me during tutoring, but clearly something was going on. I hit the button to call him back and he answered almost immediately.

Instead of being upset that he hadn't been able to reach me, which I had been braced for, Bryce crowed into the phone. "We won, Julia! The lying coward retracted all his statements and pulled the case. I'm out celebrating with the Reverend right now, but let's celebrate when I get home, okay?"

Pleasure rushed through my body. After the months of tension, all the late nights at work and stress and worry, it was finally over. I was relieved to have my charming, relaxed husband back. "I'll make something special," I said. "I'm so happy for you. Congratulations!"

Bryce whooped one more time before declaring his undying love for me and hanging up the phone. I was still giggling as I put my phone back in my purse.

When I stood up, I was enveloped in a hug by Stacy. "Isn't it great?" she said, keeping hold of my hands as she stepped back. "Every time he talked about the case, I got more worried. I wonder why the guy dropped it."

I ignored the fact that she had insinuated that Bryce talked about the case with her. He didn't even really talk about the case with me, except to say it was going badly. I shrugged. "I don't know, but I'm so glad. It was really weighing on Bryce."

Stacy nodded. "I know. I could tell." She clasped her hands together. "We need to celebrate!"

"I need to get back to the school, actually," I said, pulling my hands from hers.

"Later?"

"Celebrating with Bryce, but maybe this weekend?"

She looked disappointed but nodded. "Sounds great! We'll talk soon."

"Great, 'bye, Stace!"

I practically floated back to the school, but as soon as I crossed the threshold I knew something was up. Girls were walking in straight lines back toward their dormitories from the direction of the tutoring center, and I could hear screaming and crashing. I rushed against the crowd, worried that Nancy had gotten caught in an altercation. We had blowups from time to time, but they were usually fairly small. Only the occasional one required clearing the room.

My stomach clenched when I arrived back at the room and saw that it was Sydney on a rampage. She and Nancy were the only ones left in the room, and as I watched, Sydney picked up a desk and hurled it at the wall. I stepped forward and Nancy held out an arm to stop me.

"Careful, dear, I don't want you getting hurt."

"I'll be fine," I said, sidestepping her arm. I took another step forward. "Sydney?"

The girl turned to me, rage on her face, tears streaming down her cheeks. "Don't come any closer, Julia."

"Okay," I said, holding up my hands. "I'll just stand here, is that okay?"

Sydney didn't answer. She walked to a bookshelf and started pulling the books off. Every few books she pulled, she'd stop and rip out a few pages or rip off the cover for good measure. It was a shame, when these girls had so little, that they felt compelled to destroy. But my college psych skills came back and I thought about how over-whelming it can be to go from having no one care about you to hav-ing so many people care about you, and the people in the church and at the school were extremely caring. It was like an overload.

"Sydney," I said again, removing my heels and sitting cross-legged on the floor. She looked over at me and seemed surprised to find me down low. I didn't want to tower over her like a threat. She went back to pulling the books off the shelves without responding.

"Sydney. I know you're upset."

She snorted.

"How can I help?"

"You can start by getting that bitch out of here." She pointed to Nancy.

"Nancy is just trying to help, Sydney."

"She's a stone-cold bitch and I want her OUT," Sydney screamed, poking the air. "Or I'm gonna start chucking these books at her fake ugly face!"

"Okay," I said, trying to keep my voice calm. I looked at Nancy. "Nancy, do you mind stepping out? It would help Sydney."

Nancy frowned. "We don't give in to the whims of children, Julia."

I groaned internally. Now was not the time to make a stand. I didn't have much training for these situations, but I knew that state-ments like that would goad the girl straight into more violence. She wasn't in a place for reasoning.

Sure enough, a paperweight zoomed over my head. Nancy stepped neatly out of the way before it clattered against the wall be-hind her. I whipped my head back to look at Sydney. "Please," I said. "We don't want anyone to get hurt."

"Maybe you don't," Sydney replied, picking up a textbook and hefting it.

"Nancy." I turned back to her. "Please." I begged her with my eyes to cooperate. At this point I felt stuck between two immovable walls, and Nancy was my best option to find a crack.

Her eyes narrowed at me, but she gave a curt nod and stalked out of the room. To her credit, despite the anger radiating from her body, she closed the door with a quiet click instead of slamming it.

Sydney's back was still to me. "Sydney? She's gone." No response at first, and then her shoulders began to shake and she collapsed onto the floor in sobs. She cried as if her heart was broken. Like a child who had been abandoned in the street. My heart broke listening to those sobs, and wetness tracked down my own cheeks. "Can I come over there, Sydney?"

She didn't respond, but I crawled over anyway. It seemed the worst had passed, at least from our perspective. For Sydney, it was possible the worst was happening now. I crawled right up next to her and whispered, "Sydney, I'm going to touch your arm. Is it okay if I give you a hug?"

As an answer, as soon as I touched her shoulder, Sydney launched herself into my arms, clinging as she sobbed. I cried along with her, and I don't know how long we sat like that until the storm seemed to have passed. "Sydney?" I said. "Do you want to talk?"

She sat up. "I can't stand her," she said, her voice still wavering. "While you were gone, she said . . . she said . . ."

I smoothed her hair back from her face where it stuck to the leftover moisture from tears and sweat. "She said what?" I assumed she meant Nancy.

"She's an awful person," Sydney said, her voice barely a breath. I had to lean in to make sure I heard her correctly.

"Nancy?"

"And him. All of them."

"Sydney, are you sure—"

The door swung open and two large men filled the doorway. Sydney squeaked and burrowed further into my arms.

"Can I help you?" I asked. "We're in the middle of something."

"We're here to help," one of them said. I'd never seen him before, at the Gathering or in church or at the school. He was large enough that I thought I'd remember.

"I've got it handled, thank you," I said, my arms tightening around the trembling girl. No way was I letting her go with strange men I didn't know.

"It's fine, Julia." Nancy's voice came from behind the men, and she peeked around their bulk to give me a reassuring smile. "They're from the behavior unit. They're here to take Sydney to the closet."

I shuddered. I'd tried not to think about the closet since my initial tour before I started tutoring here. It was a tiny padded room used for girls who were misbehaving. They could be left there for hours, depending on their infraction. I thought it was a terrible use of discipline, but I knew better than to question. "I think we've got it handled, Nancy," I said. "Sydney and I were just talking a bit, getting to the bottom of things."

"That's not your place, Julia," Nancy said. "You're not a counselor."

My face reddened. "I realize that, but if she'll talk to me, why—"

"It's not appropriate." Nancy's voice was sharp and left no room for argument. The men crossed the room and each grabbed one of Sydney's arms. She immediately went wild, grabbing for my shirt, screeching and crying.

"Julia," she cried, "don't let them take me! Please! I'll do better! I'll do math! Please!"

Pressure built behind my eyes again as they dragged her to the door. My last glimpse of Sydney was the look of betrayal on her tear-stained face, and I knew I'd lost her.

Once her screams faded down the hallway, I stood up and began cleaning up the mess.

"One of the janitors will come and do that," Nancy said. "No need to bother yourself."

"It's not a bother," I said, feeling as if by putting back Sydney's mess I could somehow atone for my part in this entire debacle. I'd had her. And I'd let her go. No wonder she saw everyone else as the bad guy. Her family left her here and then she was treated as a disposable piece of property when she stepped out of line. Admittedly, it wasn't just a toe out of line. More like she flung her entire body across that line. And that required consequences. I understood that. But it still felt wrong. My stomach was a rock, and all the happiness from my phone call with Bryce had nearly disappeared.

"Julia." Nancy was beside me, and she placed a hand on my arm. "Leave it for the custodial staff to take care of."

I shook my head, fighting to maintain my composure.

"Susie is in the building today," Nancy said. "Why don't you go talk to her for a bit and then head home? I believe you have some celebrating to do."

My eyes widened and I looked at her incredulously. "How can I celebrate now?"

Nancy wrenched the book I was stacking out of my hand and grabbed my wrists, giving me a slight shake. "Because your husband did something amazing, and he deserves to have his wife's full attention and celebration tonight. This was a dreadful thing that happened, but it's not about you. Today is about Bryce. You will go talk to Susie, you will shake off whatever feelings you have left, and then you will go dote on your handsome husband and not speak of it again."

Not tell Bryce about what happened? Ever? I opened my mouth to argue.

"Never again," Nancy said. "And if you can't handle that, maybe the tutoring center isn't for you."

With that, she pulled me out of the classroom and deposited me outside Susie's room. She was right. Of course she was right. This was why I saw Susie, so I could process through things that would hold me back, and keep all the ugliness away from my marriage.

220

Taking a deep breath, I knocked and entered the room, ready to leave this afternoon behind.

My phone buzzed from my purse as I walked in the door a couple of hours later, arms full of groceries. I kicked my shoes off and rushed to put the bags on the table so I could get to the phone.

"Hello," I said breathlessly.

"Should I be jealous?" Bryce's voice teased. "Is someone else taking your breath away?"

I laughed, leaning against the table. "Only you, my love. I just got home."

"Great," he said. "I was just checking in. I should be home in an hour or so."

"Perfect. Can't wait to celebrate my brilliant husband."

"And I can't wait to ravish my gorgeous wife."

"Bryce!" My skin flushed even though I was alone in the kitchen. "I hope no one heard that!"

"They wouldn't blame me a bit," he said, "but I'm alone."

I breathed a sigh of relief. "I love you."

"Love you, too."

An hour later I stepped back to survey the table. Candles were lit and ready to go, wedding china set out, looking elegant. The house smelled like garlic from my spaghetti sauce. I used my grandma's recipe, and it was always a hit, and Bryce's favorite. Soft music played over the surround-sound speakers Bryce had installed throughout the house. I had changed into something even fancier, and was disappointed I hadn't had time to shower as well. Maybe we could shower together after dinner. My heart fluttered at the thought.

I went back to stir the sauce, tasting just a sip. Perfect.

"Julia." I jumped. I'd been so engrossed with my preparations that I'd missed Bryce's entrance.

"Darling," I said, but something in his eyes stopped me. I'd expected a cheerful greeting, but his gaze was cold, appraising. I smoothed my skirt and glanced nervously around the kitchen. What had I done wrong?

"Did you leave your shoes lying in the back room?" He held up one of my nude heels from earlier. I'd completely forgotten to put them away after rushing in to answer the phone.

I took a step toward him. "I'm so sorry, Bryce, I was coming in and the phone rang and—"

WHAM! Pain burst across the side of my face and I saw fireworks. It took me several moments to process that Bryce had just struck me across the face. With my high heel. I put a shaky hand up to my cheekbone and it came away with blood on the fingertips. Gently, I probed the spot, very near my eye. My vision had darkened, and I wasn't sure if it was from the blow or the cut.

"Put them away," Bryce said, his voice calm and colder than I'd ever heard it. He walked toward the stairs and then turned to say over his shoulder, "And don't burn the sauce again. I'd hate for the entire evening to be ruined."

Chapter 23

By the next morning, my eye had practically swollen shut. The night before, Bryce had left to change and came back as if nothing happened. He didn't mention the blow, or my eye. I spent the evening blotting my tears and the cut while Bryce ignored both, even insisting on celebratory lovemaking. I gasped when I finally looked in the mirror later, after he was asleep, and I spent half the night with a bag of frozen peas clutched to my face.

I was brushing my teeth when Bryce walked into the bathroom. He looked at me in the mirror, frowned, and looked at his watch. "I suppose we should take you to the doctor about that."

No apology. No remorse. In fact, he seemed annoyed that it would require a visit to the doctor. "It's okay," I said. "I can drive myself. I can still see out of the other eye."

"Out of the question," Bryce said. "I don't need people asking questions when I'm not there."

Ah. That was the real reason. He was worried that I would have to say what happened, which made sense. He wanted to control the situation. I knew better than to argue, so I just nodded and continued getting ready.

"I hope this doesn't take long," he grumbled as we pulled up to the clinic, and I gaped at the stranger sitting next to me in the car. Who was this man? Where had he been hiding all this time? And when could I have my husband back? He turned to me. "Listen,

Julia, this is family business, okay? No one else needs to know how I handle my affairs, so let me deal with the doctor." He didn't give me a chance to argue. I didn't know what I would have said if he had.

In the clinic, Bryce marched us straight up to the counter. The nurse in reception gasped when she looked at me. "Oh dear, my poor child, what happened?"

Bryce turned on the charm. "I'm a bit scatterbrained," he said, his tone sheepish. "Last night I was helping with dinner and I left one of the cupboards open, and my poor wife walked right into it!"

The nurse looked dubious, but copied the information down. "This happened last night?" she asked, looking at me.

"Yes," Bryce said before I could respond. "But it didn't look nearly so bad then, and she didn't want to go in. I insisted we come straight here this morning."

I could only stare at him, shock radiating out of every part of me. When I noticed the nurse watching me, I carefully schooled my features into a neutral expression. It was the best I could do. Bryce gave them all our pertinent information and filled out the forms while I waited next to him.

"The doctor will be with you soon," the nurse said. Bryce gave her a bright smile and a thank you and led me to a small couch in the waiting area. He placed a possessive arm around me, holding me close to his side. From my good eye, I could see the nurses stealing glances our way as they whispered to each other. They weren't new to this story.

"Julia Covington," a nurse called, and I stood. Bryce gripped my hand as we walked to the nurse. "Just Mrs. Covington, please," she said, her tone friendly but careful.

"She's my wife," Bryce said. "I'd prefer to go with, and I'm sure she wants me to come as well."

They both looked at me and I realized it was my turn to speak. Bryce squeezed my hand tightly enough that my fingers went numb. "Um, yes. Yes, I'd like him to come." Bryce's hold relaxed.

The nurse sighed. "Okay, then. This way." She led us through a maze of hallways, stopping to take my height and weight and herding me into the bathroom for a quick urine sample, and then into an exam room, where she instructed me to hop up on the table while Bryce took a chair, his body the picture of ease, even though I could see the tension in his eyes.

"Your blood pressure is elevated, Mrs. Covington," she said. "Are you experiencing any undue stress?"

"Well, my face hurts," I said, and the corner of her mouth twitched.

"Of course. That would cause anyone stress. Anything else?"

I shook my head. "No, things are good."

She asked me a few more questions and then left the room.

"Good girl," Bryce said, as if I were a child who had done particularly well on a spelling test. "Just keep it up for the doctor and we'll be fine."

I nodded, not looking at him, and he leaned forward, his hand finding my knee.

"You know I'm sorry, right? You moved and it almost got your eye."

As if it was my fault. I just looked at him.

"We'll talk about it later, okay, sweetheart?"

"Fine." My tone was clipped.

A knock sounded on the door and a tall woman with dark hair entered the room. "Hello, Julia, my name is Dr. Leeland. Is it okay if I call you Julia?"

"Sure," I said, shrugging.

Bryce did not look pleased as he surveyed the doctor. "What happened to Dr. Herbert?"

"He's on vacation," she said, glancing at him. "The husband, I presume?"

"Bryce Covington." He held out a hand, which she took in a perfunctory manner before dropping it.

"Lovely to meet you both. Since Dr. H. is on vacation and, Julia, you don't yet have a primary care physician at this clinic, I volunteered to step in and take you on as a patient, if that's okay. Many times women are more comfortable with a woman doctor."

"That won't be necessary," Bryce said. "We're happy to have you treat Julia today, but we'll both continue seeing Dr. Herbert."

"I believe that's up to Julia," Dr. Leeland said, not sparing Bryce a glance. "Let's see how this visit goes before we pressure her into making a decision, shall we?"

"Dr. Herbert is a member of our church and I've been a patient of his for over a decade," Bryce continued to argue. "I'm very happy with my care."

"Wilbur speaks highly of your church and the pastor in charge."

"The Reverend," Bryce corrected.

"The Reverend." Dr. Leeland was looking in my eyes with a flashlight. Her use of the name Wilbur brought forward flashes of a balding man in glasses at the Gathering, and now I knew why Bryce was so adamant that we stick with him. "Julia, can you look up for me? To the side? Other side? Down?"

She poked around a little more and frowned. "This needs stitches. How did you say it happened?"

"She—"

"I asked Julia," Dr. Leeland said, her tone sharp as she interrupted Bryce.

"I, uh, ran into the corner of an open cupboard," I said. "Silly accident, really."

"I see." She stepped back. "I'm going to go get a suture kit. I'll be right back."

Not a word was spoken while she was gone, and when she returned she had me move down to a stool so we were level with each other. "The numbing agent will deaden the skin around the cut, and you'll feel some tugging when I put the stitches in. I think two will be plenty." She injected the anesthetic and I winced, but soon half of my face was completely numb. "You're lucky you missed the eye," she said as she placed the first stitch. "Since you waited to come in, you're at higher risk for infection, so I'm going to prescribe an antibiotic as well as a pain medication. This looks quite sore."

I started to nod, and then remembered that she had a needle very close to my eye. "It is," I said instead. "Actually, the numbing stuff helps, but my entire head has been throbbing all morning."

She gave me a sympathetic look as she snipped off the second stitch and covered the cut. She disposed of the needle in the sharps container and moved the rest of the supplies to the counter before washing her hands. Crossing her arms, she leaned back against the sink and looked at me.

"Mr. Covington, I'm going to have to ask you to step out for a few minutes."

Bryce had been silent since the doctor had returned, but now he spoke out angrily. "I'm not going anywhere."

"It's customary for me to have some time alone with my patient," Dr. Leeland said, finally sparing him a glance. "You can go take care of the bill while I speak with Julia."

"She's not your patient."

Dr. Leeland shrugged. "She is today. As for the future, that's up to her."

"Whatever you have to say to her you can say in front of me," he insisted.

"Mr. Covington, I need to ask my patient some questions. It's standard procedure for these sorts of situations, and if you don't leave, I will be forced to call for help."

"That's not necessary," I said. "He can stay."

"No."

Bryce stood up, fists clenched. "You'll be hearing from me about this, *Doctor*," he said, and the venom in his voice shocked me. He stormed out, slamming the door behind him.

"Julia, you're white as a ghost, are you okay?" Dr. Leeland's brown eyes were concerned. "You should sit back down."

I hadn't even realized I'd stood up during the altercation between Bryce and Dr. Leeland. Well, it wasn't so much an altercation as an argument, but I bet that nurse would have been extremely worried about my sky-high blood pressure now.

"Put your head between your knees," Dr. Leeland instructed. The world had become sort of hazy, and the edges of my vision, at least in the eye that I could see out of, were fading. "Breathe, Julia." She demonstrated breathing with me, and after a few minutes I was able to sit up.

"I'm sorry," I laughed. "Just between this"—I indicated my face—"and that confrontation with Bryce . . . I don't do well with confrontations."

"I see," Dr. Leeland said. She pursed her lips. "Julia, I need to ask you something, and I need you to be honest with me."

"Okay," I said, already knowing I would have to lie. Bryce had, and so must I.

"How did you get that cut under your eye?"

My answer was immediate. "I ran into a cupboard. Bryce and I were cooking a celebratory dinner and he left one open. I wasn't watching where I was going and ran right into it."

She wasn't convinced. "Are you afraid to go home with your husband?"

Yesterday I wouldn't have hesitated, but today I paused, and the slight tightening of Dr. Leeland's lips told me she noticed. "No, of course not," I laughed. "I'm sure he'll spoil me the rest of the day. He feels so awful about all of this." More likely he would leave me to attend to my regular chores while he went to work.

Dr. Leeland shook her head and sighed. "I know you don't know me, but I want you to know I'm here if you need anything, Julia." She pulled a card out of her pocket. "This is a number for a local women's shelter. If you ever feel like you need to get out, get to a safe place, you can call that number and someone will come and get you. Please keep it someplace safe, where your husband won't find it."

My initial reflex was to crumple the card and throw it away, tell this doctor to stay out of our family business. I was optimistic that I'd be able to talk with the Reverend and Nancy and solve this issue so it wouldn't happen again. This version of Bryce wasn't the real one. It was a Hulkified version brought on by stress.

Still, I nodded at her and tucked the card into my bra, where Bryce wouldn't be looking anytime soon. It couldn't hurt to have it on hand, and could be a good resource for women at the church who felt threatened.

Dr. Leeland walked me out to the waiting room, where Bryce was pacing. "I'll call your prescriptions in to the pharmacy. They should be ready by the time you get there."

"Thank you," I said. Bryce glared at the doctor, took my arm, and dragged me out of the clinic. As we left, the staff at the front desk all wore identical masks of concern. I smiled to reassure them before the doors closed behind me.

As expected, Bryce dropped me off at home after we picked up my pills, and headed straight to work. My face ached, and the anesthetic around my stitches was starting to wear off, causing small stinging sensations. I took my pills and considered taking a nap, but I was too keyed up. I paced through the house, making my way up to my parlor and dropping the card Dr. Leeland had given me into the basket containing Bryce's letters. More than ever, my curiosity about the woman whose handwriting I had grown familiar with burned through me, but I had more immediate concerns.

I replayed the events of the past twenty-four hours. I prayed for clarity, that God would help me to understand why my husband had switched personalities. He hadn't been drinking. There was nothing out of control about him. In fact, it was eerie how calm and collected he was through the entire thing. The most agitated he had been was at the doctor's office, when outsiders appeared to be meddling in our life.

In one of my Bible studies with Jenny's group before I'd left the group, we'd read through some Old Testament stories about demon possession. Was it possible that Bryce was being controlled by something other than himself? Was he trapped inside himself, watching in horror as this Bryce puppet irrevocably changed our relationship?

It was far-fetched, and I wished I could talk to Jenny about it, but she no longer approached me in church, or acknowledged me in any way. I regretted that I'd let our friendship go, but Bryce and Nancy didn't seem to approve of her, and while the Reverend loved everyone in the congregation, he didn't mix with her much, which I took as tacit agreement from him that she wasn't the right sort of person to be around. Really, they only fully approved of others who attended the Gathering.

I needed to talk to someone. Maybe the Reverend had noticed something off about Bryce yesterday. They'd been together for much of the day, after all. Celebrating. Ecstatic about the results of the court case. He had office hours today. Maybe I'd just stop in and talk with him. After all, no matter what was going on with Bryce, I knew I needed help getting him back on track.

Before I could leave, my phone rang, an unfamiliar number lighting up the screen. "Hello?"

"Is this Julia Covington?" a voice asked. It was familiar, but I couldn't place the speaker.

"Yes, who is this?"

"This is Dr. Leeland," she said. "From the clinic."

As if I could forget Dr. Leeland. "I told you everything's fine, Doctor." A strange mix of gratitude and annoyance washed through me. It was nice that she was checking in, and I was glad that she was so vigilant about protecting her clients. But I didn't need protection. I'd take care of everything.

"Yes, I know," she said on a sigh. "But I wanted to call and talk to you about your urine sample results."

"Don't nurses usually do this?" I hunted through the drawer in the back room until I found my biggest pair of sunglasses. Donning them, I checked the mirror. The bruising on my cheek could almost pass as shadows wearing these. Enough to stop nosy people from asking questions.

Dr. Leeland laughed. "Yes, nurses often call when there's nothing unremarkable, but I wanted to talk with you myself. We just did some preliminary tests. You hadn't mentioned any drug or alcohol use but I was curious, so we rushed it."

"I don't do drugs, Dr. Leeland," I said, offended. "I served wine for dinner last night but barely drank any. It wasn't notable." I grabbed my purse and snatched my keys off the hook by the back door, eager to end the conversation.

"Then I wonder, Julia," Dr. Leeland said, "how you ended up with ketamine in your system."

I stopped, ignoring the clatter as my keys fell to the floor. "What are you talking about?"

"It's only a trace, so I would guess you ingested it a day or two ago, maybe Sunday, or had a very small dose."

"I—I can't deal with this right now," I said. "Thank you for letting me know."

"Julia, please, if there's something you're not telling me . . ."

"Dr. Leeland, I appreciate you filling me in on my results, but it seems to me you're overstepping. If you continue I will have to talk to my husband about the clinic we go to."

Silence from the other end, then, "I understand, Mrs. Covington. If you change your mind, you know where to find me."

"Goodbye, Doctor." I hung up, bent to pick my keys up from the floor, and calmly walked to my car.

On the way to the church, I contemplated calling my mom. We hadn't spoken in several weeks, and I could feel myself starting to break. Instead of dialing her number, I turned the car in the direction of my parents' house. I could stop by, say hello, find out how things were in their lives, ask my mom for advice in dealing with the new version of Bryce. A few minutes later, my phone rang.

"Hello?" I said after pushing the button on the steering wheel to answer. I didn't have a chance to check the number.

"Hello, my love." Bryce's voice filled the car. He sounded normal again, his tone rich and inviting, nothing like it had been earlier in the day. "I just realized I didn't kiss you goodbye when I dropped you off this morning. I owe you extra when I get home."

Despite my confusion at his switch, his words sent pleasure down my spine. My husband was nothing if not charming when he wanted to be, which I used to think was always. "I'll look forward to it," I said, my tone careful.

"What are you up to? I thought you might be napping."

"I thought about it," I said, "but I was too keyed up. I thought I'd head over to the church and check on some of the girls I tutor." I did want to peek in on Sydney after I talked with the Reverend.

"Are you heading straight for the church?" Though Bryce's voice didn't change, there was a hint of warning.

"I decided to take a little drive," I said. "I thought I might stop by my parents' place. It's been so long since I saw them." I wanted to be honest with him, especially considering what I was already keeping from him.

"That's a little rude to stop in without calling," Bryce said.

"How do you know I didn't call first?" I was probably being a little more contrary than I needed to be. I took a deep breath. "They're my parents, they won't mind."

"Julia, I think you should just head to the church. I know Nancy wanted to speak to you about an incident that happened yesterday. I wish you'd told me about it."

The incident that Nancy had told me not to burden him with on his exciting day. I was surprised she'd told him. "When did you talk to Nancy?"

"I called her after I dropped you off. I thought we should try to sit down with the Reverend and Nancy to talk about what happened."

I smiled to myself, relieved that he was going to acknowledge that something had gone wrong. "I think that's a great idea, Bryce."

"Good." The warmth in his voice was back full force, surrounding me like an embrace.

"I'll head to the church as soon as I say hi to my parents."

Bryce paused, then sighed. "I'd like for you to save your visit for another day, Julia," he said. "A lot has happened in our family the past couple days, and I'd rather we talk through it before bringing outsiders in."

"You talked to Nancy."

"She's family."

"My parents are family."

"You know what I mean." He sounded weary, as if I were a petulant child.

"I miss my parents, Bryce. We haven't even made it over for dinner since the wedding. I used to see them at least a couple times a month."

"That was before you met me, Julia. You don't need your parents as much now. You have a new family."

I frowned. I was minutes away from my parents' house. I could almost feel my mom's tight hug. "They'll always be my family, Bryce. So will Kate, if she ever decides to talk to me again."

"Julia, I think this is all stuff we need to discuss. You and I. Turn the car around and go to the church. Do not disobey me."

My jaw hurt from how tightly I clenched it. But he was right. We'd talked about this in our couples counseling and with our mentor couple. I'd also discussed with Susie what it meant to be a wife. Bryce had made a request, and I was to follow his direction. Full stop. "Fine," I said, working to keep my voice steady. "Can I at least call my parents and set up a dinner?"

"We'll talk about it later."

"Okay."

"Go talk with Nancy," Bryce said. "I think you'll feel better after you do."

"Okay."

"I love you, Julia," he said. "I only want what's best for you. Remember that."

"I know," I said. "I love you, too."

Disconnecting the call, I pulled into a driveway. I was three blocks from my parents' house, but I turned around and headed back toward the church. Back toward my home and the new family that I needed to work more diligently to fit in with. They'd accepted me, and I needed to accept them, the good and the bad.

Nancy was in the front office when I arrived. She stood immediately and held out her hands.

"Julia, let's go talk at home, okay?"

"I wanted to check on Sydney," I said, pointing toward the school.

"Oh, I looked in on her earlier," Nancy said. "She's still confined but she's calm and doing well."

I wanted to argue, but I was so tired of arguing. Physically and mentally exhausted after the past twenty-four hours. And I wished I'd stayed home to nap, given how little sleep I'd gotten the night before. So instead of telling Nancy why it was important for me to see Sydney with my own eyes, talk to her, make sure she was okay, I nodded and followed her to the door leading to her house.

Once we were seated in the sun-filled living room, Nancy called for tea, and we talked about unimportant things until it arrived. I got the sense that Nancy didn't want anyone to walk in and overhear any part of our conversation, despite the fact that those who she allowed to volunteer in her house were extremely discreet and unlikely to ever disclose anything they'd hear. My suspicions were confirmed when Nancy told her volunteer that she could have the remainder of the afternoon off.

When the volunteer had left, Nancy reached out and touched the cut on my cheek, acknowledging it for the first time. I winced, and she clucked her tongue. "What caused this?" she asked, leaning back and picking up her teacup.

I floundered, unsure if Bryce had told her the real story or the cover story.

She sipped her tea. "Bryce told me he got angry. We don't keep secrets around here." She paused. "Of course, outside of his house, you'll stick with the cupboard story. Much more believable."

My head was spinning, and not only because my pain meds were wearing off. I was relieved that I didn't have to lie to Nancy, and especially that I wouldn't be lying to the Reverend. I wasn't sure I was even capable of that. He saw through everything, and I was sure it was due to his connection with God.

"Um," I said, still struggling to say the words out loud. "Bryce hit me with a pair of my shoes. The heel cut my skin, and the doctor said if it had been only an inch closer—"

Nancy held up a hand. "I know that part," she said. "And we'll discuss the good doctor later, but my question was about what you'd done to make your husband so angry."

I frowned. "I'd left my shoes by the door instead of putting them away. He called as I was walking in and I rushed to answer the phone—" Nancy's expression cut me off this time.

"It seems like you're making excuses, Julia."

My mouth fell open. "I'm just explaining."

"And you were doing a fine job until you tried to explain away your behavior by blaming Bryce's phone call."

"But—"

"Was his phone call meant maliciously?"

"Not at all," I said. "He was calling to let me know when he'd be home so we could celebrate."

"That was very kind of him to let you know how much time you had."

"It was, but—"

"And you let yourself become distracted, is that fair to say?"

"I mean, I had to cook the meal and get everything ready, so I had a million things running through my mind."

Nancy pursed her lips. "I've been doing some reading today, Julia, and you might be interested in what I've found." She pulled out her Bible. "Proverbs is rich with these verses. 'A wife of noble character who can find? She is worth far more than rubies.' Proverbs 31:10."

"That's lovely," I said, unsure of what she was trying to tell me. We'd gone through these verses before, the ones on marriage.

"This one is a little more harsh, but I feel God is telling me to remind you," she said, flipping back a couple of pages. "'A wife of noble character is her husband's crown, but a disgraceful wife is decay to his bones.' Proverbs 12:4." She looked up at me. "Are you a crown or are you a decay, Julia?"

Her look rendered me speechless for several seconds. Censure, judgment, disappointment. As if I were the one who had failed and struck myself with a shoe. But even as one part of me fought against that judgment, another part leaned into it. It wasn't so much to ask, really, to put my shoes away, to make sure the home I made for my husband was clean and free from distractions or danger. But still, his reaction seemed out of proportion.

"Aren't there verses about a husband loving his wife and treating her as his own body?" I asked, wishing for my own Bible at that moment, or for the ability to have memorized everything of import. I was still new to all of it, as much as faith had become the center of my life.

"Be careful about using verses you're unfamiliar with, and out of context, Julia," Nancy said. "And any verses about how a husband should behave are Bryce's responsibility to review and understand. Not yours. Right now we're focusing on what you can do differently in the future."

It was the same thing Susie had said about communication with Bryce. I was responsible for my part in things, and couldn't change him. I would waste a lot of energy by focusing on how he could do things differently, and I would see no improvements, because I was only in charge of my own words and actions. I understood what Nancy was saying.

"I guess," I said, and she nodded encouragingly. "I guess I need to slow down a bit, double-check that I'm doing everything I can to keep the house looking the way Bryce likes it."

She smiled. "Excellent thought, Julia." The smile faded. "He also said you were a little contentious toward him at the doctor's office."

Guilt grew low and heavy in my stomach as I remembered how I didn't stand up to Dr. Leeland as she'd offered to be my primary physician. "I was crabby," I said. "I didn't sleep well, but I know that's no excuse. I should have stopped her right away when she tried to get involved in our private affairs."

Nancy's smile was back, and I was glad that I had pleased her. "Doctors treat injuries. They don't need the backstory. I trust you'll see Bryce's physician from now on." She sipped her tea.

"Of course," I said. A small part of me argued that Dr. Leeland had just been concerned, and that it had been nice to have someone who was concerned about what had happened, but that part had shrunk even more during my conversation with Nancy. The larger part agreed that it wasn't her business. That we could take care of it ourselves. That talking to Dr. Leeland ever again would be a mistake.

"And I think it would be best if you worshipped with us from the privacy of your home this weekend," Nancy continued. "I'm not sure your eye will be cleared up by then, and I think it would be too emotionally draining for you to answer the questions that would come your way. Much more relaxing to stay home."

She was right. I shuddered to think of having to repeat our story over and over. Better to wait until I was healed. "I'll miss the Gathering," I said.

"I know," she replied. "But the Reverend would have asked you to observe again anyway, since you're on medications. We can't fully be One with God when there are foreign elements in our system, altering our biological makeup."

It made sense, but still made me sad. The Gathering and experiencing Oneness had become highlights of my week. What kept me going even when I was feeling lonely or displaced. It was pure joy, and my fingers shook as I considered what it would be like to go a week without. Now the anguish on the faces of those who didn't achieve Oneness made a lot more sense.

Nancy and I finished our tea, and it wasn't until I was on my way out that I realized I hadn't even thought to mention Dr. Leeland's phone call, or the ketamine she'd found in my system. And I had no intention of mentioning it, either. Not yet. Not until I could do some digging of my own.

When I got home, I marched straight up to my parlor, took the card from my stationery basket, and crumpled it before throwing it into my small metal trash can. I crossed my arms and tapped my toe, staring at the trash as if it would burst into flames at any minute. Then, slowly, I uncrossed my arms and walked back over to the trash, leaning down and plucking the crumpled card from amidst the other papers inside. I opened it, smoothed as many wrinkles as possible, and placed it back in the basket.

When I went to have my stitches removed by Dr. Herbert the following week, I avoided eye contact with all the nurses, and none of them tried to speak to me. Dr. Leeland was nowhere to be found.

He starts seeing the Reverend regularly, usually at the library. The Reverend is a recruiter, looking for bright young minds to join his church. He's never been much for religion, doesn't believe in a God who allows him to live in hell, but the way the Reverend talks about it, it sounds almost plausible.

The Reverend wants to help him succeed. "You can stay here, beating up bullies, or you can aim higher. I can help." The bullies haven't bothered the boy since he broke the leader's face. The other boy needed eighteen stiches and had a broken nose, but no one told who'd done it. It would have ruined the leader's reputation, and no one would have believed the scrawny kid had managed that amount of damage.

The boy talks of his plans to get a scholarship, and the Reverend points to all the other expenses of moving away, of living elsewhere with no other support. He offers to mentor the boy, even after he leaves town, which will be soon. He is here on business, though he doesn't say what that business is, and the boy cannot fathom what business would bring such a wealthy and important man to this armpit of a place. He gives the boy a phone, tells him to keep it from his mother and her boyfriend. By now it's clear he knows the exact circumstances the boy lives in, and the boy is strangely not ashamed.

When he agrees to join the church, the Reverend is ecstatic. He leads the boy in worship, and gives him a disc that dissolves on his tongue and a sip of bitter wine and the boy is flying. He has never experienced anything like this feeling before. No one has ever shown him what he could be, the heights he could reach. Only the Reverend believes in him, accepts him unconditionally, wants to give him a better life than the one he is destined for. For the first time in his life, the boy can see beyond this town, beyond his own wretched existence. The Reverend has opened his eyes to his unlimited potential, to the unlimited possibilities that await him. He will finish school and join the Reverend and the revolution he offers, and no one will ever get the best of him again.

PART V

THEN COMES BABY

I stared at the stick in my hand, my heart racing. It had been a whim, a throwaway suspicion that had caught hold of me and wouldn't get out of my head. I hadn't really believed it was true. Or possible, at least at this point. And yet it was very clear on the display.

I was pregnant.

After my initial shock, the feeling of joy blanketed me, and I sent a prayer up thanking God for this miracle. Dr. Herbert would have to explain to Bryce how this was possible while I was on birth control, but I knew Bryce would be thrilled, even though it wasn't part of the plan. He'd always talked about wanting children after we'd been married a couple of years.

I wrapped the pregnancy test in some toilet paper and stowed it with my feminine products, which I wouldn't be needing anytime soon, it appeared. I considered calling Dr. Herbert and setting up an appointment, but Bryce would find out and I wanted to be the one to tell him. I was in the midst of putting together our first anniversary celebration dinner, and this would be the perfect addition.

Everyone had said the first year of marriage was the hardest, but I hadn't really believed them until I experienced it. It was comforting to know that it was normal to experience rough patches, and to know that with this first year behind us, we could look forward to easier years ahead. Even the past few months had eased a bit. It just took learning the rhythm of sacrifice for another person.

It had surprised me how much more demanding Bryce had been once we were married, but I talked with Nancy about it frequently. I'd forgone my sessions with Susie. She had been helpful for a time, but Nancy really understood Bryce, and it made me feel better to keep some aspects of our relationship within the family. I could be honest with Nancy in a way I couldn't be with anyone else. To the rest of the church, even those in the Gathering, our marriage had always been completely harmonious. I believed that it could be the truth eventually. We'd both learned some hard lessons.

I glanced in the mirror before heading out to run my errands. I needed a few more things for our dinner tonight, and then I would need to hurry back to cook and prepare for Bryce's arrival home. My blonde hair shimmered in the sunlight coming in through the windows. I'd lightened it even further at Nancy's suggestion, and Bryce had enjoyed it so much that I had kept lightening it until it became a shade he approved of, almost platinum blonde. We'd put in a home gym down in the basement as well, and it was now part of my daily routine to spend an hour down there, and I was in the best shape of my life. I was a model wife for Bryce.

I brushed the light scar that was the only sign of our first fight several months ago. It had healed nicely, and he hadn't drawn blood again. The Reverend had pointed out to him that it drew undue attention to our situation, and while Dr. Herbert was discreet, his staff might be less understanding. After the initial incident, the only times I went in were for my physical with Dr. Herbert and if I was ill. The staff had warmed to me, though a couple still watched me closely whenever I came. Dr. Leeland was no longer employed at the clinic, from what I could tell.

The weather was cool today, for which I was grateful, because it made it less conspicuous to wear long sleeves. Bryce had gripped my wrists a little too hard during our lovemaking a couple of nights before, and the matching green-tinged bracelets would have drawn stares. Instead of fretting about that, I fluffed my hair and dialed my phone as I headed out.

"Happy anniversary, my love," Bryce answered, his voice a caress.

"I think you wished me a happy anniversary this morning already," I teased. "Twice."

He laughed. "I do recall something along those lines. And I plan to wish you a happy anniversary a few more times before the day is over."

Shivers ran down my arms, and I smiled as I climbed into my car. "I'll hold you to that."

"Are you getting in the car?" he asked.

"Yes," I said, starting the engine as the phone switched over to the speaker. "I wanted to let you know that I'm going to the store, and then I'll probably stop at the library quickly before heading home."

"They need you at the library today?" he asked, and I worried he wouldn't sanction that stop. I'd started volunteering to help at story time at the library a few months ago, when I'd stopped tutoring at the school. I'd grown upset with how the girls were punished, even though I knew it was in their best interest. I'd asked if there were any other volunteer opportunities outside of the school, and Bryce had talked to the librarian, Vanessa, who was a part of the Gathering. It seemed there were members of the Gathering spread all throughout the city, many in positions of influence. It was nice to know that those who could make an impact were among the Chosen, doing the work of God.

"No, but I wanted to return some books," I said, glancing at the stack. "All of these biblical commentaries are so fascinating. I swear I'll never get through them all."

"Are you sure you have enough time?"

"Don't worry, sweetheart, I'll drop them off, maybe pick out another one or two, and be in and out in fifteen minutes, tops. You can have Vanessa time me."

"I don't think that'll be necessary," he said, chuckling. "Just let me know when you're home."

"I absolutely will. I love you."

"I love you, too."

We hung up, and I drove to the store, mentally going through my list. There wasn't much on it, and I was out in ten minutes. At the library, I waved hello to Vanessa and made my way upstairs and to the back corner, where the religion section was housed.

The best part about the religion section, aside from the commentaries, which I really did find very interesting, was that it was far removed from the main section, where Vanessa stayed, and it had a computer in a corner that was perfect for watching out in case she did come to check on me. Vanessa always found a reason to come and check on me at least once or twice during my visits, likely at Bryce's request. I was careful not to give her anything too juicy to report back to him.

I felt only a little guilty as I selected two new commentaries at random and made my way to the computer. I quickly looked up the title of one to read the background and reviews, and left that window open in the background while I pulled up an incognito window to do my other daily search.

Harriet Schmit, Meadowsville, NY

Of course there was nothing new. The only result that was promising, as always, was an unprotected Facebook page that was deep in memes, online games, and quizzes. Since I'd checked a few days ago, Harriet had learned that her ideal fruit was a kumquat, she should live in Georgia, and she was destined to meet a wealthy stranger in the next three months. I smirked at the last one. Maybe there was something to these quizzes.

I had the trip planned out. Meadowsville was only a two-hour drive. I could go, stake out the address that was on all the letters I still hid in my parlor, figure out if Harriet was in some way related to Bryce, and make it back in time to cook dinner before Bryce arrived home. I hadn't yet figured out a way to broach the topic with Bryce, but I wanted to check things out first. I had one more thing to do before I could put the finishing touches on my plan. Luckily, cell service was so poor in the library, there was still a bank of pay phones set up near the entry. I closed out of the computer and went downstairs to check my books out.

"Find what you were looking for?" Vanessa asked, scanning the books. "First Peter, huh? Anything interesting?"

"Just starting," I said, hoping my nervousness could pass as excitement over a new book to dive into. "The author who wrote that one also wrote my favorite commentary on John, so I'm sure I'll love it."

"Your enthusiasm has gotten me interested in reading some of these. Can you write down your favorites for me sometime?"

I nodded. "Of course. I'll bring a list when I come back next week. I need to get home and get the anniversary dinner cooking."

"That's right! Happy anniversary, Julia. I remember your wedding. It was so beautiful."

"Thank you," I said. "I had an album made at a shop here in town. I hope Bryce likes it."

"I'm sure he'll love it," Vanessa said, her tone sincere.

"That reminds me," I said, furrowing my brow as if I'd just remembered something. "The shop forgot to give me back my flash drive. I should call and see if I can stop by to grab it on my way home." I pulled a card from my purse. "Mind if I use one of the pay phones?" I asked.

"Sure," she said. "Local calls are free."

"Great!"

Once I'd rounded the corner, I pulled some coins out of my pocket. On the back of the card I'd scribbled the number I'd found in a Meadowsville online directory. It was old, as if it had been created in the days when dial-up Internet was the norm, but I hadn't been able to find anything more recent with a number attached to Harriet's name and address. I popped the coins in and dialed the number.

"Yeah?"

The woman who picked up sounded like she'd been smoking her entire life. A television blared in the background, and a dog barked over the sound.

"Hello, yes, is this the photo studio?" I kept my cover in case Vanessa was listening. Though she seemed sincere, I knew Bryce asked people to keep an eye on me. He always seemed to know what I was doing before I did it. His network was vast, which was what made this so risky. And yet, I couldn't let it go.

"Huh?" The woman was clearly confused. "Turn the fuckin' TV down, I'm on the phone!" she yelled. A deeper voice grumbled something in response, but I was unable to make out the words. "Oh, get a job," the woman muttered. Into the phone, she said, "What'd you say?"

"Who am I talking to, please?"

"This is Harriet. Harriet Schmit. Who's this?"

"Oh, I'm terribly sorry," I said. "I must have dialed the wrong number. So sorry to bother you." I hung up before she could respond.

Quickly, I dialed the number to the photo studio I'd used to make Bryce an album of our first year together. "Yes, hello, this is Julia Covington. I had a photo book made recently, and I was wondering if I'd left the flash drive with the pictures on it at your studio."

"Nope, we don't have anything in the lost and found, Mrs. Covington," the man said. "Did you check the box the album came in? Sometimes we'll throw it in there to make sure it gets back to the customer."

"I'll look there, thank you," I said. I'd known they wouldn't have it, because the flash drive was currently at the bottom of my purse, where it had been since they handed it to me when I picked up the book. "Can I leave my number in case it turns up there?"

After leaving my number, I hung up, turning around in time to see the door to the library lobby close. Either I'd missed someone opening the outside doors as well, or someone had been listening.

Chapter 25

I looked around the dining room, pleased with the result. I'd placed Bryce's present next to his chair. Twinkle lights were strung from the center chandelier to the walls all across the room, forming a canopy like the night sky, reminiscent of the night Bryce had proposed. Tall tapers flickered on the table, and soft music played from the speakers. I'd double-checked everything, down to which hook I hung the keys on, to make sure it was perfect before Bryce arrived. I wanted the night to be memorable in more ways than one.

This night was the end of a tumultuous first year of marriage, but also the beginning of the rest of our lives together. It would mark the start of a new chapter not only in the marriage, but also in our family. I'd wanted to call my mom today to let her know about the baby, but I wanted to tell Bryce first.

I really wanted to tell my parents in person, but I didn't know if I could wait for Bryce to clear his schedule to make that happen. I would be ready to burst by that time. Bryce had been strangely hesitant to ever see my parents. We'd only seen them twice outside of holidays in the past year, and when we saw them on holidays it was because they came and attended church with us, though Bryce wouldn't budge on letting me sit with them. He was adamant about staying in our spot, and wouldn't hear of displacing anyone else around us for my parents. They were always invited to the Reverend's for a meal after service, but after attending one, my parents always declined.

Bryce didn't want me going to see them without him, either. I'd suggested it a couple of times, but he thought it sent the wrong message about our marriage if I attended a family dinner without him. I suggested just meeting my mom for coffee, but he had vetoed that idea as well. So now my mom and I sent letters back and forth to share news. Bryce always got the mail and opened her letters first, and read whatever letters I sent back. He said it was in the interest of open communication, and he'd been very angry when my mother had referenced information I'd mentioned in a letter I'd sent without allowing Bryce to see it first. He'd been busy and I'd wanted to get it sent. I hadn't realized how important it was to him. But since then, it had been fine. Mom sent pictures of my nephews, and I couldn't believe how big they were getting. She never mentioned Kate anymore, and I didn't ask. It felt like I never had a sister, except for the ache around my heart when I thought of her.

I shook my head, dislodging all morose thoughts and focusing on tonight. We'd call my parents together later with the news, or tomorrow. I was sure Bryce would be as excited as I was to let everyone know, though it was early. Still, I longed to talk with my mom about it. Maybe we'd tell just close family until I was a little further along. I rubbed my belly, imagining that I could almost feel a small bump, though I knew it was impossible, and my stomach was as flat as it had ever been.

My daydreaming was interrupted by the sound of Bryce's car pulling into the garage. I tugged at my apron, hanging it in the kitchen closet as I walked past, and was ready to greet my husband as he walked in the door.

Bryce stopped as soon as he saw me, his eyes roving my body hungrily. The dark blue dress I wore clung to my tight curves. It was much shorter than anything I would wear out of the house. I only wore it for him, and he knew it. Dropping his briefcase and keys on the counter by the door, he lunged for me, crushing my mouth under his, hands sliding up and down and roaming the silky fabric.

"Happy anniversary, honey," he said as his lips moved down my throat. I leaned my head back to grant him better access. I thrilled that this passionate man had been my husband for a year and I was still able to elicit this response from him. If anything, he seemed to want me more now even than when we were first married.

"Welcome home," I said, sliding my hands under his jacket. "Let me help you with that."

A little while later, Bryce followed me into the kitchen as I smoothed my dress back into place and ran fingers through my hair, glad I hadn't twisted it into a fancy updo. Bryce swatted my rear as he walked past, looking pleased with himself in his unbuttoned shirt and pants.

"What else is on the menu?" he asked, winking at me with a lecherous gleam in his eye. "I already know what I want for dessert."

"Bryce!" I said, laughing. "You're incorrigible."

He wrapped his arms around me from behind as I tested the dishes I had set to simmer on the stove. "One of my best qualities." He pressed into me further. "But not my best feature."

"Careful or I'll burn the potatoes," I said, turning my head to give his cheek a quick peck.

"Fine," he said, releasing me. "Food now, more anniversary later."

"Deal," I said. "Go ahead and sit down, I'll bring the food out."

He leaned over and kissed me breathless before leaving the room. I could hear him exclaiming over the decorations as he entered the dining room, and it gratified me. He was in such a good mood. This was the Bryce I'd fallen in love with, the one I'd wanted to spend my life with. Unfortunately, this one didn't show up very often anymore. More days than not, Bryce was irritable and didn't want much to do with me unless he wanted sex. I wasn't even sure we'd had a real conversation in weeks beyond the day-to-day business of being married, checking in, making household decisions.

Otherwise he was on the phone or off with the Reverend, running this errand or that. I didn't think he had any other clients except for the church anymore, though he never spoke to me about it. From Stacy's remarks when I saw her, he still confided in her, which caused me to burn with jealousy. I didn't understand why my husband had become a stranger, but I worked every day to do things to please him and bring him back.

Today I had succeeded.

Dinner turned out perfectly, and Bryce praised every bite. We talked about the church and about what I was learning reading the commentaries from the library, and how I was enjoying volunteering to read to kids there as well. We played footsie under the table like we were just starting to date, and we didn't even make it to the real dessert before Bryce scooped me into his arms and carried me to the bedroom, blowing out the candles on the way.

The clock read after midnight when I stirred. I was naked, tangled in the sheets, and Bryce's arm hung heavy over my waist. Bryce had changed my plans for the evening; not that I was complaining, but I did want to share my news before we fell asleep for the night, or else I'd have to wait until tomorrow night to tell him, and it wasn't certain what kind of mood he'd be in.

I slid out from under his arm. He groaned and reached for me. "Where're you goin'?" he mumbled.

"Just going to grab dessert. I'd hate for you to miss out on the strawberry shortcake."

At that, he perked up, if slightly, opening an eye and squinting at me. "Homemade?"

"Is there another kind?"

"Okay," he said, digging his head deeper into the pillow. "But hurry back."

I threw my robe over my shoulders, belting it as I made my way downstairs. The kitchen wasn't too big of a mess, but the dining room was a bit of a disaster. I decided it was worth the extra ten minutes to clear off the table and stack the dishes in the sink. Bryce was probably sleeping again anyway, and he'd be happier coming downstairs in the morning to a cleaner room. I picked up Bryce's coat from the floor in the back room and saw a bouquet of roses wilting on the counter. I hadn't even noticed them. I found a vase and put them in water, hoping they'd perk up by morning, and then readied a tray with strawberry shortcake, two champagne flutes, and a bottle of sparkling cider. Stopping in the dining room, I grabbed the presents we'd also neglected and stacked the plates on top of them, then took the stairs very carefully.

Sure enough, Bryce hadn't moved since I'd left. I set the tray on the dresser and turned on the dimmer switch, lighting the room very slightly. Enough to see but still maintain the mood I desired. Bryce stirred as the lights came up, blinking at me from the bed as a lazy smile grew across his face.

"Ready for more?" he asked, and I almost rolled my eyes. He was like a teenager tonight.

"Let's have dessert," I said.

"That's what I'm saying," he teased, throwing off the blanket and giving me a full view in case I wasn't sure what he meant.

I laughed. "How about we have actual dessert first, and then we'll move on to second dessert."

"And maybe third."

I wasn't sure that was physically possible, but what did I know? He could give it his best shot as long as I got to tell him about the baby first. I carried the tray to the bed and set it on his lap before removing the gifts and opening the cider. Bryce watched my every move, his eyes gleaming hungrily, and I was pretty sure it wasn't for the cake. We fed each other piece by piece, and when I licked the last of the whipped cream off his thumb, his muscles coiled and I could tell he was about to pounce.

"Wait," I said, holding up my hands and sitting back. "We didn't do presents."

"They can wait," he growled.

"Come on, Bryce. Our anniversary is technically over but it's still kind of the same day. Let's open them and then you can jump me."

He paused, pretending to contemplate my request, and then nodded, eyes sparkling. "That's a deal I can take."

I handed him his gifts, keeping the small box he'd brought for me in my lap. I'd added a second gift to the album, but I pointed to the album first. "Open that one," I said.

Raising an eyebrow, he complied. His face softened when he saw what it was. "Julia," he said. "It's great." He flipped through a few pages. "Where did you get all the pictures?"

"Nancy and the Reverend shared quite a few with me. Other friends."

"Did they all know you were doing this?"

"Yup," I said. "Surprised?"

"Very," he said, and I could tell he was astonished that everyone had kept it from him. Good. The expression was genuine, and I was relieved no one had spilled the beans.

"My turn?" I asked, and he looked up, closing the book and setting it aside.

"Yes. We can look through this together tomorrow, okay?"

"It's a date." I removed the paper from around a long rectangular box. A jewelry box. I opened the top and gasped. "Bryce, its . . . it's absolutely beautiful." Winking at me from the velvet interior of the box was a necklace encrusted with diamonds and emeralds. It was delicate, not too flashy, but gorgeous and bold at the same time.

"The emeralds match your eyes," he said. "Can I help you put it on? I'd love to see you wearing only my necklace."

My entire body flushed, and my tongue went dry. I nodded, since I wasn't capable of speech, and he lifted the necklace from the box, clasping it around my neck as I lifted my hair out of the way.

He took advantage of my exposed neck to start kissing his way across my neck and shoulder. He lowered the edge of my robe, exposing more skin, and I was tempted to let him keep going.

"Just one more," I said on a groan. "One more and then I'm all yours."

"I think you're already all mine," he said, laughter in his voice. He was so right. I belonged to him.

"Please," I whispered, trying to keep my wits as he drove me wild.

Bryce leaned back on a groan. "Okay, fine. Let's look at what this last gift is."

"It's the best one," I said, pulling my robe up as I turned around. I didn't want Bryce to be distracted.

He opened the package and stared at it, confusion in his eyes. At the grocery store, there was a small clothing section. I'd found a bib that said, "Daddy's my favorite," and I'd known exactly how to share the news.

I stared at Bryce, waiting for his reaction. He stared at the bib, running his finger over the words, forehead creasing. A small muscle in his jaw twitched, and I thought he might be trying to rein in his emotion. Bryce wasn't much for crying. It filled my heart to think that he might be so joyful over our tiny miracle that he would have to work to hold back the tears. Finally, he looked up at me, but instead of pleasure in his eyes, I saw anger.

"What does this mean?"

My laugh was awkward, uncomfortable. It seemed pretty obvious the message I was trying to send. "Um, what do you think it means?"

"You're pregnant?"

I nodded. "We're going to be parents, Bryce!" I expected him to hug me, to shout for joy, to do anything but continue to stare at the bib in disbelief.

"But how is that possible?" he asked. "You're on birth control."

"Yes, and Dr. Herbert explained the risks. I've been thinking about it, and either the odds were just in our favor, or we miscalculated when it was safe to stop using condoms after my last shot."

"We?" Bryce's voice was quiet.

"I miscalculated," I corrected myself. "I'll know more once I see Dr. Herbert and find out when we conceived."

Bryce was shaking his head, still not making eye contact. "I can't believe this."

"It's a surprise, for sure," I said, scrambling for the right words. "But surely this is God's will? If we did everything we could to prevent this, and it happened anyway . . . Bryce, this is our little miracle baby." I placed my hand over my abdomen, marveling that there was life in there.

"But apparently we *didn't* do everything we could to prevent it, if you couldn't even look at a fucking *calendar* to see when you were actually protected. How could you be so stupid, Julia?"

I reared back as if he'd slapped me. He may as well have, and with the fire in his eyes it wasn't out of the realm of possibility that he still would. Bryce rarely swore. He said cuss words were a poor man's attempt at salvaging his pride. Now, though, he used them as if he'd been saying them regularly for years. I scooted as far from him as possible while still staying on the bed.

Bryce grabbed the album I'd given him and heaved it across the room, where it bounced off the wall before landing on the carpet, open, spine broken. The tray went the way of the book, cider arcing through the air, glittering in the dim light for a moment before splashing across surfaces all over the room, including Bryce's album.

"Dammit, Julia," Bryce was still ranting. "This wasn't part of the plan. We were waiting. What the hell are we supposed to do now?"

I opened my mouth, but he held up a hand. "I don't want to hear it. Happy fucking anniversary, sweetheart." He stormed out of the room, slamming the door behind him.

It was several minutes before I could move, raising shaking fingers to my face, to my neck. Though he hadn't touched me, I felt blows all over my body. I took deep breaths and set about cleaning up the mess Bryce had left behind. I didn't want to leave the room, so I used extra bath towels to wipe surfaces. Everything would have to be cleaned again tomorrow. I dabbed at the pages of the album, but they were already wrinkled beyond repair. I could probably get it reprinted, but it was so sad to see it in this state.

That's when it all hit me, what had transpired. We had gone from being giddy, happy, in love, to screaming and destruction in a matter of seconds. I'd thought bringing the news to our anniversary was the best way I could have told him, but that was when I assumed he would be as happy as I was. Instead, I'd ruined the best night we'd had in months.

Refusing to go back to the bed we'd shared less than an hour ago, I climbed into one of the chairs and curled in on myself, sobs shaking my entire body until I finally fell into an exhausted, dreamless sleep.

Her limbs feel heavy, though her spirit is soaring with a sense of freedom. She glances at the mess the bathroom has become, the puddles of water dotting the marble floor, the overturned bottles of makeup, the drawers hanging ajar. Through the open door to the bedroom, a backpack sits on the bed, zippered mouth gaping, waiting to be filled with the clothes strewn about. He would be so angry to see how disorganized everything is. Everything has a place. Business, possessions, people. To him, there is little difference between the latter two.

Chapter 26

Bryce left early the next morning, before I was even awake. He hadn't been back to the bedroom, but there was a note on the door that said simply, "Tell no one." I showered and straightened the bedroom as best I could before going back downstairs, though I needed to go back to make sure all the glass had been cleared away. As I'd anticipated, there was no saving the album, and I made a mental note to call the company and have it reprinted.

I went about my tasks robotically, washing the dishes from the night before, taking down the twinkle lights and throwing the candlesticks away. Within a couple of hours, all evidence of our celebration and subsequent altercation was erased, and everything was as it should be. In its place. Including me. The numbness that had gotten me through the morning was wearing off, and I needed distraction.

Remembering the commentaries I'd picked up from the library, I decided to immerse myself in study. I'd left them in the car in my hurry to get everything ready for Bryce, and I headed for the garage to retrieve them. Though I wasn't going anywhere, my hand automatically reached for my keys on the hook, as they did every time I left the house. Except this time they met only air. I paused with the door to the garage half-open, staring at the empty key hooks in confusion. Had I forgotten to bring the keys in with me?

I hurried to my car. The commentaries were there in the

passenger seat, where I'd left them, but the keys were nowhere. I thought back to the day before, and I knew for certain I'd brought them in, because I'd double-checked to make sure they were on the correct hook before Bryce got home. Had he taken them? If so, it certainly wasn't by mistake.

Back inside the house, I searched for my phone to text Bryce about the keys. It wasn't on the charger, or in the kitchen or bedroom. It appeared my phone had gone the way of my keys, and I couldn't even call to confirm that my husband had, in effect, grounded me.

I made my way to my parlor and pulled out my Bible, desperate to find some justification for Bryce's behavior. Had I disobeyed him in some way? It wasn't even certain that it had been my faulty math that caused the pregnancy. I could simply be one of the rare instances where it didn't work. Even Dr. Herbert had cautioned that the shot, while one of the most effective methods of birth control, was still not one hundred percent effective. Nothing was. And Bryce refused to double up methods.

No, I shook my head at myself. I wasn't going to blame Bryce. In fact, I didn't want to blame anyone. I wanted to thank God for this miracle, for this life growing inside of me. It was something to be celebrated, not mourned, not blamed upon someone. It had been a shock, certainly, but I knew Bryce would come around. I closed my Bible and sank to my knees next to the chair, sending up prayers of thanks to God, and begging for His intervention in Bryce's heart to show him that this was a good thing, that our child would be the best thing in our marriage yet.

It was midafternoon when the doorbell rang. Only a few people had the code to the gate, so I wasn't surprised to see Nancy standing on the front steps, holding a casserole dish.

"Bryce said he wasn't sure you'd be up for making dinner," she commented as I invited her inside. "So I had Margot whip up an extra helping of our dinner for you."

"Thank you, Nancy, that's very kind," I said. "I was so focused on getting things ready for our dinner last night, I hadn't planned for the rest of the week. I was going to go to the store today, but . . ."

She smiled, sympathy in her eyes. "Well, now you don't have to worry about it." She breezed through to the kitchen as if she owned the place, setting the casserole in the fridge. "Instructions are written on the foil. Just pop it in about forty-five minutes before you plan to eat."

I dropped into a chair. "I don't know when we're going to eat," I said, tears threatening. "I don't have my phone." I hadn't anticipated the hollow feeling that being left completely cut off would leave me with. Bryce had even taken his laptop. I'd almost crushed Nancy in a hug when she arrived, would have if she hadn't been holding the dish, and it had only been a few hours.

"Bryce will be home around six, dear," Nancy said. "And you'll work it all out."

"Did he . . ." I looked at her, wondering how much he had told her.

"Of course, and I'm tickled pink to be a grandmother." She took the seat next to me, reached over and patted my stomach, which felt a little weird, but also comforting. Nancy was supportive of my baby, even if Bryce wasn't yet. And if Nancy was, Bryce would be. I sighed, feeling a weight lift from my shoulders.

"I just wish he'd talked to me first," I said. "It's our baby."

"He's angry, Julia. Surely you can understand that." Nancy's voice was as smooth and logical as ever, but this time her words grated on me, dissipating the appreciation I'd felt toward her only seconds earlier.

"Actually, Nancy, I don't understand this time." I stood up and began pacing the kitchen. "I understand that it was shocking. I understand that it wasn't how we'd planned it. But I don't understand how this miracle could elicit such rage." I spun to face her. "He acted like this was my fault, that I'd done it on purpose. To what end?"

"Isn't it your fault?"

My jaw dropped. "No. It's not. And my *baby* is not something I want to spend time blaming or being blamed for. He or she is loved, wanted, welcomed already." I slumped back against the counter. "At least by one of its parents." I looked down at her. "Did he say why he took my things?"

Nancy stood. "Bryce was afraid you wouldn't act responsibly. He thought you might do something irrational, like call your parents, or try to visit them."

I crossed my arms, unwilling to admit that I had thought to do just that before I'd realized I was stranded.

"Part of being a wife is being willing to take responsibility where it's needed. Bryce needs to be able to trust you. And he did trust that you knew your body and could make sure to do your part to stay with the plan the two of you had laid out together." Nancy folded her hands in front of her. "I can see now why he was so upset."

Anger bubbled through my veins. "Was I supposed to just not let myself become pregnant? Is that how this works?"

She shrugged. "The Reverend and I chose not to have children of our own. We decided we could best serve God by ministering to the lost children of others. We took every precaution, and trusted each other to do our respective parts. If I'd screwed up, we never would have met Bryce."

They'd mentioned that decision long ago, back when I'd first met them. "How did you meet Bryce?" I asked. "You've never told me that full story. Only that you connected with him as a teenager and helped him get into a good school. No one talks about the family he came from."

"If Bryce wanted you to know about that, Julia, he would tell you. If I were you, I'd focus on your current family affairs instead of digging up things best left buried." Nancy's rebuke was sharp, but instead of quelling under it as I normally would, my residual anger and sudden certainty that they were all hiding something from me caused me to stand up straighter.

"Thank you for the casserole, Nancy," I said. "I think I need to spend some time in prayer, considering ways to be a better wife through this situation." The words tasted bitter on my tongue, but they did the trick.

Nancy stepped forward and hugged me, her arms stiff, her embrace cold. "Once you and Bryce talk through everything, let's have dinner to celebrate. I can't wait to start designing the nursery!" With a wave and a swirl of expensive perfume, she was gone.

As soon as her car engine started out front, I sank back into the kitchen chair and buried my face in my hands. My entire being was a riot of emotions, bombarding every part of me. My thoughts, my beliefs, everything was suddenly cast into the harshest light possible, the light of questioning and doubt, things I'd learned over the past year and a half never to allow into my heart. But now that they were there, I had a difficult time dispelling them.

Dinner was ready by the time Bryce got home a few hours later. The table was set and I was pulling the dish out of the oven when the garage door opened. I continued what I was doing, ignoring my husband as he stepped inside and dropped his briefcase on the counter, though my heart hammered in my chest. I watched out of the corner of my eye as he put two sets of keys on the key hooks, and as he stepped into the kitchen and pulled his phone out of his pocket to plug into the charger before pulling my phone out of his briefcase and setting it next to his.

He stood watching me as I carried the casserole and side dishes to the table, and as I filled the water glasses. I'd decided we would eat in the kitchen tonight. I wasn't ready to be with him in the dining room again. I was surprised when he silently took his seat instead of berating me for my attitude. I expected some sort of commentary on my unwifely behavior, but he simply waited for me to take my seat across from him before holding out his hand.

"Let's pray, darling," he said, and I hesitantly placed my palm in his.

His grip was firm as he began to pray. "Dear God, thank you for this food that was prepared for us, for the gentle hands that made this meal possible, and for the generous feet that brought it directly to our door." His hand tightened around mine. "We pray that you would be with us despite the toxic spirit that lies between us, and that you would speak truth to our souls so that our lips would speak truth to each other." My fingers were tingling, losing feeling, and still he squeezed tighter, ignoring my efforts to loosen his hold. "We pray forgiveness for the words and deeds that led us here, and that you would be present as we take responsibility and change the plans you have laid out for us." I could no longer concentrate on the words coming from Bryce's mouth as my fingers were crushed in his hand. My eyes popped open to find him watching me even as he prayed. The iciness I saw in them frightened me more than the increasing pressure on my fingers, but I refused to cry out. Instead, I bit the inside of my cheek until finally, mercifully, he released my fingers and my gaze. "Amen."

Without another word, Bryce began eating as I cradled my hand in my lap. Refusing to let him see weakness, I took my fork in my left hand and ate as well, though the casserole was tasteless. After we'd eaten in silence for a few minutes, Bryce finally spoke.

"It was nice of Nancy to bring a casserole."

I nodded. "It was."

"You should be able to make it to the store tomorrow."

"Will I?"

"Yes, Julia." He tone reflected irritation. "I only took your keys today to make sure you didn't do something drastic before we had a chance to talk."

"We could have talked last night."

"I wasn't in a good place to talk last night."

I took another bite, chewing slowly as my anger burned. "And you're in a good place to talk now?"

"I think it's important that we do talk."

"Okay." I put my fork down and gave him my full attention. "What shall we talk about?"

"We're having a baby."

I resisted the urge to roll my eyes. "We are."

"That's going to change things around here."

"Indeed."

He wiped his mouth, narrowing his eyes at me. "Are you being purposely disrespectful, or is this a side effect of pregnancy?"

Widening my eyes, I gave him my most innocent look. "I'm not trying to be disrespectful at all. I'm just trying to follow your lead. How would you like me to respond?"

"What are we supposed to do now, Julia?" Bryce asked, and I saw the first chink in his armor. He looked almost . . . sad. Which annoyed me more.

"Bryce," I said, leaning forward, earnest. There was still time to salvage the situation, and I was seized by a sudden determination to do just that. I could set aside my anger and disappointment at his reaction if he could set aside his determination to find someone to blame and just be happy about the baby. "I don't know how it happened. I don't know if I miscalculated, or if it was a fluke, or a miracle. But I'm not sorry."

His brow furrowed, and he opened his mouth to speak, but I laid a finger over his lips, surprised when he allowed it.

"I will apologize for the change in plans, only because I know how important our plans are to you. But maybe . . . maybe this is God's plan? He doesn't make mistakes."

"But people do."

"Fair enough." I nodded. "But I can't look at our baby as a mistake, Bryce." I grabbed his hand with my uninjured one and pulled it to my stomach. "Our baby is in there. A bit of you and a bit of me. What could be better? God will use our baby in amazing ways. I'm sure of it."

Bryce's features softened as he stared at our hands on my stomach, and I saw the moment it became real for him. And the next moment, when the wall went back up. He frowned and snatched his hand away, scooting back and standing up.

"I have some work to do. I'll call and make an appointment with Dr. Herbert for next week to see if you're actually pregnant, and we'll decide where to go from there." He stalked out of the kitchen.

Tears pricked my eyes as I sat back in my chair, deflated. I'd seen him for a moment, the man I married, the man who could be excited about the baby. And then he was gone. Whisked away by this stranger who inhabited Bryce's body now. Unless the man I married was the myth, and this was the real Bryce. The thought was too depressing to dwell on for long, and I busied myself cleaning up one-handed before wrapping my hand in an ice pack and retiring to my parlor for the rest of the evening.

Chapter 27

I t had been a while since I'd spent time in the café after church. I'd been either at the Gathering or observing since before the wedding. In some ways I was gratified to see my old Bible study still hung out there after service . . . less so when Jenny gave a vague wave and turned back to the group without greeting me fully. Not that I blamed her—or any of them—for the irritated looks they sent my way. I'd abandoned them for a different group, hadn't even spoken to most of them in over a year. It would have been ridiculous for me to expect them to welcome me back, to open up as if I'd never left.

Still, I wished that they had.

I got a mug of hot tea and sat in a chair in the corner, watching the people in the lobby socialize in groups, hug, laugh, chat, and then eventually trickle out of the building. The Bible study group left, and I was the only one in the café. I knew the barista only stayed because I was still there, but I couldn't get myself to move, though Nancy had said I could wait at their house.

I'd been asked not to attend the Gathering for the time being. Not knowing my condition, it wouldn't be safe for me to attempt Oneness, and given the conflict between Bryce and myself, it might hinder his chance at Oneness if I was in the same room. In fact, Nancy explained, if Dr. Herbert confirmed the pregnancy, I would not be invited back until after the baby was born and I was deemed ready again. Apparently my spirit would be too focused on growing the child to connect with God in the same way. "Pregnancy is its own form of Oneness, Julia," the Reverend had said. "A beautiful miracle that only women are able to experience. It only makes sense that you would give Bryce every opportunity to continue communing with God in this way for the duration of your pregnancy."

My spirit missed the connection with God. It had become almost an addiction, and so much a staple of my life that I didn't know what to do with myself, knowing that elsewhere in this building, God was granting His presence to a group of people, but that I wasn't allowed to be there. Now I knew why they didn't tell the greater congregation about their Chosen group. It could definitely foster resentment if people knew what they were missing.

Time slowed to a crawl until Bryce showed up to bring me to lunch with the Reverend and Nancy. He'd barely spoken to me for the rest of the week, but around other people he was as congenial as ever. He tucked my arm under his as we walked through the church, held doors for me, and pulled my chair out for me at lunch.

Once we'd all been served and prayers had been said, the Reverend looked at us. "How is everything?"

I wanted to answer, to rant about how Bryce acted like I didn't exist, how he was acting like a child because I was pregnant and he didn't want me to be, but instead I looked at Bryce, deferring the question to him.

"It could be better," he admitted. "But we're working through it."

I snorted.

"Julia," the Reverend said. "That was very unbecoming. Do you have something to add to Bryce's assessment?"

Suddenly I felt like I was a teenager again, being scolded by my mother for being rude to my aunt Ruth. "No, Reverend."

"Are you sure?"

I looked at Bryce, and there was warning in his eyes, but a glance at the Reverend sealed my decision. The Reverend's expression was open, curious, sympathetic, and I wanted him to understand my side. I didn't want him to think I was just acting immature and refusing to respect my husband. "Actually, I'm very saddened by how this week has gone."

"How so, Julia?"

"I assume you know about our news," I said, and the Reverend inclined his head to indicate that he did. "I was very excited, and Bryce became so angry that it scared me. He still refuses to talk to me until I take the blame. I don't feel like he's fully recognizing what a miracle the baby is, and how God can use every situation to His glory."

The Reverend leaned back. "I understand your disappointment, Julia, and I think Bryce does, too." He folded his hands, searching for the words he wanted to use. "I wonder if you're being a bit stubborn as well, as you're accusing Bryce of being."

I opened my mouth to argue, but he held up a hand. "Just hear me out, okay?"

My mouth snapped shut with a click of my teeth and I nodded.

"God has been very explicit with me and with Bryce about the plans for our lives. It's a gift that we do not take lightly, as most are stuck blindly feeling their way. It's like having night vision goggles on a dark path. We know exactly where we are meant to go, and what is waiting for us if we follow our assigned path."

"I get that," I said. "I know that you have a special connection with God, and I respect that."

"Good," the Reverend continued. "And now I need you to hear the next part." He took a deep breath. "When you became pregnant, it was like you grabbed Bryce by the arm and yanked him off the path he was trying to lead you down. He could see the path, see the goal, in a way that you couldn't possibly understand, and now you've pulled him off the path, into the brambles, and along a path that was not laid out by God. It will take some adjustment for him to accept that this is the path he's on now."

Bryce had been silent during the Reverend's explanation, but now he turned to me, genuine emotion in his eyes for the first time since I'd announced the pregnancy. "I wish I could have explained it that well. I don't mean to take it out on you, Julia, but your carelessness has pointed us in a direction that is . . . unexpected. I promise I will try to do better, but I need your understanding as well."

I almost had to bite my tongue to keep from screaming when he mentioned my carelessness, but I knew that would just get us back to where we started, so instead I nodded. "I'm sorry," I said, the words tasting like vomit on their way out. "I'll try harder."

And I would. As much as I resented making the apology, I knew it was necessary to move forward. I needed Bryce's support for the pregnancy, and the baby needed him to be a proud and happy father. So I would swallow my pride for the sake of my child.

But I was more determined than ever to figure out my husband's past, and why everyone was so intent on hiding it from me.

Chapter 28

I waited until things calmed down a bit before putting my plan into action. If everything went well, I could talk to the woman who had sent the letters, figure out what Bryce was hiding, and hopefully move on. I prayed it was something minor that he was simply embarrassed about. But I knew I couldn't move forward without figuring it out, and there was no way I could talk to Bryce about it again.

Bryce was a little less crabby than he had been when I first told him about the pregnancy, but little things would still set him off. I stayed to my own corners of the house for the most part, except when we ate dinner and when we slept. After getting the confirmation from Dr. Herbert that I was, indeed, pregnant, the first thing Bryce wanted to know was about sexual activity. The good doctor had clapped him on the back and assured him that it was completely safe to resume activity, which Bryce took to heart as soon as we got home from the appointment.

There was no connection anymore, however. He was emotionally distant from me in a way that he'd never been before. He used my body, but it was just sex. I couldn't shake the feeling that if I could just figure out his past, I could reconnect with him so that we could look forward to a brighter future.

The morning my plan was to take effect was like any other morning. I made Bryce breakfast and he grunted a thank-you before opening the paper. Twenty minutes later and he was out the door.

Normally I would have started with a workout and progressed to chores, but instead I grabbed my purse and jumped in the car once I was sure Bryce had a good head start.

I hadn't driven out of the city since our honeymoon, hadn't even been out of our neighborhood in months. My bubble had grown very small, and as I passed the city limits and sped into the open countryside, it felt a bit like flying. I turned the radio up and appreciated the rolling hills and curving roads. I allowed my mind to wander away from the church and Bryce and everything that kept me pinned down, and I imagined that I lived out here, in the open air, that I was free to run barefoot through the grass or sit in a sheep pen and read a book. Free to be dirty, to be frivolous, to waste time.

Too soon, I started seeing signs for Meadowsville. Population eight hundred. According to the GPS on the car, the address on the envelopes was on the outer edges of the town, almost out in the country, but still in view of the town. I drove slowly through the town, surprised at how dusty and grungy it looked compared to the countryside. There was a diner that appeared to be the only eating establishment in town, and a small grocery store. A seedy-looking motel completed the main street area, and then I was driving back out of the town. I crested a hill, and at the bottom stood a lonely-looking shack under the shade of a giant tree.

Bingo.

I parked in front of the house and sat in the car, squinting at the windows to see if there was any sign of life. A curtain fluttered, and a dog barked. There were no neighbors to speak of, as if the very town stayed as far away from this house as it could. Taking a deep breath, I screwed up my courage and got out of the car. A crude cement pathway led through a gate, which was falling off its hinges, and up to a faded green door behind a tattered screen door. The lawn was dotted with piles of dog poop, as if no one could be bothered to clean up after the animal. As I passed under the tree, I saw the remains of what may have been a tree house at one point, though only a few boards hung from the branches.

Once I approached, the dog inside started barking with enthusiasm.

"Shut up, ya mutt!" someone screamed at him.

Before I could knock, the inner door swung open. A woman filled the doorway, peering at me through the screen door, wearing faded jeans and a Mickey Mouse T-shirt. Her hair was pulled back, but graying strands that had escaped the rubber band hung limply around her face. The wrinkles in her face were deep, and the skin sagged as if her face used to fill it out better. She took a drag from her cigarette, emphasizing the hollowness of her cheekbones. "Yeah?"

I smoothed the front of my blouse nervously. I'd wanted to dress nice, but not too nice; however, I wished I'd worn a pair of jeans. Or even sweat pants. My yellow capris and white blouse were a violent contrast to her outfit. "Are you Harriet Schmit?"

"Who's askin'?"

My fingers shook as I extended a hand. "My name is Julia Covington," I said. "I'm married to Bryce Covington." I searched her face for any sign of recognition, but she remained dispassionate. Her face was somewhat shadowed, and I took a tiny step back, hoping she would reflect my movements.

"So?" she said, staying where she was. "That fancy-pants name s'posed to impress me?" She turned around. "Bruno! Shut up!" The dog had continued barking but it was muffled. "Locked him in the bedroom. He hates that but I didn't figure you'd want dog prints all over that pretty outfit."

"Th-thank you," I said, clearing my throat. "Um, do you think I could come in?"

She regarded me, leaning forward to peer around me and look at my car. I gasped when I saw her eyes. Only one other person had eyes that blue. Eyes that were pinned to me after I made the noise. "What did you say you needed, Miss, uh . . ."

"Covington," I said. "Mrs. Julia Covington. Um." I should have rehearsed this part. I was so focused on getting here, I didn't give much thought to what I would say. "Listen, Ms. Schmit."

"Harriet."

"Harriet. You can call me Julia." I sent her a tentative smile. "I'm trying to find out some information about my husband, and I think you might be able to help me."

She frowned. "What did you say his name was?"

"Bryce, but—"

"Don't know no Bryce. Sorry, Julia." She stepped back as if to close the door. I reached into my purse, pulling out the letter I'd stuffed in there before leaving.

"Wait," I said, waving the envelope at her. "Do you recognize this? Did you send this?"

Harriet froze, eyes wide as she looked at the envelope, then she snatched it from my hand. "Where'd you get this?"

"In a box of my husband's things," I said. "It was with what looked like childhood memorabilia." I paused. I already sounded like the sneaky wife. I probably was the sneaky wife. "My husband is very closed about his past. I used these letters to track you down in hopes that you could help."

"Your husband's name is Bryce?" she whispered, still staring at the envelope.

"It is."

"Anything stand out about him?"

I tried to decipher what she meant. "Dark hair, two dimples . . . his eyes are the exact color of yours."

She clutched the envelope to her chest. "Bruce," she gasped. "That's why I couldn't find him. He changed his name. Of course."

Her eyes were miles away, as if I wasn't even standing there. "Harriet," I said, trying to bring her back. I reached out and touched her hand softly, and she jumped. "Harriet. If Bryce and Bruce are the same person, I think you can help me."

She nodded and turned, as if in a trance, walking back into the house. I followed, looking behind me, feeling watched, though I knew nobody was there.

Harriet set the tray with iced tea and cookies on the coffee table, and her hands shook, clinking the glasses together. "Sorry it's not more fancy," she said, hands fluttering uselessly. "I wasn't expecting no one."

I infused my voice with as much sincerity as possible. "I'm sorry I didn't call. It's my fault for catching you off guard."

I perched on the couch as she sank into the recliner next to me. Everything was covered in blankets, and a thick layer of dark dog hair carpeted the floor and every surface. I regretted wearing yellow and white even more. I'd have to get home and get a load of laundry started before Bryce returned.

Harriet sat back and stared at me, her eyes roving over every feature. "So you're Bruce's wife. He got himself a pretty one."

I averted my gaze, focusing on a particularly large clump of dog hair under the TV. "Thank you. He's a very handsome man."

She pursed her lips. "Do you . . . I mean, can I . . ."

I pulled out my phone. "Would you like to see a picture?"

Nodding, she wrung her hands anxiously. I pulled up a picture from our wedding and showed it to her. She stared, tears filling her eyes and spilling over. I scrolled through several pictures of the two of us, and soon she was smiling, tears flowing freely. "He was always so handsome," she said. "Scrawny, but mostly because he was always runnin' and we didn't have much to give him to bulk up." She looked at me. "Is he a good husband?"

I hesitated. This was not the time to get into my marital issues. "The happiest day of my life was when I married your son."

A smile split her face. "You guys have any kids?"

My heart stuttered. "Um, actually, we just found out we're expecting our first."

Harriet glanced down at my stomach. "You can't tell."

"It's still early," I said, rubbing my abdomen. "But he's in there. Or she."

She reached out to clasp my hand. "Bruce will be such a great daddy."

Squeezing her hand back, I didn't comment. "You said that he was always running? Was he on the track team?"

"Oh no, nothing like that." She laughed. "He was always gettin' picked on by this group o' boys. They picked on the little 'uns. He didn't think I knew, but I knew."

"What else can you tell me about him?" I asked, leaning forward. Already this was helping. Poor Bryce, picked on. No wonder he worked so hard to stay at the top and in control.

"He was always workin' on his homework, always writin' somethin'. He was such a mama's boy when he was little, but after Sissy came along, he grew up fast. Had to." She shrugged, guilt radiating from her entire body. "I wasn't the best mama to him. I let a lot of bad people into this house. Maybe if I'd done a better job, he woulda stuck around."

"He has a sister?"

Another smile. "Brenda. Though we all called her Sissy." The smile fell, and the difference in her face when she was smiling and when she was frowning was dramatic. She'd been a beautiful woman once. "She calls every few months now. Ran off with her high school boyfriend. She was never the same after Bruce left. Nightmares for months. Course, that could have more to do with Dwayne."

"Dwayne?"

She looked at me, almost seeming startled to see me there, as if she'd been sucked into the past for a short time. "Guy I dated back when Bruce was still here. Let him move in and everything. I did that a lot back when Bruce's dad and me were on the rocks. He'd move out and I'd move in a replacement. Hard on the kids, I suppose, but I needed help."

My heart hurt as the picture of Bryce's childhood became a little clearer, and I had to work to keep a neutral expression on my face. I didn't want Harriet to feel that I was judging her in any way. All I wanted were answers. "Why did Bruce leave?" Using his real name felt strange on my tongue, but it was how she remembered him.

Her brows veed, and her eyes turned stormy, just like Bryce's did when he got angry, but her anger wasn't directed toward me. "It was that man."

"Dwayne?" I guessed.

"No," she said, her voice taking on a protective note. "I mean. Sure. Dwayne wasn't the best guy, but he didn't deserve that. And that man got hold of Bruce and he changed."

"What man?"

"He was a church man. A pastor or something. Showed up in town one day and 'fore you knew it Bruce was with him all the time. It wasn't right, a grown man and a teenage boy hangin' out. But Bruce seemed happier and I had my own issues. And then that night . . ."

I'd scooted so far forward on the couch that I was in danger of falling off. "What night?"

"The night Bruce left." Harriet was answering my questions, but she had drifted off again. I was sure she was back at that night, and tears spilled down her cheeks at whatever she was remembering. "It was the night Dwayne died."

"I'm so sorry," I said, reaching over and covering her hand with mine. Her cigarette burned between her fingers, forgotten, and I reached over and plucked it out of her hand, resting it in an overflowing ashtray. "You lost Dwayne and Bruce in the same night? What—what happened to Dwayne?"

Harriet's eyes found mine and focused in. "Bruce killed him."

———

An hour later, I was speeding home, my mind a jumble of everything I had learned from Harriet. She'd told me about how Dwayne's death was an accident, that Bryce had been defending her. She'd told the cops he hadn't even been there, that she'd wielded the bat that struck the deadly blow in self-defense. It was a pretty open-and-shut case, but by the time all the dust had cleared, there was no trace of Bruce.

Her voice shook as she told me about how the Reverend showed up, in that calm way of his, and took her son away without so much as a note to tell her where he was. How, months later, she'd jumped for joy to receive a letter from Bruce with some money in it and vague assurances that he was doing well. He'd kept a PO box for a while, which is where she'd sent all the letters, but then they started coming back to her and she hadn't heard from him again. There'd been no explanation from him and no contact since.

She'd begged me to stay when I stood to leave, and asked for some sort of contact information. I regretted giving my real name, and Bryce's, and counted on Harriet's apparently patchy memory to forget our last name, at least. If she tracked him down now, it would all be over. He'd find out what I'd done.

I wished more than anything that Bryce could have confided this to me himself. How much better might I have understood him if I'd known how he grew up? He didn't have the family relationships I had, despite what he said about the Reverend and Nancy. I might have been more patient, more understanding, helped him learn rather than expecting him to know how to be a husband automatically.

Insistent beeping brought me out of my reverie, and I saw the low-tire-pressure light blink on two seconds before a loud bang caused my car to swerve back and forth across the road. My heart beating out of my chest, I managed to guide the car to a stop on the shoulder. The road was deserted, so I got out to see that my front tire had blown.

"Shit."

Climbing back in my car, I pulled out my phone. Normally I would call Bryce, but I couldn't tell him where I was. I dug through my purse for the AAA card, breathing a sigh of relief when I found it. Hopefully I could get the tow set up before I let Bryce know I would be late.

Thanks to GPS, I was able to tell AAA exactly where I was. Unfortunately, they wouldn't be able to get a truck out to me for a couple of hours. They suggested I call a friend to pick me up and leave the key.

"Thanks for nothing," I grumbled into the phone after hanging up. At that moment, my phone dinged with an incoming text. Bryce. Shit shit shit.

> *Where are you?*

> *Went for a drive. Had some car trouble. Everything okay?*

> *Fine. What's wrong with the car?*

> *Flat tire. Called tow truck.*

> *Need me to come?*

> *No, I'll wait. Dinner may be late.*

> *I'll pick something up.*

> *Thank you. See you at home.*

Love you, Julia.

I love you, Bryce.

I breathed a sigh of relief. He didn't seem to suspect anything, and he was downright cheerful compared to his usual texting style lately. If I could get home and smooth things over, maybe we could get back in rhythm. At least now I had an excuse to smell like cigarette smoke. Bryce didn't have to know whether my tow truck guy was a cigarette-smoking dog owner.

It was almost three hours before the tow truck came. I'd hoped he'd just change the tire there, but he insisted on towing it to the garage and having the guys there change it. Thankfully, they did a much quicker job and had me on my way twenty minutes after arriving.

Still, darkness had fallen by the time I pulled into the garage, feeling dirty, smelly, and emotionally spent. I didn't care what Bryce had brought home. I had missed lunch and I was famished. I was ready to eat and then soak in the tub for an hour before falling into bed. I hoped Bryce wasn't in the mood for more than sleeping.

No lights were on downstairs when I walked in, which I found strange. I expected Bryce to at least have left a couple of lights on, even if he got distracted in his study. Cold Chinese sat on the table, several containers tipped as if they'd been tossed there carelessly.

"Bryce?" I called. The study was empty as well, but I heard a creak from upstairs, so I headed in that direction, hoping I wasn't walking in on an intruder. My heart beat rapidly in my chest, and my breaths came in short gasps. The only light upstairs spilled from my parlor door and my heart stuttered as I came to the doorway.

Bryce sat in the middle of the room, spinning in my chair. The room looked as if it had been hit by a tornado. Every drawer had been dumped, every book thrown off the shelves, and on the desk sat the stack of letters and the tiny wrinkled card Dr. Leeland had given me so long ago I'd almost forgotten about it.

Torn between wanting to explain and wanting to flee, I stood frozen in the doorway, watching as Bryce planted his feet to bring the spinning chair to a stop. He rose, and every muscle in his body was coiled tight. He advanced toward me, and the look in his eyes was pure rage. Spinning on my heel, I ran back into the hallway and down the stairs. I didn't know where I was going, but I knew I had to get away. I pulled open the front door and slammed it behind me, sprinting down the stairs and cutting across the grass. I stumbled through the shadows created by the large overhanging branches of the giant trees lining the driveway. The moon peeked through in small patches like spotlights, illuminating my path. I'd almost reached the gate when the front door slammed again.

My shaking fingers took three tries to punch in the correct code, and at the sound of the gate creaking open, the steady footfalls heading in my direction became faster, more urgent. I slipped through the gate, catching my blouse on the rough metal. Wrenching myself free, I hazarded a glance back, and saw that he was no longer far behind. As I began to run again, so did he, his large steps dwarfing my own. As he pursued me down the street, he closed the gap, and it felt as if I were running in slow motion. I glanced over my shoulder once more, and it cost me. I tripped over the edge of the sidewalk and fell into the soft grass of a carefully manicured lawn. He was on me in seconds.

He pinned me to the ground facedown, breathing hard. "How *dare* you run out on me," he hissed, his breath hot on my ear.

I struggled against him, straining to rid myself of his oppressive weight, but soon I realized it was useless, and I allowed myself to go limp. Sensing surrender, he eased himself off me and rolled me onto my back, holding my wrists as he loomed over me. Bryce pulled me into a sitting position and crouched in front of me. "Come back to the house on your own, or I'll carry you back," he said in a calm voice that didn't match the expression on his face or the weight of his words.

281

I didn't doubt that he would do just that, and my head dropped in defeat. I allowed him to help me to my feet. He brushed the grass off our clothes and ran a gentle hand down my cheek, lingering on a spot that was tender after being pushed into the grass.

"Let's go inside, darling," Bryce said. "We have important things to talk about."

I allowed my husband to tuck my arm under his own and lead me back toward the beautiful house that in that moment felt more like a prison. As he closed the gate behind us, I realized that the gate wasn't there so much to keep people from getting in, but to keep them from getting out.

His door bangs open and Sissy runs into his bedroom, skidding under the bed before he can register anything more than the terror on her face. This fight is worse than the others. Sounds of his mother begging float through his open door. She never begs. She gives as good as she gets, and he never feels sorry for her. This time, concern he didn't know existed in his body flares to life, along with the need to protect his family. He tells his sister to stay where she is and closes the door behind him as he rushes out to the living room.

He rarely comes into this room, so he's not sure if the mess is from the altercation or if it's just how his mother and her boyfriend live. The argument is about his father, who has popped up in town again. Not that the boy would know. He is inconsequential to his biological father. But his father always goes after his mother, and always runs whatever man she has living with her out of town. He'll move in for a while before abandoning them again.

The boyfriend growls at the boy to leave. Their fight is their personal business. He calls the boy's mother a series of degrading names, and swipes at her with a baseball bat. The boy approaches, putting himself between his mother and her boyfriend. The man swings a warning shot, catching the boy on the arm as he raises it in defense, knocking him to the ground. The boy is surprised at the pain, and he is sure his arm is broken. A rage fills him, and as the boyfriend towers over him, threatening to rain more blows on him as his mother screams in the background, the boy is also filled with calm. He welcomes the rage. And he knows the calm comes from elsewhere. It is similar to being One, and he knows his next moves are divinely ordained.

As the bat falls, the boy reaches up with both hands, wrenching it from the man, whose face fills with surprise and confusion as he stumbles back. He grabs for the bat as the boy rises, but his reflexes are dulled by alcohol and the boy steps neatly out of the way. More threatening words fly from the boyfriend's mouth, but they wash over the boy like a summer rain. His arm doesn't even hurt anymore. He smiles at the man, who stops talking and looks at him dumbly.

His vacant look turns to terror as the boy raises the bat, and the expression pulls a laugh from the boy's belly. He was never much good at baseball, but the bat swings true and catches the man on the side of the head. He tumbles like a giant oak, catching the other side of his head on the coffee table as he goes down, and is still. Home run.

His mother's screams change as she rushes to her boyfriend's side. Not her son's. She doesn't look for her daughter. She screams and tries to wake her boyfriend, but he won't wake. His eyes are open, dark orbs staring into nothingness. His dad won't have to run this one out of town. The boy has taken care of it. Protected his family, ungrateful as they will be. He gazes at his mother in disgust before heading back to his room. He pulls Sissy from under his bed and comforts her before tucking her in.

He digs through his bag to find the phone the Reverend gave him and dials a number. In ten minutes, the Reverend walks into the room. Sissy is asleep. He tells the boy to pack what he wants to take. He has taken care of his mother and she will sleep until morning. She hasn't called the police yet. The Reverend holds the bat, the only evidence of the boy's involvement.

The boy doesn't look back as they drive away from the shack. It was never really home. His only twinge of regret is for Sissy, who will have to deal with the aftermath without him.

The Reverend would not allow him to bring her along. He vows to take care of her from afar, as the Reverend had planned to do for him. They drive out of town, and as the lights from the place of nightmares blink out in the rearview mirror, the boy sleeps, deep and dreamless.

Chapter 29

As soon as we were back in the house, Bryce turned on me, shoving me against the door.

"Where were you today, Julia?" he demanded, his eyes wild.

"I went for a drive," I said, my voice small. I didn't know why I was lying to him. He obviously knew where I'd been, but some protective instinct kept me from admitting it. Belatedly I remembered that one of his hobbies was to check in on the location of my phone. I couldn't believe I'd been so careless.

He slammed me against the door again, and I saw stars. His hand came around my throat. "Like hell, you lying bitch. Where. The fuck. Were you?" With each word, he slammed my head against the door again. My vision swam.

"Bryce, I—" I gasped, finding it hard to focus, hard to breathe.

Releasing my neck, he gripped my arm in an iron vise and dragged me up the stairs. He threw me at the chair, and I missed, tumbling to the ground. He didn't move to help as I levered myself up, trying to climb into the chair while my head continued spinning. When I'd finally seated myself, he stepped forward, bracketing my body with his hands on both arms of the chair.

"Let's try a different question and see if you can get that one right." Backing away, he picked up the stack of letters from the desk. "Where did you find these?"

The words seemed to catch in my throat, but I forced them out. "In one of the boxes I went through when you moved in."

He pinched the bridge of his nose. "You've had these for *over a year* and you never thought to mention it?"

There was no good response, so I just shook my head. "I'm sorry," I said, though little sound came out of my mouth. Tears streamed unchecked down my face, and my entire body ached.

"Did you go see her?"

I nodded. "I just—"

"I *told* you I didn't talk about my past, Julia. I asked you to stay out of it. And you couldn't, could you? You just had to go and stick your nose where it didn't belong, didn't you?"

I just stared at him, not sure what sort of answer, if any, he wanted from me.

"What was it like? Was there still dog shit everywhere? Was good ol' Ma taking care of her latest live-in? Were they screaming at each other? Did it smell like an armpit? Do you feel sorry for me now, Julia, growing up like that? Do I have your *pity*?"

"No, Bryce, I—"

"I don't want your fucking pity!" he yelled. "Bruce doesn't exist anymore. I left him behind. He's dead. You should have left him that way."

"I'm sorry—"

"Did she tell you about the guy? What happened the night I left?"

My wide eyes told him all he needed to know. He laughed, then swooped in close, rolling the chair back until it hit the wall.

"Does it frighten you to be married to a murderer, sweetheart? Does it make you shudder to think that these hands that have been all over your body were also used to take a man's life?"

My head wobbled back and forth, a denial. "It was an accident," I said, my voice small, wavering.

He laughed again, louder this time. "Is that what she said? I suppose it looked that way. Maybe it was an accident. But make no mistake, dear wife. I wanted him dead. And then he was."

Bryce walked over to the table and picked up the card with the shelter name on it. "Were you thinking of leaving me, Julia?"

"No," I said. "Never. Dr. Leeland—"

"Ah, the bitch doctor gave it to you. Of course. But why'd you keep it? Why not toss it right away if you had no intention of using it?"

"I don't know," I said. "I just . . . I don't know. I should have thrown it out."

He smiled and pulled a lighter from his pocket. Picking up the letters, he held the lighter to the edge of the top envelope and the ancient paper immediately caught, the fire greedily moving down the stack. Bryce threw the stack in the metal trash can, the card following closely behind. He watched it for a few more seconds, then turned to me. "Better put that out," he said. "I'd hate for you to get burned."

Without another word, he turned and walked from the room. I listened to his footsteps descend the stairs and head into the study. Only then did I move. I ran on unsteady feet to the bathroom, filled the bathroom trash can with water, and came back to dump it on the fire. Once it was out, I closed the door to my parlor, locked it, and slumped against the wall, sobbing.

I ached when I woke up the next morning. I'd fallen asleep in my parlor, and the chaos around me when I opened my eyes brought on a fresh wave of tears. I couldn't look at the mess, or the ashes that were all that remained of the letters, so I slipped out of the room and closed the door behind me. The house was silent, and I couldn't even hear birds singing outside. It was as if every living creature in the vicinity mourned what had happened the night before.

When I entered the bedroom, I was surprised to see that the

bed looked slept in, at least on Bryce's side. He'd left it for me to fix, which I did, automatically. I passed the mirror and realized that I was still filthy from the day before. I stripped out of my clothes, not bothering with a hamper. They would go straight into the trash. A bath had sounded good the night before, but I just wanted to get clean, so I stepped into the shower and turned it on as hot as I could handle it, scrubbing every inch of my body, wincing as I came across sore spots.

Stepping out of the shower, I examined myself in the mirror, noticing the shadowy spots that I'd hoped were dirt, but which hadn't washed off in the scalding water. Bruises from head to toe, with distinctive finger bands around my neck. I chose my outfit carefully to cover up the bruising, including a lightweight scarf.

I wasn't surprised that Bryce hadn't cleaned up the food from the night before; nor was it a shock to see that my car keys were once again gone, along with my phone. I cleaned up the Chinese food and poured myself a bowl of cereal. I'd been on autopilot this morning, but I needed to figure out what to do now.

Bryce could come home tonight completely normal, or on another rampage. There was no way to tell. His pattern would suggest that he might sulk for a while but then go back to normal, and if I stayed in line, he'd have no reason to flip out on me again. But hard as I tried, I always seemed to do something wrong. And now that I knew the full extent of where his anger could lead . . . I shuddered.

Not for the first time recently, I longed to talk to my mom. She didn't even know about the baby yet. If I could just talk with her, mother to daughter, maybe I could sort things out. Maybe I would tell her everything about our relationship, maybe not. But I needed her.

Rising from my chair, I walked over to the pantry and pulled out the flour container. Reaching into the white powder, I felt around until I found the plastic baggie. I dusted it off before opening it and pulling out a spare key for my car. I'd had it made after Bryce had taken my keys the last time. Not to disobey him, but in case of an emergency. Today, I deemed going to see my parents as an emergency, consequences be damned. Besides, if Bryce had my phone, he couldn't track me anyway. I'd be there and back before he even knew I was gone.

When I pulled up in front of my parents' house, I didn't hesitate before launching myself out of the car. It didn't occur to me until I was ringing the bell that they might not be home, but my fears were short-lived as the door swung open. My mom's expression changed from surprise to delight as she recognized me and immediately pulled me into a hug. I melted into her arms, tears leaking from the corners of my eyes as she held me. I wasn't sure how long we stood there like that, rocking back and forth. My dad, hearing the commotion, found us like that and soon his great big arms surrounded both of us.

A while later, my mom had settled us at the table and was making waffles. "You look so skinny, Jules," she said, and it had been so long since anyone had used my nickname I closed my eyes in pure pleasure at the sound. "You need to eat something."

"I eat, Mom," I said, smiling. This was what I needed, what I'd been missing. How had I let Bryce keep me from this for so long?

I asked my dad about his job, which he'd started working part-time in preparation for retirement, which was how he happened to be home today. We made small talk while Mom loaded me up on waffles before coming and taking the chair next to mine.

When I'd eaten as much as I could, Mom took my hand. "What's going on, Julia?" she asked. "We never see you or hear from you anymore. We miss you."

"I miss you guys, too," I said, a lump forming in my throat. "And I want to try to see you more, especially since"—I looked down, rubbing my belly—"you're going to be grandparents again."

Mom stared at me for a moment, and then her entire face lit up. "Oh, Julia! Sweetheart! I'm so excited for you! When are you due? Boy or girl? How did Bryce react?"

I answered her questions as best I could. It was still too early to tell most of those things, other than the due date. January. I avoided her question about Bryce, but she was perceptive.

"Julia? How are things with your husband?" she asked.

She was so sincere, and in that moment I was ashamed. I couldn't tell her how badly things were going. I couldn't confess that my husband berated me and critiqued everything I did and occasionally used me as a punching bag, and that it was okay because the Bible said I had to be a good wife. It sounded ridiculous even in my head.

"Things are fine," I said, raising one shoulder. "The first year had its rough moments, but we're working on it."

Mom studied me, as moms do, and didn't seem to believe me, but as she opened her mouth to say something, the doorbell rang. I knew even before I heard his voice that he was here.

"Julia! There you are!" Bryce followed my dad into the living room. "I came home for lunch and my lovely wife was missing. Plus, she forgot her phone at home," he said, waving my phone at me. "Pregnancy brain, right? Thank goodness for GPS on your car." He grinned at my parents, turning the charm on high. "I'm assuming she told you the great news?"

"Yes, Bryce," my mother said, rising to give him a hug. "Congratulations!"

He glared at me over my mother's shoulder and made a slight movement with his head, making it clear I was to come to him. I stood and walked over to them, and Bryce quickly pulled me under his arm. "We'd hoped to share the news together, over dinner, but our schedules are just so crazy."

My dad crossed his arms over his chest. "Seems to be a problem a lot since you two got married."

"We'll definitely try to do better," Bryce lied. "I'm going to work fewer hours at the firm now that we have an addition coming. Family is first, after all."

"Please do," Mom said. "We miss you."

Bryce looked at his watch. "I'm sorry to steal her away, but I only have a short time left for lunch. Is it okay if we leave Julia's car here? We'll pick it up later."

"Of course," Mom said.

"Julia, give them the key in case they need to move it."

Taking a deep breath, I fished the spare key from my pocket. I was the only one who noticed the slight narrowing of his eyes as I handed it to my dad.

Reaching out, I gathered my mom into another hug. "It was so good to see you. I love you, Mom."

"Come back soon, okay? Or at least call."

I nodded and turned to my dad. "Daddy, I love you."

"We're always here for you, Jules. Anything you need."

"I know."

And then Bryce was tugging on my arm and the door was closing between me and my parents, and I had no idea when I'd see them again. Bryce led me to his car, opening the passenger door for me before rounding the hood and sliding behind the wheel. I waved at my parents through the window and we drove away.

"That was risky, Julia," Bryce said after we'd driven a few blocks. "What did you tell them?"

"Nothing," I said. "I told them about the baby. That's it."

He scoffed. "Really? You make a copy of your car key and go running to your parents at the first sign of trouble and I'm supposed to believe you weren't trying to escape?"

"I wasn't," I said, and sighed. "I still want to make this work, Bryce. I just wanted to talk to my mom. You never let me talk to her."

"Because she's an outsider. She doesn't understand how our family works. She wouldn't have been able to give you the help you need. If you need to talk to someone, I'll have Nancy come over."

"I can go see her at the church."

"No. I'm dropping you at home and I'll have Nancy stop by."

Fuming, I stared out my window. The transparent reflection

staring back at me was of a stranger, and in that moment, the fight left me.

"Whatever you think is best," I said, and his gaze whipped to mine, surprised flickering across his face. "But maybe she could come by tomorrow. I have some cleaning to do, and then I'd really like a nap."

He didn't say anything for the rest of the drive home. I considered myself lucky to have escaped an angrier tongue-lashing, but it seemed he believed me about not telling my parents the details of our fights.

Before I got out of the car back at the house, Bryce leaned over, pushing my hair out of my face and kissing me softly on the lips. "You know I only want us to be happy, right? Everything I do is for us and for God."

I nodded, my hand on the door handle.

"I'll have Nancy stop by tomorrow. If you make a list of groceries we need, I'll have someone bring them to her to drop off with you."

Apparently I wouldn't be going anyplace anytime soon.

"Okay," I said.

"I'll bring something home tonight. Maybe we'll try Chinese again?" He winked at me, and I gave up trying to figure out his moods.

"Sounds good."

"Take it easy today, sweetheart," he said. "I'll see you tonight."

He waited until I'd entered the house and closed the door behind me before driving away.

Bryce did have my car picked up from my parents' house later. Someone picked it up and drove it to a storage facility one suburb over. "For safekeeping," he said.

It was no longer clear who he was trying to keep safe.

The water is a deep red now, but still she remains submerged, only head, toes, and rounded belly breaking the surface. She rubs a pruney hand over her swollen abdomen. This is for the child. She couldn't bring a baby into this life. It wouldn't have been fair. He would have found a way to control the child the way he controlled everything in his world. Even if it hadn't been part of his plan, he would have reshaped their child the way he had reshaped her. It would have grown to be just like him, the beauty on the outside masking the danger within, like Snow White's poisoned apple. It's better this way. They're all better this way.

PART VI

BREAKING FREE

Chapter 30

Time passed, and we fell back into a pattern of sorts. My body had healed, but my spirit was completely broken. I didn't know what to believe anymore. In public, Bryce was the doting husband. After church every Sunday, he walked me to the Reverend's house, where I waited for them to finish with the Gathering. He led all conversations with other members of the congregation, and I smiled and nodded, taking my cues from him. I learned how long I could keep a smile pasted on my face before excusing myself for a moment. I was never allowed to get far from Bryce when there were others around.

At home, Bryce was in a better temperament. It helped that I didn't question him anymore. I didn't have the energy. I understood that my vital role was to be the best wife to Bryce that I could, to keep him happy. He'd returned my phone, but with all the numbers erased except a select few, and Internet access disabled.

Most days, I spent the morning cleaning the house and working out, trying to keep myself from gaining too much baby weight. In the afternoons, Nancy often stopped by for a visit, or I was allowed to walk the three blocks to the library, as long as I kept my phone on me and let Bryce know when I was going, though Bryce had made sure Vanessa revoked my computer access while I was there. I still participated in reading with kids sometimes, but mostly I went to the religion section, as I had for months, and read through commentaries. I'd branched out to researching other religions, though I was careful about that, knowing that Vanessa reported back to Bryce. But she rarely bothered me, and at least it got me out of the house.

Dinners were full of Bryce telling me all about his day. In some ways, he was more open with me now that he had complete control over me than he had ever been before. He finally trusted me enough to open up to me fully. It was ironic. I learned that my husband was as ruthless in his job as he was in our marriage. He represented any number of shady things going on within the church, and laughed over the deals he was able to make. That was how he'd won the case that had threatened to expose the Reverend and the Gathering the last time. They'd gotten dirt on the guy and leaned on him until he caved. In fact, he was back attending the church again, though not part of the Gathering. And that wasn't the first time they'd used their considerable influence to get out of sticky situations. It became a game for me to figure out just how to react to keep him talking about each person, each case. I filed all the information away, though I wasn't sure why. I had no one to tell.

Bryce had also finally accepted the pregnancy. He told me that God had illuminated a new path for him, and that the baby was indeed a miracle. He spoke excitedly about the baby's future, how he would raise it and give it all the things he didn't have as a child. He spoke openly about his childhood now, too, even up to the day that he left. I learned about Sissy, and how he had tried to protect her, and yet I was unmoved. Even as he talked, I couldn't reconcile the boy he described with the man I had married or with the man my husband had become. He even talked about his decision to cut ties with his family, to stop sending the letters and close the PO box. The Reverend required a clean slate before Bryce could become who he was meant to be. The letters he'd kept had been his one concession.

I didn't hear from Harriet, as I thought I might. I didn't ask

Bryce if he'd done anything about her, or if she'd reached out to him. She'd seemed so hopeful that my visit could be the start of a relationship with her adult son, even as I told her that he didn't know I had come. I was sure that she would look up our names, which would lead her to his law firm, as I had discovered in my initial searches so long ago, and try to connect. If she did, he didn't tell me about it. Maybe her patchy memory had been a blessing after all.

One morning, before he left, Bryce turned to me. "The past few weeks have been wonderful, Julia," he said, grasping my shoulders. "I feel like we can finally be completely honest with each other. No more secrets."

I nodded. "No more secrets."

"That's my girl." He kissed me and started humming on his way out the door as I turned to clean the dishes.

It was a beautiful afternoon for a walk, so I texted Bryce to tell him I'd be going to the library, and set out. It was usually pretty quiet on my walk. Our neighborhood wasn't the type to have children playing out front, and the houses were set far enough back from the street that I wouldn't have been able to chat with anyone anyway. There were very few other pedestrians, especially in the middle of the day, but the sun was shining and the birds sang from the trees, so I took my time.

Vanessa greeted me when I entered the library. "Nice day?"

"Gorgeous," I said. I didn't have any books to return. I didn't check them out anymore. I just read while I was here. It wasn't a story time day, so I waved at Vanessa and headed upstairs.

The religion section remained my sanctuary. The computer in the corner had been removed, replaced with a cozy reading area. I had marveled at my husband's influence the first time I saw the new setup, but I really shouldn't have been surprised. If he'd told the library to throw all computers out and use kerosene lamps only for light, they would have done it in a heartbeat. He had dirt on everyone who worked here. It was part of how they got their jobs.

I picked up a book on Buddhism before settling into the new reading area. I'd tell Bryce about it later. He didn't mind my hobby, encouraged it really, as long as I talked with him about what I learned so he could tell me all the ways it was wrong. He thrived on being right.

I was immersed in an introductory chapter to Noble Truths when someone else entered the section. Normally no one bothered me, but occasionally someone else wandered in. I heard the footsteps, but didn't look up. I didn't want to engage with anyone, and if I ignored them, typically they'd find their books and leave without initiating small talk.

"Julia? Julia Hawthorne?"

Startled, I looked up to see a man with brown eyes and shaggy blond hair peering at me, a disbelieving smile on his familiar-looking face.

"Tim?" I dropped the book I was reading and jumped up, throwing my arms around his neck before I caught myself and stepped back, still reeling in surprise. "Tim Wilson. I can't believe it! What are you doing here?"

"Looking for books," he said, gesturing at the shelves. "I'm taking a religion class as an elective for my master's degree."

"Wow! A master's degree in what?"

"Counseling," he said. "It's for my cultural competency credit. I want to be able to understand anyone who comes through my door, at least a little."

I shook my head. He was so familiar, though it had been years since I'd seen him. "That's great, Tim. What have you been up to? How long has it been?"

He scrunched his face, like he always used to when he was working a math problem out in his head. "Since graduation? So ten years? Give or take."

"That long, huh? No wonder you look so old."

"Hey." He lightly punched my shoulder, and I immediately

stepped back, my heart pounding. "Oh, hey, sorry," he said, holding up his hands at the panic on my face. "Didn't mean to hurt you."

"Uh, you didn't," I said, rubbing my hand down my arm, cursing my jumpiness. "Listen, I should be going, but it was really great to see you."

"Wait," Tim said. "Can I get your number so we can catch up? I'd love for you to meet my wife, and I know my parents would like to see you again."

"'Bye, Tim!" I called over my shoulder, pretending I hadn't heard him. I waved at Vanessa on my way out, and didn't slow down until I'd rounded the corner at the end of the block. Once I was sure he wasn't following me, my feet dragged the rest of the way home.

Seeing Tim had been like a breath of fresh air and a splash of cold water all at once. We'd been good friends in high school, but lost touch once we went to college, as happens with even some of the greatest friendships. But in high school, we'd been almost inseparable. Always at each other's house, practically part of each other's family. I'd seen him on holidays for a while, but then he'd studied abroad and I'd stopped coming home and our only point of contact was social media. He was one of those people whose lives I'd always looked at wistfully, scrolling through his pictures from his time in other countries, smiling at his wedding photos, but who felt like someone from another lifetime. Like the person I knew didn't even exist anymore.

Except he did, and seeing him brought back all those memories, of the person he'd been . . . of the person *I'd* been. High school me wouldn't recognize the person I'd become. But then, high school me probably couldn't fathom living in a giant house and being married to a man as attractive as Bryce. I really couldn't complain about my life.

I couldn't explain why I'd run from Tim, however. He'd been playful when he'd cuffed my arm, teasing like we always had, but my heart had almost exploded out of my chest, my lungs constricted, and I needed to find an exit immediately. I didn't care if it looked rude or hurt his feelings. All I cared about was escape. From Tim. Removed from the situation now, it seemed ridiculous, and I did feel a little bad, but it was probably for the best. Tim wouldn't understand the life I was leading, and I didn't need him to. He was from my past, and it was better if he stayed there.

When I got home, I decided to make an extra-special dinner for Bryce, since I had some extra time. He oohed and aahed over the homemade ravioli and sauce, and we ate in silence for a few minutes before he struck up a conversation.

"How was the library today?"

I kept my features schooled even as my heart sped up. He knew. Not that there was anything to hide, but guilt sat like a rock in my belly anyway. "It was fine," I said. "I started to read a book on Buddhism but I started to feel sick, so I came back home."

His brow furrowed in concern. "Are you feeling better now? Was it morning sickness?"

I nodded, though I was past that stage. "Probably. I felt better after my walk home. Fresh air always helps. I'm glad I'm able to walk to the library."

"I'm happy you're feeling better," he said, taking another bite. He chewed thoughtfully. "Anything else interesting?"

It was on the tip of my tongue to tell him I'd run into an old friend, but for some reason I felt protective of Tim. It was nothing, but I knew instinctively that Bryce would not be happy that I'd spoken to him at all, though it had only been a few sentences. I worried that he would restrict my visits to the library, or ask me to stay where Vanessa was stationed, and I needed my sanctuary. So instead I just shook my head. "Nope. Pretty uneventful. How was your day?"

He looked at me for only a moment before launching into his latest case. He believed me. He knew he had me totally cowed. He was confident that I wouldn't keep anything from him. That knowledge fanned a spark of defiance I thought had been snuffed out. It was a small thing, keeping my high school friend from him, but it was something. I was still my own person. Still me, at least in small part. For now.

I waited a few days before returning to the library. Not that I thought Tim would come looking for me, but just to be sure. And as much as I loved the sanctuary of the religion section, I decided to peruse some other areas. I ended up in a section I'd never explored before. It was full of medical textbooks, and I was getting ready to keep moving when I saw a pharmacology textbook.

Though I'd never brought it up with Bryce or Nancy or the Reverend, it had always bothered me that I never figured out what Dr. Leeland had been talking about when she mentioned ketamine, all those months ago. I'd been so intent on making sure everything was perfect, on pleasing Bryce and the Reverend, that I'd stuffed that bit of information into the back of my brain. I barely thought of it anymore, but when it did come up it was like an itch I couldn't quite reach. There was something to it, but I'd never taken the time to fully explore it.

Taking the textbook to a table, I opened it and began leafing through until I found it.

> *Ketamine—dissociative anesthetic, some hallucino-genic effects, can cause distortion of sight and sound, users report feeling out of control and disconnected from environment—effects often last 30–60 minutes—often used in veterinary clinics.*

I continued scanning the page, reading through street names and abuses of the drug, but my eyes got stuck on one sentence. *Several common types of experiences with ketamine have been reported, including what users call simply "God," based on the hallucination that they have met their maker.*

My heart raced as I read the sentence over and over. Was it possible? Had I been drugged? Had we all been drugged? And if so, who knew about it? Did Bryce know? Or was it one of those things they would tell me was to help out as I got started, to "open my mind" to Oneness with God? Through all of this I had been questioning what I was doing wrong, why I was in this situation, and I had concluded that this was the life God planned for me. After all, it's what Bryce saw. It's what the Reverend saw. And in all of that, I always knew it had to be true because I had experienced it for myself. I wasn't making that up, the Oneness with God.

Maybe it was all a lie.

"There you are." Tim's voice cut through my chaotic thoughts, and I looked up at him with wide eyes, slamming the book shut in surprise. His expression turned to one of concern. "Hey, are you okay? I saw you come in, but I didn't know if you wanted to talk to me or not . . . you ran away so quickly the other day."

Trying to gather myself, I took a deep breath. "I'm fine. Just . . . doing some reading."

He squinted at the book on the table. "You're reading a pharmacology textbook."

"I was curious."

He slid into the chair across from me and moved his hand as if to cover my shaking fingers, but pulled back. "Is there something wrong, Julia? Are you taking medication or thinking about it?"

This was ludicrous. He was so nosy. "No, Tim, I just heard the name of a drug the other day and I was curious about what it did. That's all. I don't have a drug problem."

Leaning back in his chair, he crossed his arms over his chest. "Okay, hey, didn't mean to upset you. Although you looked pretty upset before I even said your name."

"Why are you here, Tim?" I asked, irritation slicing through my words.

"Just wanted to say hi," he said, sliding his chair back. "I thought maybe something had happened the other day that made you run away, but I guess it really was just me. I thought I was being paranoid."

"I didn't run away."

"You left rubber tracks on the carpet with how fast you peeled outta here."

I couldn't help the smile that quirked up the side of my mouth. "You always were dramatic."

Standing, he stretched. "I'll get out of your hair. It was great seeing you. Best of luck with everything." He gestured to the textbook, a twinkle in his eye.

"Wait, Tim," I said, holding out a hand. "You can stay. It's just a little weird running into someone from my past. I haven't talked to anyone from high school in years."

"All the more reason to catch up!" He plopped back into his chair.

"So tell me about your life," I said. "I know you traveled around Asia and South America, and I know you're married, but I quit social media a while back so now you need to fill me in the old-fashioned way."

Tim laughed and started talking about his travels, about his wife, Mary, about his family. It was like old times, chatting for hours in his parents' basement. "And now I'm in grad school, which is completely insane. I'm in my last year, though, doing an internship counseling out of a church."

My nose wrinkled. I hadn't fully processed what I had learned today, but even hearing the word "church" put a bad taste in my mouth. He noticed my look and his mouth turned up at one corner. "Not religious? Even though I found you in the religion section the other day?"

I shook my head. "Actually, my husband and his family are very religious. They run the Church of the Life here in town."

It was his turn to wrinkle his nose. "I hear weird things about that church."

I laughed. "It's not all bad." And that was true. When I thought about most of the people who attended the church, they were good people. But knowing what was under the surface, I didn't know if I could buy into any of it anymore. Although I didn't really have a choice.

Fingers snapped in front of my face and I jumped. "You looked a million miles away for a second there," Tim said.

I blinked, coming back to the present. "Sorry. Just thinking. I've spent the past couple years being deeply devoted to the church and to God, but I just don't know what I believe anymore." I clapped a hand over my mouth. I couldn't believe I'd said that out loud. If Vanessa heard me, or any of the other patrons who could speak to Bryce . . .

Realizing where I was, I jumped up. "I need to go, Tim, I'm sorry." I looked at my watch. I should have left half an hour ago. I sent a quick text to Bryce.

> *Got immersed in a book and lost track of time. Be home soon.*

His reply came immediately. `I can pick you up. I'm on my way.`

My heart pounded. I turned to Tim. "I'm going to head out, but you need to stay back here, maybe go around and come out a different section."

He laughed, but then seemed to realize I was serious. "Are you embarrassed to be seen with me?"

"My husband . . ." I lowered my voice and looked around. "He gets a little jealous, and we know a lot of the people here. I'd hate for them to get the wrong idea."

"About us?" Tim laughed again. "We're just old friends."

Bryce would be pulling up any moment. "Please, Tim. For me."

Concern creased his forehead as he nodded. "Okay. Will I see you again?"

I smiled. "I hope so." Then I turned and hurried to where Bryce was waiting out front, completely forgetting to put away the textbook I'd been reading.

Chapter 31

At lunch on Sunday with the Reverend and Nancy, I had a more difficult time holding my composure, but it was more important than ever that I did. It wasn't just Bryce and me who were guests, but a random assortment of others who had come from the Gathering. I watched each of them closely to see if I could recognize signs that they'd been drugged. As always, everyone was smiling and euphoric from their experience, but was that the same thing as having been drugged? And if the effects were short-lived, did that mean that they wouldn't show any outward signs?

"So, Julia." Dr. Herbert was sitting across the table from me, next to Nancy. "I understand you've developed an interest in pharmaceuticals."

I raised an eyebrow at him. I could take this opportunity to let them know I knew what was going on, but then, I wasn't sure what they'd do. I knew enough about Bryce's work at this point that I wouldn't put it past them to somehow frame me for some wrongdoing, if they didn't do something worse. As it was, nobody would know I was missing for weeks or longer. These people were the only ones who knew the status of my well-being.

Except Tim. Tim would notice now. He would realize that I wasn't at the library and he would contact my parents, especially since I'd told him Bryce was the jealous sort. I shouldn't have said that. It might have made him suspicious. I hoped that he would be back this week so I could explain that I'd just been paranoid. I didn't want him involved in any of this. But still. It was nice knowing that if I disappeared, he would notice.

"I'm not sure what you mean, Doctor," I said, taking a bite of the salmon that had been prepared for lunch. It was perfect, as always.

Bryce chuckled next to me. "Vanessa mentioned that she put away a pharmacology textbook you'd been looking at the other day. I mentioned in passing to the doctor that perhaps you'd like to learn more."

My cheeks heated, but for once I was glad, because it looked like I was embarrassed rather than frightened that they'd found out what I'd been looking at. "Oh, that," I said, patting my mouth with my napkin and taking a drink of water. "I've read many of the books in the religion section, and I got to thinking that I hadn't explored much. I made a game out of it and picked at random." I shrugged, allowing a small laugh to escape my lips. "I could not have picked a more boring section to end up in. I'll have to be more selective next time."

Laughs floated around the table, and I breathed a silent sigh of relief. "Well, let me know if you change your mind," Dr. Herbert said.

"You'll be the first one I call," I said, and he winked before focusing back on his plate. I kept an eye on Bryce out of the corner of my eye. I couldn't decide if he knew about the ketamine or not, or if he did, whether he suspected I now knew the truth as well. But Bryce's face remained calm and relaxed, none of the telltale signs of irritation or anger hinting that he was holding back.

The conversation swirled around other topics, but an itch between my shoulder blades told me I was being watched. I glanced around the table, but everyone seemed to be engrossed in their own conversations until I met the Reverend's eyes.

He studied me with cool calculation, a look I'd never seen on his face sending shivers down my spine. I'd always felt completely at ease with the Reverend, from the moment we'd first met. He seemed to have that charisma, which I'd later attributed to being connected with God. He drew people in, made them feel important, was able to convince them of just about anything.

But I saw through him now. Being a broken woman meant that people often spoke around me as if I didn't exist, and I'd learned to listen, not only to Bryce, but to what others were saying. I'd gleaned that the Gathering was not only a way for the Reverend to control others, to hold power, but also gave him incredible amounts of influence over vast resources. It was no coincidence that the "Chosen" also happened to be the wealthiest and most influential people in the city. The Reverend, Bryce, even Nancy had collected dirt on each of them, and they weren't above using blackmail to grow the church . . . or to grow their bank accounts.

My eyes narrowed as I looked back at the Reverend. I had all this information bubbling within me, but I couldn't do anything with it. They had me completely tied up, no escape routes available. I was at Bryce's whims, which meant I was at the Reverend's whims.

Was it a sign that I was no longer under his spell that I could see the iciness in his eyes? Or was he giving up the pretense? Did he realize that I knew his secret? Knew what he was doing to these people? How he was controlling them? He rested his chin on his hands, his fingers steepled over his lips, and it was as if time stopped. As if we were the only two in the room. As if he saw every part of me, every thought in my head, every question I'd ever asked, every doubt I'd ever squashed. And then he smiled.

Instead of leaving me feeling comforted, my entire body went numb at that smile. It wasn't a smile of acceptance, of comfort. It was a smile of pure evil.

Tim wasn't at the library on Monday or Tuesday. I didn't go Wednesday, because I'd never gone more than three days in a week, and I didn't want Bryce to be suspicious. Nancy visited Wednesday, and asked several times if I was feeling okay. I clearly wasn't putting on my act as well anymore.

Once I'd peeled that first layer back, exposed the fact that it was very likely my experience at the Gathering was unnatural instead of a natural connection with my Creator, everything else began to un- ravel. I began to hear the disharmonious notes in everything Nancy and the Reverend said. The subtle ways they made me feel as if everything I did was wrong, that everything Bryce did was for me and for God. Nothing rang true anymore. And yet I was so entan- gled in their web that I saw no way out.

The worst part was that everything I'd believed in, the faith I'd built over the past two years, was shattered. I didn't know what I believed. Before Bryce, I had some sense that there was a God some- place, that Someone was out there, but now . . . if this was what the church was built on, lies and deception, I wanted nothing to do with it.

I didn't see Tim again until the following week. It was getting harder and harder to pull it together all the time, and I'd begged off early from lunch with the Reverend and Nancy after church the day before to go home and lie down. Bryce was worried about me, and wanted to set up an appointment with Dr. Herbert, but I assured him it was normal pregnancy fatigue. When I texted him to tell him I was going to the library today, he was concerned, and I knew to expect Vanessa to pop in more often.

"Hello, Vanessa," I said, giving her my most cheerful greeting as I walked in. "How are you?"

"I'm great, Julia, thank you." Her gaze flicked up and down my body, as if looking for signs of illness or exhaustion. They paused on my belly, just starting to round out a bit. "Bryce said you were under the weather yesterday."

"I had a good nap and slept great last night," I lied. Bryce had woken me for sex and I hadn't been able to get back to sleep after.

Thank goodness for all of the makeup tips I got from Stacy. The bags under my eyes weren't visible at all. "I just get tired a little easier, but I'm feeling wonderful today."

Vanessa smiled. "I'm glad. Back up to the religion section today, or back to exploring?" She'd talked to Bryce.

"Not sure," I said. "Maybe I'll find a novel and curl up in a corner for a bit. Are the kids still coming in for reading time today?"

"They are. Want me to find you?"

"That's okay," I said. "I can always hear when they show up." Children weren't known for being quiet, even in the library.

I wandered up to my normal spot, which was empty, as it usually was. I continued walking, slowly perusing the books until the sound of children's voices floated up from below. I descended the stairs and greeted the children and their families. Many were members of the church, but not of the Gathering, so they recognized me from there.

The children's librarian, Doreen, always read a book, and then a fleet of volunteers, myself included, took children aside one-on-one or in small groups to read some books of their choosing. The parents were free to browse through the library or even run out for coffee during the hour-long event. It was very different from my tutoring, and I enjoyed it immensely.

Today, my mind was on other things. I kept my eye on the front door as I listened to the story Doreen read, hoping Tim would come in. Maybe he was done with his research. I'd hoped he would return, but I realized he didn't necessarily say when or if he would be back.

My desire to see Tim surprised me, but it wasn't an attraction. He represented everything I wasn't, everything I missed. When I felt myself being pulled under again by the doctrine of the Reverend, I remembered the feeling I had when I'd looked up and seen Tim for the first time, like coming up for air when I hadn't even realized I was drowning. He was my beacon, my cue that maybe not everyone was always watching, always finding ways to manipulate. Tim felt safe, in a way that no one else had for a long time.

"Miss Julia?" A small girl in blonde pigtails tugged on my sleeve. "Will you read to me?"

I hadn't even realized Doreen was finished. The kids were all splitting up with the other volunteers. I crouched down to the little girl's height. "I would be happy to, Lydia," I said, recalling her name as I looked into her wide green eyes. She held out a Dr. Seuss book, which I loved reading. "Should we go over to one of the chairs?" I asked. I patted my belly. "It's not as easy for me to get up and down as it used to be." In truth, I was barely showing and could still maneuver easily, but the joke made Lydia giggle.

"Are you gonna have a baby, Miss Julia?"

"I am! Unless it's a kitten."

More giggles. "Are you excited? I was excited when my baby bruvver was borned."

"Very excited."

We walked to a squashy chair, where I sat down and pulled her into my lap. She leaned her head on my shoulder and pointed at her favorite pages as we went. We read through three books before the time was up. She jumped off my lap and waved. "Bye, Miss Julia! Bye, baby kitten!" She blew a kiss at my belly and scurried away. Contentment flowed through me. I couldn't wait to meet my own child, to hear the giggles, to see the world through a child's eyes again. It seemed like a much brighter place when children looked at it.

Vanessa was preoccupied at the front desk, and I took the opportunity to slip into the back part of the library and use a different set of stairs to go back up to the religion section. Even if Tim didn't show today, I had another hour before I had to head home. Maybe I would find that novel I'd told Vanessa I was considering.

All my plans for the novel were wiped away when I entered the section and found Tim immersed in a book at one of the study tables. He didn't see me right away, so I tiptoed across the floor and peered over his shoulder.

"Bees?" I asked, and laughed when he jumped.

"For a pregnant lady, you sure move quietly, like a pregnant ninja," he said, pushing the chair across from him out with his foot. "Have a seat. Take a load off."

I lowered myself into the chair and gestured to the book again. "You're interested in bees?"

"Actually, I have a hive on an acreage outside of town. I'm hoping to expand eventually."

Leaning back, I raised an eyebrow at him. "You're a beekeeper?"

"Guilty. Remind me to show you a picture of me in my bee suit sometime."

"Do you have a bonnet and everything?"

"It matches."

We both laughed, and it was easy. Easy to talk to him, easy to be with him. I didn't feel like I had to watch what I said, or avoid certain topics. He spent the next hour teaching me about bees and hives and the setup he had to extract honey. "You and your husband can come help us extract next year."

I snorted. "I can't see Bryce extracting honey." I thought for a moment. "I'd like to see him in that bee suit, though."

My phone buzzed. "Speak of the devil," I said, and smirked at my own joke, though Tim just looked confused. "I gotta go. But I'll be back Thursday if you're around."

"Always need to study," Tim said. "I might be around."

I was humming when Bryce walked in later that evening.

"Sorry I'm late, sweetheart," he said, kissing me on the cheek. "Had to wrap a few things up."

"It's okay," I said. "I kept the chicken warm."

I took it out of the oven and danced it out into the dining room.

Bryce watched me, a bemused look on his face. "You're in an awfully good mood," he said.

I twirled one last time before taking my seat across from him. "I did story time today at the library. Do you remember little Lydia from church?"

He shook his head. Of course he didn't. Her parents weren't important enough for him to know, and he had little time for children. He likely wouldn't have much time for his own, other than to make sure he or she was doing exactly what they were supposed to do.

"Well, she's the cutest thing, blonde hair and green eyes. Anyway, she asked me specifically to read to her and was asking about the baby and it just got me thinking how excited I am to meet the little one." I rubbed a hand over my belly, something that had become an almost unconscious act since I started showing.

"I'm glad you had a good day," Bryce said, and went back to his chicken. He didn't offer any information about his day, and I didn't ask. Instead, I immersed myself in my daydreams of what our child would look like, and what kind of person they would be.

That night, I dreamed of the baby. A little girl with blonde hair, even though neither Bryce nor I was naturally blonde. She skipped away from me, and I reached for her, but couldn't quite get to her. I called out, "Wait!" and she stopped, but when she turned around, her eyes glowed red, and she bared a mouth full of sharp teeth at me.

I woke up sweating, breathing hard. Bryce slept soundly next to me, but I lay awake for the rest of the night, unable to get the monstrous face out of my mind.

Chapter 32

T im found me in my normal spot two days later, frantically flipping through baby books. Vanessa had helped me find a stack of them and I'd been looking up pregnancy dreams and effects of drugs on babies for the past hour.

"You look like you're on a mission," Tim said, dropping into the chair across from me. He tilted his head to look at the titles. "Everything okay with the baby?"

"I don't know," I said, slamming one book shut and pulling another toward me. I'd also stopped by and grabbed the pharmacology textbook I'd read before, but it didn't have any insight into the effects of ketamine on an unborn baby. If I was able to get on a computer, I could research it, but since I couldn't, I had to stick to old methods.

Unless . . .

I looked up at Tim. "How much do you know about hallucinogens? Specifically ketamine?"

"You in the market?" he asked, his tone careful despite the teasing words.

"No. I just . . . never mind."

"Julia," he said, reaching his hand to cover the page I was scanning. Since the first day when I'd fled, Tim made sure not to actually touch me, which I appreciated. It wasn't that I felt threatened by him. I just felt dirty, and I didn't want it to rub off. "What is this about?"

"Nothing," I said. "I just had a question."

"Did you try the Internet?" He was joking around as if it was a silly question.

"No, I'm not allowed access to the Internet."

Tim sat back, stunned, but I didn't even care about hiding the weirdness of my life from him at this point. "What do you mean, you're not allowed?"

"I mean that I looked up stuff that Bryce wasn't happy about and he asked for my access to be cut off at the library. The only computer at home is a laptop in his study, which I'm not allowed to enter if he's not there, and my phone's data is blocked."

Tim was shaking his head in disbelief as I talked. "That's insane. What were you looking up? Porn?"

My head jerked up at that. "No," I said. "I looked up his mother." I went back to flipping through my books. I had likely been dosed with ketamine at least a few times before I realized I was pregnant. Now I understood why I wasn't allowed to participate in the Gathering during my pregnancy, and probably while I was nursing. I was desperate enough at this point to call Nancy and just ask her if she knew what the effects were, or even Dr. Herbert. What would they say if at Sunday dinner I just asked what they knew about the effects of ketamine in utero?

"Julia." This time Tim did touch me, his fingers only lightly brushing the skin on the back of my hand. I froze, and then jerked my hand away. He moved his arm back to his side of the table. "Do you want me to go look it up?"

Paranoid thoughts rushed through my head. What if Vanessa was tracking everyone's searches? Did she know? Did everyone know but me? Or was it just the Reverend and Nancy? Did Bryce know? Or was that one secret the Reverend kept from him? It was important that I find out.

"Okay," I said. "But use the back stairway and one of the computers in the study area, not the main area. If Vanessa sees . . ."

"If Vanessa sees, I'll tell her I'm doing research for one of my clients. Given that I've only spoken to her when I check books out, I don't think she'll have much interest in what I'm looking up."

I just hoped she hadn't realized I was spending time with him here. It was pretty risky, now that I thought about it, but I also wasn't willing to give him up just yet. "Okay. I'll keep looking here."

He nodded and slipped away to the back. I kept reading through the books, and a few minutes later I heard footsteps coming closer. Not the heavy footfalls of a man, but the gentle clip-clop of Vanessa's flats. I was grateful Tim had offered to go look things up, because it would have been a disaster for her to find him here with me.

"How's everything going, Julia?" Vanessa asked. "Are you finding what you were looking for?"

"Yes, thank you," I said, tucking the textbook under my pile. I didn't need her telling Bryce that I was looking at it again after I'd brushed it off before. He would definitely grow suspicious then, whether he knew about the ketamine or not. "I just got to thinking that I didn't know if I was doing everything I was supposed to be doing." Laughing, I turned one of the books to show her the pages. "Apparently it's an early sign of nesting, suddenly needing to prepare and protect the baby. So I guess I found out that I'm normal!"

"That has to be a relief." Her eyes ran over my stacks of books. "Can I put any of these back for you?"

"Nope, I'm not sure which ones I've looked at yet. I'll bring them down when I'm done."

"No need," Vanessa said. "I can just collect them after you leave." She turned to head back downstairs and then looked back. "You know, Julia. We do have lots of tables on the first level. You wouldn't have to lug stacks of books up here."

"I know," I said, shrugging. "But I like it here. It's quiet and I'm almost always by myself."

"Okay, if you're sure," she said, lifting a shoulder. "Let me know if you need anything else."

"Will do!" I saluted her, and cringed, glad that she'd already turned her back before she'd seen the salute. That wasn't exactly acting natural.

A few minutes later, Tim was back, a sheaf of papers in his hands. "I can look more later, but from what I found, I don't think you have too much to worry about. There's not much on ketamine use, but it's been classified as safe to use in limited amounts during pregnancy."

All the tension rushed out of my body at once as I grabbed the papers from Tim and scanned them. There were more tests in animals, since it was typically used by veterinarians, but while there were some possible side effects, there wasn't enough evidence to make it statistically significant, especially if the exposure was early on.

A tear dropped on the paper in front of me, and I hadn't even realized I was crying. I quickly wiped my cheeks, but it was too late. Tim stared at me, his eyes burning with concern. "What is it, Julia? Please tell me."

I shook my head. I wouldn't bring him into this. I couldn't put him at risk. "It's nothing."

"Hey," he said, his voice almost a whisper. "Remember when you wrecked your mom's car and you didn't know what to do? Who did you call?"

I shook my head again, refusing to answer.

"What about the time you got caught cheating off of Lizzie Lamb's Spanish quiz and got suspended? Who helped you convince your parents it was a school holiday?"

My eyes fluttered closed. I was cracking.

"And who beat up Mason Grimes when he got a little handsy at Homecoming?"

"You did," I whispered.

"What was that?"

"You did," I repeated, louder. "But, Tim, you can't save me this time."

His features clouded over, but then he locked his gaze with mine. "Try me."

I didn't mean to tell him everything. I meant to give him a quick background, make up a story about how I might have gotten ketamine in my system, leave the church out of it, but before I knew it, the entire story came spilling out. His face grew more and more stormy as I talked, his fists and jaw clenching unconsciously when I talked about Bryce's treatment of me.

When I finished, he was silent for a moment, eyes closed as his chest rose and fell rapidly. When he opened his eyes, they were bleak. "I can't believe you've been dealing with all of this alone, Julia. I wish I'd known . . ." He shook his head. "What can I do? How can I help?"

"You can't do anything," I said. "It was enough of a risk for me to tell you, but promise me. Promise me you will do nothing."

"I can't, Julia. I can't just let you walk away knowing what you're going home to."

"If you want to see me again, you have to. Because if Bryce suspects I've breathed even a word of this to you, to anyone, he'll put me under total house arrest."

"We can call the police."

"And tell them what? I promise you now, I'll deny everything if you call the police. And I'll still get in trouble. I'm not prepared to bring anyone else into it."

"Why not?" he said, his voice strained with defeat. I knew then that my secrets were safe, at least for now.

I thought about it. "I don't know," I said. "I think part of me still hopes I can find a way to work it out." I held up a hand as he started to speak. "Don't say it. I know. I've seen all the Lifetime movies. Just . . . it's enough for now that someone else knows, you know? It helps. You helped."

He nodded. "Okay." But he didn't look convinced. His entire face was shadowed with worry.

Standing, I stretched. "I need to go. Will you take the printouts with you?"

He nodded. "Need a ride?"

"No, we can't be seen together. You know that. Everyone will suspect the worst."

He shook his head, disgusted.

"I'll see you soon, okay?" I waved at him and hurried to the medical section, where I returned the textbook. By the time Vanessa got up there to search through my books, she'd only find books a frantic mother-to-be might look through. She could report that to Bryce all she wanted.

The next several weeks fell into a rhythm. Seeing Tim at least once a week helped me to put on a happy face for the remainder of the week. He brought his wife, Mary, to meet me. She was a petite brunette who seemed a perfect match for Tim. When Tim got very busy with end-of-term tests and papers, it was Mary who met me at the library, who talked to me about life and her adventures, and my hopes for the baby.

At home, Bryce grew more agitated again, but it didn't seem directed at me, though I ended up getting the brunt of it. He yelled more than he spoke, if he was acknowledging me at all. He rarely touched me anymore, which I was okay with.

On the day of my appointment to find out the sex of the baby, Nancy pulled into the drive instead of Bryce when it was time to go. I didn't ask any questions, just slid into the passenger seat.

"Bryce was held up," Nancy said. "Held up" was their favorite excuse. It covered anything from actually being busy to just not wanting to do something. With Bryce's mood lately, I guessed his excuse was closer to the latter today.

"Okay," I said, staring out the window.

"He wanted to come," Nancy said.

Sure he did. That's why he'd called, apologized, and told me how much he regretting missing this important milestone. Except he hadn't. I hadn't heard from him all day. "Of course," I said to Nancy. "What father wouldn't want to be present for this?"

"Exactly." She reached over and patted my knee, completely missing my sarcasm. Of course she did. They all assumed I was still toeing the line, still just as naïve to what they were doing as I had ever been.

After conversations with Tim and Mary, however, I knew even more. I should have done my research before getting sucked into the Church of the Life. But I wasn't sure it would have made any difference. Bryce had me from the moment I first saw him. My friends and family tried to warn me, but they all gave up on me because I pushed them away. I had only myself to blame for my current situation.

Dr. Herbert greeted us happily, unfazed by Bryce's absence. I had asked once if there was another doctor I would be seeing for the pregnancy, and Dr. Herbert had acted offended that I'd even suggested it. "I can do all that, Julia. I wouldn't hear of you seeing anyone else!"

The gel Dr. Herbert poured over my rounded belly was cold, and I shivered. Nancy held my hand as he spread it out and used the wand to find the heartbeat and check anatomy. After a while he looked at me, eyes shining. "Do you want to know?"

I nodded. "Please."

"It's a girl."

There is no one to call. She has been removed from her circle of friends as cleanly as an amputated limb. Or perhaps they are the amputated limb, as she often feels the ghost of their presence, the urge to reach out, to make plans to dance all night and sing bad karaoke as they used to. But none of them would come now, even if he hadn't removed each of their names from her address book. She shunned them. Pushed them away. Told them they weren't good enough for her new glamorous life. In their stead he had placed various models of the same type of person, approved by him, just as cold and controlled as he wanted her to be. None of them would come, either. They would be scandalized.

Like a lightning bolt, the fuzz in her brain clears. There is one person who never fell under his spell, who might understand her choice. Who would help her. With trembling fingers, she reaches for her phone on the ledge and dials a number she still remembers despite not using it for months. When the other person picks up, she sighs in relief as tears run down her cheeks.

Chapter 33

"Here, take this," Tim said, pressing something into my palm.
"What is it?" I opened my hand to see a small phone.

"My number and Mary's number are already programmed in. We're the only ones who have that number, but keep it on silent. There's a password programmed in." He handed me a charger and a piece of paper with a six-digit code on it. "Memorize it and throw the paper away on your way home."

"What's this for, Tim?"

He paced the religion section, agitated. "I've got a bad feeling, Julia. The things you've been telling me, Bryce closing off, being more irritable. I've heard things aren't going well for the church. There's a movement to expose what's really going on there, but it's very underground. I can't even get a read on what they want to expose, or who. But I hate the idea of you being trapped there."

"This really isn't necessary," I said, trying to hand the phone back.

"He's right," Mary said. "Our prayer group has been feeling it, too. It would really make us feel better if you had a way to contact us. Only use it if you need it."

Sighing, I nodded, trying to figure out a good place to keep it. I could hide it in the tampon box. It hadn't been used in months anyway, and was buried at the back of the bathroom closet. Bryce would never look there. "Thank you."

I was grateful for my friends, and I trusted their instincts, though

I thought they were being a little paranoid now. Ever since I'd told Tim about what was happening he'd been digging around, researching the church, asking people who had left what was going on. The majority had positive experiences, but there were a select few who clammed up as soon as he mentioned the name. I was more worried for him than I was for myself. He was going to get himself into trouble.

Tim and Mary had also been pivotal in helping me reclaim my faith. I realized that my faith had been based on something completely false, on the Reverend and on Bryce. It was tempting to turn my back on religion entirely, but they had helped me find the places in myself where I'd developed my own ideas, read and created my own understanding instead of just listening to what the Reverend said. I didn't know if it would stick, but it was something.

The couple left soon after giving me the phone, passing Vanessa on their way down. My heart sank when I saw her. "I see them around quite often," she said. "What were you talking about?"

"Oh, they were just asking questions about the church," I said. "They're new to the area and wanted to know about where they could worship."

Vanessa's eyes narrowed. "He's been in here quite a bit. They can't be that new."

I shrugged. "Maybe they just haven't gotten around to finding a place yet. They've seen me hanging out in this section, so they thought I could help." Laughing, I said, "I guess that's what I get for hanging out in the religion section!"

Vanessa still looked suspicious, but she only said, "Are you checking anything out today?"

"No," I said. "I think I'm going to head home, though. It's amazing how much this little girl is taking out of me."

The Reverend had announced our news to the entire church last Sunday, and I'd been receiving cards all week. I didn't see Bryce's face when he learned the baby was a girl, but I could sense that he was disappointed. I assumed he imagined a son he could mold into an image of himself. I couldn't help but think that my body had formed her into a girl on purpose, to protect her from that. Or maybe there really was a God.

I walked home, my footsteps hurried, and rushed upstairs as soon as I got there. I closed the door to the bathroom and slipped the phone Tim had given me into the tampon box. I used the bathroom for good measure, and was drying my hands as I walked out and saw Bryce seated on the edge of the bed. I jumped.

"Bryce," I said, putting a hand over my heart. "You startled me."

"Why did you close the door?" he asked.

"What?"

"Why did you close the door to the bathroom? You don't close it when I'm here. Why close it when you're alone?"

He was too calm. "There's too much space," I said. "When I'm alone I prefer to keep the door closed so I'm not constantly listening for sounds elsewhere in the house. I used to freak myself out a lot."

"You never told me that."

"You never asked."

"Who is Tim Wilson?"

I swore my heart stopped for a moment. "Who?"

"The man you've been meeting at the library for the past several months."

My head was already shaking in denial. "Bryce, I'm not—"

"Don't lie to me!" he bellowed, standing and looming over me. "Vanessa told me she's seen you together multiple times."

I held up my hands. "Okay. Okay, listen. Tim is a friend from high school. We ran into each other a few weeks ago and now we sit together if we're at the library at the same time. That's it."

"Are you sleeping with him?"

"No!" I should have guessed that was where his mind would go, but I was still shocked. "It's never been like that with Tim. He even brings his wife a lot of the time. I was going to suggest we have them over for dinner soon."

He smelled my lie immediately. "How convenient that you were going to talk to me about them right about the time I tell you I know all about your little affair."

"We're not having an affair, Bryce. I haven't done anything wrong."

"You kept it from me. That tells me that you knew it was wrong."

"I knew you would react like this! That's why I didn't tell you!" I knew I was saying all the wrong things. I should have sat down and let him yell himself out, and then begged forgiveness. It would have been the safer route, but fear for Tim had overtaken my common sense. I needed Bryce to understand that there was nothing going on, and when he didn't, I got even more angry. "You don't have to believe me, Bryce; I know I'm telling the truth." I spun on my heel and marched toward the door. "I'm going to go make dinner. Maybe we can have an adult conversation by the time it's ready."

"Don't you walk away from me, Julia," Bryce said, stomping after me. I kept walking down the hallway, and he caught up to me at the stairs, grabbing my arm painfully.

"Let go," I said. "I'm sorry I raised my voice, and I'm sorry I didn't tell you about my high school friend, but I need you to be calmer when we talk about this."

His face was pure rage, and his eyes narrowed to slits only a moment before he released me with a shove and I was airborne, tumbling down the stairs. My only thought as I rolled was to protect my little girl, and I curled around my stomach, shielding it from the worst of the fall. My head came into contact with the floor at the bottom in spectacular fashion, fireworks bursting in my vision before it went blurry. The last thing I saw before everything went dark was the shiny tip of Bryce's dress shoe as he knelt to check my pulse.

"Everything seems fine with the baby," Dr. Herbert said. "You were lucky. You need to be more careful with your chores." He looked at

Bryce, who held my hand in an iron grip. "Maybe you should bring the laundry down from now on. Just carry the basket for her."

"Of course, Doctor," Bryce said. "I told her to ask for help if she needed it. I'll insist from now on."

Dr. Herbert nodded his approval. "As for the mother, I think we can rule out concussion."

"But I passed out," I said, startling both men. I hadn't spoken since they'd brought me in. "It was only for a few seconds, but I was definitely out."

"We can monitor you if you'd like," the doctor said. "But none of my tests indicate brain trauma. Likely you were shocked by your fall and your brain needed a quick break. I think Bryce can take care of you just as well from home."

"Of course I can," Bryce said. "And you'll be more comfortable, too, sweetheart. Better our bed than this uncomfortable hospital bed. What thread count are these sheets anyway, Doc?" he joked, and Dr. Herbert laughed along with him.

I was desperate to stay in the hospital, but it was useless to insist. Bryce wouldn't allow it. He had refused to leave my side since the paramedics arrived, even riding in the ambulance with me. The Reverend was waiting to bring us home. Hopelessness overwhelmed me as they talked through my discharge. I knew once I entered that house again, I wouldn't be coming out for a very long time.

Every time we had a big altercation, it served as almost a reset button for Bryce. He was extra attentive over the next several days, even taking time off work. He wouldn't hear of me leaving the bed, and insisted I call him even when I needed to use the bathroom. I had no chance to contact Tim or Mary and let them know what had happened. I had no way of warning them that Bryce knew about our meetings.

Finally, the following Monday, Bryce decided I was well enough for him to leave me. "Nancy will be here in a couple hours. Go back to bed until she gets here. I've changed the security code, and I'll be locking you in, but she knows how to get in, so don't worry about it." He gave instructions with equal parts concern and warning. To a casual listener, he was the doting husband. But I heard the other message loud and clear. *Don't leave the house. I'll know if you try.*

I watched from an upstairs window as he drove away, and then rushed to the bathroom, digging out the phone I'd hidden there almost a week ago. Thankfully Tim had included the plug, as it was completely dead. I plugged it in by a window where I could watch for Bryce or Nancy, and for once I was glad there were no alternate routes onto the property.

When the phone had powered on, I wasn't surprised to see that I had missed a handful of calls from Tim. He hadn't left any messages, but there was one voice mail from Mary.

"Tim's been in an accident," she said. "A hit and run. He's in the hospital. I thought you should know." She sniffed into the phone. "He's been worried about you, so I'll keep trying to reach you." She sounded completely distraught. The message was from Friday, after I'd been under house arrest for several days. There were no more messages from Mary, though, and I assumed the worst.

I dialed her back and she answered almost immediately. "Julia?"

"Mary! What's going on?"

"Oh, thank God," she said, then covered the mouthpiece to say something to whoever else was with her. "Are you okay?" she asked, speaking to me again.

"That's a matter of opinion," I said. "I had an . . . accident last week. My husband has been home taking care of me and this is the first time he's left me alone since then."

"What happened?"

I relayed the series of events. I had nothing to hide from her, and I had a sneaking suspicion that Tim's accident was related to mine. "Is Tim okay?"

"In a manner of speaking," she said. "He's lucky, really, but he broke one of his legs and a few ribs, and had some internal bleeding. I can't even remember all the details. I'm just grateful he's awake and he'll be fine." She took the phone away from her ear again to speak to someone in the background. Tim, I now assumed. "He wants to talk to you."

Before I could agree, Tim's voice came over the line. "Julia? I'm so glad you're okay."

"Same," I said. "I'm so sorry for all of this."

He didn't ask why I was sorry. He knew as well as I did that Bryce was somehow at fault, or else it was an awfully big coincidence. "You had nothing to do with it, Julia. You can't blame yourself."

"I dragged you into my awful world."

He laughed. "I kicked my way in." I could hear Mary agreeing in the background. "Mary says that I don't know when to keep my nose to myself, but I think she loves that about me."

"I bet she doesn't love that about you right now, cooped up in that hospital bed."

"Hey," he said. "I needed a break. I just go to extremes to get the breaks I need."

"If you say so."

"Julia." Tim's tone grew serious. "You have to get out of there. You need to go someplace far away. Someplace where he can't find you. The more desperate he gets to keep you, the more scared I am that he's going to do something extreme."

I'd been thinking along the same lines. I knew he was right, but leaving was almost harder than staying. Where would I go? I couldn't put my parents at risk. I'd have to start over. No money, no friends . . . I'd have to create a new identity, and I didn't know where to even start.

"If you won't leave for you," Tim said, "leave for that baby girl. She deserves better than to be born into fear."

A sense of peace overtook me at his words, and I knew then that he was right. I needed to leave. "Okay," I said. "By the end of the week I'll be out. I'll have to wait until he leaves me without a baby-sitter, but I think I can act broken enough that he'll buy it. That's what he wants to see."

As if on cue, Nancy's car pulled into the driveway. I hadn't heard the gate, but it was difficult to hear from up here. "I have to go," I said. "I'll keep you posted."

I had barely stowed the phone and climbed back into bed before I heard Nancy's footsteps on the stairs. She opened the door quietly and I feigned sleep. She walked into the room and came to stand in front of me, running a hand down my cheek before making her way around the room, opening and closing drawers quietly. She was looking for something, but I didn't know what. She went into the bathroom and I heard rustling, but it didn't sound like she found my hiding spot. After a few minutes of snooping, she left. I rolled over and stared at the ceiling, already trying to choreograph my exit.

I knew I couldn't take much, and there wasn't much I wanted. A change of clothes and a few toiletries. I packed in my mind every day, switching items around, trying to figure out the most economical way to fit things into a bag. I couldn't very well roll a suitcase down the street, so I would use a backpack. I had nothing left from my life before Bryce. He'd gotten rid of it all. And I wanted nothing to remember this life by, only what I absolutely needed before I could get back on my feet. I would have no money and no possessions, but I would be free.

It was Friday before I had my opportunity. I'd done my best impression of a broken woman all week, lying in bed, staring at the ceiling. I heard Bryce on the phone with Nancy, telling her to stay home and get stuff done. He brought me a tray a little while later. "This can't last much longer, Julia," he said. "But here's something for lunch. Just a sandwich. I'll be back around dinnertime. Tomorrow we get dressed, okay?"

I rolled my head to face him and stretched my mouth into a small smile. "I'll try," I said. "If you think it's best."

"I do," he said, leaning over to kiss my forehead. "You need to get moving and keep the baby healthy."

"I know."

"I've been thinking," Bryce said, sitting on the edge of the bed. All I wanted him to do was leave. "Maybe if we picked a name for the baby, it would help energize you. You're not alone here, after all. She's here to keep you company."

"That's true," I said, struggling into a sitting position. "We could talk about names."

"I was thinking we could name her after Nancy," Bryce said. "She's been such a huge help to you. It would certainly honor her."

"Oh," I said. "Well, yes, that would be nice. We can definitely add it to the list."

He frowned. "I really think it would be nice if we could tell her this weekend that we're naming the baby after her. I'd hoped you wouldn't fight me on it."

"No, I'm not fighting you at all, Bryce," I said, widening my eyes. "Nancy is the perfect name."

He smiled, satisfied. "She'll be so excited."

I nodded and closed my eyes as he leaned in to kiss me again.

"Last day of lazing around, okay?" Bryce warned, as if I had just been on a vacation instead of recovering from his assault.

"Promise," I said, and I actually meant it.

As soon as he left the house, I crept to the front window and watched him drive to the gate. I opened the window just a little to make sure I heard the gate open and close, and then rushed to the bathroom to take a quick shower. It was time.

I retrieved Tim's phone and called them to tell them I was leaving. I'd check in again when I was safe. I tossed the phone on the bed as I surveyed my closet. My other phone was in the bathroom, but I knew I wouldn't be bringing that one along.

Heavy footfalls on the steps were the first sign that I'd been discovered. I froze, trying to decide how to play it. There wasn't time to shove everything back in the closet, and if he already suspected that I was up to something, he'd find the half-packed bag anyway. So instead of hiding or running, I continued to fold clothes and place them in my backpack, more deliberate than frantic. There was no reason to hurry now that he was here.

I should have expected it. He knew everything. My every move, my every thought. He knew what I was going to do before I did. I'm not sure what gave it away. Maybe he really did have a connection with a higher power who ratted me out. Maybe he'd bugged the house. Either way, he came storming into the bedroom, ready for a fight.

"Where the hell do you think you're going?" he demanded, chest heaving in agitation.

There was no point in denial. We were past playing games with each other. "I'm leaving," I said, keeping my voice as calm as I could.

He stilled. "You're not leaving."

I sighed and continued packing, ignoring him as he stalked closer. In my heart, I'd known it would come to this. That's why I hadn't allowed Mary to come and get me. Why I hadn't contacted anyone else, involved anyone else. There was no way he would let me leave. Not if he had any control over it. It would disrupt his plan. Make him look bad. He grabbed the shirt I was folding and whipped it across the room.

"You. Are. Not. Leaving," he said, and I appreciated how he controlled the rage simmering beneath his measured words. "Pick up the room and get yourself cleaned up. I'm going to drop you off at the church for the day. We'll discuss this later." His voice held a menacing promise. I knew what later would bring. And I refused to cower in a ball of nerves for the entire day waiting for the other shoe to drop.

"We can discuss it now," I said, picking up another shirt. "I'm leaving, and you can't stop me. I'll send you the divorce papers when I'm settled." I dropped the shirt into the bag and reached to remove my wedding ring.

His hand shot out, grasping my wrist to the point of pain, preventing me from removing the ring. I gasped, struggling against his hold. "You belong to me," he hissed. "You will stay until I tell you to go, which will never happen. We will stay married. You will give birth to our child. And everyone around us will know how happy we are."

I wrenched my hand away, rubbing the bruised skin. I knew this was only the beginning. He could have held on to me if he'd wanted to, but he had something more planned. Something worse. Barely taking his eyes from me, he reached into his pocket and dialed his phone.

"Yes, hello, I'm not going to be able to come into the office today," he said, then paused to listen. "Yes, Julia's just not feeling great still. I'll check in later in case anything comes up." He hung up and tossed the phone on the bed, then did a double take as he spotted the other phone. He picked it up. "Where did this come from?"

I sent up a prayer of thanks that he couldn't unlock it, and wouldn't be able to connect it with Tim and Mary. Unless they called. My anxiety spiked.

"Unlock it," he said, holding it out to me. "Let's see what you've been up to."

Taking the phone with shaking hands, I said a silent apology before taking it and breaking it in two. It was good it was an old-style flip phone, as it was easily ripped in half. "It was just something I picked up," I said. "Not worth anything to you."

He shook his head. "You shouldn't have done that. But information can be retrieved. Don't worry."

"Just let me go," I pleaded, hating the taste of begging on my tongue, a hint of hysteria creeping into my voice despite my attempts to remain calm. "It doesn't have to be like this."

Bryce smiled that chilling smile, and I couldn't believe I used to find him charming. "Oh, but it does," he said. "How else will you learn?"

Darting around him, I raced for the door. He intercepted me, backing me toward the antique desk in the corner of the room. "Please," I whispered as I bumped into the desk behind me, and my fingers grappled across the surface, searching only moments before wrapping around their target.

He came to stand toe to toe with me, raising his hand and caressing my cheek. Even still, after all of this, I had to resist the urge to lean into his touch, to draw strength. But his strength was cruelty, not comfort, and as he wound up his other hand to deliver the first blow, I turned my head and sank my teeth deep into the soft flesh of his palm.

Yowling, he took a step back and I ducked under his arm, running into the bathroom, where I had left the other phone, trying to slam the door behind me. He was too quick, and shoved a foot in before I could get the door shut.

"That was a big mistake," he said, no longer concealing the anger in his voice. He forced the door open and lunged for me at the same time as I brought my arm forward to stop him. A surprised look crossed his face, and he backed away, gazing in confusion at the bone handle of the letter opener now protruding from his chest. He held out his arms toward me, but stumbled back, tripping over the edge of the tub and falling in.

Chest still moving up and down, Bryce watched me, and I him. I knew in that moment, saw in his eyes, that it was never going to stop. Even if I got away, he would come after me. Until he caught me. Until I was once again under his control. I would never be free. Calmly, I stepped over to the tub and turned on the water. He began to make weak flailing motions as the water rose up over his face. I climbed in beside him, using my legs to hold him under. And I watched as the light went out from those crystal-blue eyes, the ones that hid the demon that surely lived inside of him.

"Till death do us part," I whispered.

The doorbell peals frantically, as if the person on the other side of the door is just holding their finger on the button. She doesn't move. There is a spare key under the flower pot. Not an original spot. He never knew she kept one there. If he had found out, it would have been good for at least two bruises. Maybe more.

Minutes later, footsteps pound on the stairs, and a voice calls out for her. Still, she remains quiet. Everything is about to change. She takes a deep breath as the footsteps move closer.

When her sister enters the bathroom, she gasps. "What have you done?"

Epilogue

EVER AFTER

Chapter 34

The police had arrived, and the paramedics. Kate hadn't left my side since she came into the bathroom. I wore different clothes, my old soaking-wet set stained with blood and taken for evidence. My sister squeezed my hand, and I found the strength I craved, the strength I looked for in all the wrong places. If only I had known then.

They wheeled the body out, covered by a sheet, but with a weird tent where the letter opener raised the fabric. One perfectly manicured hand peeked from under the sheet, harmless now. I rubbed my belly, feeling small flutters of movement within. A paramedic crouched in front of me.

"We need to take you to the hospital," he said, his voice gentle. "Your sister can come along in the ambulance."

I nodded, not letting go of Kate's hand even as they loaded me onto a gurney and rolled it out of the house. I knew I'd never return. There was nothing here I wanted. I sandwiched my sister's hand between both of mine. Everything I needed was right here. And I was free.

Acknowledgments

Writing a book doesn't happen in a vacuum. This book especially has been a labor of love and a community effort.

To my indomitable agent, Sharon Pelletier: I couldn't ask for a better partner in this adventure. Or a better source of GIFs sent at just the right moment. I hope you know you're stuck with me now.

To Sara Minnich and the entire Putnam team: you continually make something I thought was pretty great even better. Your advice and experience have been invaluable, and have made this publishing ride as smooth as possible. Sara, you are my word Yoda, and I'm so grateful for the work you've done on these books.

To my cousin, Dana Pryor, who several years ago gave me a scene—a woman in a bathtub—and let me run with it. That scene became a short story, and that short story grew into this book. Thank you for being my muse, Dana, and one of my best friends.

To my parents: each time I tell you I'm starting a new book, I'm sure you brace yourselves. Thank you for sticking with me through the highs and the lows, and for believing in me all the way. And to the rest of my family, brothers, sisters, aunts, uncles, cousins, and grandparents, who tell everyone they meet that they should read my books: thanks for being the best street team there ever was.

To my friends in the real world and my imaginary social media friends and those who have become both: thanks for the continual cheerleading and support. I wouldn't be where I am without you guys. You complete me.

I am blessed to work at an agency that supports this "second job" of mine and is generous with their time and support. I can't imagine a better place to work than Orchard Place.

And, finally, I thank God for all the opportunities I've been blessed with and the stories I have to tell. Truly none of this is possible without Him.